SCANDAL *at*
the HOUSE OF RUSSELL

Never Marry
a Viscount

Also by Anne Stuart

Historicals

Romantic Suspense

Collaborations

ANTHOLOGIES

Burning Bright

Date with a Devil

What Lies Beneath

Night and Day

Valentine Babies

My Secret Admirer

Sisters and Secrets

Summer Love

New Year's Resolution: Baby

New Year's Resolution: Husband

One Night with a Rogue

Strangers in the Night

Highland Fling

To Love and to Honor

My Valentine

Silhouette Shadows

CATEGORY ROMANCE

Wild Thing

The Right Man

A Dark and Stormy Night

The Soldier and the Baby

Cinderman

Falling Angel

One More Valentine

Rafe's Revenge

Heat Lightning

Chasing Trouble

Night of the Phantom

Lazarus Rising / reprinted as

Here Come the Grooms

Angel's Wings

Rancho Diablo / reprinted as

Western Lovers: Once a Cowboy

Crazy Like a Fox / reprinted as

Born in the USA

Glass Houses / reprinted as Men at Work

Cry for the Moon

Partners in Crime

Blue Sage / reprinted as

    Western Lovers: Ranch Rogues

Bewitching Hour

Rocky Road / reprinted in

    Men Made in America #19

Banish Misfortune

Housebound

Museum Piece

Heart's Ease

Chain of Love

The Fall of Maggie Brown

Winter's Edge

Catspaw II

Hand in Glove

Catspaw

Tangled Lies / reprinted in

    Men Made in America #11

Now You See Him

Special Gifts

Break the Night

Against the Wind

NOVELLAS

The Wicked House of Rohan

Risk the Night

Married to It (prequel to

    Fire and Ice)

SCANDAL *at*
the HOUSE OF RUSSELL

Never Marry a Viscount

ANNE STUART

Montlake
Romance

Text copyright © 2014 Anne Kristine Stuart Ohlrogge

Published by Montlake Romance, Seattle

www.apub.com

ISBN-13: 9781477824092
ISBN-10: 147782409X

Cover design by Mumtaz Mustafa

Library of Congress Control Number: 2014903119

Printed in the United States of America

To the fabulous editors at Montlake—JoVon Sotak,
Charlotte Herscher, and Elizabeth Ridley

CHAPTER ONE
Renwick, 1869

SOPHIA EULALIE RUSSELL SLIPPED silently out the back door of Nanny Gruen's tiny cottage. She had bread and cheese wrapped in a cloth—her own bread, and a magnificent loaf, if she should say so herself—and for the next few hours she could do exactly what she wanted. Nanny Gruen had settled herself for what she called "a little lay-down," and the old woman fondly assumed that her one-time charge would obey the rules.

Nanny had forgotten that Sophie never obeyed rules when she deemed them ridiculous, or inconvenient, and today she had every intention of giving in to temptation. After all, it wasn't as if anyone would notice, or even care.

Nanny Gruen's cottage was on the very edge of the massive estate of Renwick, not far from the town of Basking Wells. The ancestral home of the Griffiths family, it had come into the hands of Sophie's father, Eustace Russell, shipping magnate, in a card game. The wastrel heir, the second Viscount Griffiths, wasn't able to deed the land over legally, but Russell had won life rights to the place, and it was there he'd brought his bride, raised his three daughters,

1

and lived most of his life. When the girls' old nanny retired he gave her a cottage and a small living on the edge of the estate.

That, of course, was before he'd been murdered, Sophie thought grimly, making her way through the thick bushes toward the path that led up Beekman's Tor, the high ledge overlooking the valley and the estate of Renwick that had once been theirs. They'd lost it when their father died, as well as the house in London, and the three sisters had been tossed out on their own, their father's reputation in disgrace. Not only had he died in a suspicious carriage accident out on Dartmoor, where he never should have been in the first place, but he'd embezzled every penny he could from Russell Shipping, the business he'd started and made thrive.

The sisters had huddled together in a miserable flat on the edge of the slums in London, until her eldest sister, Bryony, had come up with a brilliant idea. They would each enter the household of one of the men they suspected of destroying their father. Well, in truth, Bryony had thought she might be the one to enter each household, but Sophie's bossy middle sister, Maddy, put a stop to that. Bryony became housekeeper to one of their father's major investors, Adrian Bruton, the Earl of Kilmartyn. Maddy, losing patience, crossed the countryside to become a maid in the household of a former pirate and sea captain who'd once served their father.

And Sophie had been left behind while her sisters had adventures. She had absolutely no interest in changing beds or counting linens. She'd forgotten how very boring it could be, left as a social pariah on the edge of the estate. The Griffithses weren't even aware of her presence, and Nanny wanted to keep it that way. Not that Sophie could blame her. The Griffithses had no obligation to honor Eustace Russell's bequest, and they could have turfed the old woman out at any time.

So Sophie crept through the bushes and kept a sharp eye out for anyone who might interfere with her secret indulgence.

It was a rough climb to the top of the tor, and Sophie's sturdy black shoes slipped on the rocks again and again, but she was used to it and knew the best footholds and places to stop and rest. By the time she reached the top she could see all over the fertile valley that had once been theirs. She could see the crystalline blue pool of water in what used to be the rose garden. In a few moments, with luck, she'd see the man who swam in that cool, clear water, back and forth.

It had been a sheer accident when she'd first spied him. Bryony had just written that she had married her suspect, Kilmartyn, and she was presently somewhere on the Continent, keeping abreast of the overzealous police inquiry into the death of Kilmartyn's first wife. Maddy was incommunicado, presumably still dealing with their ancient suspect. There was one more name on their short list of suspects, and that man was about to come into view.

Alexander Griffiths, the new viscount, had a reputation that was far from stellar. His first wife had died under mysterious circumstances more than a decade before, and he'd lived far to the north, never venturing into society, presumably haunted by guilt. He was certainly haunted by something, Sophie thought, dropping down to her favorite spot of grass on the ledge and taking out her cheese and bread. The one thing no one had ever told her was how exquisitely beautiful he was.

She'd had one season in London; she'd seen any number of handsome young men, been pursued by them. She'd been blessed by a combination of physical perfection that had left her the toast of London for a brief, glorious period, but unfortunately she had found all of those handsome young men shallow and boring. And then her father had died and everything had changed.

Alexander Griffiths was a far cry from the pretty young men of London, though he was physically quite stunning. She'd always thought of him as the Dark Viscount, a man of mystery, of deep secrets, perfectly in line with the gothic romances she devoured. She had a great fondness for maniacs in dungeons, and until she'd seen Alexander Griffiths she'd had every hope he'd kept a madman or a reanimated corpse in a laboratory.

But no one who looked like that was likely to be a brooding maniac, though she still persisted in thinking of him as the Dark Viscount. After all, his coloring was dark, and he still had a mysterious background.

She'd never been very close to the man, but she had excellent eyesight as well as the spyglass she'd managed to sneak out of her house when they were confiscating everything. She could see him quite clearly—the high cheekbones, the overlong dark hair, the sharp blade of a nose, and strong chin. And she could see the shadows in his eyes.

Sophie congratulated herself that he had no idea he was being watched. Ever since she'd stumbled onto this ledge during one of her more restless walks, she'd been drawn back to the place, back to him. If she could have convinced Nanny that walking for several hours in the rain was her idea of fun she would have gone out in inclement weather. She was certain the Dark Viscount wouldn't let a little rain stop him.

But today was a clear spring day, warmer than usual, and he would be there; she knew he would.

He swam in his smalls, something that both relieved and annoyed Sophie. She was curious—that was what brought her out to the tor every day. Curious about their neighbor, who might have killed both his wife and her own father, curious how such evil could reside in such a glorious form. She was undeniably curious about the male form itself, something she'd never seen in such scantily dressed, glorious condition.

The first time she'd spotted him she'd been frozen, motionless, staring at the figure in the distance as he plowed through the water with an almost desperate intensity, back and forth, back and forth.

The second time, she'd brought the spyglass, lying prone in the grass and watching with fascination as he pulled himself from the water.

His skin was darker than what she was used to, possibly from exposure to the sun during his swimming. His body was lean, hard, and she could see the flat stomach, the delineation of muscles, the water dripping off his golden flesh.

He shoved his wet hair back from his face, pushing away the water that clung to him. She had almost been afraid to peer more closely, in case he wore nothing at all, but Sophie, in general, was afraid of very little, and she'd looked, following the thin line of hair downward.

The linen of his underdrawers clung to him, outlining that part that a proper young lady was supposed to pretend didn't exist until it got slammed into her on her wedding night. Her friends had told her the most unpleasant stories about it, and sooner or later she was going to have to face one herself. She was going to marry someone young, handsome, and manageable, with pots of money—and a title wouldn't hurt—but she planned to be reasonable about it. A plain "Mr." might be more easily handled than a lord.

The Dark Viscount did happen to fit a few of her criteria, but he might have killed her father, and if he was truly in the habit of doing away with his wives then the less she had to do with him, the better.

But still, it wouldn't hurt to look. She and her sisters had stared at the sketches of the Elgin Marbles with avid fascination, none of the girls evincing any particular fondness for that foreign part of the male anatomy.

The wet underclothing was plastered against something larger than what she'd observed on statues, but nevertheless nothing so very terrifying, and through the thin cloth she could see dark hair surrounding the small bulge in front of him. She hadn't noticed that on the statues—perhaps the ancient Greeks were hairless down there.

Did they shave? Such a bizarre notion! Nonetheless, the hair made perfect sense—her own, more hidden parts were protected by soft golden curls. His legs were very long, and the hair on them was flattened by the water. He must be tall. She didn't like men looming over her—she preferred shorter, paler men. But still she watched, every day when she could escape Nanny's careful eye.

Sometime, she was sure of it, he would dispense with his under-drawers, and she would get a clear view of what would loom so large, so to speak, in her married life. Once he did that, she promised herself, her questions would be answered and she would come no more.

She stretched out on the grass, spyglass beside her in case this was the day, waiting for one of the French doors to open and the Dark Viscount, the usurper who had taken her beloved family home from her, to walk out on the terrace where she'd once played with her dolls.

He would come out, fully clothed, and strip in the full light of day. Sophie could imagine the housemaids peeping from the windows and giggling.

Of course, housemaids tended to be foolish creatures, easily seduced by their masters, and someone like Viscount Griffiths would be able to take his pick.

It was a good thing she wasn't so easily enamored.

He was late. She rolled onto her back, staring at the bright sky in frustration. He was a man who adhered strictly to his own schedule—had something disrupted it? The day was fine; surely he wouldn't be so selfish and annoying as to skip his swim, not after she'd had to endure such an arduous climb. Why, if he failed her this time she might refuse to ever come again.

She laughed at herself. It was a good thing he didn't know he had an audience, or he probably would never come out at all. That, or send his footman to scour the countryside looking for the tres-passer.

Which might call attention to Nanny Gruen and threaten her comfortable retirement. Sophie was being selfish and she knew it, risking so much out of simple curiosity. She needed to head straight back to the cottage and stay within its environs. If she wanted to go for a walk, the village wasn't far away.

She began to climb to her feet, when a flash of reflected sunlight hit her and she realized the door was opening at last. She immediately dropped back down again, picked up her spyglass, and began to focus.

• •

Alexander Montgomery Griffiths, Viscount Griffiths, stepped into the sunlight of the West Terrace, Lady Christabel Forrester on his arm. He wished to Christ the stupid female wasn't still here, particularly in their current state of mourning, but his stepmother had invited her, and he'd been too weary to try to thwart Adelia again. He was wearing his blacks, and Lady Christabel had donned a black lace ribbon around her sleeve as a sign of respect, even though she'd never met the recently departed, and her high-pitched voice was subdued enough that he could usually ignore her, as he'd managed to do for the three days she'd already been there.

Alexander still couldn't believe he was gone. His charming, troubled, scapegrace brother, lost forever.

He glanced longingly at the pool of clear water dappled with sunlight on this spring afternoon, the first clear day in almost a week. What would the boring and proper Lady Christabel do if he suddenly shucked off his clothes and dove into it? It was tempting. He needed to do something to drive the grief from his mind. He needed to get away from her.

He doubted she'd have the calm, dedicated curiosity of the woman on the tor. Oh, he was sure from almost the first day that he was being spied on. The servants knew well enough to stay away from the west side of the house when he went for one of his punishing swims—Dickens saw to it.

No, this watcher was farther away. His first thought had been logical—one of his many enemies, looking for a chance to finish him off.

It wasn't until he was well into his third glass of Scots whisky that he remembered that his enemies, though virulent, were simply not that numerous. His late wife's extended family, holding the firm conviction that he'd murdered Jessamine, comprised most of them. Much as he'd longed to strangle his wife on numerous occasions, he had had nothing to do with her precipitous fall from the top floor of the decrepit old manor house that had been his previous residence. Thank God for his brother, who'd stood beside him and kept him sane through that hideous period.

And now his brother was presumed dead. Everyone was gone, with the dubious exception of Adelia, his stepmother.

His brother had been his heir and Alexander hadn't planned on remarrying. Now he was going to have to rethink the matter, and Lady Christabel knew it.

She was still talking. Lady Christabel was an unending source of conversation, none of it interesting, and yet Adelia seemed to think he'd consider marrying her. He glanced down at her while she nattered on. She was pretty enough, he supposed, though ever since his marriage he hadn't been fooled by the perfection of a woman's face.

If only she'd shut the fuck up he might consider it.

He didn't bother to glance up in the direction of the tor. He wouldn't see anything, and for all he knew he could be going mad. He was convinced the woman watched him while he swam, and whether she was a figment of his imagination or real, it didn't matter. His instincts told him the watcher was distinctly female, and he'd always trusted his instincts, even if this time he might be completely delusional. He didn't give a damn.

". . . And I think it would be an excellent idea, don't you?" Lady Christabel nattered on.

She continued, and he shut out the annoying chirp of her voice, looking at the pool with longing. The dratted woman was clinging to his arm, but he was quite capable of ignoring her existence—the drone of her words, the insistent clutch of her soft white fingers.

Perhaps he *should* marry her. It would be convenient to have an available woman under his roof, particularly since it turned out that there was absolutely no need to pay attention to this vapid, talkative creature—she just kept going on by herself.

For some reason he glanced toward the tor. Was he imagining anger from his watcher, jealousy, even? He had come up with a mental picture of her, a cross between the toothy, horse-mad spinster daughter of the local squire and Adelia's put-upon companion, Regina Throckton.

Miss Throckton had as little use for the male of the species as did the horse-loving Miss Clover, though the squire had been making halfhearted efforts to throw her at his head.

"And I know you agree with me," Lady Christabel was saying.

Alexander knew on principle that he didn't, but he made a noncommittal sound in the back of his throat and continued onward, the lady's gloved hand clamped firmly onto his arm.

Was the silly creature out of her mind? And what were her parents thinking? They were sending her into the arms of a man who may very well have murdered his first wife, flinging her off the rotting roof of Montgomery Manor? Though he could certainly sympathize with wanting to silence Christabel.

But such was the way of society, he thought with carefully veiled contempt. Before he'd inherited the title and the small fortune he'd been quickly able to double, he was persona non grata. Now women would travel to the heart of the countryside to fling themselves at him.

He glanced up at the tor again. Who the hell was up there? He could feel real anger radiating toward him—he hadn't noticed that before.

He needed to find out. First he had to get rid of Lady Christabel and the tiresome brother who'd accompanied her.

And then, by God, he would go after his watcher and beat the truth out of her.

The thought put him in a much better mood. "Shall we return to the house, Lady Christabel?" he said abruptly and she halted, rattled. He must have interrupted her mid-spate.

She blinked, her mouth open. She should have expressed her displeasure, but he was rich, single, entitled, and by all accounts good-looking, so of course she ignored his rudeness. The new Viscount Griffiths was known for his eccentricities, his unsettling behavior, his cynical discourse. Clearly she was going to overlook it for the chance to be a viscountess rather than simply the daughter of an earl.

"An excellent idea, my lord, and I was thinking about Elliott Ponsonby's second wife and how she . . ."

Alexander turned his back on the tor and moved toward the house.

Sophie rolled over on her back, her spyglass abandoned beside her, irritated beyond belief. Who was that woman beside him, holding his arm in such a proprietary manner? She hadn't heard that the Viscount planned to marry, but the woman was treating him like her own personal possession. A good thing, Sophie told herself. If the Dark Viscount was caught up in a new marriage he wouldn't be paying attention to anything else. If there was only some way she could follow her sisters' example and make her way into his household, she, too, could find out whether this man had had anything to do with their father's disgrace.

She scrambled to her feet, gathering up the tea towel that had held her lunch and her spyglass. It was time she got back to the cottage or Nanny would begin to wonder.

But she would come back tomorrow to see whether the unexpected blond woman was still here, whether the Dark Viscount would no longer go for his swims in the bright golden sunlight of a late spring afternoon. The rest she would figure out later.

CHAPTER TWO

THE MIDDAY SUN WAS warm, and it shouldn't have surprised Sophie that there was no smoke billowing out of the chimney in Nanny Gruen's fairytale cottage in the woods. They were eating later, and Nanny knew that if there was one thing Sophie approached with enthusiasm, it was cooking. She'd already planned on trying out a variation of brook trout à l'anglaise, and while Nanny cheerfully peeled potatoes and did any of the simple work, she was just as happy to give over the task of cooking. Nanny's sister had been a cook, and they'd never gotten along, so she did her best to keep out of the kitchens as much as she could.

While Sophie had dutifully learned the despised chores of taking care of such a small household, the only thing that interested her was cooking. Baking, to be precise, but she could derive almost as much pleasure from a roasted guinea fowl in a lemon cream sauce with a hint of saffron as she could from a gâteau with crème fraîche and fondant, and Nanny was more than happy with the division of duties.

Sophie had wrapped the spyglass in the tea towel, not wanting to risk any questions. But the sight of Elsie Crowell, Nanny's longtime friend, standing in the tiny doorway made her drop it, and she heard the glass crack with an ominous sound.

"Where have you been?" Miss Crowell demanded. "I was about ready to send a search party after you. You're lucky I chose to visit Bessie today or who knows what might have happened."

A cold chill ran through Sophie's body, but she moved forward, leaving the spyglass in the dirt. "Is something wrong? Is Nanny all right?"

"No thanks to you," Miss Crowell said with a sniff. "As far as the doctor can tell, she tripped on the uneven flooring. She was facedown when I got here, and who knows how long she'd been lying there?"

"You got the doctor in?" Sophie was aghast. Nanny must be gravely ill. Doctors were fiendishly expensive, and no one hired one unless the matter was dire.

"Bessie is very dear to me," Miss Crowell said stiffly. "Needless to say, I paid him—we all know what happened to your father's great fortune. Fortunately Dr. Madeira assures me she'll recover completely after a stint in a nursing home. Her leg is broken, and old bones don't heal as quickly, but when she is able to leave she is coming to my house, not back here to this wretched little place."

Sophie's back stiffened. For one thing, Nanny's cottage was snug and adorable. For another, Miss Crowell was a wealthy spinster who liked to have her own way, and she'd been trying to talk Nanny into moving in with her for years.

But Sophie was just as good at having her own way, and she had never liked Miss Crowell. "Nanny likes being independent. She's never said a word about wanting to leave here."

"Of course she didn't. Not while she had you to look after. I would think you'd be ashamed of yourself, taking advantage of a poor old woman. She's earned her rest. She told me she would join me once you girls were safely settled, but of course that will never happen. You're all as wild and reckless as your wicked father."

Sophie smiled angelically, the look that her sisters had learned to dread. "My wicked father?" she echoed in a dulcet voice.

"You know as well as I do that he stole all that money from his shipping company, and if he hadn't had a carriage accident on his way to the Continent no one would ever know what happened to him." She sniffed disapprovingly. "As for your sisters, they're no better than they should be. Your eldest sister has run off with a murderer, and even in our tiny village we heard the rumors about your sister Maddy's behavior. And where is that young woman, may I ask?"

Living with a pirate and pretending to be a maid, Sophie was tempted to say, just to watch Miss Crowell's pale, protuberant eyes pop out still further. "You may not ask," she said instead, all affability. "Exactly where is Nanny at the moment? I need to see her."

"That wouldn't be good for her. Dr. Madeira agrees with me that Bessie needs complete rest. She's to have no visitors."

"She'll worry about me," Sophie protested.

"No, she won't. I've assured her that you'll be looked after."

"I don't need looking after." Whether or not that was strictly true was a matter of opinion, she thought fairly. She had no money, no notion of how to replenish the dwindling food supplies, and she'd never been terribly good at lighting the recalcitrant old stove. However, she wasn't without resources. She could always join a traveling circus, or perhaps start a career on the London stage . . .

"You're going to have to find somewhere else to go, Miss Sophie," Elsie said. "They will hear about Bessie's accident up at the big house and that nosy steward of his lordship will be making inquiries in the village, no doubt hoping she won't return and they can get rid of the last trace of your family's occupancy at Renwick. Not that your father wasn't an excellent landlord before his descent into crime, far better than the Griffithses ever were, but there's naught that can be done about that at this point—there's no way you can get Renwick back. It legally belongs to the Griffiths family, and it would never have left their hands if the old master hadn't been such a wastrel and gambler."

At least Miss Crowell was equally disapproving of all the inhabitants of the great house of Renwick, Sophie thought, keeping her deceptively sweet smile on her face.

"Now, I was thinking there were a number of possibilities for you," the elderly woman was saying. "The vicar knows of a post as governess to a family with six children, up north. They've had trouble retaining someone, or they'd never consider a girl as young and pretty as you are, but beggars can't be choosers."

"I'd rather starve," Sophie said flatly, never particularly fond of children.

"Do you have any family besides your sisters?"

"None." She didn't even blink, consigning her distant cousins to perdition. "And I have no idea where my sisters are." That wasn't strictly true, though the details were fuzzy.

"If only your family hadn't held Renwick for so many years," Miss Crowell lamented. "Not that there'd be a place for you—there are no children and Mrs. Griffiths's companion is her first cousin. You'd be better off looking for genteel employment in London."

The very thought of genteel employment gave Sophie cold chills, and she didn't bother to inquire how she was even supposed to get there in the first place. "When is Nanny coming home?"

"My dear, haven't you been listening? She's not going to. And even if she wanted to, Lord Griffiths's steward might make certain she can't. In the meantime she's very well settled into the nursing home right now, and when she's well enough she can share my little home for the rest of her days. We've always found each other most convivial."

Sophie didn't miss the glaring fact that Miss Crowell's "little home," a house with at least four bedrooms, didn't have room for her.

"Nanny likes her independence," she said carefully.

"She's worked hard all her life." Miss Crowell was firm. "It's time for someone to take care of her. Her only worry is about you, but I'll set her mind at ease."

"You will?"

"I'll tell her you're going to join one of your sisters."

Sophie wrinkled her nose. "And you think she'll believe it?"

"Why should I lie to her?"

"Why indeed?" Sophie purred. "But unfortunately, even if I had the money for such a journey, my sister is in no position to have me come stay with her."

"I have enough set aside," Miss Crowell announced smugly. "And the boy will drive you into Upper Pelham, where you can catch the stage, either to Plymouth or back to London. It's your choice."

"But I have to see Nanny first . . ."

"I can't allow that. She doesn't need the extra worry. Better if you simply leave."

"Without a word to her?"

The elderly Miss Crowell had a gleam of triumph in her faded blue eyes. "She has no illusions about you, my dear. Everyone knows you're a shallow, selfish beauty who thinks of no one but herself."

Sophie gave her a feral smile, and Miss Crowell took an involuntary step back. "Yes, I am pretty, aren't I?" she said smoothly. "I trust if I send a letter to Nanny from . . . Plymouth, you'll give it to her?"

"Of course," Miss Crowell said, clearly affronted. It would go in the fire, Sophie thought.

She would have fought more, but Miss Crowell really was going to give Nanny the life she deserved. They were good friends, and Miss Crowell's income even afforded a couple of servants. Nanny would live out her life in grand style.

"It shouldn't take you long to get ready," Miss Crowell continued. "You don't have much—I gather when your father stole all that money, his creditors stripped you of everything, including most of your clothing. Young Jacky will be by with his cart in a few hours—you should be ready."

Young Jacky's cart smelled of dung. "Of course," Sophie murmured, plotting revenge. "I'll be ready."

The fool woman believed her.

• •

It didn't take long for her to pack her two plain dresses—dyed black and now laundered to an indiscriminate shade between brown and dark blue—her hairbrush and toiletries and the fine lace undergarments that they hadn't been able to take from her. Her emerald ear bobs that had been a sixteenth-birthday present from Papa made up the sum of her earthly possessions—she, the toast of London, the beautiful, gay, young heiress who'd had a personal maid, a laundry maid responsible for the ornate gowns that were long gone, and a hairdresser she shared with her sisters. Her siblings had managed well enough with their own hair since their fall from grace—she'd had nothing but trouble with her unruly mane of blond curls.

She was just about to fasten the small satchel when at the last minute she threw in Nanny's voluminous aprons. Nanny wouldn't need them when she moved into the comparable lap of luxury that was Miss Crowell's village home.

She snapped the satchel closed, taking a long look around her. The answer had come to her, simple and obvious. She hoisted up her bag and started the long walk across the fields she had once known, down the lanes, to the house that had been her own such a short time ago.

• •

Sophie went unerringly to the kitchen door, making her way through the neat gardens full of vegetables and herbs. Bryony would be glad of that, Sophie thought as she marched by. The new servants the usurper had brought in were keeping the place in good shape.

She knocked firmly on the door. She could hear noise beyond, the clanging of pots and pans, and for the briefest moment her courage failed her.

But only for a moment. Anything Maddy and Bryony did, she could do as well or better. It had been more than a month since she'd heard from either of her sisters, and she couldn't wait forever. She rapped on the door again and, receiving no answer, pushed it open.

It looked as if a whirlwind had hit the large kitchen of Renwick. Chaos reigned, servants were rushing to and fro, and no one even noticed the young woman standing there.

A stocky, rough-hewn man who could only be the butler was busy fanning a harassed-looking woman who'd collapsed in a chair, red-faced and weeping. Three kitchen maids stood in the background wringing their hands, rather like a Greek chorus in one of those interminably long plays she'd seen in London. On the wide table in the center of the room stood a huge bowl, dough rising over the top, three pastry crusts half rolled out, the corpses of half a dozen pheasants still with their feathers, and the place was blazingly hot from the huge stove, which seemed to be cooking absolutely nothing.

People rushed past her, ignoring her, and Sophie, who preferred to be the center of attention, dropped her valise, walked into the center of the kitchen, and took a large wooden ladle from the table, clanging it against an empty iron pot.

There was instant silence as all eyes were on her. Sophie straightened her back, wishing for not the first time that her height were a bit more impressive. She was about to embark on a series of unlikely little lies in order to find a place at Renwick, when the properly dressed butler dropped the fan he'd been using, straightened his waistcoat, and stepped forward. He looked more like a prizefighter than a butler, but his manner was perfection.

"I beg your pardon," he said with great deference, shocking Sophie into a prolonged silence. No one had treated her with deference since her father died. "Of course you must be Madame Camille. We were afraid you weren't coming."

Madame Camille? Should she attempt a French accent? Their mother had been French, so there was the likelihood that she could manage it, but it would be difficult. "You were?" she said in a nondescript voice, neither French nor English, neither haughty nor subservient.

The butler didn't appear to notice. "When you failed to appear at the inn, Mrs. Griffiths was quite put out, and we were afraid you'd changed your mind. But you're here now, thank God, and I apologize that you were forced to find your way here on your own. I hope you're not too tired."

Everyone in the kitchen was following this polite inquiry in fascinated silence. "It was quite easy," she said with great truthfulness.

"I am relieved to hear it. Where would you like to start?"

All right, his attitude was respectful bordering on obsequious, so Madame Camille clearly had some authority. If the current owner's stepmother was put out, did that mean she was supposed to be a lady's maid? She was supposedly French, after all. She wasn't quite sure why she'd decided to approach Renwick—perhaps it had been the distant hope that she could find some sort of employment, but the idea of being a maid most definitely did not appeal, though she supposed she could manage, having had her own maid for most of her life. While she was useless at taking care of her own hair, she had managed to do a creditable job with her sisters', and she could put together a flattering toilette, though her laundry skills were definitely lacking.

How far could she carry this off? If she made a wrong move, would she be turfed out on her ear? And would that be any worse than the position she was already in?

"First, I would like to see my accommodations, Mr. . . . ?"

"Dickens, Madame Camille." A frown crossed his brow. "I thought you were French?"

"Half-French," she said truthfully. "And I have spent many years in England."

"Very good, madame." For some reason Dickens took it in stride. "You'll find your quarters quite satisfactory, I expect. Mrs. Griffiths had them done up new just for you. She'll be so pleased to hear you've arrived."

Sophie took a calming breath. "Will she?" If she just kept answering everything with a question, she might manage to carry off this masquerade, at least for a bit. At least long enough to figure out what she was going to do next. Not to mention get a good long look at the third man they had considered capable of destroying their family.

"Your reputation precedes you. When Mrs. Griffiths advertised for a new chef, she didn't think that the great Madame Camille would condescend to leave France and work at Renwick."

Sophie almost kissed his balding head. In one short speech he'd given her everything she needed to know, and instead of waiting on the notorious harridan she was to have her own kitchen. Bliss!

"I felt like returning to the land of my birth," she said.

Dickens's high forehead creased. "But madame is French."

Bugger! Sophie thought, using the curse she learned from Bryony. "Half-French," she corrected. "And my parents lived here when I was born."

It satisfied the man. Not that he seemed suspicious, merely curious. "Were your parents in service, madame? You seem so very young to have such an impeccable reputation, if you'll pardon my saying so."

Well, there was that, she thought. But if there was one thing she could do well, it was lie. "But of course," she said with great dignity. "My father was a great chef, and my mother his assistant. I learned to cook at their knee. Knees. I have had my own kitchen since I was very young."

"Well, you're a blessing from above," Dickens said. He turned to the red-faced, tearful woman he'd been fanning. "Did you hear that, Prunella? We don't have to worry about Mrs. Griffiths coming in here again." He turned back to Sophie. "Mrs. Griffiths has very high standards," he said with an effort at tact, "and our lack of a chef has been . . . challenging for all of us."

"I've tried me best," Prunella said tearfully, "but I never claimed to be able to do more than plain country cooking, and was that good enough for her high and mightiness? Oh, no, she had to storm down here like the harpy she is and berate us and . . ."

"Prunella." Dickens's voice was admonitory. "We do not speak of our employers in that fashion, particularly in front of . . ." He jerked his head toward Sophie in a gesture that was supposed to be subtle.

Sophie wanted to giggle, but she preserved her sober mien. "I presume my rooms are nearby?"

"Yes, madame. I wondered if I might dare ask . . ." His words trailed off as a commotion came from the far end of the cavernous room, and the seated woman immediately leapt up, the butler straightened, and the three maids scattered like the frightened mice they suddenly resembled. Sophie held her place, calm and imperturbable in the face of this chaotic household. She wasn't sure whom she was expecting to stride into the kitchen, the housekeeper or perhaps even a return visit from the viscount's notorious mother, Mrs. Griffiths. The last thing she expected was Viscount Griffiths himself.

She'd never seen him up close, and she was frozen, staring at him in astonishment. She knew far too well the beautiful body that lay beneath all those proper layers of clothing, the bone and sinew, the golden skin, the long, long legs and strong shoulders. Her view of his face had suffered from the distance, but now, even in the murky light of the kitchen, she could see him better than she ever had before.

Up close, he was even more handsome than she'd thought him,

dangerously so. Up close she could see the high cheekbones, sharply delineated, the dark, satanic eyebrows, the strong, narrow nose and thin-lipped mouth. He had dark hair, worn too long, and she still couldn't guess the color of his eyes—his lids were drooping almost lazily as he surveyed the kitchen inhabitants.

"Hard at work, I see," he drawled in a lazy voice. "I gather my stepmother was in here earlier, causing a fuss. My apologies to all of you. She has come to me, and I regret to inform you that Mrs. Griffiths has decided to fire you all and bring in new staff from London." There was a shocked silence in the room as everyone seemed to diminish slightly. He looked out over them—he was taller even than the huge, burly butler, and even if he hadn't been, he would have given the impression of height. He seemed at ease, almost casual, as he stood in the doorway of the kitchen.

"The good news is," he continued, "that I never listen to my stepmother, not to mention the fact that she's alienated so many employment agencies in London and everyone around here that it's unlikely we'd be able to find anyone to work this huge monstrosity."

Monstrosity, Sophie thought with instant outrage. If he disliked Renwick so much, he should have left it alone. For a moment she felt his eyes on her, and she quickly schooled her expression into one of subservience, congratulating herself on her acting ability.

"So you are all reprieved for the time being, though I might suggest you keep your distance from Mrs. Griffiths if you can help it. I've told her to stay away from the kitchens, but I have no faith that she will listen to me."

Dickens stepped forward. "Yes, my lord," he said with great dignity. "And we're most grateful that you've chosen to support us . . . ."

"Oh, you know me, Dickens. I'm only interested in my own comfort, and being without servants would have a dreadful effect on it. We do, however, have an outstanding problem."

"My lord?"

Sophie felt his eyes glance over her bowed head once more. He couldn't know she was new here—people simply did not pay that much attention to their servants. "The chef . . ."

"He walked out two days ago," Dickens said, interrupting his employer. Sophie's eyebrows rose as she waited for the viscount to address such impertinence, but he seemed to take it in stride.

And Dickens had drawn the viscount's attention away from her, Sophie thought gratefully, trying to sink back into the shadows.

"That explains the slight improvement in the quality of what's on the table. However, it won't suffice, and if that young lady continues to try to sneak away, I'm going to be very cross." It was all said in a lazy drawl, and it took Sophie a moment to realize he was talking about her. She came to a dead stop, frozen, as she felt the heat of a blush rise to her cheeks. Where had that come from? She'd never blushed during her triumphant season, unless she'd done so on purpose to abash some young suitor.

She squared her shoulders and stepped forward, removing the hat that was far too dashing for a mere servant but the only one she owned, and met his lazy gaze with a completely spurious serenity. "Were you referring to me, your lordship?" she said in an even voice. "I must confess I am the new cook, so if you have requests or complaints you'd best address them to me."

He had abandoned Dickens and Prunella, who seemed to fade into the distance as the Dark Viscount turned, surveying her with deceptively benign interest. "Are you indeed?" he murmured, strolling toward her. The servants she'd been trying to hide behind had scattered, leaving her standing alone. She met his gaze steadily, knowing a servant should lower her eyes, not giving a damn. "And where did you pop up from?"

"London," she said. "Although I'm French, I've lived in England half my life. Your mother hired me." She only hoped she'd gotten that part right.

23

"Not my mother, my stepmother. That hag is no blood relative of mine," he said in perfect French, devoid of the usually terrible accent the British aristocracy employed, as if learning the words was imposition enough. Why bother with pronunciation?

But she knew her own French was equal to or better than the Dark Viscount's. "I beg your pardon, *monsieur le vicomte*," she said in the same language, "but I am unaware of these things. I can assure you I am an excellent chef, skilled in many areas." She sent up a mental prayer in the midst of this. So far her skill, or perhaps it was her luck, had been golden. Everything she'd cooked for Nanny, for her sisters, for herself, had been quite spectacular. She seemed to have a gift, or perhaps the fates had decided to reward her after taking everything else away from her.

He was watching her, his lazy gaze traveling from the top of the mussed golden hair down the length of her small, curvy body to the expensive shoes peeping out from the dusty hem of her dress. It was a good thing he was a man, and therefore unable to guess at the original cost of the stylish hat she was holding, the kid gloves, the expensive dress. And no one ever looked at the faces of servants.

But he was looking at her face, and his seemingly casual regard was anything but. It made her want to squirm. "And you just arrived from London, madame?" he continued in French.

"Yes, *monsieur le vicomte*. I promise you, I am more than able to fulfill anything you require of me."

A look flashed in his eyes, and she saw, at last, that they were an odd, clear gray, almost the color of the scrubbed stone floor beneath her feet. "We'll wait a bit on that, shall we?" He had switched back to English. "We have houseguests at the moment—Lady Christabel Forrester and her brother. I intend to get rid of them as soon as I can, but in the meantime, remember that we are a house of mourning. Frivolous confections and ornate menus would not be appropriate."

"I am so sorry for your bereavement." She uttered the proper terms that had been drilled into her since childhood—Nanny Gruen had been determined to teach her "poor, motherless chicks" the right way to go on in society.

The viscount raised one of those satanic eyebrows at her words and she could have kicked herself. "It shouldn't concern the staff. My brother had yet to visit this mausoleum, so any sign of mourning would be a superficial platitude. Nonetheless, things will be quite subdued here for the time being, and your menus should reflect that." He continued to stare at her, as if trying to place her.

She knew for a fact that he had never seen her—she would have been vitally aware if she'd been anywhere closer to him than the tor overlooking the valley setting of Renwick. She refused to lower her eyes—cooks were at the upper end of the strict servant caste system, and she wasn't going to let him cow her. "Yes, sir," she said.

He watched her for a moment longer, then turned away. "I trust this will be the last time I have to waste my time with household matters—I have no fondness for kitchen visits. We'll have something simple tonight—four courses will suffice. Lady Christabel doesn't eat much, and Mrs. Griffiths is distraught with grief. What's your name?"

The last question came so abruptly that it took her a moment to realize he was speaking to her. Dickens jumped in. "This is Madame Camille . . ."

"I don't believe I asked you, Dickens." His calm voice stopped Dickens abruptly. "Your name." It was an order, not a question, and his indolent air had left, his stare hard and uncomfortable.

She took an instinctive step forward, simply because she wanted to step back. She couldn't let him frighten her. "I am Madame Camille . . ." For a moment her mind went blank. He would want a last name, and she hadn't had the sense to think of one. She could only hope the real Madame Camille went by her first name alone.

"Delatour." It was stupid of her, her own personal amusement. Camille of the tor. It would mean nothing to him.

His expression didn't change. "Walk with me, madame."

"I have yet to see my rooms, to wash the dust of travel from me," she said calmly, and heard the indrawn breaths of shock around her. Did no one tell this man no?

If they did, he didn't listen. "That doesn't signify. Dickens will see to your things. Come."

Oh, damn, blast, and bugger, she thought furiously, outwardly obedient. The last thing she needed was someone pawing through her valise. Clearly the Dark Viscount was going to haul her off whether she agreed or not, so she simply smiled at Dickens, who'd managed to edge to her side without ever getting in between her and the viscount. She handed him her hat and valise, then stripped off her expensive gloves, slowly. "I should be back shortly. If you'd have one of the footmen leave these in my room, I would appreciate it," she said. "I prefer to deal with my things personally."

"Certainly, madame."

She brushed at her heavy skirts, shaking them a bit, and turned to face the lord of the manor. *"Monsieur le vicomte?"* she said politely.

Like a fool she waited for him to hold out his arm for her, but of course he simply turned and strode from the room, expecting her to follow. He had long legs, she was small, and she had no choice but to break into a little run before he disappeared from sight. *Blast the man.* Gorgeous or not, he was rapidly sinking in her esteem.

With a soft French curse under her breath, she rushed from the room, chasing her nemesis.

CHAPTER THREE

"MOST OF THE SERVANTS understand the word *merde*," Alexander said in a casual voice, not bothering to turn back to the girl as he strode along the corridor. "Words like that tend to be universal."

The so-called cook said nothing, merely rushed to keep up with him. He could have slowed down, he supposed, but he had a certain cynical enjoyment in having her hurry after him. They moved through the narrow hallways, directly out into the stable yard. He could see the various grooms watching them with curiosity, but he knew they would duck their heads if he glanced their way. They were all properly cowed, he thought with grim amusement. The murderous viscount was afoot.

He glanced at the petite creature he'd found in his kitchen, of all places. If she were a cook he'd eat his hat, which would probably taste better than some of the things that had appeared on his table in the last fortnight. Their previous chef had a fondness for his brandy and presumably no taste buds. Alexander had endured it for as long as he could stand it, but it wasn't until Dickens had murmured something about the uproar in the servants' hall that he decided to do something about it. After all, he didn't really give a damn about food, and enjoyed watching his stepmother fume. But he wanted a fire in his bedroom and clean sheets and a general sort of tidiness, and the servants wanted decent food.

Adelia had apparently made some sort of arrangement for a cook, but for weeks no one had appeared. Alexander had been making his own arrangements for more important appetites, but he'd never expected this.

He marched her out past the stone walls, onto the paths leading to the gardens, saying nothing until they were well out of earshot. And then he stopped so abruptly she barreled into him, unable to slow her momentum.

She was a gorgeous handful. She smelled like spring—fresh grass and wild roses, and her golden blond hair was a haphazard mop of curls that was about to tumble down around her perfect face.

Well, nothing was truly perfect, but she was absolutely enchanting. Her eyes were a brilliant dark blue, her lips adorably kissable, her nose small and pert. In truth, she was the loveliest thing he'd seen since he could remember, and that in itself presented a problem. When he'd talked to Mrs. Lefton he thought he'd made things clear.

He caught the girl by the arms, but not before she slammed up against him with her light weight, and he enjoyed the feel of her breasts against him for a brief moment, the soft sound of surprise from that lovely mouth. He wanted to drink that sound from her, cover her mouth with his, but he needed to be absolutely certain his suspicions were correct.

"Did Mrs. Lefton send you?" he demanded abruptly, reluctantly releasing her.

She took a step back, rubbing her arms as if he'd left a mark. She looked up at him fearlessly, so unlike anyone in the servant class. There was only a moment's hesitation. "Of course," she said.

He looked her up and down, slowly, circling her like a panther about to attack its prey. She was too young, too short, too pretty. He'd told Mrs. Lefton he wanted someone older, who'd spent enough time on her back to know what was expected of her. He'd said tall—he hated bending over women all the time. Besides, there were some sexual variations he had in mind that required someone tall enough, though no woman was going to reach his six foot three inches. He'd stated that he wanted someone appealing to look at, but no great beauty with aspirations. And here he was, left with a mistress who not only was everything he hadn't asked for, but who also appeared to think she could pass herself off as his cook.

He'd had every intention of setting her up in her own cottage on the estate to make visits easier—in fact, he'd promised Mrs. Lefton that as part of their financial arrangement. So what the hell was she doing in his house, among his servants?

"You aren't what I expected," he said eventually.

"No?" she questioned brightly. "What did you expect?"

Jesus, she was saucy. Mistresses were supposed to be subtle and almost invisible when they had their clothes on. He ought to send her back.

"How old are you?" he demanded abruptly.

"Twenty."

Better than he would have thought, though a good twelve years younger than he was. She should have said, "Twenty, my lord," but then he hated the damned title anyway. It was just interesting how lacking in etiquette she was.

"I'm not sure you'll do. You're pretty enough, but I'm concerned about this cooking business. Can you even cook?"

A series of unreadable expressions flashed across her face, and if he didn't know that it was almost impossible, he would have thought she was angry with him. Mistresses don't get angry with their keepers, at least not in the early days. Later on in a settled relationship they would throw little fits that could only be calmed with an expensive piece of jewelry, but most had the sense not to light into their lovers before they'd even gone to their bed.

This one clearly had enough sense; he could tell she swallowed her instinctive retort to give him an icy smile. "I am a most excellent cook, my lord." The words were bitten off, but it didn't matter. He was used to women fawning over him. He had no illusions about his looks—he was by all accounts a very handsome man with a strong, fit body. Add to that his recent inheritance of both title and fortune, and women were ready to lie down for him at the snap of the fingers. In fact, Christabel had made several hints.

But he was no fool. Once you bedded a well-bred virgin you were trapped into marriage, and he had no interest in repeating that particular mistake. He'd yet to see a successful one—his parents had disliked each other, though in truth he could barely remember his real mother, only the sound of his parents' fights. Mason Griffiths's second marriage, to Adelia Casoby, hadn't been any better, with only the arrival of his younger brother improving things for a bit. Until Adelia decided Alexander was some sort of threat to his younger brother's well-being and had tried to do something about it. Dickens had been his father's answer to that, companion and bodyguard, and he'd been with Alexander ever since, even accompanying him to Oxford.

Despite the fact that it would please his stepmother, Alexander had had every intention of dying without issue, leaving all this to his brother. They both would have loved it far more than he did, and Adelia would have adored being the mother of a young viscount. Of course, that was presuming Alexander died early, which Adelia had been doing her best to see to. But now his brother was dead, and everything had changed.

"Will I do?"

He was shocked out of his abstraction by the sweet, soft voice of the creature in front of him. He gave her his most haughty stare. "I beg your pardon?"

"I said, 'Will I do?'" she repeated in a slightly aggrieved tone. "My lord," she added as an afterthought.

"That remains to be seen." He wasn't going to make this easy for her, but the more she startled him, annoyed him, the more interested he became. Perhaps he'd been wrong in asking for an experienced courtesan to set in place as his mistress. This young thing could scarcely have much experience—she still carried a bewitching innocence about her that he realized had to be completely spurious. He could feel his blood stirring in his veins.

"I assure you, I'm a very good cook," she said, a trace of uncertainty in her voice.

"That's really the least of my worries. I had planned to set you up in a small house on my estate, but I don't think that will do."

There was a sudden, surprising flash of anger in those dulcet eyes. "If you think you're going to turf out some old retainer and stuff me into her cottage then you'll find . . ."

He stopped her with a lift of his hand and a cool smile. "Hardly. There are a number of small houses connected to this estate, which, frankly, is too damned big. There's a small dower house to which my stepmother refuses to retire, but that's neither here nor there. She's not the dowager viscountess, much as it grieves her, and I don't trust her out of my sight. I suppose for the time being you may stay in the cook's quarters until we see if you can carry off this charade."

She looked at him, dumbstruck. "Charade?" she echoed.

He shook his head. "Never mind. You're here now. It remains to be seen whether you'll be staying. Fortunately for you my stepmother does not keep country hours. She prefers to dine at nine o'clock precisely, and her companion sees to her substantial teas in the afternoon. But if I were you, I'd get moving. It's already late afternoon."

"I believe it was your idea to take me away from my work," she pointed out.

He looked down at her, unexpectedly amused by her haughty demeanor. She was due for a set-down, but he wasn't quite ready to administer it. "You are dismissed, Miss . . . what are you calling yourself?"

It seemed to take her a moment to remember. "M-madame Camille."

"My lord," he prompted. "You are dismissed, Madame Camille."

She didn't like that, he noticed. He hadn't had such a firecracker in his bed for a long time—he'd gotten used to placid females who did what he told them to do and took their dismissal gracefully. This one wasn't going to make anything easy, and he ought to get rid of her right now.

But he wasn't going to do so. In the darkness of losing the one member of his family he liked, he needed the distraction, and this woman would damned well provide it.

"Go," he said again, while she hesitated, probably wondering how far she could push him.

"Yes," she said between admirably gritted teeth. "My lord."

He waited until she was out of sight before he gave in to laughter.

• •

She was pretty enough! Sophie fumed. *Pretty!* Why didn't he go all the way and tell her she was nice as well. No one in her entire life had insulted Sophie with such a lackluster turn of phrase. *Pretty. Faugh!*

It was a good thing she'd spent most of her life in these halls, or she'd have no idea how to get back to the kitchen. She certainly wasn't waiting around for that man to show her. He was the most disagreeable creature it had ever been her misfortune to meet, and if he turned out to be a villain and a murderer then she would be perfectly happy, no matter how good he looked without his clothes on. A trace of her bad mood lifted at that shocking thought, and she almost giggled. The disdainful viscount would be livid if he knew she'd been spying on him while he swam. The thought of his fury cheered her.

But what in the world had he been talking about? She'd gone along with whatever he said—Mrs. Lefton must be the woman who ran the employment agency—but what had Sophie's looks to do with anything? She was pretty enough! She made a growling noise low in her throat.

She certainly didn't want to be set up in the dower house. The very idea of such a thing was outrageous—who put a cook in the dower house? Of course the dower house had been empty during their years of occupancy, but Bryony had always made certain it was kept clean and in good repair, and occasionally guests would use it. It was far, far too grand for a cook. Besides, she needed to be in the house, be as close to the Dark Viscount as she could bring herself to be, if she wanted to find out the breadth of his crimes. Everyone said he'd thrown his first wife off the battlements of his house, though there hadn't been enough evidence to go further than an enquiry. It had been the talk of London, even though Mr. Griffiths, as he'd been at the time, had never bothered much with society.

Fortunately there were no battlements at Renwick. Besides, why should he want to throw her off? Certainly he'd be displeased if he found out she was lying to him and the employment agency hadn't sent her, but that would hardly countenance murder, now would it? Unless he really had killed her father as well, and she found out something that would incriminate him.

Which was exactly what she planned to do. She was counting on being able to carry this off for at least a few days. Clearly the real Madame Camille had changed her mind about working so far out in the countryside, and even if the employment agency sent someone else, it would take a while. Besides, hadn't he announced that his stepmother had outraged all the employment agencies in London? Perhaps that was why the famed Madame Camille hadn't shown up.

Her sisters thought Sophie was too young and self-absorbed to be of any help in finding out what truly happened to their father, but she'd show them. Without getting tossed from the battlements.

When she reached the kitchen she found everyone as she'd left them, the bread dough still puffing over the bowl, the piecrusts half-rolled, the pheasants unplucked. It was unfortunate she was so short, Sophie thought, removing her shawl and placing it on the back of one chair. It took a little more effort to convince people to do what you wanted. She usually relied on a winning smile and mild flirtation to get anything she desired, but she could hardly flirt with the viscount's other servants.

There was a pile of clean, starched aprons over by the ironing board, and a full basket beneath it, but the laundry maid had ceased her efforts and was sitting back with a cup of tea in her hand.

Sophie took an apron from the pile and threw it over her head, tying it with quick efficiency. And then she pulled out a chair and climbed on it so that she towered over all of them, and began the work of rallying her troops. "Gather round, everyone, and prepare yourselves, my companions of the cuisine. You are about to work harder than you ever have before, and if you fail to do so, I'll convince his lordship that better workers are easily found."

It was almost funny to see how fast they could move when they had incentive. Funny that a twenty-year-old who'd never been able to tell her sisters what to do suddenly had a staff of more than a dozen to obey her every whim. She was going to like being back here, most especially in the kitchen.

From what she'd observed in her dash down the corridors after the viscount, it appeared that someone had redecorated the lovely old walls of Renwick with garish, "modern" colors and chinoiserie furniture that was just a bit terrifying. But the kitchens were the same, thank God, the kitchens where she used to play under Cook's watchful eye. These were the kitchens where she'd learned to cook, much to her sisters' amusement. Such industry was very unlike the baby sister they tended to underestimate.

She looked out over her busy army of workers, searching for a familiar face. The Russells had usually brought their own servants down from London with them, including the chef and kitchen staff, keeping only a caretaker and his wife on the estate, as well as the gardeners. As far as she knew they were all gone now—the new mistress of the house, the Dark Viscount's stepmother, had fired the few remaining servants, but Sophie needed to be careful she didn't run into anyone she knew.

The other servants in the house were all strangers to her. She'd never spent much time in the gardens anyway; if any of those workers had remained, they wouldn't know her.

She hopped down from her chair and approached the suddenly industrious woman who'd been in tears when Sophie had first arrived. She'd always had an excellent memory, for names, for recipes, for artists, and this one was easy. "Prunella," she addressed her in a gentler voice. "Or should I call you something else?"

The woman looked up, flushed but pleased. "Prunella's good enough for me, Madame Camille. We're right glad to have you here. It's been . . . difficult."

"The master of the house seems a bit challenging," she said softly, aware that Dickens was just out of earshot, overseeing the defeathering of the pheasants.

"Eh, he's not so bad. It's his stepmama who's the real problem. Has tantrums, she does. His lordship's fair enough most of the time, unless he's been pushed too far." She gave Sophie a searching look. "I don't think he's going to be too mad at you, madame."

It felt absurd to be called "madame" at her age, but that was the role she'd stepped into and she had to accept it. "We'll see. I imagine a good dinner will go a great deal toward making both the viscount and his mother more sanguine. What did you have planned?"

Prunella's face fell. "Game pie," she said. "With a cream of turnip soup, buttered cod for the fish course, and bread pudding for dessert. Problem is, Mrs. Griffiths don't care for turnips, and she thinks cod is déclassé, or so she says, and I was going to give them turnips for the vegetable course but they'll have already had them, and . . ."

Sophie put a calming hand on the woman's burly arm. "Not to worry, Prunella. We'll figure something out. What about the joint?"

Prunella looked as if she were about to start crying again. "That's the problem, miss."

Miss sounded a lot more comfortable than madame, so Sophie didn't bother to correct her. "What is?"

"I have no idea how to cook a roast. I was never in charge of cooking for the gentry, you know, just helping out the chef and taking care of the staff's meals."

"Well," Sophie said with far more confidence than she was actually feeling, "you're going to learn. By the time I'm finished with you, you'll be able to feed the queen herself."

The big woman looked down at Sophie doubtfully. "I'll trust you, miss. We've got a side of beef and half a lamb in the cold room, plus Toby can get us anything we want from the butcher's."

"The lamb," Sophie said instantly, having at least a passing familiarity with it. "We'll need a clear soup as well, and I have a new sauce for the fish that will disguise its humble origins, something with just a hint of lemon. We have lemons, I hope?"

"Yes, miss. But Mrs. Griffiths still won't like it, knowing it's cod."

"Then we'll tell her it's Dover sole, and she'll be delighted," Sophie said briskly, ignoring Prunella's shocked sound. "The lamb we'll roast simply—I'd love to stud it with garlic but I doubt the lady of the house would thank me for it. The weather's been fine enough that I expect we already have spinach in the garden—send someone to see to that."

"Oh, we do, miss. But it's very small."

"Then have him or her pick twice the amount. The smallest are the sweetest. What else? Oh, yes, the turnip soup. We'll add curry and call it something creative. Let's add a mushroom soufflé for good measure. Then on to dessert. I'm very good at desserts."

Prunella was looking at her in mingled awe and apprehension. "Mrs. Griffiths is very partial to chocolate," she volunteered. "His lordship, not so much. He's the reason we have lemon on hand. He likes a fruit dish."

"It's too late to manage both," Sophie said briskly. "I'll make a chocolate torte so decadent Mrs. Griffiths will think she's died and gone to heaven, and that should keep her from bothering us, and too bad for the Dark . . . for his lordship." She wanted to kick herself. She had to stop thinking of him as the Dark Viscount, or sooner or later she was going to slip.

"Yes, miss. Where would you like me to start?"

Oh, lord. Never had she had her own kitchen. There had always been someone else to oversee things, to answer questions, and now it was all up to her.

She straightened her back, rising to her full five feet and half an inch, almost. "We'll roast the lamb on a spit—do we have a boy to turn it?"

Prunella looked doubtful. "I misremember who . . ."

"It doesn't matter. We'll put a chair by the hearth and whoever is tired can sit and turn it. I imagine some of the maids have been up since dawn and . . ." She looked around her. "Is there a housekeeper? I shouldn't wish to trample on her authority."

"No, miss. Mr. Dickens is in charge of everything. He's been with his lordship since the beginning of time and he's a good butler. He sees to things, and he's fair."

"Has it always been this way?"

"Yes, miss. Apparently housekeepers and upper servants tended to develop an affection for Mrs. Griffiths's son, the late Mr. Griffiths, and the old lady don't like that."

"His brother? Is that why the house is in mourning?"

"Indeed, yes, miss. So I think your choice of a chocolate torte is a more fitting one. There's something more funereal about chocolate, isn't there?"

Not the way I make it, Sophie thought. Though given the Dark Viscount's vaguely threatening demeanor, she could always add some rat poison. No, that wouldn't do—it was his stepmother who liked chocolate. He wouldn't touch her glorious creation.

Which suited her perfectly. She didn't particularly want to waste her best efforts on an unworthy audience, but there was the pretty young lady who'd been clinging to him, Mrs. Griffiths, and . . . "How many for dinner?" she asked suddenly.

"Six," Prunella said promptly. "The viscount and his step-mama, Miss Forrester and her brother, and I believe the vicar and his wife are coming as well. Which won't put his lordship in any good mood."

"He doesn't like the vicar?"

"He doesn't believe in God and he's going to hell," Prunella said in a whisper so loud that Dickens looked up from his spot at the end of the long table.

"Are you gossiping again, Prunella?" he said severely. "You know there's to be no gossip in this household."

Sophie considered climbing on a chair again, but decided she'd already made her point. "She was filling me in on some of the details of the household, Mr. Dickens," she said. "And while I bow to your responsibility for the entire household, I must remind you that the kitchen environs are under the rule of the cook. This is *my* kitchen, and I believe I shall make the rules." Dickens began to frown, but

Sophie sailed on with a sweet smile. "However, I agree with you about unnecessary gossip. I do need to know who makes up this household and how many people will sit down to dinner, and the more we learn about our . . ."—she almost choked on the word—". . . betters, the more efficiently we'll be able to serve them. Don't you agree?"

Dickens was bedazzled by her smile. "Oh, yes, Madame Camille."

Too bad the Dark Viscount wasn't as easily conquered. "Are the pheasants almost ready for the ovens?"

Dickens was staring at her, momentarily besotted, and she wondered whether she'd given him too sweet a smile. "Just a moment, Madame Camille."

"Very good, Mr. Dickens. I appreciate your helpfulness more than I can say."

She now had a slave for life, she thought, almost ruefully. But a champion like Dickens could come in very handy.

CHAPTER FOUR

ALEXANDER WOULD HAVE GIVEN ten years off his life to barricade himself in his library, away from the chattering voices of his unwanted houseguests. Christabel was bad enough, with her meaningful looks and clinging hands. Her brother Fred was simply an ass, always saying the wrong thing and then letting loose with his braying laughter. Alexander had had no choice but to drink deeply in order to simply bear his presence, or he might have ended up strangling the idiot the next time he made one of his foolish, usually offensive, jokes.

Alexander couldn't even mourn his brother properly, not when he was forced to play host. Adelia had decided she was prostrate with grief, though she managed to join them for dinner. Adelia was a gourmand, whose once-luscious curves, the ones that had blinded his father into an unfortunate second marriage, had now turned to something less appealing, but since her mealtime conversation consisted of sniffs and artfully muffled sobs, she'd made the situation even worse. Now, to top it all off, they had that prating fool of a vicar and his sanctimonious wife coming to dinner, to offer succor to the bereaved, even though it had been two weeks since they'd received the terrible news from his brother's manservant.

At least he had . . . what was her name? It was no more Camille than his was Robin Hood. He'd like nothing better than to parade her into the dining room and introduce her to all as his new mistress, but he'd have to be very drunk to do that, and he still had a headache from last night's libations. No, he was going to have to get through dinner and foolish conversation and earnest homilies and awful jokes, and then he would go in search of the gorgeous creature Mrs. Lefton had sent him and forget everything as he stripped those ugly, proper clothes from her sweet little body.

He needed exercise. If he couldn't swim, couldn't even walk without Christabel tagging along, then at least he could fuck, hard. Despite the girl's apparent fragility, Alexander knew full well that Mrs. Lefton would never send him anyone not up to his own particular needs, which were powerful and often. Mrs. Lefton had a reputation to uphold, after all.

He felt his headache begin to recede a bit. The Lefton's prices were steep, and this one would be very expensive indeed, something that worried him not one bit. After all, he'd inherited an obscene fortune as well as the damned title and this huge house. He just wondered idly whether he'd be required to pay her an additional salary as his cook, and whether Mrs. Lefton would take her very large percentage out of that as well. He would feel sorry for the girl, except that she was no one's victim, and she was here under her own free will, and he would be paying so much that even her share would be impressive. He wouldn't be surprised if she ended up eventually taking over for the aging Mrs. Lefton. She seemed to be a young woman who got what she wanted.

He could feel his shoulders relax as his groin tightened. She was going to keep him delightfully busy, busy enough that he could forget the things that plagued him. The sudden, unexplained influx of money, a worrisomely large sum courtesy of his brother, and now there would be no explanation. The details of his brother's death troubled him as well, not to mention the watcher from the tor, the old pensioner who'd broken her hip and left her cottage empty, the houseguests who wouldn't leave; all of these dragged at him.

No, he didn't need to think about anything but the sweetness that lay between his new mistress's thighs. He was going to send Mrs. Lefton a bonus this time. Apparently she knew what he needed better than he knew himself.

He only hoped the girl would be as enthusiastic about some of the things he had in mind as he was.

He found he was looking forward to dinner for the first time in weeks, months, perhaps years. Tonight was a different matter entirely, he thought as he dressed in the evening clothes that Adelia insisted upon. It wasn't the food itself that interested him; it was whether Madame Camille could manage to pull off a creditable meal or whether the ensuing repast would sink to the depths of their exceedingly talentless erstwhile chef. Or would she offer the plain country food that had been their lot since Adelia had fired the last one? In truth, that plain country food had managed to tempt his appetite just a bit—he liked his food simple and recognizable, given that sauces were usually just an attempt to cover spoiled meat. What if Adelia decided to fire her on the spot? He wouldn't put it past her—his stepmama had a temper that had betrayed her too often in public. He would simply have to air their dirty linen by contradicting her. No one was sending Madame Camille anywhere, even if she served creamed worms on toast points.

If the dinner was a debacle, he would take perverse pleasure in calling his flustered faux chef to the table to compliment her on the magnificence of her repast, a gesture often made when a cook had outdone herself. It would drive Adelia mad, and that was enough to make him smile. Now that his brother was gone there was no real reason to have to suffer his stepmother's presence. Despite her complaints, she would never be the dowager countess, and it would take nothing but a fair chunk of his abundant wealth to get her settled elsewhere. He couldn't think of a better way to spend his money.

He moved to look out over the gardens, the shimmer of the pool as the wind teased the surface. The hell with his houseguests—if they wouldn't leave tomorrow he would swim anyway, in his small-clothes or perhaps in nothing at all. Anything to get rid of them. The early summer days were too unusually fine to miss the chance to be out there. Besides, his watcher must be getting impatient.

● ●

"You're late, Alexander," Adelia said tartly when he finally wandered into what she persisted in calling the Roman Salon, simply because there was a rather battered bust of Cicero adorning one alcove. At least, he presumed it was Cicero—he couldn't be quite sure since the fellow was missing both a nose and an ear, clearly having been hurled at something or someone in the past by his drunken uncle. Marble could be more fragile than one would think, though harder than a human head. He could only hope the old reprobate hadn't killed someone.

Or maybe it had been tossed by what Adelia fondly referred to as the Usurpers, the shipowner's family, apparently a gaggle of girls and a criminal father. None of that mattered. What mattered was annoying Adelia. "My toilette took time," he murmured as he bent over Lady Christabel's frail white hand.

"The ladies should realize it takes us time to look up to snuff as well," Freddy announced.

Adelia made a face but Christabel giggled. "You do look magnificent, my lord," she said in her soft, breathy voice, turning her hand under his to capture it. "It was definitely worth the effort. May I hope it was for me?"

Oh, lord, he thought with an internal groan. "In truth, I have a particular, hopeless longing for the vicar's wife," he announced with a self-deprecating smile, just as that stout, elderly female entered the room, accompanied by her stern husband.

"Alexander! You go too far!" Adelia hissed.

"Were you talking about me?" Mrs. Constable demanded suspiciously.

"Only expressing my admiration for your forthright opinions," he said silkily, giving her the smile that dazzled every female he'd ever met, except for the one downstairs who was being paid to be dazzled.

The stern Mrs. Constable was far from immune, and she turned a becoming shade of pink. "My husband wishes I were more tactful," she said.

"My dear!" Mr. Constable said reprovingly.

"Tact is for the morally corrupt," said Alexander.

"I agree," said that lady, "and I—"

"Good evening, Mrs. Constable." Adelia failed to rise, as was her right as the bereaved mother, and both the vicar and his wife converged on her, making soothing noises.

Alexander turned back to Lady Christabel and her brother as the least of all evils. For some reason Adelia's justifiable grief over her lost son infuriated him, mocking his own pain. But then, everything about the woman infuriated him and always had. Perhaps it was simply that he couldn't despise her grief; he was much happier hating the woman who had tricked his father into marriage and then done her best to get rid of him.

He should have sent her packing long ago. There was no way to prove she'd had anything to do with the various accidents that had befallen him before Dickens had come to look after him. But he loved his younger brother, and he simply couldn't have left him to Adelia's tender mercies.

Once his father had died, his brother had been under his protection, but there was no way Alexander could deny the boy his mother, particularly since he'd just lost his father. And so he endured the woman, for his brother's sake. That time was coming to an end, and his relief made him feel guilty.

This evening was going to be endless. He hadn't decided whether he was going to make the trek down into the kitchens to find the cook's quarters, or if he was going to summon her to his bedchamber like a regal satyr. Or whether he'd put it off for a day or two, long enough to get the Forresters out of the house and to come up with a comfortable plan. By then he'd know whether they could manage to stomach her cooking or if he needed to end that particular charade and cart her off to the dower house. He could think of no reason why she'd want to cook, when she could earn her living much more pleasantly on her back. But perhaps she wanted to leave the life of a whore and thought cooking a more respectable occupation. Either way, it didn't matter. He didn't care about the way her mind worked, he only cared about what lay under those ugly clothes.

It was going to be a long night, and even if he had no particular interest in food, for once he was hungry. Starving, in fact, all his appetites awakened by that pert little miss in his kitchen. Anticipation usually made the reward that much sweeter.

"Word has it you've a sweet little crumpet downstairs," Freddy was saying, and Christabel, who still had a proprietary hand on Alexander's arm, suddenly dug her fingernails into his evening jacket.

"You seem to be more conversant with my staff than I am, Freddy," he said, so mildly that the fool might have missed the edge of danger in his voice. "But if you think the maidservants are fair game, I must inform you that they're out of bounds. I doubt they're a particularly virtuous bunch, but Adelia transported them all from London, and it would be too expensive to replace them." *How the hell had Freddy found out about Madame Camille so quickly? Probably through his valet,* Alexander realized.

"Wouldn't think of it, old man," Freddy said with a leer. "It's the cook I'm talking about. You know the one. You were seen deep in conversation out in the stable yard. I hear she's quite gorgeous."

Christabel had now released his arm, and for that Alexander could have kissed the foolish ass. "Don't be gauche, Freddy darling," she said, her irritation profound. "Mrs. Griffiths is in no condition to see to menus, and I gather Lord Griffiths doesn't hire a housekeeper. Why don't you?" She was turning some of her ire on him, and the question was accusatory.

"Actually, I tend to molest all the female servants and we simply couldn't find one pretty enough to suit me."

Freddy's braying laugh rang out. "Don't believe him, sis. The new viscount isn't known for his indulgences, at least not out here. Now, Mrs. Lefton's establishment . . ."

"This is hardly fit conversation for either the drawing room or your sister's ears," Alexander said, losing some of his amusement. "Bad taste, old boy."

Oh, things are getting even better, he thought, as Christabel stiffened. The one thing more important than snagging his unwilling hand in marriage was her devotion to her spoiled younger brother, and any hint of disapproval raised her hackles like a bitch with a favored pup.

"I hardly think my brother needs to be lectured on proper conduct by a newly minted peer who's lived most of his life in the wilds of . . . of . . ."

"Yorkshire," he said with real enjoyment.

She faltered for a moment, but rallied. "Well, society there is hardly like that of London."

"I am chastened," he murmured. "Perhaps I'd better make certain my stepmama is not tiring."

But Christabel wasn't to be deprived of her goal so easily. She gave what she obviously hoped was a light laugh. "Well, of course it takes a little time to acquire the proper mien of a viscount. A wife of the proper background could be immense help."

For a moment he was struck dumb, a rare occurrence for him. She was even more gauche than her brother with his mention of well-known brothels. He gave her his devastating smile. "You're right, of course. Someone with discretion and delicacy would fill the bill quite nicely." It was said so sweetly that Lady Christabel wasn't certain whether she'd been insulted or not. "Let me see what's keeping dinner."

"That new cook of yours," Freddy said with a laugh, loud enough for Adelia to hear and cease her posturings for a moment.

"A new chef?" She almost brightened.

"Indeed, Mama." He liked to call her that, simply to annoy her. "She just arrived this afternoon, so I have no idea whether she's managed to improve our menu as yet."

"Gorgeous little thing, I've heard," Freddy said, and Alexander briefly considered strangling him.

Adelia's beady eyes narrowed. "To my mind the best cooks are large, ugly, and usually male. If she can't improve our repast then I'll know what to do."

Probably eat her, Alexander thought without shame.

"Then why don't we find out just how good she is?" he suggested, and signaled to Dickens, who was standing at attention near the door, flanked by the handsome footmen Adelia had insisted upon.

"Yes," said Adelia, rising majestically and taking the reverend's proffered arm. "I could manage something sustaining." And she began her journey toward the large dining hall.

Here I come, ready or not. The child's game came into his head as he took Lady Christabel's arm, leaving Freddy to follow up with the redoubtable Mrs. Constable. His little darling was about to have a baptism by fire. He could only hope she wouldn't go up in flames.

CHAPTER FIVE

SOPHIE WAS RATTLED. SHE had never cooked so many things at once, never had other cooks under her direction apart from her willing sisters, and the kind of repast required for a small dinner party in a home the size of Renwick had been momentarily daunting. The one blessing was that most of the staff knew what they were doing—they simply needed direction, and Sophie, as the baby sister of her family, had always loved the rare chance of getting other people to do her bidding. It turned out Prunella had a lovely light hand with pastry, and another woman proved more than capable with the game birds once Sophie adjusted the herbs. She had planned to let Dickens know when she was ready to serve the meal, but that decision was taken out of her hands, and she had no choice but to let the first course, a clear soup, go out unadorned by the sculpted toast she'd planned.

Another of the staff, a young man just promoted from the ignominious position of "boy," proved to have a talent for arranging food on the elegant china, and it needed only her touch with a feathering of freshly shredded basil to complete the fish course just as the soup dishes began to return to the scullery. They were gratifyingly empty, but then she remembered the swill bucket upstairs in the butler's pantry, and she could have cursed. How would she know what met with approval and what didn't if she couldn't see what they'd actually eaten?

She almost laughed. She was taking this job, this enormous task, far too seriously. After all, this was hardly her life's work, and they would give her at least a two-week trial. The Dark Viscount didn't look like someone who was likely to turn her out without notice, even if she sent burnt, unpalatable food upstairs. And she knew very well that her food was a great deal more than palatable.

Indeed, she seemed to have a magic touch. The roast of lamb came off the spit at just the right time to sit and regather its juices before carving, the pheasant pies came from the oven golden and fragrant, and she watched course after course disappear upstairs with a wistful longing. This was her kitchen—she owned it, she acknowledged, as she never had when Renwick had been their home.

But it had been her dining hall as well. Not that she wanted to sit down with the Dark Viscount, but she would have given almost anything to hear their reactions to her creations. She knew her food was good, bordering on magnificent, but she couldn't count on the man having as good taste as she had.

The dessert went last, her own personal triumph. At the last minute she'd given up on chocolate, and gone with something that had turned her family silent in awe. Tiny puffed pastries in the shape of a swan, filled with custard, they were so beautiful one hesitated to touch them, and they dissolved in the mouth like a heavenly cloud. She had sent up twice the number needed, reserving the last dozen for the serving staff to enjoy after clearing up, but one of the footmen came haring down with the demand for more. *A good sign,* she thought, watching them go wistfully.

She hadn't expected the summons to appear upstairs. Oh, to be sure, her father had often called Cook up to the dining room to compliment her on an especially good meal, but this didn't seem that kind of household, not for such a friendly gesture. She started for the door, ready to follow Dickens, when Prunella stopped her.

"Your apron, miss," she said, holding out her hand. "And you might want to brush some of the flour off your face. You have to look neat and proper for the quality."

Sophie controlled her instinctive snort and ripped off the apron and the sleeve protectors, dusting her face with her hands. Her hair was coming loose, but Dickens was impatient and there was no time to fix it, so she scampered up the stairs after the butler, her heart pounding. Was there some sort of problem with the meal? Was she going to be tossed out on her rump?

Dickens pushed the door in the butler's pantry open and announced in loud, gravelly tones, "Madame Camille, my lord."

She froze, and Dickens gave her a little push as the majestic woman at the end of the table began to speak. She had small, dark eyes that reminded Sophie of a rodent, and she wanted to squirm in distaste. She stayed still. "Madame Camille, I am so happy you agreed to my entreaties. The meal was quite . . ." Her voice trailed off, and Sophie stood in the middle of the dining hall, the space familiar and yet unfamiliar, as six pairs of eyes stared at her with astonishment.

Oh, bugger, Sophie thought, coming up with the worst curse she knew. *They know I'm not Madame Camille, and they're going to demand who I really am and I'd better come up with a reasonable lie, fast, but who could I be because I'm obviously not a regular servant and what reason would I have for showing up here . . . ?*

Finally the lady continued, but there was an assessing look in her eye. "Well, I must say, when I wrote you I didn't realize you were quite so young. You are not at all what I imagined, Madame Camille. You've developed quite a reputation in your short years on earth."

Bugger, bugger, bugger. She held her breath.

"But I can see why. The meal was magnificent, though the soup was perhaps a bit plain, and I might have wanted a richer sauce for the lamb. But the vol-au-vent swans were a poem, though you should have made more of them."

In her relief Sophie noticed that the woman's massive bosom was liberally dusted with the flaky pastry, and could well imagine where the last twelve had gone. This must be the Dark Viscount's stepmother, Mrs. Griffiths.

She was damned if she was going to curtsey. If they all thought she was some magnificent, famed chef then she would have the self-esteem not to cower. She gave the woman a small bow of acknowledgment. "You are very kind, madame."

The pretty young woman she'd spied clutching the viscount's arm earlier was looking at her with undisguised dislike, the young man who resembled her and was most likely her brother was almost drooling, but she'd been in society long enough to understand both of those reactions.

"Yes, indeed, an excellent meal, Madame Camille," said an unctuous voice, and her eyes went to the older man in the clerical collar. He was new to the living since the Russells had owned Renwick, and thank God he'd considered himself too important to make calls on the lesser members of his congregation, such as a retired nanny and her temporary wards. There was no chance he'd recognize her.

She hadn't yet looked at the head of the table, and the lord of the manor was silent. Maybe she could simply thank them and back out of the room before things got complicated.

"A dream," trilled the woman across from the vicar, clearly his wife.

And then he spoke, his deep, slightly cynical voice sending peculiar sensations down her spine. "Yes, indeed, Madame Camille," Viscount Griffiths said. "You more than exceeded our expectations. We all look forward to seeing what else you might be capable of."

She turned to him. She had no choice, and she met his cool, saturnine gaze across the table. "Thank you, my lord." Maybe she ought to say she was honored, but she wasn't going to do it. There were limits to how much she was willing to grovel, and her meal *had* been wonderful.

"Particularly on such short notice," said the pretty female, not as pretty with that sour expression on her face. "You just arrived, did you not?"

"I did, my lady." It was a stab in the dark, but the woman held herself like someone with a title and a stick up her arse.

"Well, you'll be kept quite busy in the kitchen, I imagine," the woman continued, and Sophie knew she'd guessed right. It was a good thing she'd never run into this particular female in society or she'd be in deep trouble. "We shan't be likely to see you abovestairs again."

"I believe you're incorrect, Lady Christabel," the viscount over-rode her. "I will wish to approve her menus, as my stepmother is too prostrate with grief to attend to such mundane details. But the time I spend closeted with my new . . . cook should be of no concern to you."

The woman's face flamed, and Sophie was at a loss to understand why, any more than she could guess the meaning of his hesitation before calling her his cook. Was he suggesting she was anything more than that? She would soon set him straight on that particular detail. In some households the sexual favors of female servants were a foregone conclusion, but such had never been the case at Renwick when they'd owned it, and she wasn't going to let it happen now. With no housekeeper, she was the senior female servant, and she was damned if she was going to let him have his lecherous way with anyone, including herself.

Though he didn't look particularly lecherous. He was watching with that same dark stillness, lightened by the faint trace of amusement, as if he found the entire situation funny. Sophie could see no possible sign of humor in it, and she wondered if the man was slightly mad. That would explain why he killed his wife, but what else would it explain?

Except that he wasn't mad—she knew that perfectly well. He simply didn't care what anyone at the table thought, which was almost more shocking than madness itself.

"You're dismissed, Madame Camille," he said, watching her with that odd light in his eyes. "But I shall wish to confer with you as soon as possible. Tonight might be difficult, but by tomorrow my guests will make their inevitable departure and you'll be more rested."

There was an immediate babble of protest. Mrs. Griffiths announced her ability to monitor the menus in a tone far different from her previous failing accents; the young man was asserting that he and his sister weren't demanded elsewhere at the moment; the young woman was whining to the viscount; the vicar was looking across at his wife with a certain resignation; and Sophie wanted to clap her hands over her ears and scream for them all to be quiet.

Alexander Griffiths's voice silenced everyone. "You must look to your health in this time of grief, Mama," he said, and there was no missing the cynicism in his voice. "And Lady Christabel, you and your brother have been too generous in keeping us company in this house of mourning, but I know you'll be relieved to be on your way."

"No such thing, my lord," Lady Christabel said with a false laugh. "I wish to provide succor to you in this time of need."

Alexander Griffiths let his slow, insolent gaze slide down Lady Christabel's fashionably flat front, then lifted his lids to look at Sophie's more generous curves. No one in the room could miss such a blatant, wordless insult.

Lady Christabel's face turned crimson, her brother began to bluster, and even Sophie could feel the heat rise in her cheeks.

There was nothing she could do, and her presence only made the situation worse. "If you'll excuse me, Mrs. Griffiths, my lord, I still have work to see to." Before anyone could grant her permission, she simply slipped past Dickens's back, through the butler's pantry, and down the curving stairs into the kitchens.

She hadn't been upstairs that long, but the place was already spotless. Prunella met her as she reached the bottom of the stairs and led her into the kitchen. The staff met her with a round of enthusiastic applause, and for a moment Sophie felt almost tearful. The fulsome compliments of those idiots upstairs meant nothing. This was the real tribute.

She applauded them in return, and Prunella brought her to the table, where a blessedly fresh pot of tea and the final two vol-au-vent swans awaited her. "You've done a right fine job, miss," Prunella said heartily. "We all agree, and we'll follow you wherever you lead us. Not to worry about any trouble from hereabouts. We'll be more than happy to see you safe."

Sophie was sinking gratefully into the chair—her feet and her back were suddenly aching, now that the excitement had died down, and she looked up into Prunella's eyes. What was this now? First the viscount making odd suggestions, and now the kitchen staff was hinting at knowledge they could not have. Not a single one of them was from the area; none of them had ever worked in the house during the thirty years the Russell family had been in residence. No one could know.

She had no choice but to let it go. She was far too weary to figure it out. She hadn't even had time to unpack, and right now all she wanted was a hot bath and the chance to crawl into bed. "You are all very kind," she said, and this time she meant it.

Dickens had reappeared. "The party has disbanded, and there will be no need to bring tea and coffee for the ladies, nor port for the gentlemen. I can say with certainty that the Lady Christabel and Lord Frederic will be leaving in the morning, which means Mrs. Griffiths will soon go back to having a tray in her room and our meals should be a great deal simpler. Thank you, Madame Camille, for a truly inspired dinner. The rest of you, you're finished for the evening."

Sophie had taken her first sip of the tea, perfectly brewed, as she listened to Dickens. The rest of them were finished for the evening? What did that mean for her?

Dickens waited until the last of the staff departed, even giving Prunella a meaningful eye as she hovered protectively.

"You don't have to do anything you don't want to do," Prunella announced stubbornly as she headed for the stairs that would lead her up to the attics. "And don't let Mr. Dickens tell you anything different."

Sophie braced herself. *What next*, she thought wearily.

Dickens waited until Prunella disappeared. "His lordship wishes to see you in the library at half past eleven." The butler made it sound like the voice of God had decreed it.

"I don't think so." She drained her tea, then poured herself another cup.

"I will show you— I beg your pardon?" Dickens blinked at her and her arrant blasphemy.

She took another sip from the tea, then reached for one of the swans. "I said I don't think so. I am weary, and I intend to go straight to my bed once I finish my tea. I expect tomorrow will be a long day, and I have no intention of lengthening this one."

"But his lordship—"

"Can go hang," Sophie said ruthlessly.

"Madame Camille!"

"Mr. Dickens," she replied in a civil tone. "Please tell his lordship that I'll be happy to wait on him in the morning at any time he requires. But right now I need my rest."

Dickens didn't look happy, but he knew an unshakable decision when he heard it. "Yes, madame," he said.

She felt a smile curve her mouth. "Come along, Mr. Dickens, how bad will it be? It's not your fault I'm being a recalcitrant female—he won't blame you."

The butler didn't appear any too certain of that fact. "Yes, madame," he said again. "We usually put out breakfast at nine in the morning, but with the Forresters leaving we might provide earlier trays. I doubt they'll want to sit at table with his lordship again."

"It got that much worse after I left?" she said sympathetically.

"Immeasurably," said Dickens. "I'll go and give your reply to his lordship, though perhaps I'll be more diplomatic. My rooms are on this floor as well, though at the far end past the stillroom, the plate room, and the cheese room. If you need anything you have only to ask."

"Thank you, Mr. Dickens. You've been very kind. And please don't blame Prunella for looking out for me. She was only being kind."

It was a mere guess, but Dickens's expression verified it. There was something rather sweet going on between the cook's right hand and the burly butler. "Miss Prunella is a very kind woman."

"She is indeed. Good night, Mr. Dickens."

"Good night, madame."

She watched him go, then took her dishes to the scullery and washed them. She didn't need to—most kitchen workers would have left them for the scullery maids to deal with in the morning, but they'd all worked so hard, Sophie had no intention of leaving them with any more work.

It had been the longest, most eventful day of her life. Tomorrow couldn't help but be easier.

The cook's quarters were luxurious by servants' standards. There was a small sitting room with cast-off furniture, a bedroom with a nice, large bed, and even a bathing room and water closet. She remembered something about Bryony insisting the servants needed bathing facilities and their father protesting it was a waste of money in a house they didn't even own, but right now she could bless Bryony's stubbornness. The tub was deep and the hot water abundant, and she slipped into it with a sigh of relief as every muscle in her body began to relax and her mind ran past the events of the day.

She would need to get word to Nanny, somehow, without the interfering Miss Crowell becoming involved. She also needed to understand the Dark Viscount's cryptic statements about the employment agent, Mrs. Lefton, and what was expected from her. She should have gone with Dickens to meet with the viscount. After all, he was her employer, and normally she would work on menus with whomever was in charge—usually the housekeeper and lady of the house.

But there was no housekeeper, and the mistress, Alexander Griffiths's stepmother, was apparently prostrate with grief, though not so prostrate she couldn't devour an astonishing number of vol-au-vent swans. A midnight meeting with his lordship was therefore logical.

But she didn't want to do it. She leaned back in the tub and closed her eyes. Seeing him close up had been a shock. The man was mesmerizing, with his dark gray eyes lit with just a trace of wicked humor, the high cheekbones and narrow nose and, oh my God, his mouth. She was obsessed with his mouth, with its faintly mocking curve. And she didn't even want to think about the lean, powerful body up close.

She slid lower into the tub with a moan. What was wrong with her? There'd been a score of men falling at her feet, plain men, handsome men, even a couple of too-exquisitely beautiful men who could have made her life a complete misery. She hadn't wanted any of them—they'd been playthings to tease and set against each other.

Now that she could no longer have any man she wanted, she suddenly wanted one. It was a shocking thought, and she wished she could deny it, but the more she tried to talk herself out of it, the worse it got, and she finally gave up.

"So he's pretty," she said out loud. "So you're obsessed with him, and have been for weeks. What else have you got to be obsessed with? He's the first good-looking man of quality you've been around in months, and he has all that romantic, broody stuff going on, with the long hair and the fascinating eyes. You're just bored. In London you wouldn't look twice."

But she would, and she knew it. He was the kind of man who drew the eye, and that secret twist of humor kept her attention focused. So what? During the long hours of dinner preparations Prunella had talked, of course, answering her questions about the household and its ways with a low voice. Apparently the viscount didn't touch the staff, even the prettiest, youngest ones, and he made certain no one else did. Which meant she was safe from importunate male attention, particularly from the master of the house.

Such a relief, she thought, grimacing. It would certainly keep things simpler, knowing he had no intention of pressing advances on her. Knowing he'd never touch her with the long, elegant hands she'd noticed at the dinner table while the argument railed around her. Knowing she'd never feel all that golden skin against hers, nor the touch of his mouth. She wouldn't wipe the cynicism from his eyes and the sarcastic bent from his speech. She would cook for him, and discover just where all this money had come from, and whether he'd been in London or had any confederates connected to Russell Shipping. And then she'd leave. Once she had a place to go.

Right now Nanny Gruen's cottage was empty, her sisters were God knew where, and she was on her own. She pulled on the lace nightdress she'd managed to sneak out under her petticoats when they'd been summarily evicted from their town house, and climbed into the cool, clean-smelling sheets. She could probably thank Prunella for that. It wasn't a warm night, but there were plenty of quilts and blankets on the bed, and she moved to open one of the high-set windows just a bit, to let the scent of the night air into the room. Odd, but she'd always thought she'd hated being outdoors. It turned out she simply disliked parading around in a crowded public park. She loved the wild expanses around this house, and she'd spent years not realizing it.

She slid into bed with a sigh of relief. Renwick had never been Sophie's favorite place in the world, though her sisters had adored it.

She'd preferred the excitement of town life. But now, being in London was the very last thing she wanted, not because of the shame her father had brought down on them all, but simply because she'd feel stifled. She breathed in the smell of the countryside, slowly, evenly, as she drifted into sleep. And if the last thing she thought of was Alexander Griffiths's beautiful hands, no one had to know.

Alexander leaned back in the leather chair, a glass of Scots whisky cradled in his hands, and controlled his urge to strangle someone. What the hell was going on in his household? These matters were supposed to be very simple, and instead it was growing more and more complicated.

A man had needs. Hell, he had needs, strong needs, and his months-long period of celibacy had made him twitchy. The last time he'd been able to indulge himself had been at Mrs. Lefton's discreet, elegant town house with its absolute richness of female flesh, and he'd taken full advantage of it. The problem was, he hated London, and he was hardly going to travel all that distance simply to scratch an itch.

He had no intention of trifling with anyone in the village of Basking Wells; he refused to touch the servants, and while there were usually a number of interested widows, this place was too damned small to get involved. Besides, the two possibilities didn't appeal to him—Mrs. Richards had a laugh like a screeching bird and Mrs. Densey was too thin. He liked curves on a woman. Something to hold on to, to lose himself in.

Importing a mistress from London seemed only logical, even if it was sight unseen. Mrs. Lefton was a brilliant entrepreneur, and she knew his tastes very well—he'd put his complete faith in her ability to send a pliable female with a willingness for experimentation, a woman of enough years that she'd have ideas of her own without showing the wear such a life takes on a woman. Though indeed, most of Mrs. Lefton's employees did very well for themselves, retiring at an early age with a comfortable income and their health intact. Some married, some ended up in a private relationship. But then, Mrs. Lefton knew the value of the commodity she sold.

She'd made a huge mistake this time. That . . . that girl couldn't have been plying her trade for more than a year or two. At least, he certainly hoped not. The ones who'd been at it from childhood had a certain emptiness in their eyes, for all their agreeable smiles and willing bodies, that left him feeling empty as well. No, this one was new at her game, not what he'd requested.

She was also small, when he liked a tall woman, and far too beautiful. He'd wanted a bed partner who was both enthusiastic and pleasant to look at, not a woman who struck a room dumb even in ugly clothes and with her hair a mess beneath her restrictive cap. Beauties were tedious—they expected too much and drew too much attention to themselves. He wanted discretion and no demands. Not much chance of that with the young stunner he'd suddenly acquired.

She was rude, which was a shock as well. How dare she refuse to come to him tonight? Oh, Dickens had phrased it tactfully enough, but Alexander could read between the lines. She'd simply said no, and thought she could get away with it.

She'd been astonishingly pert in the stable yard as well, and she'd watched him out of her magnificent blue eyes with wariness and something else that he couldn't quite define. In the dining hall tonight he'd been intensely aware of her attention beneath her unreadable expression. It had been almost physical, and if the very sight of her hadn't already made him hard beneath the table, that connection would have done it.

He took another sip, letting the whisky burn his tongue and slide down his throat like rough silk, and then he laughed. He knew what his gorgeous little cook's problem was.

She was as attracted to him as he was to her, and it unnerved her. He could sense it, that raw pulse of connection running between them, and as vain as it made him feel, he had no doubt he was right. He'd been in this game long enough to recognize the signs, even if she herself didn't.

She was young, the blush of innocence barely off her cheeks, so new at this that she expected it to be simply a job, to lie on her back and make the right sounds and the right smiles and then be done with it, but she'd looked at him and something had shaken her. The same thing that had shaken him. He knew it with every instinct he trusted.

And so she was rude, and she was running.

His bad temper began to evaporate as he considered this. He knew women tended to find him pleasing—even without the title and the fortune, they had flocked to him, and he had only to beckon to have them wind up in his bed. It was simply the luck of the draw—nothing he could be proud of. In fact, his face would have been the better for a few scars, perhaps a broken nose, something to mar the prettiness that his brother had always teased him about.

But he didn't want to think about his lost brother, someone who had troubled him as much as he'd loved him. He took another sip. He wanted to think about the beautiful bundle of contradictions who was supposed to fill his bed and his erotic fantasies, not his kitchen and his stepmother's appetites. She was supposed to distract him from the unanswered questions that had plagued his relationship with his adoring younger brother.

Indeed, a woman who could cook like that had no need to earn her living on her back, and so he would tell her once he was finished with her. He could even help her get a decent job. The Lefton wouldn't thank him for that, but tant pis. He was generous with the women who'd shared their favors, and he would be generous with this one.

Once he got her past her skittishness. Indeed, she was like a beautiful, unbroken colt, uncertain of the reins and halter, but knowing the man had sugar and carrots and other lovely things to tempt her.

And he would tempt her. He would tame her, he would ride her, and he might even introduce her to variations he kept for rare occasions when he and his partner were feeling particularly adventurous.

He had things to teach her, and he found he enjoyed the idea. He might be wrong, of course, and her intense regard could come from a profound, instant dislike, but he didn't think so. He recognized all the signs of sexual interest, even if a so-called professional didn't.

Or perhaps she was afraid of it. Life as a prostitute was probably easier if you didn't feel anything for the client.

He frowned. *Prostitute* was an ugly word—it made him think of back alleyways and disease-riddled women, and this girl was so young, so fresh, so beautiful. She had a gloriously untouched quality about her. Mrs. Lefton would charge him a fortune, unless . . .

It was always possible that the girl was never particularly amenable to the path she'd chosen. Lefton might have sent her to him to break her. If so, Lefton was in for a surprise. Alexander had no interest in breaking a woman's spirit, in crushing her rebellion. In fact, he intended to enjoy it.

If he were a decent man he'd find a house full of women who needed a brilliant cook—anywhere else and she'd have the men on her the moment she dropped her guard. But even in a convent there'd be trouble, and he knew it. She was better off with him. He liked only willing females, and if there was anything she didn't like, he wouldn't insist.

He'd give her this night to get settled. He hadn't even figured out how he was going to arrange things—he was hardly going to creep down into the kitchens like some predatory old man. Nor could she come to his rooms—while he was as far away as he could be from his despised stepmother, she was still under the same roof, and he'd rather not have to think of her at all when he was deep between his not-French cook's legs.

There were certainly enough bedrooms in this place to suffice. He'd have her put in one of the bedrooms where the daughters of the criminal shipbuilder had slept. They were innocent rooms, made for pretty girls, and she'd like them. He could even give her her pick. The idea of taking her in such a bastion of innocence would have made him hard if he weren't already sporting a painful erection. He'd like to take her in every room in this huge house—stretched across that scarred table in the kitchen, the desk across the room from him, in the straw in the stable yards, in the attics. The thought of her straddling him on this comfortable chair almost finished him off, and he laughed ruefully.

In the end, Mrs. Lefton was quite brilliant. She'd sent him the unexpected, and he had the worst case of blue balls since he was a randy stripling. This was going to be a game of cat and mouse, just what he needed to take his mind off the loss of his worrisome brother.

Because Rufus was gone, drowned off the coast of France, and life had to go on.

CHAPTER SIX

SOPHIE ALWAYS WOKE UP slowly, needing time to lie abed and face the demands of the upcoming day. She was sleeping so peacefully that when the rapping on her door threatened her slumber she simply turned over in the comfortable bed and pulled a feather pillow over her head.

Her respite didn't last long. The next thing she knew the pillow was pulled from her head and someone was shaking her shoulder. "You need to get up now, miss," came an unknown and unwanted voice. "We're already at work on the breakfast trays and the bread's started, but you need to get up to oversee things."

Oversee what? Who is this woman and what is she talking about? All Sophie wanted to do was sleep, and sleep she would, damn it, and the strange woman could go . . .

She bolted upright, trying to focus her sleep-filled eyes as memory came back with an unwelcome rush. She was at Renwick, albeit in the basement, and she had work to do.

"I've brought you both tea and coffee, miss," said the woman, whom Sophie recognized as her ally, Prunella. "And sweet rolls from yesterday. But you must get up."

"I'll take the coffee," she said, swinging her legs around to the side of the bed. Thank heavens she'd bathed the night before, or she would be unable to face the day. "I'll be out in five minutes." She yawned hugely. "Are the breakfast trays ready?"

"Not yet, miss. It's only just past six, and even if the Forresters are leaving today, I expect they won't call for them until eight at least."

"Six?" Sophie, an inveterate late sleeper, echoed in horror. "In the morning?"

"Yes, miss. I don't think anyone begrudges you sleeping so late, but there are decisions to be made, and I think the viscount will wish to see you."

Of course he would, she thought with a grimace. She had her work cut out for her in that area.

She was no innocent—she'd been kissed, a number of times, and found it pleasant. She'd been the toast of London; she recognized the signs of male interest. She could comfort herself with Prunella's assurance that he never touched the female servants, but there was still that look in his dark, mocking eyes that she found so unsettling.

What would she have done if she'd met him in London, she thought as she hastily began donning the layers of clothing. He would have been one of the many men seeking her attention, wanting her hand in marriage and a piece of her father's fortune. She would have ignored him, of course. She liked simple, shallow men whom she could move around like figures on a chessboard.

Or would she? Would it have made all the difference if she'd met him a year ago, when she was the beautiful Miss Sophia Russell, the toast of the season? Would she have . . . ?

It was all moot at this point. She laced up her corset, loosely. It was hot, hard work in the kitchen, and she wasn't about to tie herself in so she couldn't breathe. At least the basement kitchen stayed cooler than the upper floors.

It must have been closer to ten minutes before she sailed out of her rooms and into the kitchen, fortified by the hastily downed coffee and sweet rolls. Everyone was busy in the early morning light, but each person she passed smiled at her and said, "Good morning, miss," in such a friendly way that by the time she reached the long table, she was feeling a bit bemused. They'd been polite enough yesterday, but wary. For some reason this morning they were on her side.

The two footmen leapt to their feet as she approached. "Good morning, miss," they parroted, and she wondered if she ought to correct them, remind them that she was "madame." No, it was easier this way, and she was used to being called "miss." That one bit of familiarity would make this masquerade a little easier.

"Good morning, staff," she said, loud enough for everyone to hear. "We've got a busy day ahead of us. I need to learn your schedule and you need to learn mine. Has everyone had breakfast already?"

"No, miss," replied one of the maids by the stove. "Gracie and me usually wait till after the trays go up."

"And you are?"

"Maude, miss. The trays are ready—once they ring for them, Gracie makes the tea while I take care of the toast and fruit. If someone wants something more filling they come down to breakfast." She colored. "But you know that, miss."

For a moment Sophie felt uneasy. Why would they think she'd know such a thing if she'd never been a guest? But then, a cook should be aware of details like that, shouldn't she?

"Then the two of you sit and eat something. I overslept and I've already had my breakfast, and I can handle things if anyone rings."

"Oh, but miss . . . !" Gracie squeaked a protest.

"Don't worry. It hasn't been that long since I was the one doing trays first thing in the morning," she said cheerfully, pouring herself another cup of coffee from the pot on the massive range. In fact, it hadn't been that long since she herself had received breakfast trays. She just had to start thinking of things backwards-to. Arsey-versey, her father would have said, though never when he was out in public.

She could do it. She *would* do it. Failure simply wasn't a possibility.

No one rang for a tray for a full hour, while Sophie thought bitterly of the sleep she could have had. The girl who had made the dough for the day's bread had done a good job—it was silky and elastic to the touch, even after the second rising. The morning toast was best made from yesterday's bread, so there was no need to panic if the loaves weren't formed yet.

She set Maude to work once she'd finished eating her meal of porridge and milk. While the footmen scattered with the trays and the scullery maids began the washing, Sophie surveyed her army of three: Prunella, head kitchen maid, who had tried to fill in, Gracie, a sturdy young girl most likely shy of twenty, and her friend Maude. They were city girls, all of them, imported by the Griffithses to run the kitchens of Renwick. There'd been a bit of umbrage in the village over it, but her father had also brought his own servants when he came to stay, and the people of the prosperous little village had no need of jobs.

"I should check the larder," she said, when they were at last alone. "I need to come up with menus for his lordship, and quickly, and I need to know what we have and what we'll need. And how we'll get it," she added. Such details were totally foreign to her— Bryony knew how to organize a household, but Sophie had never bothered learning such mundane details. She'd always expected she'd marry and have a housekeeper to handle such chores.

"I'm sorry, miss," Prunella said. "It's my job to keep the inventory up to date, but what with having to take over the cooking I've been that busy . . . Normally you wouldn't have to bother with looking into the larder and the pantries."

Good to know, Sophie thought. *The cook doesn't take inventory.* She covered herself. "In a new house I always like to inspect the food storage anyway. To make sure the grains are properly preserved from mice, that the meats and dairy are kept cool." She had a sudden, horrifying thought. "Do they have their main meal in the evening when there are no guests, or in the middle of the day?" If she had to come up with a full seven- or eight-course meal in the next four hours, she was going to be frantic.

"Oh, things will be much simpler when the Forresters are gone," Prunella said. "Mrs. Griffiths has been taking a tray in her room for the last few weeks, ever since word came about Mr. Griffiths."

Sophie remembered the gossip in the village. "That would be the viscount's brother who recently died?"

"His half brother, miss. He was lost at sea, or so we've heard, and Mrs. Griffiths is that upset. She doesn't like her stepson one tiny bit, so I think she's using the excuse to avoid him, but it makes things simpler for us all. Though she does like a heavy tray."

A real cook would stop her staff from gossiping, but Sophie had no intention of doing so. She needed to find out everything she could about the Dark Viscount. So his stepmother hated him, and his half brother had died. Could Alexander Griffiths have anything to do with his own brother's death? If he was the murderous criminal they had suspected, then it wouldn't be beyond him. First his wife, then her father, then his brother? It seemed inconceivable, but evil could come in beautiful packages. She pushed the thought away for the moment.

"And the viscount?" she asked. "He must dine in the hall."

"No, miss. The new viscount ain't much for ceremony. He'll have us bring a tray in the library, but half the time he doesn't touch it but goes off riding instead, at all hours of the day and night. As for luncheon, it's trays again. Mrs. Griffiths is the one we've got to please, and sooner or later she'll start coming back downstairs to eat."

"And does her stepson join her then?" It was an innocent enough question.

"If he has to. He don't like her much; that's for sure."

It was impossible to tell from Prunella's voice which side of the battle she preferred. Despite Sophie's very real misgivings about the Dark Viscount, the memory of his stepmother was disconcerting. There'd been too much arguing for her to get more than a quick glimpse at the older woman, but Sophie's impression had been full of misgivings.

"Well, then, we'd better get to work." At the last minute she remembered something Bryony had said, and she offered it with an air of triumph. "A good servant needs to be prepared for everything."

Prunella looked at her for a moment, her eyebrow raised, and Sophie felt another trickle of unease. "Indeed, yes, miss," Prunella said eventually. "I'll just get my inventory and then we can update it while you look things over."

The pantry wasn't bad, though Sophie rearranged things to her liking. The bins of flour and sugar were well filled and shielded in tin to keep vermin out; there were dried apples and pears, aging cheeses and bottles of oil and vinegar, jars and jars of preserves and honey, and several dozen eggs.

"Lamb with rosemary for luncheon, starting with a crisp chestnut soup, followed by smoked trout and finished off with a round of roasted asparagus and an apple charlotte," she said decisively. "Where's the larder?"

"This way, miss," Gracie, who had followed along with Maude, announced, and started for the door, only to hear Dickens's calm voice sounding oddly panicked.

"Deliveries," he gasped.

"Oh, we should go out and supervise," Sophie said, starting to move past the maid, when Prunella suddenly dragged her arm and moved her back into the small room, with Maude slamming the door and leaning back against it.

"We should recount the jars of honey," Prunella announced firmly. "I believe I am way off. And did anyone see a bottle of wine? Open and half gone."

Sophie looked at her in surprise, both for her words and her odd behavior. Was she a drinker? "I counted eighteen," she said flatly. "And there was no wine."

"That's a serious situation," Prunella announced. "Someone's been here getting into the wine. The footmen know better, and I can't imagine anyone else doing it. I wouldn't want to face Mr. Dickens, telling him wine has gone missing."

"Wouldn't the wine be in the cellar, with Mr. Dickens keeping the keys?" Sophie asked. She could hear voices outside the room, the sound of things moving around. "You know, I really should be out there if they're delivering food. I need to choose what looks the freshest before I come up with a menu."

There was a panicked look in Maude's eyes, and she glanced at Prunella uneasily. The senior maid took over with suspicious smoothness. "I'm sure you can trust Dickens. He usually oversees deliveries of everything, including food. Nothing to worry about. Unlike this missing wine . . ."

"But I intend to change things," Sophie said stubbornly. If she was going to finally have a chance to throw herself into cooking anything she wanted and hang the budget, then she needed to pick and choose.

"God bless you, miss, and I'm sure that will be fine with Mr. Dickens. But we'd best make sure about the wine. Mr. Dickens takes inebriation very seriously indeed, miss."

"I haven't seen anyone inebriated."

Prunella looked at Maude and Gracie with almost a flash of amusement. "Yes, miss, but you're the newest one here. If wine goes missing for the first time, then you'd be the obvious suspect, and doubtless they'd double-check your credentials and . . ."

"Never mind," Sophie said hastily. "I didn't touch the wine, and I certainly wouldn't have expected to find any among the cooking supplies. Not that I have anything against wine in certain dishes—in fact, I applaud it. But I didn't touch it."

"I'm sure Mr. Dickens realizes that," Gracie piped up. "But maybe we'll just make certain it hasn't fallen somewhere."

Sophie was about to tell her that Gracie could make certain while Sophie met with the vendors who came to the kitchen door, when something stopped her. Some look that was moving between the three of her staff, a warning expression, and she hesitated. Did she trust these three strangers who'd been kind to her? What were her own instincts telling her to do?

She dropped to her knees and peered under one row of shelving. "I don't see anything under this one, but that doesn't mean it's not here." She sat back on her bum and looked up at the three. "A little help?"

The three of them immediately sank to the floor, and the next half hour was spent crawling around on the spotlessly clean pantry floor, giggling and squashing spiders and indulging in the kind of harmless gossip that wiped away the last of Sophie's misgivings. For some reason her kitchen staff didn't want her out in the room when the deliveries were made. She would trust them.

She heard the soft, rhythmic rap on the door, so quiet that she might have missed it if Maude hadn't immediately lifted her head like a bloodhound scenting a rabbit. She sat back, trying for a casual expression. "I think we might see what's been delivered, miss."

Sophie raised an eyebrow as she scrambled to her feet. "Oh, really? It's safe?" she said with only mild sarcasm. "Then by all means." She pushed open the door, and this time no one got in her way.

The long center table in the kitchen was covered with food. A huge basket of fresh peas that had probably come from the Martins' farm, as well as the spinach and mushrooms, plus a haunch of beef whose proper aging could only be the work of Delbert the butcher. There were fresh spring potatoes, newly dug, from the Bonethwistles' potato farm, and an order of wine that would have come from London but may or may not have moved through the hands of Jacky, the lad who owned the delivery cart.

In other words, her masquerade would have been over almost as soon as it had begun, and she glanced at her suddenly industrious kitchen staff. She could happily bless them. She had no idea what was going on with them earlier, what they were trying to hide from her, but she didn't care. The most logical explanation was that someone was skimming off the deliveries—they were receiving short rations or someone was taking food from the kitchen. Either way, she'd put a stop to it. No one had expected her arrival, and plans had already been in place. She would simply have to make it clear to the girls that she would tolerate no dishonesty when it came to the kitchen staff.

She suddenly realized her own hypocrisy, and she wanted to laugh. No one was allowed to be dishonest but the cook herself, lying to get the job, lying about her name, her age, her identity. She was no one to point a finger of blame. One did what one had to do. Her father had taught her that.

Which was why she wasn't as convinced as her sisters that her father was an innocent man. He'd started his life as a laborer, a shipbuilder, and he'd built his business and amassed his fortune much too quickly to have followed all the rules. It had been his business in the beginning, and still bore his name—he could have justified stripping it of its assets.

But he never would have taken the money and run off, abandoning his daughters. And there was still no explanation as to why he was alone in the middle of Dartmoor, and where all that money had gone.

"I'll add this to the inventory," Prunella volunteered. "Unless there's something you'd rather have me do."

Sophie glanced at the heavy-laden table, determined not to look overwhelmed. "You never told me what kind of meal the family prefers for the midday."

"None of us has been in service to them for that long," Prunella said. "But the first cook brought a big book of recipes with her, and she left it behind when she quit."

"And why did she quit?"

"Didn't like the countryside," Maude volunteered. "She had family back in Surrey."

"Ah," Sophie said, hoping to sound wise. "And where is this miraculous book of recipes?"

Indeed, *miraculous* was the word for it. When Prunella finally unearthed the massive tome, it was filled with the answers to, if not all her prayers, at least a goodly portion of them. It contained full instructions for the traditional French service à la russe, which amused her. If it were Russian, how could it be French? There were hors d'oeuvres and soups, fish and entrees, joints, game, and vegetables and even a long treatise on various sweets and removes. Nothing she couldn't improve with a slight adjustment here, a major substitution there. She was about to set Gracie and Maude to washing and chopping the vegetables when a familiar voice came from the stable yard, one that sent cold chills down her spine.

"Yoo-hoo," came Miss Crowell's dulcet tones. "I'm here with the flowers."

Sophie was momentarily turned to stone. She'd forgotten that Miss Crowell's magnificent gardens provided cut flowers for Renwick—the cutting gardens had been dug up and transplanted for the viscount's swimming pond and they hadn't had time to accustom themselves to their new home. Miss Crowell had been supplementing, but not for a moment had Sophie considered that the old hag would deliver them herself.

It happened so fast Sophie barely had time to react. One moment she was standing in the middle of the kitchen, listening to Miss Crowell's stalwart footsteps, and in the next Dickens himself had taken her and shoved her back into the pantry, slamming the door behind her.

"Ah, Miss Crowell." Dickens greeted her with his usual dignity, not like someone who had manhandled the new cook into the larder. "You're early today."

"I have a dear friend who's going to come to live with me, and I have a lot of things to do to get ready." Her voice carried perfectly through the thick door. "You may have heard of her—the nanny who worked for the former residents of this lovely house."

"Mrs. Gruen," Dickens supplied smoothly. "Yes, we know of her. She suffered an accident, didn't she?"

"She did indeed. She broke her leg, but it's an ill wind that blows no one good. As soon as she's well enough, she's going to come live with me while she recuperates, and I don't intend to let her leave to scrimp and slave on her own. And that wretched Russell girl has decamped, thank heavens."

"Has she indeed?" Dickens might be talking about an absolute stranger, but Sophie knew that he wasn't. He knew exactly who the wretched Russell girl was, and where she was hiding at the moment. Suddenly their secrecy all made sense. They'd been protecting her. "I heard she was a quite pleasant young lady."

Even through the thick wood Miss Crowell's contemptuous snort was audible. "That's as may be," she said loftily, "but she has no place around here anymore. I sent her off yesterday. Mrs. Gruen doesn't need to be worried about a former charge, and I imagine the viscount will be glad to have the use of the cottage back."

"I can't imagine why," Dickens said in a repressive tone. "Renwick is a very profitable estate, and there is no need for more tenant farmers. Indeed, his lordship has very advanced ideas about land ownership and cultivation, and if memory serves me, that cottage is too small to be of much use for a family. I believe his lordship was more than happy to have Mrs. Gruen continue to reside there, and I doubt he would have minded if Miss Russell had remained while Mrs. Gruen was in hospital."

Sophie could almost feel Miss Crowell's frustration. "Well, that's as may be," she said finally, "but she's gone, and good riddance. And you're wrong about the viscount—he would have made certain Sophie Russell was out on her . . . was out the moment he heard. He'd never struck me as a particularly charitable gentleman, particularly when it came to the family who stole his birthright."

"Stole his birthright?" Dickens sounded almost affronted. "I fear you've been reading too many novels, Miss Crowell. He's always known this house would return to him sooner or later, and he wouldn't have blamed a young girl for the bad behavior of his own relatives and hers."

Miss Crowell made a little *phhfft* sound. "You just be sure to let me know if she attempts to make contact with the viscount. She wasn't certain of her destination and I wouldn't put it past the minx to try to wheedle her way into his good graces."

"I don't believe his lordship has any good graces," Dickens announced in a lugubrious tone, and Sophie wanted to laugh. As far as she could see, the milk of human kindness had been drained and replaced with the sour curdle of mockery and sarcasm in Viscount Griffiths's veins.

The voices faded away, and she heard the heavy outer door close with a thud. She counted to one hundred, first in French and then in Latin, just to make herself wait long enough, and then she slowly pushed open the inner door once more.

No one raised his head when she stepped back into the kitchen. Gracie was cutting the flowers, Maude and Prunella were busy with the vegetables, and Mr. Dickens was arranging the stems in a vase.

"Does everyone know?" she asked quietly.

Mr. Dickens looked up from his task. "Only the servants, miss. You can't keep anything a secret from the servants, and the goings-on in the village are as well known to us as they are to those who live there."

"Are you going to tell anyone?"

Dickens looked affronted. "Begging your pardon, miss, but haven't we gone out of our way to keep you from being seen by the townspeople? You'll be able to live here in safety and anonymity for as long as you wish. There's no reason why his lordship or his stepmother should have to find out anything."

For some reason Sophie, who was fiercely against tears, felt suddenly weepy. It had been so long since she'd felt that anyone had been on her side, apart from her sisters and Nanny, that she would have sagged back against the door if she weren't determined not to show weakness. She was safe here. The other servants were watching out for her. She had nothing to worry about.

"Madame Camille," came Alexander Griffiths's drawling voice from the stairwell. "Are you finally willing to grant me a moment of your time?"

Oh, shite.

CHAPTER SEVEN

HIS NEW MISTRESS-CUM-COOK WAS looking both very beautiful and completely panicked for the moment, and Alexander wasn't sure whether to be amused or annoyed. A moment later she turned to face him, her beautiful face bland and expressionless, like a woman, no, a girl, wearing a mask. How many of the women he'd bedded had worn masks like this one? Probably all of them—this one was simply too inexperienced to have perfected the art.

He'd asked for experience, and it was hard to believe Lydia Lefton would have dared send him someone so far from his expectations. "In the library," he said. "Now."

He saw the brief flash of annoyance in those dark blue eyes, and oddly enough some of his own irritation faded. The more she failed to live up to his expectations, the more entertaining he found her, and he was beginning to realize he'd been bored for a long time. She was a perfect distraction from thinking about Rufus, thinking about the harridan upstairs, and with the thoughtful application of just the right incentive she would prove even more entertaining. He was very good at finding incentives.

He strode through the hallway, not bothering to moderate his long-legged stride, knowing it would require an effort for her to keep up with him. With luck she'd arrive at his library flushed and breathless and just the tiniest bit overheated, and he could begin to unbutton that ridiculously high-necked dress.

He moved into the ancient study that smelled of books and leather and generations of wood smoke, the one room he refused to let Adelia work her hideous taste on, and was about to close the door when a small, slim hand reached out and caught it. Looking down at his new mistress in surprise, he saw that she was neither out of breath nor flushed. Since the women of his acquaintance earned their living in bed, they were usually fairly indolent with their clothes on, but Madame Camille, or whatever she was calling herself, seemed ridiculously fit.

He stepped back, into the room, but she made no effort to follow, standing there with her back stiff. "Did you change your mind, my lord?" she asked, just slightly caustic. "I can always return to the kitchen—I have a great deal to do there and . . ."

"Sit down," he said mildly enough.

"I'd rather stand."

For a moment he was speechless, not quite as amused. "I don't give a fuck what you'd rather do," he said, and if he hadn't been watching her so closely he wouldn't have noticed the slight wince at his crude word. What kind of whore was she, to be uncomfortable with the word best suited to her chosen profession?

She came into the room, taking her own sweet time about it, as if to make sure he realized that he didn't cow her. It was a waste of time on her part—he knew just how much he did and didn't intimidate her. She glanced around the room, then went directly to the most comfortable chair in the place, the ancient green leather chair he usually sat in to read. The girl had taste as well as temerity.

He moved around to the far side of the desk and sat. Having a piece of furniture between them kept their positions clear—master and servant, no matter how good a chair she'd chosen. "Do you wish to remain in my employ, Miss . . . ? What the hell should I call you?"

This time she flinched, and he knew that no matter how standoffish she was being, she wanted to be here. "I am known as Madame Camille."

"You don't strike me as a Frenchwoman."

"My mother was French. Madame will suffice."

He'd been trying to intimidate her, but at that he laughed. "I don't think so. What's your name? Your real name?"

He'd taken her off guard, and he could see her mentally scrambling. He snapped at her. "Now!"

"S-Sophie."

"You don't look like a Sophie," he said. He'd be damned if that was her real name—it was too innocent. "But it will do. I must say, my dear Sophie, that I question your interest in the role you've been sent to fill."

"You're wrong." And then she added, "my lord," as if she realized how abrupt she sounded. "I am most determined to provide satisfaction."

He leaned back, letting his mouth curve in a mocking smile. "Now why have I been doubting that?"

"I don't know, my lord. I never undertake something without throwing myself into it completely, and I promise you that you will have absolutely no complaints about my . . . my cooking." She stammered over the words. So they were going to speak in code, were they?

"Oh, I expect you're an excellent . . . ah . . . cook. Mrs. Lefton would never have sent me a candidate who was unqualified. But there seems to be a certain lack of enthusiasm for some of the duties the job entails."

"Oh, no, my lord." She was putting energy into it, her eyes wide and guileless, and yet he was still having his doubts. Oh, he wanted her, quite badly. But she wasn't the comfortable, undemanding creature he'd requested. "You will find that your faith in Mrs. Lefton's judgment is not misplaced," she continued. "I will stop at nothing in my efforts to please you. I am very creative, and I promise to astonish your senses with delights you haven't even dreamed of."

She was so earnest, and his problem had always been his imagination. He could already guess just how she could astonish his senses, and it was a good thing he was sitting behind the desk as he felt himself begin to stir. That was odd. He was no randy boy to sport a hard-on from nothing more than a mild sexual innuendo, but here he was, wanting nothing more than to leap across the surface of his desk and drag her down onto the floor. He raised an eyebrow. "Indeed?"

She didn't blush—clearly she was more brazen than she had first appeared. "I will stop at nothing in my efforts to please you, my lord."

His grin was wry. "Mrs. Lefton would expect nothing less."

She nodded vigorously, showing more enthusiasm. "Her employees have to meet her exacting standards, and I know she has always been most impressed with my work."

He considered this for a moment. He'd always wondered how women of the night received their training, and just assumed it was from experience, starting with their first lovers. The thought that Mrs. Lefton might have had firsthand knowledge of his new mistress gave him an odd feeling. While in general he found the idea of women pleasuring each other to be perfectly acceptable and even exciting, he didn't like the thought of that raddled old hag touching Sophie.

Sophie. Maybe that was a good name for her after all.

"I really want this position," she added.

He couldn't repress a grin. "Which one?" He could think of half a dozen positions without even trying.

Sophie didn't appear to share his extremely vulgar sense of humor. "The position for which I was hired," she said with great dignity.

"I was thinking of more than one."

She looked at him blankly, and his amusement began to turn to irritation again. He wasn't used to having to work for a woman— that was the point in paying for it. No misconceptions, no polite lies or even the necessity of charm, though he'd been told he had his own, barbed brand of charm.

Unfortunately it was already too late—he wanted her, he wanted her now, and she was watching him with a cool expression that suggested half his innuendoes were going right over her head, when he knew that was impossible.

"I have very strong appetites," he said slowly. "It takes a great deal to leave me sated, and I bore easily."

"I promise my efforts won't leave you bored," she said.

He let his eyes drift down over her body. He could tell that the dress she was wearing had once been very good quality, and it had survived a hurried trip to a dye bath to turn it a rusty shade between black and brown. He certainly hoped she had something more becoming in her trunks, because this masquerade, while amusing, was most definitely finite. The only one in this household who cared about food was Adelia, and he'd just as soon poison the bitch as she had once tried to poison him. With Rufus gone there was no longer any reason to tolerate her. He'd promised his father he'd look after her, and deathbed promises weren't to be broken lightly, but Adelia was someone who could be bought off quite easily. As long as he kept funneling money in her direction, he wouldn't have to see the vicious cow.

In the meantime he had more pleasant things to think about, such as the gorgeous, prickling creature in front of him. "I could be up all night," he murmured, thinking of his unruly member, "and do nothing but eat."

She didn't even blush. For all her seemingly untouched appearance, she must have seen and heard a great deal in her young life not to react to his salacious comments. Once again he wondered if she'd been a child whore, and the thought sickened him.

But no, she didn't have that dead expression in her eyes. "How long have you been doing this?" he said abruptly.

"Long enough, my lord. I promise you will find me more than competent for anything your appetites desire." Again she looked at him with that absolute earnestness that many of the most unblushing whores couldn't carry off.

"Competent, eh?" he echoed. Lord knows one wanted a competent whore, he thought wryly.

"More than competent," she corrected him. "In fact, you might even call me inspired when the occasion merits it."

He laughed. "Well, I shall simply have to see that the occasion merits it. You're dismissed, Sophie." To his surprise he found himself rising, as if a lady were leaving the room. While he tended to treat his mistresses with absolute courtesy outside the bedroom, it would look extremely odd if he started rising for his cook. But sitting back down would be too awkward, so he skirted the desk as she rose, wanting to get closer to her. He wanted a taste of that lovely mouth of hers; he wanted to bite and lick her. He moved swiftly, before she had time to back away, and the chair was behind her legs, trapping her there.

She was suddenly breathing deeply, as if she were actually nervous, when up till now she'd been ridiculously calm. And she smelled . . . different. She smelled of soap, rather than scent, with a touch of vanilla sugar about her that suddenly reminded him of his childhood days in the kitchen, begging Cook for a taste of the sweet dough, when he was young and nothing bad had happened.

Of course, Cook had never looked like Sophie.

He bent down, because she was shorter than he'd ordered, ready to take her mouth, when there came a sharp rapping at the door.

He should have ignored it, but it startled him enough that she was able to back away and open the door before he could stop her.

It was good, reliable Dickens, and Alexander wished him to the devil and back again. But he'd already taken a step toward his desk, and Alexander had no intention of having his butler and old friend think he'd caught the master in flagrante delicto with the new cook.

"I beg your pardon, your lordship," Dickens said, looking disturbed. "But we've received word from the man you hired to look into your brother's death."

"Of course," he said, mentally dismissing Sophie. Temporarily. "Is he here?"

"No, my lord. But there's correspondence."

He'd been so distracted he hadn't noticed Dickens was holding a silver salver with the morning post on it. "You may go, Madame Camille," he said carelessly as he reached for the letter. "But I'll most definitely have need of your talents later on."

She bobbed a curtsey, something she clearly didn't have much practice in, and whisked herself out the door. And then he thought of nothing else but the private detective's neatly penned words.

CHAPTER EIGHT

FORTUNATELY DICKENS DIDN'T SEEM determined to race through the corridors of Renwick like his master, and Sophie had no trouble following in his wake, her mind reeling. She had to be imagining what had just happened in the Dark Viscount's library. She'd been frozen, looking up at him, and she'd had the sudden thought that he was going to kiss her, that he was going to put that hard, mocking mouth against hers, and the very thought made her feel hot inside, and she wasn't sure why. It was almost as if she'd wanted him to kiss her.

But that was impossible. He'd asked her all the right questions; he'd seemed much more interested in her qualifications as a cook than last evening's meal had suggested, though heaven knows his guests might have put a damper on his appetite. Strong appetites, he'd said, and she wondered why that felt unnerving. There were men in society who had little interest in anything but food, but they tended to be corpulent, and the viscount was, if anything, a little too lean. She only wished she'd had a closer look at him when he swam. From the distance he'd seemed fit, muscled and strong, but up close there was a whipcord energy about him that was too hard, too unforgiving. God help the woman who drew his attentions, she thought piously, a little shiver of longing running down her spine.

Dickens had stopped in front of the baize door that led to the servants' staircase, and she halted her headlong pace, almost running into him as he stood waiting for her. "Miss Russell . . ." he began.

"You shouldn't call me that," she said hastily. "Someone might hear you. Like an idiot I just told his lordship that my real name was Sophie, so you may as well call me that, unless you prefer Madame Camille . . ."

"Miss Sophie," Dickens said, clearly determined to be formal. "Might I suggest you keep your distance from the viscount? While he has never once interfered with any of the staff under my protection, you are obviously not in the usual way. I have complete faith in his honor in this matter, but it might be prudent to keep temptation out of his reach."

She blinked. "Do you think he has . . . er . . . designs on me?"

"It's difficult to say, but it never hurts to err on the side of caution. I'll speak to Prunella—she'll come up with excuses if he asks for you. As I said, it would be completely unlike him, but I feel responsible for you. I should send you on your way, but we at Renwick are well aware of the difficult position you are in. I would never forgive myself if something happened to you."

She smiled up at him gratefully. "I think you're mistaken. The Dark . . . the viscount is far too proud to be interested in me. I've been the object of men's flirtations since I was fifteen years old, and I assure you Viscount Griffiths is showing none of the signs." It was true; that heavy, intense gaze was something totally unfamiliar.

"He doesn't wish to court you, Miss Sophie. I'm concerned that he wishes to bed you. Pardon my plain speaking, but you're on the other side now, and gentlemen do not always behave with perfect propriety. To my knowledge the master has never lowered himself to interfere with the servants, but I merely wished to caution you."

He had to be wrong, but Sophie felt a rush of gratitude. People were looking out for her, caring for her well-being. She was no longer so alone. "Thank you, Mr. Dickens. I'll be very careful."

He gave a slight bow. "I also need to inform you that you are to stay away from the east aspect of the house in the afternoons. This is a rule for all the members of the household. His lordship swims in the reflecting pool in what I gather used to be the rose garden, and he insists on no witnesses."

The loss of Bryony's roses still rankled. "Why?" she said, trying to damp down her anger. "Does he swim in the altogether?"

Dickens looked faintly shocked. "Certainly not, miss! He just doesn't wish to be spied upon."

"I couldn't care less about spying on the man," she said airily, for the moment forgetting that she'd spent the last month going to a great deal of effort to do just that.

"Of course, miss. And when you come up with a few days' worth of menus, I'll be the one to take them to his lordship, to spare you."

"His lordship, not his mother?"

"Mrs. Griffiths is his stepmother, and there's no love lost between the two of them. She has a much more avid interest in food, and the viscount prefers to thwart her."

"Childish of him."

"We do not criticize our . . ." Dickens stopped as he realized what he was about to say. He sighed. "It's best not to discuss those abovestairs. I beg your pardon, miss, but I worry about you."

It was pure instinct on her part. She reached up and gave him a kiss on his rough cheek, and he flushed in embarrassment. "You're very—"

"Do I interrupt?" The viscount's soft voice did just that, and Sophie and the butler sprang apart, suddenly guilty.

Sophie recovered her composure faster. "I was thanking Mr. Dickens for his excellent guidance, my lord." She was quite proud of herself for remembering the "my lord" part. "He was informing me that everyone avoids the east aspect of the house in the afternoons while you partake of your improving exercises." She was hoping to goad him, just the tiniest bit, not for her sake but to pay him back for startling Dickens.

But Alexander Griffiths simply gave her that wicked smile. "Oh, they're hardly improving. They're more a matter of . . . maintenance. My temper is far more sanguine when I'm able to get a bit of exercise. Otherwise I'm an absolute bear, aren't I, Dickens?"

"Good heavens, no, my lord!" Dickens managed to protest.

"Why don't you ride, as most gentlemen do?" Sophie said curiously, then realized her mistake as both of the men turned to stare at her, Dickens with horrified eyes, the viscount with wry amusement.

"I do appreciate your concern, but I ride when I wish to go someplace. I happen to have a particular affinity for water. My mother used to say I was part seal."

Sophie blinked, picturing the mean-looking dowager she'd seen the night before, then reminded herself that the woman was his stepmother. "I thought seals preferred the ocean to freshwater." She heard Dickens's shocked intake of breath, but it was too late to do anything about it.

"You should come with me, Madame Camille," the butler said hastily, clamping a hand on her arm.

It was removed a second later by the viscount. "I'm afraid Cook and I hadn't quite finished our conversation when you interrupted us, Dickens," the viscount said in a silken voice. "I'll send her along in a moment."

Dickens was looking distressed. "I don't mind waiting, my lord. Madame Camille is new to the house and she might not be able to find her way . . ."

"This staircase leads directly down to the kitchens. You know better than I how dim-witted she might be, but I imagine it would be fairly difficult to lose her way in such a short distance."

Dickens cast a worried glance at Sophie's fulminating countenance. "Yes, my lord," he said helplessly, and slipped behind the baize door.

"Dim-witted?" Sophie echoed, her voice deceptively dulcet. "Have I given you any particular reason to suspect I'm devoid of my full complement of wits?"

That half smile again. "I knew it would annoy you. How do you like being called 'Cook'?"

She barely managed to control her glare—she hadn't liked it at all and he knew it. "Do you always bully your servants the way you did Dickens?"

"Oh, you give him too little credit. Dickens has been looking after me since I was fourteen years old and he's used to my ways. He's wise enough to know when to keep his mouth shut. A trick you could learn."

"Why should I keep my mouth shut?" she said recklessly. "I'm your employee, not your slave, and you're paying a very great deal for my wisdom and experience, not to mention my creativity." At least she assumed he was. Too bad she was unlikely to see any of it. Since the mysterious Mrs. Lefton seemed to have made the arrangements for the viscount's new chef, then most likely the money went to her first. Even if it did trickle down to Sophie, she would probably be gone well before her first month's wages were due.

"So you are," he murmured thoughtfully, letting those stormy gray eyes run down her body, and that familiar unease and anticipation swept through her.

He wouldn't touch her, she reminded herself. Dickens had sworn he never touched the female staff. It was a blessed relief, she reminded herself for not the first time. "So what else did you wish to say to me, your lordship?" She didn't bother disguising the note of impatience that crept into her voice. Even knowing she was perfectly safe from importunate advances still didn't quiet her uneasiness in his presence, the strange restlessness that she couldn't understand.

"Just this," he said in a lazy voice, and before she had any idea what he intended he reached out and pulled her up against him, his other arm coming round her waist.

It was almost as if she'd been slammed against a hard object, though in fact he was only flesh and blood. Extremely firm, well-muscled flesh and blood, and there was no way her breath could have been knocked out of her by his unexpected move, and yet suddenly she couldn't breathe.

She'd managed to raise her arms, to push against him, but it did no good. He was very strong, and she was trapped.

She looked up, way up into his eyes, steeling herself not to react to the stark, elegant beauty of his face. She knew her own eyes were cool, her expression undaunted, but she could feel her lower lip tremble slightly, the one part of her she couldn't control, and she bit down hard on it to try to still the telltale sign.

She couldn't read his expression—he was adept at being enigmatic, and he simply stared down at her for a long moment, as if he could read her soul beyond the determined, bland expression she was trying so hard to master.

"Yes, my lord?" she prompted impatiently, hoping her cool words would bring him to his senses and he'd release her. She'd made a fatal miscalculation.

He caught her chin in one large, hard hand, holding her still, and when he put his mouth over hers, she froze in shock.

This kiss wasn't like any other she'd ever experienced. His lips weren't soft, tentative, worshipful. His mouth was hard, damp, covering hers as he tipped her head back, and she let out an involuntary gasp of shock. This wasn't right. He didn't touch his servants; she was perfectly safe.

He lifted his head, and she let out her pent-up breath in a whoosh. He was looking down at her critically, *critically*, as if she'd just presented him with an undercooked capon. "Surely you can kiss better than that," he said with a hint of asperity. "Open your mouth."

He still had her trapped against him, and the heat of his body through the too-few layers of clothes was calling to her. She needed to put a stop to this immediately, she reminded herself. "Why?"

He raised an eyebrow. "Why?" he echoed, almost nonplussed. "Are you really asking me why you should open your mouth when I kiss you?"

"You are correct, *my lord*"—she put an ironic emphasis on his title—"although it's of little importance, since I have no intention of letting you kiss me again, and I am most certainly not going to kiss you. Please release me."

For a moment he seemed almost baffled. "You're not going to kiss me?"

"Absolutely not. Ever." Her voice was firm. "Now if we're finished here I need to return to the kitchens to begin preparing dinner."

"Not quite finished, my dear Sophie," he said in an amused tone that sent shivers of alarm down her spine. "Were you or were you not sent here by Mrs. Lefton?"

She'd already told him that she had been—she could hardly take it back. Maybe the mysterious Mrs. Lefton specialized in cooks who kissed their masters. "Mrs. Lefton sent me." She didn't even blink at the blatant untruth.

"And did she, or did she not, send you here for a specific reason?" His soft voice was almost dangerous, but his hold on her had gentled slightly. Not that she made the mistake of thinking she could tear herself out of his arms. If she tried, those arms would tighten once again. She was going nowhere until he was ready to release her.

"Yes, my lord. And I promise to fill my position to the absolute best of my abilities." She swallowed, then continued doggedly onward. "But I have my own ways of doing things. I promise you will have nothing to complain about with what I offer you." She was feeling reckless—she hadn't even cooked him a full sixteen-course meal, and yet she had complete faith in her abilities if he just gave her enough time to try. "I swear to you that by the time I'm finished, you will be struck silent with awe and admiration."

He simply blinked in astonishment. And then he threw back his head and laughed, and for once the sound was different, clear and loud, with none of the irony and mockery that seemed to lace his speech and his humor. "My dear Sophie," he bent down to murmur in her ear, "your promises whet my appetite to an alarming extent. If you're able to fulfill them even half as well as you insist you can, then I imagine we'll get along very well."

If she let out a sigh of relief he'd feel it, so she simply nodded. She'd earned a reprieve, and once he tasted her Poulet à l'Ancienne with its cream sauce just lightly touched with lemon and capers, her place of honor would be assured for as long as she wished to stay.

"In the meantime you need to release me, your lordship. How would it look to the other servants if they happened to see me in such an odd position?"

He glanced down with a lazy expression at their bodies pressed close together. "I can think of many odder, more interesting positions," he said, and the mocking humor was back. "And they'll find out soon enough."

She was too busy trying to wriggle out of his arms to pay attention to what he was saying, and this time he let her go, stepping back from her. "Do keep away from the east lawn," he added affably. "Or you may not be able to wait until tonight."

She had absolutely no idea what he was talking about, and she wondered for a moment if the man were slightly . . . *eccentric* was the polite term for it. *Moon-mad* might be closer.

"I intend to spend the rest of the day and night in the kitchen," she said firmly, backing away from him, hoping she wasn't going to trip. She wasn't going to turn around and run—that was assured. Never turn your back on the enemy, Papa had always said, and whether the Dark Viscount had had anything to do with Papa's death or not, he was most definitely the enemy.

"Not the entire night," he said, and before she realized it he'd pushed her up against the baize door, caught her mouth with his, and his tongue was there, touching hers with an intimacy that astonished her. What strange perversions had the man come up with?

She'd never been kissed like this. It felt almost unbearably intimate, and she froze, wild thoughts careening through her brain. She should be furious, disgusted, outraged. Instead she felt an odd trickle of arousal begin to burn in her belly, and lower still. She could feel her body soften against his, as if she could mold herself against his hard frame, and she recognized, to her dismay, that she liked this. No, more than liked it. She wanted the kiss to last forever. This was what she'd been waiting for during her long, endless season in London, this rush of need, of emotion that was sweeping her off her feet, leaving her moon-mad herself.

He lifted his head, far too soon, pausing for a moment as he stared down at her, a quizzical expression on his face. As if he found the kiss as astonishing as she did.

Before she could shove him away, before she could close her eyes and drift into the strange, enticing promise of that indecent kind of kiss, he released her. "You'll need to get used to it," he said cryptically.

A moment later he was gone, leaving her standing alone in the hallway, unable to move.

Get used to what? What in the world had just happened? She felt confused, flushed, nervous, and excited, all from a strange kind of kiss that surely wasn't even English. She realized she was trembling, and she quickly pulled herself together. She was no weak-minded miss to dissolve when a strange man kissed her. Except that the Dark Viscount wasn't simply a stranger at all. Whether she liked it or not, he was someone who mattered to her, mattered a great deal.

She pushed open the green baize door and then leaned against the other side, trying to catch her breath and still her racing pulses. It wasn't as if she hadn't been kissed before. She'd allowed a select few of her most devoted swains that privilege, and at night she'd talked to Maddy, comparing one against another in hopes of being able to choose a suitable husband. Life would have been so much simpler if she hadn't been so choosy. A husband would have had no choice but to support her sisters as well as herself when their world had been destroyed, and since she had had no intention of marrying anyone without a fortune, a title, and a great deal of influence, both socially and politically, their problems would have been over before they'd started.

But no, she'd kept finding fault with each one of them, all for one thing or another that in retrospect seemed ridiculous. She hadn't liked Reginald Grant's protuberant Adam's apple. Cecil Hargreaves had an annoying laugh, Nigel Pennysworth cleared his throat constantly, Sir Richard Thompson had been too dour, Lord Kindor smiled too much. While their attention had been flattering, she couldn't imagine spending the rest of her life with any one, much less sharing the mysterious activities of the bedchamber with him.

Not that those activities were that mysterious. Both Bryony and Maddy had explained them to her, but neither of them had spoken from experience. Her maid had offered up a few shocking tidbits, such as the fact that some men and women actually put their mouths *there,* and derived great pleasure from it. As someone particularly interested in the taste of things, Sophie couldn't help but be appalled by such a notion, but maybe if one washed down the flavor with wine or a sweet custard one might not notice.

And of course she had no idea what the actual member itself looked like, apart from the sisters' surreptitious and intense study of the Elgin Marbles. If it were rather like a piece of liver in texture then it might do well with bacon.

That was when she realized the appalling absurdity of what she was doing, coming up with a menu for raw . . . raw cock, that's what the stable lads had called it. There were other words too, but she didn't want to think about it. She didn't want to think about putting her mouth on a piece of raw liver; she didn't want to think about naked bodies.

Except his . . .

She still hadn't seen the Dark Viscount in the altogether, and she'd promised herself she would, sooner or later. Now that she'd put herself in such close proximity to him, it might not be such a wise idea, but she'd made a promise to herself the first day she'd gone tromping around on that outcropping and come across the view down in the valley, and a promise was a promise.

She probably ought to see what she could do to solve the mystery of her father's fall from grace, to see whether Alexander Griffiths had anything to do with it. Once she'd determined his innocence, and only then, would she sneak out into the east garden, hide behind the few sad, remaining rose bushes and take in the full glory of his body.

It would make her eventual marriage to whomever was lucky enough to win her favors much easier to deal with. Knowledge was power, Bryony always used to say, and Maddy had seconded it. Who was she to go against her sisters' wisdom?

She could hear the staff down in the kitchen, the quiet sounds of someone chopping on the wooden block, the slap and thump of dough being worked, the smell of chicken stock wafting up. She would make the Dark Viscount the most magnificent meal he'd ever enjoyed, and then she'd sleep the sleep of the just, knowing she'd lived up to her extravagant promises.

She reached up and touched her mouth, her fingertips soft against her lips. He'd kissed her. Deep, open-mouthed. How very odd. Not odd that he'd wanted to kiss her—most men did, and for no earthly reason besides her fortunate combination of face and figure. But that he would do so when he found his female staff to be beyond the pale, that he'd kissed her so intensely, shocked her. Presumably he thought too much of his own consequence to dabble with the lower orders.

But that didn't explain why he'd kissed her like that. It was no hastily snatched kiss and a pinch on the bottom. It felt like a lover's kiss.

She'd find out eventually. One thing at a time. First, produce a meal to silence all his sly innuendoes and ill-advised flirtatiousness and ensure her job was secure. Secondly, see if she could figure out where the money had come from to refurbish an already well-ordered house with such bad taste. It didn't appear as if any amount of money had been spared, though at least the kitchens were still as they had been. But money had come from somewhere, and the Griffiths family fortune had been decimated by the last viscount's gambling and profligate ways. The current viscount, his nephew, had lived in much more modest circumstances somewhere up north, and as far as she knew the only thing of value that came with the title was Renwick.

She reached the bottom of the stairs, surveying her army of workers, and belatedly she put her hand to her mouth. It felt as if his kiss still lingered, and she scrubbed at her lips surreptitiously. It was time to sweep the Dark Viscount and his Dark Doings from her mind, at least for the next few hours. She had to create a magical meal to ensure her position here, and she was ready to begin.

•••••••••••••••••••••••••••••••••

Ten hours later Sophie had collapsed on the chair she'd had one of the footmen drag in from a storeroom, her stockinged feet propped up on the stool. She shouldn't have removed her shoes in front of the few remaining staff, but it was that or die on the spot, and she preferred to live.

She had never worked so hard in her entire life. Compared to her first night here, this evening's meal was a full-blown feast, despite Dickens's contention that his Dark Lordship would be eating alone and could make do with a tray. She had something to prove, and prove it she would, with the very best of her art and abilities. Besides, there were twenty-seven servants belowstairs who would happily partake of the leftovers.

Twenty-seven other servants, she reminded herself. She was a servant too, at Alexander Griffiths's beck and call. At least this sumptuous meal would leave no doubt as to her qualifications.

Everyone belowstairs had been wonderful. She could bless them all—they'd taken her directions, and when she'd made a mistake they'd helped her, all with a kind, odd protectiveness. She'd felt a little like a baby chick encircled by a crowd of hens and roosters, scaring off any predator.

She summoned up a weary sigh at the fanciful thought. The only predator in this household was abovestairs, and while she'd managed to keep the thought of him out of her mind during the intense, exhausting work, now she was too tired to fight it.

The man was attracted to her. That came as no surprise, having had most of London at her feet during her one season. He was a man who didn't touch the women in his employ, but he'd touched her once already, kissed her, his hard mouth against her, kissed her with his . . . his tongue, and that strange, barbaric kiss had lingered, and nothing seemed to drive it away. No matter what she ate, what she drank, she could still feel his kiss in her mouth.

She would simply have to be firm with him, she told herself, closing her eyes as she leaned back in the chair. She could feel her hair escaping the white cap she'd worn, drifting around her shoulders, and she was finally beginning to cool off from her time spent huddled over the massive coal-fired range. The dinner had been a triumph, and she'd been summoned once more to the table, to be properly lauded.

The viscount would have been alone at that table, and she wasn't going to spend another moment in his company if she could help it. It was bad enough that he'd wormed his way into her daydreams. Dickens had made her excuses, and she had complete faith that he'd come up with something plausible. He'd reported back that the viscount, who usually ate very little, had sampled everything and been gratifyingly amazed at the results. He'd closed his eyes and savored, said Tim, one of the footmen who'd served dinner, and Sophie could picture him with an almost erotic look of pleasure on his face.

Not that she was familiar with erotic looks of pleasure, she reminded herself. But it was easy to imagine it on Viscount Griffith's cool, handsome face, with its high, aristocratic cheekbones and saturnine mouth. The mouth that had kissed her.

Damn, she was back to that again! She stirred, opening her eyes. She could hear quiet noises in the scullery as the maids finished up the final bits of their work. Dickens had already counted the silver and plate; the trays were laid out for the morning, the worktable scrubbed clean. No one would have thought they'd waged a massive culinary battle just a few short hours ago, and would again tomorrow.

She felt rather than saw Dickens approach her. She'd wanted to help, but Prunella had reminded her of the fierce hierarchy of the kitchen, and Sophie had sunk into her chair with blessed relief.

"You should retire, Miss Sophie," Dickens said. "The majority of the staff have already gone up to their rooms, and I can oversee the last little bits of cleanup."

"You're a god among men, Mr. Dickens," she murmured, "but frankly, I don't know if I'll ever be able to move from this chair."

Dickens made an odd, rusty sound that she rightly identified as a laugh. "I can call one of the footmen back and have you carried to your room."

"A lovely idea, but I'll forgo the offer." The noise in the scullery had ceased, and the two maids headed for the narrow staircase that led directly to the servants' quarters. The only access to the main house was through the kitchen stairs, which was something Bryony had set in place, Sophie remembered hazily. A gentleman houseguest of their father's had taken advantage of one of the pretty maids, and Bryony had decided to limit their access. Perhaps tomorrow Sophie would see about sleeping up there as well. Not that she really had anything to fear from the Dark Viscount—he was just amusing himself, like a great, sleek cat baiting a poor mouse.

Except that she was far from mouselike, and she wasn't going to be batted around for his entertainment. The next time he tried to kiss her, she was going to use her knee on his privates, and then he'd leave her alone.

Or discharge her, but she wasn't going to worry about that. She was hardly going to trade her virtue for a chance to discover whether or not Alexander, Viscount Griffiths, was a criminal, and her sisters would kill her if she did. Her virginity, along with her beauty and her acceptable lineage, were her stock in trade, her bargaining chips. She couldn't play them recklessly.

"You go on to bed, Mr. Dickens," she continued, trying to put the idea of her virginity and Alexander's dark, predatory eyes out of her mind. "I'll be fine. I'll just rest here a bit."

"If that's all," he said. "Tim is on duty for the night if anyone needs anything, so don't worry if one of the bells rings—he'll take care of it."

As if his words had set things in motion, the harsh sound of a bell broke through the late-night hush in the kitchen. Dickens turned to look at the board, and he made a face. "It's his lordship.

I'll take care of it." He started toward the stairs, when Tim appeared, looking slightly rattled.

"His lordship wants to see Miss Sophie," he said breathlessly. "He says he wants what she promised him."

Sophie sat up, suddenly alarmed. What was that annoying man demanding now? She'd given him everything she'd promised: a wonderful dinner to enrapture his senses. What else could the dratted creature want?

"Tell him I've gone to bed," she said, not moving from her chair.

Tim cleared his throat. "Um, miss . . . I don't think that's going to do. He said I was to send you upstairs right and proper and no dawdling. He says he's ready for the dessert you promised him."

What the hell was he talking about? She'd already offered him dried apple tart, a blancmange, a lemon torte laced with cognac, and even an arrangement of spring berries and Chantilly cream. What else could he possibly be demanding?

She pushed herself up from the chair, groaning as her back ached and her feet hurt. How could women twice her age do this three times a day without complaint?

Dickens was looking befuddled. "I fail to understand. I believe I personally carried a tray of exquisite sweets to the table. He should have no need for more food."

"He told me he grew famished at all hours of the day and night," Sophie said.

Dickens looked doubtful. "That's news to me, miss, and I've been with his lordship since he was fourteen. It's his stepmama who seems to have an unquenchable desire for sweetmeats and the like." He turned and frowned at the footman. "Are you sure it wasn't Mrs. Griffiths who asked for Miss Sophie?"

Tim shook his head. "No, sir, Mr. Dickens. And I will say his lordship looked hungry."

Dickens shrugged. "Very well, I'll assemble a tray and you can carry it up."

"Begging your pardon, Mr. Dickens, but he specifically demanded Miss Sophie. He's not going to be any too happy to see me return without her."

"Well, then, you'll just have to deal with it," Dickens said reprovingly. "We do our best for those upstairs, but sooner or later we find ourselves disappointing them. You may as well get used to it."

Sophie didn't move. Her instincts, powerful enough to keep her still, warned her to run. To go into her rooms and lock and bar the door, which was ridiculous. As if the Dark Viscount would come prowling down to the basement in search of his errant cook!

Then again, he'd kissed her. The problem with Alexander Griffiths was that *she* wanted to kiss *him*. Wanted to kiss him the way he'd kissed her, that intimate, open-mouthed possession that seemed to reach throughout her entire body. Oh, to be sure, her previous adventures in the art had been willing. She'd hoped she could tell who would make the best husband, though Maddy had told her caustically that she was being absurd. Perhaps she was, but if she had to go through the mortification and discomfort of lying naked in a bed with a man, she ought to at least enjoy kissing him.

And she had, mostly. Those closed-mouthed, chaste salutes on her lips had been, on the whole, pleasant, though nothing had moved her to want more. At least, not until a few short hours ago, when Alexander Griffiths had pushed her up against the baize door and kissed her with a thoroughness that she could still feel imprinted on her mouth.

Damn the man.

"Never mind, Tim," she said wearily, struggling to her feet. "I'm up now, and I may as well face the dratted man."

"We don't refer to our employer in that manner, Miss Sophie," Dickens said reprovingly. "And I think it would be best if you kept your distance, particularly at this hour. One never knows if his lordship has been drinking—there are nights when the black moods are upon him and he imbibes a little too freely."

"I assure you, Mr. Dickens, that I am more than adept at dealing with gentlemen who are a bit castaway," she said briskly, assembling a tray of such sumptuous sweets that the man's eyes would glaze over and he wouldn't even notice who had brought them. "But I appreciate your concern."

"Miss Sophie . . ." he continued, but she'd already started up the stairs to the main floor. The sooner she got this over with, the sooner she could seek her bed and sleep the sleep of the just. And she wouldn't dream about that man at all. Not for a moment.

The halls were deserted. Not that they'd been teeming with servants before, she thought, but there was something almost eerie about the quiet that night. The moon was almost full, and it cast shadows through the French doors that lined the hallway to the viscount's study. She could hear her skirts swish as she walked, a quiet rustle of cloth and the silken petticoats she'd managed to keep with her when she and her sisters had been thrown into the streets. All the rest was silence.

His door was ajar, and light spilled out into the hallway. Sophie paused, rethinking her impulsive gesture. She was returning to the presence of a man who had kissed her. Not just kissed her, but shaken her to her very core. For all that everyone kept insisting that he would never trifle with a servant, he'd done just that earlier in the day, and what made her think that in the dark of night he'd be any different? She'd been a fool to come out—his behavior, his mouth, earlier in the day should have been warning enough. She should have listened to Dickens, who seemed to know the viscount better than anyone, and stayed safely in the confines of the kitchen. But some wicked, dangerous part of her wanted to go, she realized ruefully.

It was then, and only then, that she recognized the other sound that had been missing from her precipitous trip up the back stairs to the Dark Viscount's library—the sound of footsteps. She'd slipped off her sturdy black shoes when she'd dropped into the rocking chair in a state of exhaustion, and she'd been in such a hurry to get back to him that she'd completely forgotten to put them back on. *Idiote!* She cursed herself, mortification sweeping over her. How could she have been so stupid?

She started to back away from the half-open door, very slowly, like a young deer facing a hungry tiger. Not that tigers and deer lived together, she reminded herself with a trace of asperity, and as long as she was going to be so fanciful it served her right . . .

"Are you going to hover out there forever or are you coming in?" Alexander Griffiths's caustic voice came from inside the room, and Sophie considered running for only the briefest moment. She had never been a coward, and she wasn't going to let a saturnine creature like the Dark Viscount intimidate her, no matter how physically beautiful he might be.

Straightening her shoulders, she pushed open the door and then stopped, filled with misgivings. Perhaps it wasn't too late to run.

CHAPTER NINE

HER EMPLOYER WAS SPRAWLED on the large sofa in front of the fire, his long legs stretched out in front of him. His hair was tousled, and it was much too long for fashion, but clearly that was of no consequence to him. Most men had some sort of facial hair, but he was clean-shaven as well, and he was watching her out of those dark gray eyes.

He'd discarded his coat and cravat, and his white shirt was partially unbuttoned. His smooth, tanned flesh should have come as no shock—she'd seen it any number of times as she'd watched him from her perch up on the tor. She eyed him warily as she approached, the tray clutched in her hands.

"I've brought you the dessert you requested," she said stiffly. She looked around for a table to set it on, but the only one was across the room, so she moved in front of him, setting the tray down on the seat of a leather chair, planning to go and fetch the table for him.

"So you did," he said lazily, his eyes drifting down her body in a manner that was both insulting and oddly exhilarating. "I find I'm quite . . . famished."

She did her best to ignore him, bustling around with an efficient air. She still couldn't get used to the fact that gentlemen didn't rise when she came into a room; they simply lay sprawled on a sofa watching her out of predatory eyes. No man would appear in her presence without his jacket or cravat, but then, no man would have kissed her as he'd kissed her earlier in the day, no man . . .

Before she realized his intention she found herself yanked off her feet, falling onto his lap with a decided *oomph*. She struggled to get up, but he captured her flailing arms very quickly, holding her still so she could do little more than glare up into his face.

"What do you think you're doing?" she demanded frostily.

"Having dessert." Sliding his hand behind her neck, beneath her tangled hair, he drew her mouth to his, slanting his own over it.

Reaction spiked through her, though it wasn't the outrage she expected. Her hands still shoved at him, uselessly, but everything inside her seemed to soften and flow, and she wanted to wrap her arms around him, she wanted to push her hands through his too-long hair, she wanted to kiss his mouth and his hard jaw and his eyelids.

He lifted his head, looking down at her, a little breathless. "Don't be tiresome, Sophie," he said in a voice that was too cool, given the circumstances. "It's just a kiss."

She would have disputed that if he hadn't covered her mouth once more. This was a great deal more than a simple kiss. His hard, warm body seemed to surround her, and she found he no longer bound her hands, so that she was clinging to his arms, to the fine, soft linen of his shirt. She wanted to move closer, up against him; she wanted to kiss him back. Somewhere in the depths of her fuzzy brain she knew it would be a very bad idea. It had taken her far too long to realize it, but she'd been thinking about kissing Alexander Griffiths for weeks now. Whenever she lay on her stomach in the grass and watched his lean, beautiful body cut through the water that had decimated Bryony's rose garden, she'd wondered what it would like to be kissed by him. To be held in his arms, against his bare chest. To feel his skin, smooth and warm beneath her fingertips.

He'd moved his mouth away from hers, trailing soft, biting kisses down her neck, and she was awash in a myriad of strange reactions. Her stomach knotted with longing, her chest ached, her . . . her breasts seemed to grow sensitive beneath the layers of garments, and worst of all, between her legs she was growing hot, damp. She wanted to rub against something, like a cat needing to be stroked, and even her shame couldn't stop her.

"But I brought you dessert," she said helplessly, then realized how stupid that sounded.

He laughed softly, the sound simply adding to her crazy mix of stimulation. "So you did," he said, "and it's delicious." To her shock he leaned down and licked her lower lip with a slow, lascivious sweep of his tongue, and she heard a panicky little moan in the room that could only have come from her.

She wasn't sure how he did it, but he somehow managed to shift her off his lap and onto the sofa, with his long, powerful body stretched out over her, his legs between hers, between the layers of skirts, one hand cradling her chin, holding her face still for his deep, tempting kisses, the other trailing down her bodice to the sensible row of buttons half-hidden by the apron she had yet to remove. She knew she ought to object, but the feather cushions were soft beneath her, and he was so warm and hard and strong above her, shielding her, cocooning her, that she didn't want to move. She closed her eyes to the dim light and let him coax her mouth open, allowing his tongue to take possession of hers as his long fingers touched the skin of her throat and she burned, her hips rising against him of their own accord. He laughed that wicked, throaty laugh again.

"That's right, sweetheart," he murmured against her ear, his voice low and seductive. "You know what you want." He was struggling with the next button down, but it was hidden by the apron. "Though why the hell you thought this was proper attire for the occasion is beyond me."

She was actually feeling dizzy, she, who never fainted no matter how tightly she was laced. "What else would I wear?" she asked weakly.

He reached up behind her neck and with a short, brutal jerk he ripped the ties that held the apron at her neck, yanking the linen down to expose the front of her dress. "Preferably nothing at all."

Somehow, through the maze of desire, the words penetrated, just as she felt his hand on her leg, slowly lifting her heavy skirts, and with a shriek she shoved him, rolling off beneath him and landing hard on the parquet flooring.

It was sheer chance she'd been able to do it—he hadn't been expecting anything but blind acquiescence, the bastard. Before he could gather his wits she'd scrambled away, racing for the door.

She expected he'd reach it first, catch her, hold her there, put those mesmerizing hands on her body, kiss her again. God, she wanted him to kiss her again! She wanted to lose herself in the heat of his mouth, his tongue. She didn't want to behave herself, to think clearly—she needed his hands on her. But he simply stayed where he was on the sofa, watching her out of lazy, half-closed eyes. "What do you think you're doing?"

"Going down to my rooms, sir," she said, her shaky voice sadly lacking in dignity. "I seem to have mistaken your appetites."

"You know perfectly well what I'm hungry for. Are you coming back here?"

"No. This is . . . this is . . ." Words failed her. During their brief tussle on the sofa she hadn't had the chance to touch his skin, or to kiss him back, or do the things she'd wanted to do. But she was most certainly not getting any closer to him right now. There was no telling what he might do, and she suspected that this time she wouldn't stop him. "This is unacceptable," she managed to say, and then her evil genius prompted her. "It goes against the terms of my contract with Mrs. Lefton."

He frowned for a moment. "Perhaps you'd best acquaint me with the details of that contract. This is all very entertaining, but I begin to tire of the shy virgin act. If you enjoy games, let's play something else. You can be the naughty governess and I'll be the lecherous master."

"You already are the lecherous master," she snapped. For some reason his casual words hurt. "And someone else will have to be your naughty governess. I'm going to bed."

"That was exactly what I was suggesting . . ." he began, when she whisked herself out the door and closed it none too gently behind her. She set off at a run, down the endless hallways, expecting him to materialize behind her, his breath at the back of her neck, his hands reaching for her, pulling her to him, but there was no sound of pursuit, and she told herself she was relieved. She practically fell down the narrow, circular stairs to the kitchen, which now lay deserted, no sign of Dickens or Tim, only the glow of the bright moon lighting the place.

She should have tried to lock the baize door, though most likely it locked only from the outside, assuming it locked at all. She stilled, taking a deep breath and looking around her. The trays had been set for the morning, the whole area was spotless, and while the windows had been opened to let the smells and the steam of the night's cooking dissipate, she could still sense the lovely fragrance of apples and a hint of lamb.

Clearly everyone was entirely wrong, and the Dark Viscount had no qualms at all about putting his hands on his female servants. She should have known. She was doubtless just one of many, a novelty because she was new. Now she was going to have to spend her time avoiding him until he found someone else to lavish his attentions on.

For some reason the notion didn't feel particularly comfortable. She didn't want him doing that sort of thing with anyone else, kissing her, pulling her beneath him on the soft, old sofa.

She realized with sudden shock that there was one room that hadn't been changed by what she assumed was Mrs. Griffiths's doubtful taste. The library was the same, though the position of the desk had been moved so that its occupant would have a clear view of the lawns and what used to be the rose garden.

And the sofa he'd pressed her into had been the very same sofa where she'd curled up and read thrilling romances, and dreamed of being swept off her feet with the wonder of a chaste, worshipful kiss.

There had been nothing chaste or worshipful about Alexander's kiss. It had been carnal, demanding, shocking, and she hugged herself, trying to force the longing out of her body. Curse the man! She didn't need this kind of complication. She didn't need the confusion that flooded her, the wicked thoughts that kept dancing in her mind. She needed her old life, where she'd been in control of her body and the men around her.

She had to remember that he was the enemy, or at least, close enough. He had taken Renwick away from them. It didn't matter that it had legally belonged to him, the terms of her father's possession broken by his death. Alexander had supposedly killed his first wife, threw her off the battlements of his other house. He was a villain, wasn't he?

There was a very good chance he had killed her father and stolen the liquid assets of Russell Shipping. He might be a very bad man indeed—all signs pointed to it. She needed to be extremely careful, ignore those random urges that were disgraceful, and remember who she was. She was Miss Sophia Russell, not some chippie to be taken by the first lecherous man to put his hands on her.

Except that other lecherous men had put their hands on her, or at least tried. Once the scandal had broken, she and her sisters had lost any claim to proper courtesy or etiquette. They had been fair game, and Maddy had left more than one importunate gentleman bent over and moaning with pain. Sophie hadn't had to be quite so physical—she'd been able to slip away without anyone realizing she'd escaped.

Slipping away this time might be more difficult, when the truth was, she didn't want to. She shook her head at her own foolishness. She had a lock on her bedroom door, and a chair to lodge beneath the knob, and she would use both. She stripped off her clothes and bathed in cool water, hoping to bring down the fever inside her. All it did was give her a chill. With a sigh she pulled on her lace-trimmed nightdress and crawled beneath the damp sheets. When she'd been a lady, someone had warmed her sheets for her with a warming pan. It might be that simple courtesy that she missed most of all. She needed a warm bed and warm covers to wrap around her. She needed to sleep, and forget what had happened in that too-familiar room.

All she could do was lie there, eyes open in the dark, and wait.

....

Damn the girl! What kind of game was she playing? Whatever it was, it grew extremely tedious. He needed sex; he needed to shove his cock into someplace tight and willing, and he wanted it to be Sophie. Again, he had to consider Mrs. Lefton's surprising ability. She'd sent him someone the complete opposite of what he'd wanted, and it was exactly what he needed.

He'd grown bored with sex over the last year or so. Six years ago, after Jessamine had died and he'd faced the ignominy of a trial, he'd decided to go away, travel the world. Rufus had come with him, and his brother had been more than conversant with the ways of the world.

Rufus had called it a Whoreson's Grand Tour, and they'd managed to sleep with Venetian courtesans and French aristocrats, though they were thin on the ground these days. Alexander had taken opera dancers and royalty and streetwalkers to his bed; he'd dabbled in a world of bondage and pain for pleasure, and he was still bored. He'd ordered Miss Sophie as one might order a sack of flour, just for the convenience of it, and instead of taking care of his physical urges, it was starting to become an obsession. *She* was starting to become an obsession.

He'd played games before—women seemed to like them—though never with a hired partner. Some women couldn't achieve their peak without being spanked, or pretending to be a captive princess or some such bollocks. That was the advantage of whores— one didn't have to go through all that rigmarole. You snapped your fingers and they were there. It was up to them to do all the work to entertain, not him.

Though in fact, Sophie was doing just that. He couldn't remember wanting a woman more in his life, not even when he was young and foolishly, desperately in love with Jessamine. Mrs. Lefton's delicious morsel was a positive genius in building his desire to a dangerously explosive point, and he knew that when he had her, while he doubted it could be as gratifying as this pent-up frustration suggested, it would still be quite . . . satisfactory.

She was going to cost him a pretty penny, and she was worth every bit of it. She'd managed to distract him from his younger brother's death, and his own, unthinkable guilt, guilt that came from relief that . . . no, he wasn't going to let those thoughts in. When she was around he could think of nothing but her—the taste of her, the feel of her, the sheer, saucy effrontery of her.

This whole cooking business was a charade, he thought as he reached for the lemon torte. He was going to have to find someone to take her place once this game was played out. He certainly had no intention of arranging his desires around the demands of the kitchen, and there were at least two suitable houses on the estate that would do for her. He took a bite, and let the mélange of flavors dance against his tongue, and he closed his eyes and savored it. Well, perhaps he'd still allow her to bake. Only for him, of course.

He finished the piece of cake, then reached for the apple tart with hard sauce. He was naturally lean, but a few months of Sophie's fell hand and he'd become as roly-poly as a judge. He laughed at the thought, finished most of the tart, and set the plate back down on the tray, half-tempted to have the footman order her back once more. Her behavior amused him, though he supposed the letter Dickens had brought him accounted for some of his sanguine mood. There was a good chance Rufus might have survived.

He should have viewed that possibility with unadulterated joy. But there was nothing simple about his relationship with Rufus, nothing straightforward about his younger brother, and never had been.

Rufus had always been the charming one, the naughty one, the occasionally devious one, and Alexander had learned long ago not to underestimate him. Indeed, he'd worried about him for the last few years, when he'd disappear for months at a time and return in the middle of the night, with odd injuries like burns on his hands or a broken leg.

And the money had been a concern as well. Soon after Alexander had unexpectedly come into the title and the debts that came with it, Rufus had somehow managed to unearth a huge amount of money. He'd been evasive, insisting it was simply part of the inheritance that had gotten overlooked, and in the end Alexander had taken the money and made a great deal more, enough that he could easily return the original money to Rufus and not even notice its loss.

If Rufus was truly dead then Alexander wouldn't be able to return the money, nor would he ever have an answer as to where it had come from. Much as he hated to distrust his brother, there was no avoiding the fact that Rufus's sense of honor was extremely elastic. It was entirely possible he'd stolen that money, and Alexander was duty-bound to return it, if he only knew the source.

If Rufus was still alive then he would get those answers, but that brought with it an even worse problem. What do you do when you know someone is a criminal? Do you turn him in, or let him continue with his activities? And if he didn't stop Rufus, someone else might, someone who might use lethal force.

Those moral questions had been unimportant while he believed Rufus was dead. If his brother really had managed to escape death once more, then there would have to be an unpleasant reckoning before long, one he dreaded.

He'd been tempted not to say anything to Adelia about the possibility of Rufus's survival, but in the end even his contempt for her couldn't make him cruel. If Adelia loved anyone above herself it was her son, and he couldn't keep the possibility of hope away from her, whether she deserved it or not.

Time would tell. For now, he was going to do the one thing that could cool his body down and enable him to sleep. Pushing off from the sofa, he went in search of the night air and the clear, cool water.

CHAPTER TEN

SOPHIE HADN'T SLEPT WELL. Every time she drifted off she would reawaken with a start, feeling his mouth on hers, his hands holding her. At one point she even got up and lit the lamps again, peering through the shadows in her rooms. He wasn't there, of course. She wasn't sure whether that was a relief or a disappointment.

Breakfast had been a simple enough matter, with the viscount and his stepmother taking trays in their rooms. Sophie could only be glad her employer hadn't decided she should be the one to serve him. The thought of the man still in bed, lying amidst rumpled white sheets, was disturbing. Would he wear a decent nightshirt and cap to bed? She knew he wouldn't. The man would sleep in nothing but all that hard, bronzed skin, and he would probably enjoy trying to embarrass her if she entered his rooms.

Once the trays had gone, the rest of the household sat down for their morning meal, and by the time it was finished and the staff had been dispersed to their duties, Sophie was considering slipping off to her room when Dickens returned to the kitchens, a grim look on his face as he approached her.

Sophie felt her stomach knot in distress. Had Alexander Griffiths found out who she was? She'd hoped for an easy day of it, given that she'd already come up with a week's worth of menus and Prunella had started in on the bread, but she simply squared her shoulders and waited for Dickens to make his pronouncement.

"You're wanted upstairs, miss," he said in a gloomy voice.

"I expected as much." The viscount presumably didn't like being told no. Despite the assurances of the rest of the staff that her employer didn't poach among the serving class, Alexander Griffiths had proved them wrong. Not only had she refused his advances, she'd all but shoved him onto the floor and run.

Well, to be utterly truthful, refusing hadn't truly been the case. She was putting up a good fight against the seductive gleam in his eyes, the clever touch of his hands, the wicked demands of his mouth, but sooner or later she was going to lose unless she came up with better defenses. Oh, she could fight off the Dark Viscount—wife-murderer, possible embezzler and killer of her own father—with no little effort. It was fighting off her own untoward desires that were leading her down a path to her own destruction.

She had no dowry. Her name, her real name, was tarnished. Her sisters had scattered. All she had was her face and her innocence, and that wasn't going to last long at this rate. If he started in at this hour in the morning she would probably need to hit him over the head with a skillet.

"What does he want?" she asked, not bothering to hide her grumpy mood.

"Not his lordship, Miss Sophie. In fact, he's gone out for the day and left no word as to when he might return. If he's gone down to London we won't see him for days, I should think. No, it's Mrs. Griffiths who wants to see you."

Sophie didn't even have time to feel relief over the viscount's disappearance before the thought of his stepmother made her heart sink. Here was a different danger entirely, and she wasn't looking forward to facing the woman.

"She'll want to see the menus, and she'll probably ask you a dozen questions you won't want to answer," Dickens continued morosely. "I'll do my best to remain with you in case she proves difficult."

"I thought you told me the viscount approves the menus," Sophie said.

"The moment he leaves, Mrs. Griffiths tries to take charge. She's gotten rid of any number of servants during the few months they've been in residence, particularly anyone for whom his lordship shows a . . . a partiality."

The very last thing she was going to do was question the viscount's partiality for her. "So she could dismiss me?"

"No, miss. I don't think even she would dare."

She almost asked him why not, but wisdom stopped her. "Just give me a moment to tidy up," she said, untying her apron and heading toward her room. There was always the possibility that she and Mrs. Griffiths could form some kind of alliance against the viscount. Apparently they despised each other, and the old woman would probably be more than happy to help find proof that would discredit the man.

Sophie had no intention of helping his stepmother. It didn't matter if the man was guilty of every last thing she suspected him of—she wasn't going to side with that harridan. If he truly had anything to do with her father's death, then she would find it out on her own.

Sophie followed Dickens up the winding stairs to the front hall, then followed him up narrow servants' stairs, taking time to peek in at the various floors before moving on. While the ground level of Renwick had been redecorated, the higher floors were still the same, though Sophie imagined it wouldn't be long before those were torn apart as well. It was hard to believe her father had been dead for less than three months, that just last winter she'd been the spoiled and pampered Miss Sophie Russell, sought after and adored. Mrs. Griffiths had taken over the apartments on the third floor that had once belonged to her father, which struck Sophie as decidedly odd. Those were the best rooms in the house—why wasn't the viscount living in them? Exactly which rooms had he claimed? The three sisters had slept in rooms on the second floor, and along with those rooms there were three guest chambers. The third floor held guest rooms as well, but none of them had a dressing room and water closet as her father's had.

She followed Dickens up the last flight of stairs, casting surreptitious glances around her. The lack of a housekeeper showed here—while the hallways were clean, there was a certain lack of polish and refinement that her older sister, Bryony, would never have tolerated. But then, the maids who worked at Renwick had known the place well, unlike the new staff.

It gave Sophie an odd feeling to be standing outside her father's door, waiting, as Dickens gave a muted scratch against the thick walnut, and Sophie's mouth went dry in sudden alarm. *It's not Alexander*, she told herself, and then realized with shock that she'd thought of him in terms of his Christian name. He was the viscount, the Dark Viscount, the Damned Viscount, *damned* as in *doomed*, and she needed to remember that, even if he was frighteningly adept at making her forget.

"Come in, Dickens."

If the woman had looked intimidating from her place of honor at the bottom of the table, she looked even more unnerving in Sophie's father's old rooms. These had been redecorated as well, though the job had clearly been a hasty, slapdash affair. The walls were now an unfortunate shade of salmon, unfortunate because it made Mrs. Griffiths's high color look almost apoplectic. Her hair was arranged in such a complicated array of dubiously blond curls that Sophie suspected it might be a wig, and her black mourning dress was bedecked with enough jet and bead to weigh down a clipper ship, a notion accentuated by her massive bosom. A woman sat to one side, a worried expression on her face, and Sophie recognized the proverbial lady's companion. Though the companion looked more well bred than the lady.

Mrs. Griffiths said nothing as she ran her dark, beady eyes down Sophie's body, and her pursed mouth tightened. Sophie felt Dickens give her a surreptitious push, and she entered the room, deciding to give the woman her very best curtsey.

Those small eyes darkened further, and belatedly Sophie realized her mistake. She wasn't familiar with the polite bob of a maidservant—she'd just given Mrs. Griffiths her elaborate, presented-at-court curtsey, only a shade less deferent than the curtain call of an opera dancer, and it must have looked overdone. "Mrs. Griffiths?" she asked in a polite little voice. *This was not going to go well.*

"Madame Camille," Mrs. Griffiths said in a stiff tone, and it took Sophie a moment to remember that that was her purported name.

"Yes, ma'am?"

"I trust you've brought at least a month's worth of menus with you for my perusal?"

No mistress of the house would ask for a month of menus—too much depended on what might come in season, and whether there were last-minute visitors. The woman next to Mrs. Griffiths put out a hand.

"Adelia," she said in a hushed voice, "a month is simply not done. Better you ask for a week at most."

Mrs. Griffiths's high color darkened, and Sophie immediately guessed what was going on. The companion, whose clothes were more tasteful and whose hair was more subdued, was clearly more conversant with polite society, and she was both a companion and a social tutor. And Mrs. Griffiths didn't like it one tiny bit.

"Cousin Mary, I believe I am the lady of the house, and if I asked for a month of menus then I expect my expensive, highly recommended cook to provide them. I do not see any papers in your hands, Madame Camille."

Sophie could feel Dickens about to speak, but she quickly stepped forward. She wasn't going to let him fall on a sword for her like some Roman general. "I beg your pardon, Mrs. Griffiths," she said in her most humble voice, "but I already presented the menus to his lordship. You probably aren't aware that he's gone out, and for some reason he's locked his study." It was a shot in the dark, but a lucky one. Alexander didn't trust his stepmother—it only made sense that he'd utilize locked doors to keep her out.

"Has he gone out?" Mrs. Griffiths said airily. "I hadn't realized. Dickens, you must have a key for the study."

"No, ma'am, I'm afraid I don't," Dickens said regretfully. "His lordship took the extras from me and the housekeeper's chatelaine. Said he didn't want anyone rummaging through his papers."

Mrs. Griffiths's teeth were large and rather terrifying. "Surely he didn't mean his dear stepmama in that injunction."

"Surely not, ma'am. But the fact remains that the doors are locked and I have no way of retrieving the menus."

The mean little eyes, like raisins in the midst of a suet pudding, swung back to Sophie. "And you didn't think to make a copy?" she demanded. "Most irresponsible of you."

A month's worth of menus consisting of innumerable courses would have taken more time than she'd been in residence, and a copy would have been impossible, as the old woman well knew.

Except that she wasn't an old woman. She had to be somewhere in her fifties, an age when one could certainly look well preserved if one tried. She was a formidable woman, tall, sturdily built, but her taste was somehow off. The black dress showed far too much cleavage, her maquillage was overdone, and she wore far too many rings on her plump fingers.

"I beg your pardon, Mrs. Griffiths," Sophie said in her most humble voice, no matter how much it galled her. "I'm still learning my way around here."

"It seems to me that you're having trouble knowing your *place*," she said. "If you think my stepson is a likely candidate for protector then you're wrong. He's a pinchpenny miser, with only a cursory interest in females. In truth, I believe he prefers males, but of course that is something we don't discuss."

Sophie blinked. It took all her concentration to keep her face entirely blank at the woman's absurd statement. "Indeed, ma'am," she murmured. She'd never seen a man less likely to prefer his own kind, though it would certainly make her life easier if he did. But why would Mrs. Griffiths lie about such a thing?

Clearly the woman had been looking for a more dramatic reaction. "Yes, well, I'm not convinced that you will suit us here. Your reputation led me to believe we'd be fed something quite extraordinary, but so far it's only been . . . adequate."

Well, that was undoubtedly a lie. "I'm sorry, ma'am," she murmured. "Perhaps you could provide me with some direction." Women like Mrs. Griffiths liked to control things—Sophie could see it in her hard little eyes. Resistance would be a waste of time.

"I shouldn't have to provide you direction," the woman snapped. "You were hired for that purpose. If you cannot fulfill your position then you'd be better off departing before you make a shambles of things. In fact, my stepson was most displeased with you, and let me warn you that he is a difficult, no, a dangerous man when he's angry. You would be wise to leave here before he returns, or I can't answer for your safety. He has a history of brutality against women, you know."

Sophie blinked again. She and her sisters had often played cards, betting their pin money, and she'd always won, due to her enigmatic expression. Dealing with this woman's outrageousness was harder than she would have thought.

"I never listen to rumors, madame," she murmured politely. She could try calling her "my lady," but instead of stoking her vanity, it might anger the woman. "And his lordship has yet to express any displeasure with the meals I've prepared. I would hardly think he'd be so unfair as to dismiss me without giving me a full chance."

Impossibly, the old woman's eyes narrowed further. "I cannot speak for your safety if you insist on staying."

Sophie said nothing. It was clear that the woman didn't have the power to dismiss her, but she was doing everything she could, short of saying so. Mrs. Griffiths fixed her with a dark look. "You'd best be very careful, Madame Camille. Even if my stepson is generally uninterested in females, he will occasionally lapse, and I tell you, in great confidence, that there have been severe injuries with the women he's . . . he's been intimate with."

At this the companion made a noise. It was a small, strangled sound of protest, as if this was too far even for her.

Sophie nodded politely. "Then I will ensure that his lordship keeps his hands off the kitchen staff. Good servants are so hard to find."

Mrs. Griffiths automatically reached for another biscuit, then glared at the empty plate as if it were to blame. "He won't touch the servants," she said. "He never does."

Sophie smiled sweetly. "That is reassuring, ma'am. Which means that I and my staff are safe from any importunities, and if his lordship is feeling amorous, he's more likely to look for companionship in the stable than the kitchen."

"He likes men, not animals!" Mrs. Griffiths snapped.

"As long as he's uninterested in women, it's none of my concern. You've been most kind in instructing me about the household, Mrs.

Griffiths. I look forward to hearing more of your thoughts about the meals in the future." She gave her a curtsey, trying more for a polite little bob than the full-court obeisance, and then departed before her employer realized that Sophie had dismissed *her*.

Dickens followed her down the wide marble staircase, wise enough not to remain behind and bear the brunt of Mrs. Griffiths's displeasure. "I'm not certain that was particularly smart of you, Miss Sophie," he said in an undertone. "We do our best to placate Mrs. Griffiths whenever possible. She can be a very vindictive woman."

"Clearly," Sophie said. She wanted to add, "And she's a liar as well," but she stopped herself. Really, she could hardly discuss something as intimate as sexual proclivities with a man old enough to be her father, when she wasn't even supposed to know about such things. In truth, she didn't know much. If only her sisters were here—Maddy had faultless instincts when it came to something like that, warning her off one or two extremely handsome young men who had courted her.

If Alexander Griffiths was interested only in men for bedsport, then why had he kissed her like that? No, she didn't want to think about his kisses. They were too distracting. She needed to stay down in the kitchen and . . .

"What was that, Miss Sophie?" Dickens said as she let out an unbidden curse.

"Nothing, Mr. Dickens," she murmured, mentally kicking herself. "I just remembered that I wanted to make a tarte au l'onion tonight and I have to check the egg supply."

"Our chickens, quails, and ducks lay far more than we can use, Miss Sophie."

"That's a relief." But Sophie wasn't relieved at all. She'd been so caught up in the pleasure of having her own limitless kitchen, not to mention being distracted by the bewitching, nerve-racking presence of the Dark Viscount, that she had forgotten why she was here. Not to cook, not to find shelter when she'd lost her temporary home, though both of those were lovely. She was here to find out whether Alexander Griffiths, Viscount Griffiths, had had anything to do with her father's disgrace and death. Where had all his money come from?

And if the man was gone for a number of days, now was the time to find out.

She didn't want to. She wanted to go back to her wonderful kitchen and her helpers and create masterpieces, even if the only audience was that horrid old woman on the third floor. At least Mrs. Griffiths's silent companion would enjoy them as well. She'd make enough for her kitchen staff, rather than feed them something cheaper and plainer. At least for as long as she remained here, they would eat like peers of the realm.

"Do you have any idea where his lordship went, or how long he'll be gone?" Sophie asked in what she hoped was a casual voice. "Shall I expect him for dinner?"

"It's unlikely," Dickens replied. "He goes into town fairly regularly and stays away a night or two. I imagine this is one of those . . . er . . . occasions."

"Really? Where does he go?" She didn't bother pretending to be uninterested. Where would the viscount disappear to without telling his stepmother?

"He . . . that is . . . his lordship . . . er . . ." Dickens was looking uneasy. "A man has certain needs, miss, and he . . ."

"Oh," Sophie said, finally understanding. "You mean he goes out and finds a whore for a couple of nights?"

Dickens cleared his throat. "He doesn't wish to . . . er . . . mingle with anyone in the area. He says it's soiling his own nest."

More proof that she was safe from his advances. Which made the fact that he'd kissed her, twice, all the more puzzling. Perhaps his stepmother hadn't lied, that he preferred men, and the companionship he found in town was of the male gender. But still, why had he kissed her?

It wouldn't happen again. She wasn't going anywhere near him without Dickens in tow.

Clearly she was living on borrowed time. Either Alexander Griffiths would return, refuse to take no for an answer, and she'd have to run away, or his evil stepmother would find some excuse to dismiss her. If he was gone for two nights then now was the time to act, whether she wanted to or not.

• •

Sophie could feel his hands on her face, her neck. They were smooth, cool, slightly calloused, not the soft, pampered hands of the men she had danced with. He slid his hands over her breasts, his fingers dancing across her hardened nipples, and she wanted to reach up and pull the chemise down to her waist, exposing herself to the feel of his skin against hers. He leaned over and put his mouth against hers, and she knew he was wet from the pool with cool water on his golden skin, and she wanted to taste the water, to drink it, and she opened her mouth for his tongue, reaching up for him . . .

The chair beneath her creaked, and she awoke with a start. She was alone in the kitchen, sitting by the fire in her ridiculously comfortable chair. Dinner was finished, everything put away, and only one tray was set for the morning. Which meant he wasn't expected to return that night. Sophie shook the last remnants of the dream from her brain and rose, wandering around the dimly lit, deserted kitchen, making a last-minute inspection. She was delighted that he'd gone out to find more agreeable companionship, she told herself. If the man had to pay for physical affection, then it only served him right if it was cold and heartless.

Except she knew very well he wouldn't have to pay. The majority of the women on staff, and possibly a number of the men, would have gladly accepted his advances, not to mention the married women and widows in the surrounding areas. Wealthy, handsome viscounts were not in abundance—despite suspicions surrounding his first wife's death, she imagined that most young women of proper upbringing and lineage would leap at the chance to marry him.

She didn't like the idea. In fact, it put her in an extremely bad mood, whether she pictured him in the arms of a painted courtesan or kissing the hand of some simpering young lady. God knew there were plenty of girls who simpered. Blushed and stammered oh so prettily while they hid behind their fans. They weren't as beautiful as she was—that wasn't vanity but simply a fact. But they were much more compliant.

Sophie had never simpered in her life, except in moments of extreme sarcasm. For all that she was planning a traditional life with a wealthy, titled husband, she had no intention of being a shadow. Her sisters had always been strong, and Sophie liked to think of herself as the strongest.

Of course, a wicked thought came creeping into her mind— Alexander Griffiths was rich and titled, and he fit the criteria for husband material. Not to mention divinely, dangerously attractive. *Dangerous* was the word—she was being distracted by the nice gothic air of brooding and mystery that went with his gorgeous face and even more gorgeous body.

She was attracted to the danger he represented, even as she was horrified by it. She couldn't stop thinking about him. She dreamed of him at night. She kept expecting him to stride into the kitchen. Her nipples were still hard from her dream, and she thought she could taste his cool mouth on hers.

She needed to get away from here.

Of course, that was the difficulty. She had a small amount of money—Maddy had given it to her with strict instructions before she took off in search of her pirate. It would be enough for a ride on the public coach to London, though she had no idea what she'd do when she got there. She could follow Maddy to Devonport, just outside of Plymouth, but if Maddy was working as a housemaid she could scarcely bring her sister in. Besides, Sophie had absolutely no intention of scrubbing and sweeping and making beds. Cooking was one thing—it was a glorious task for the senses. Any tedium could be passed along to Prunella or one of the kitchen maids, though in truth nothing felt tedious in the kitchen. The cutting of vegetables, the kneading of dough—they were among the many routines that were balm for the soul.

Perhaps Mrs. Griffiths would be interested in bribing her to leave. For some reason the old woman didn't want her here, and for the proper financial remuneration Sophie should be able to go. She wasn't equipped to sort through papers and discover some heinous plot. She was a creature of emotion and passion, given to listening to her instincts when it came to people. She wasn't made to fathom complicated plots and obscure motives. There was no reason for Alexander to kill her father. To be sure, he gained ownership of this house, but it was an expensive house to maintain, and the previous viscount had gambled away all the money before he finally parted with the place.

And yet the new viscount, coming from an obscure background to the north, somehow managed to support this grand house and more servants than her father had ever hired, plus pay for unnecessary refurbishing. Not to mention the fact that rooting up the rose garden and putting in a reflecting pool would have been an absurd expense.

Unless, of course, he'd wound up with the majority of the assets of Russell Shipping, assets that had disappeared without a trace.

She closed her eyes, trying to picture him with a sardonic smile on his face, but instead she saw him as she'd first seen him, in his smalls as he'd climbed from the pool, water dripping off every inch of bronzed, muscled skin, glinting in the afternoon sunlight like some kind of golden god.

The sudden, distressed noise startled her, even though it had come from her own mouth. This was not good, not good at all. She had always prided herself on being a pragmatic creature, and first of all she had to protect herself. If he kissed her again she might not be able to stop him from doing more, and she knew full well what "more" would be. She knew, because for the first time in her life she felt the same kind of longing, in her chest, her belly, between her legs. She wanted to touch and taste that skin, and self-discipline had never been her strong suit. She needed to get out of there, fast.

There was no need to panic—he was gone for at least the night. Plenty of time to take off in the morning. She stretched her kinked muscles and removed the starched cap and apron. She'd already dispensed with her shoes the moment she'd sat down in the chair, much to Dickens's shock and disapproval, but after a day on her feet in front of a hot stove she needed to be barefoot.

In fact, she needed to be outside. She'd discovered an unexpected love for the outdoors once she'd moved in with Nanny. In the past she'd always remained in the country house, playing card games or charades or amateur theatricals with her sisters. The other two tended to ride and walk, but Sophie preferred to keep her porcelain complexion unblemished by the sun.

But once in the cramped quarters of Nanny's cottage she'd had no choice but to escape, and she'd discovered there was nothing she liked better than hiking up the hills that surrounded Renwick.

If she'd stayed put in the cottage she never would have seen Alexander Griffiths swimming, and much as she'd like to believe otherwise, she knew that was a major reason she'd chosen to come to Renwick.

Then again, her sisters had distrusted him as one of the three major suspects in their father's death. But Bryony had married the first of the suspects, presumably exonerating him, and Maddy had been off investigating Eustace Russell's privateer captain for so long Sophie suspected she'd not only decided the ancient mariner was innocent, but she'd probably fallen in love with someone as well.

Not for one moment did she consider that Maddy might be in trouble herself. Maddy was indomitable—she let nothing get in her way. If the old sea dog turned out to be nefarious then Maddy would simply deal with it, Maddy-style. The fact that she hadn't returned, hadn't been heard of in almost a month, didn't bother Sophie. If there was one person who could take care of herself it was Maddy.

It wasn't fair. Her sisters were off, having adventures, falling in love, and Sophie was . . .

Doing the same thing. Oh, not the love part, absolutely not. Not ever. She wasn't going to make the mistake of falling in love—women did very foolish things for love. No, she was going to be completely ruthless, marry whomever made the most advantageous offer, and live like a queen in the very best part of London. The Dark Viscount could marry a simpering female and stay out here and she'd never think of him again.

Oh, well, maybe she would. When she was on her back, doing her duty for Queen and Country, with some anonymous, pleasant gentleman laboring away, she might just close her eyes and dwell on the very wicked thought of Alexander Griffiths doing such shameful things to her, and no one need ever know.

Bugger! She was doing it again. She had to leave here before she became totally besotted. She was falling in love with him, and it made no sense. It wasn't simply the undeniable attraction of his face and body; it wasn't just his decadent kisses. He was cynical, inexplicable, and he was all she could think about. She could only hope that once away from him she could forget all about him and the unnerving way he made her feel.

At times his odd conversation convinced her he was half-mad. It didn't matter. She knew, deep in her heart, that she was falling in love with him, emotions rampaging through her that she'd never felt before. She had to get out of here before it was too late.

Loving someone was a dire mistake. She'd seen what happened to Maddy, and Sophie's heart had broken for her, despite their constant bickering. She never wanted that to happen to her, and the only way to avoid it was to never fall in love. Men were too powerful as it was. If she were so weak as to fall in love, she'd have no defenses left. The wolves would eat her alive.

No, Alexander wasn't the man for her. Someday she'd look back on him as a temporary weakness, and she'd wonder, what if . . . ? But that was as close as she was getting to his bed, no matter how much fear and desire were warring within her. She needed someone amenable, someone she could control. Not a wild heart like the one she knew beat beneath Alexander's cool exterior.

She started up the winding stairs to the ground floor of the house, her bare feet silent on the wooden treads. She would have had a hard time seeing if it weren't for the brightness of the full moon sending mullioned shadows through the uncurtained windows. A delicious little shiver ran through her. People did foolish things on the night of the full moon. They danced around bonfires and celebrated pagan rituals. She paused to look out the French doors that led onto the terrace and the pool beyond. The water glimmered in the bright moonlight, and she was tempted, so tempted to go out, to dance barefoot in the moonlight, to slip into the cool, silken water. What harm would it do? She wasn't going to find out a thing from shuffling through Alexander's books, and he'd probably notice someone had been snooping. And she certainly wasn't about to search his bedroom. The very last place she wanted to go was near his bed. She was better off not knowing which room it was in.

She looked up into the sky. The moon was so bright she could barely see the stars, though a few clouds reflected the silvery light. She would be leaving this beautiful place, back to the city where you never looked at the sky, presuming you could even see it through the smoke and haze, and she felt a sudden clarity settle over her. She had to leave, much as she hated to, leave before Alexander could return and tempt her once more. But for her last night she would go out and enjoy herself in the night air.

The door was locked, which amused her. They'd never locked the doors when they'd lived here. There were enough strong servants around to repel any intruder, and besides, this was the country, safe and peaceful.

She unlocked it and slipped outside, then stood still, breathing in the night air. And it was warm, unusually so, with a soft breeze that carried with it the scent of apple blossoms and newly turned earth, and Sophie let out a soft laugh of pure joy as she turned her face up to the moon. Tonight, with no one to watch her, she'd be a pagan. Tomorrow she'd be on her way to London and find her way from there.

She moved into the first part of the complex garden layout. The pool was just beyond, gleaming in the moonlight, but she took an abrupt turn to the right, still distressed about the destruction of Bryony's roses. A familiar scent drifted to her, and she walked ahead into what had once been a cutting garden, and stopped, momentarily stunned by her discovery.

There were the roses, everywhere, the early ones blooming and adding a delicious flavor to the night air, the masses of later varieties leafing out and getting ready to bud. They had all been carefully transplanted, thriving in their new setting instead of lost forever.

Sophie felt tears sting her eyes, and she fought them back. She never cried. Never ever ever, not when word came that their father had died, not when they'd been evicted with only the clothes on their backs. Not when Bryony had come up with this harebrained scheme to become servants to find out what had happened to their father and she'd sent them off to stay with Nanny Gruen. Not when Maddy had left her as well.

But the scent of roses on the warm night air ripped away her last defenses, and she wanted to weep with the sheer beauty of it, and the loss of so much.

It only lasted a moment. She rubbed her eyes with stern hands, then reached back and released her hair from its tight coils, stuffing the tortoiseshell pins in her pocket. She shook the mass free, and another weight lifted from her as it rippled down her back. She plucked a fragrant pink rose—one of her favorites, though she forgot the fancy name Bryony had given it—carefully picked off its thorns, and stuck it behind her ear, letting the scent surround her. This was her last night here. Tomorrow she would take her carefully hoarded money and leave this place, questions unanswered, heart intact.

It had been so long since she'd danced. She began to hum, the Strauss waltz that had been the very last thing she had danced to, the night before their world had collapsed. She couldn't even remember her partner, but she remembered the waltz, and she moved through the garden, her eyes half-closed, reliving that dance, her imaginary partner bending over her, tall, commanding, with devilish eyebrows and mocking eyes . . .

She stopped immediately. She was not going to indulge in any more fantasies—they had become too dangerous. She would not pretend she was dancing with Alexander Griffiths. She was never going to see him again, thank God; she'd be gone before he returned from his nights of debauchery. She needed to let go.

Still humming, she moved through the gardens, touching a leaf here, a blossom there. She had never appreciated these when she'd lived here, and now they were lost to her. But not tonight. Tonight they were hers alone.

She hummed, and moved, a graceful half dance, circling the carefully laid-out gardens until she ended, to her surprise, at the long, shallow pool. The moonlight was mirrored on the glassy water, and somewhere in the back of her mind she remembered the term *moonling*. Hadn't it come from a fool who saw the moon reflected in a pool of water and drowned trying to catch it?

She was a moonling, all right. Reaching for what she could not have, almost drowning in the process. She stood at the far end of the pool, not even glancing up at the darkened house. Everyone would be asleep by now. She couldn't catch the moon, but she could swim with it. Let the cool water that had caressed the Dark Viscount's skin caress hers as well. She didn't know why that was important, but it was. Illogical as it was, she wanted some kind of imprint on her flesh to take with her, even as the rest of her was forced to forget.

She tilted her head back, looking up at the bright circle of the moon, just as a cloud scudded over it, momentarily plunging the night into darkness, and her hands stilled, just as she was about to reach for the buttons at her throat, the so-convenient buttons that enabled her to dress and undress herself. She should go back inside. She should pack her valise, write a note for Prunella and Dickens, and then try to get what sleep she could until morning.

But the cloud moved, the silver moonlight bathed her, and the reflection in the pool called to her. *Come to me. I am yours. Catch me, moonling.*

She began to unbutton her dress. It dropped to the grass, followed by her loosely tied corset, her petticoats, her stockings and garters. At the last moment she pulled off her shift and pantalets, so she was shockingly naked in the moonlight, and she didn't care. Let them look.

She laughed to herself. Brave of her, considering everyone was either asleep or gone. It was a very strange sensation, to let the night wind caress her bare flesh. She looked down into the pool. She couldn't swim, but it wasn't very deep. She sat down on the side and slipped into the cool, lovely water.

It felt glorious. No wonder he swam whenever he could—the feel of the water surrounding her body was a sensation so astonishing that she could stay there forever. She moved, feeling the water flow about her as sheer joy filled her heart. This water could seduce her just as surely as Alexander could, and she needed to get out, to dry herself and get dressed before it was too late.

She slid out, reluctantly, and rose, squeezing the water out of the ends of her hair. Her flannel petticoat did as good a job as a towel in drying her, and she pulled on her shift, then looked at the massive pile of clothes, including her discarded corset and her shoes. The thought of putting all that on again was too much. Without a backwards glance she left it, heading toward Bryony's roses, her bare feet dancing across the damp grass.

CHAPTER ELEVEN

ALEXANDER GRIFFITHS WAS IN a strange mood. He'd left the small, discreet house in the nearby town of Whiston without partaking of any of the young ladies' charms. He'd been more than ready to avail himself of a particularly fetching young thing, small, rounded, with blue eyes and a mass of blond hair. But the blond hair was too brassy, the blue eyes too flat, the curves too curvy, and her pretty little mouth had smiled at him instead of offering him saucy rejections. Then again, he'd been paying her for her smiles.

In the end he walked away. Damn it, he was paying Madame Sophie for her smiles, and what had it gotten him? A damned case of blue balls and an obsession that was destroying his ability to concentrate on anything else.

Which in its own way was a good thing. It gave him less time to think about Rufus and the possibility that he had survived. Faced with the possibility of Rufus's reappearance, reality had settled in. He expected the worst—he'd learned that early on. He'd grown up with few memories of his mother and learned from Adelia's tender mercies much about the goodness of women and the possibility of happy endings. If he'd had any doubts, his fragile, beautiful young wife had taken care of those. His marriage had been a cold, empty thing, with Jessamine flirting with every male except her own husband. She'd married him for the title, and it was taking him too long to inherit it, and a woman like Jessamine didn't want to live immured in the country with no one to appreciate her. She'd hated him, and he'd begun to hate her.

The furor surrounding her death had finished him off. "Death under suspicious circumstances," the coroner had ruled, and everyone had eyed him accusingly. But no one had dared say the words—he'd simply been shunned, whispered about, even as Rufus had staunchly supported him.

Then came the title, the house, and the money. The title was no surprise—his great-uncle, the magnificently wasteful second Viscount Griffiths, had never married, and Alexander's father had been his only brother. His father had been in excellent health and could have lived for decades longer, but instead he'd died when Rufus was seven, drowned trying to save his younger son. Rufus had been a strong swimmer, even at that early age, but he'd developed a cramp, and their father had been the one to die.

For years Alexander had been saddled with Adelia and her incessant demands for money. In any other circumstances he would have given her anything she wanted, as long as she disappeared from his life; he'd promised his father he'd look after her, and for his half brother's sake he put up with the woman. He had the cynical suspicion she'd wanted everything, including the title for her son, and he'd learned to be very careful.

If Rufus was truly dead—and Alexander still had his doubts there'd been any deus ex machina to save him—then he could finally dispense with the witch. Perhaps now she'd be amenable to a generous settlement. He'd once even considered offering her Renwick, but he'd changed his mind about that. Oddly enough, the moment he stepped inside, it had felt like home, and despite Adelia's elaborate redecorating, he'd claimed it in his heart.

Normally he wouldn't have cared about his surroundings, as long as they were neat and clean, and he let Adelia do what she wanted in a few of the public rooms, but she was allowed nowhere near his private areas.

The change he'd made, and the most important one, was the transplanting of the rose garden and the pool. Even his father's death by drowning couldn't halt his love for being in the water, and his ancient Scottish nanny had told him tales of the selkies and sea people. He used to wish he had webbed toes.

The only way to make Renwick perfect would be to get rid of Adelia, and presuming Rufus didn't return from the grave, he'd figure out a way to do it short of cold-blooded murder.

Madame . . . though it must be Mademoiselle . . . Sophie was a different matter.

He should get rid of her, too. Much as her games distracted him and built his appetite, his obsession with her was becoming too strong. He didn't like being a slave to his senses, and he hadn't asked for a challenge. He'd ordered a comfortable woman to ease him and stay quietly in a nearby cottage, ready to service him and to make life simpler. Instead he got someone moving into his house and his kitchen but doing everything she could to avoid his bed.

A wise man would send the girl packing. He didn't need those kinds of complications in his life, particularly when it came to women. Every relationship he'd had with women had been fraught with hysterics and treachery and violence. He'd wanted a woman for one reason alone, and the offering Mrs. Lefton had sent him was giving him everything but.

Somehow over the last few days he'd lost control of the situation, seduced by her cooking and the addictive taste of her mouth and, yes, even her sass. The first step in regaining his life would be to get rid of her. He could even stomach the unappetizing results from the kitchen if he didn't have this constant . . . need for her. It was a bad word—he didn't want to *need* anything. Need made you weak, made you vulnerable, and then the tigers would pounce.

In the end he was glad he'd left the overscented whorehouse. The night air was warm, and the moon so bright he could see clearly enough to ride at a comfortable pace, and the moon was still high in the sky when he returned to his darkened estate.

No one was up, not even a footman. It didn't surprise him— he'd told them not to leave someone waiting around for no reason, and when he went out on his visits it usually took him a couple of days to slake his hunger. Thinking of Sophie, he found himself grinning. It would take more than that to have enough of her.

He needed to send her away, and that's exactly what he would do. Damn the food, damn his stripling lust. He wasn't in the mood for adventures right now.

A sleepy stable hand appeared just as he was about to take care of his own horse, and Alexander gladly handed over the reins. He was tired; he needed his own bed.

The house was still as he entered, and he breathed a sigh of relief. Not that he wasn't fond of Dickens, who'd been with him since just before his father died, but there were times when he really got tired of being hovered over, particularly by a man half a head shorter than he was. He strode through the halls at a leisurely pace, dispensing of his coat and his jacket, unknotting his cravat and tossing that as well. One of the efficient maids would make his mess disappear long before anyone else awoke, though Dickens would give him a wounded look.

A glass of brandy and a good cigar would end the night to perfection. The door to his office was open, and he sat down behind his desk, pulling off his boots with a grunt. Sitting back, he stared at his moonlit office, at the sofa where he'd had Sophie beneath him for too short a time. In fact, he couldn't stop thinking about her. He needed to get rid of her, before this entire thing got out of hand.

Getting up, he went over and poured himself a generous snifter of brandy, not giving a damn that he was ruining the bouquet of it by overfilling the glass. He needed alcohol if he was going to sleep tonight, enough alcohol that he wouldn't dream about Sophie. He tossed the contents back with a disrespectful shudder, then refilled the glass, repeating the action. The third was a reasonable amount, one he could savor, his offering to Bacchus as appreciation for the nectar of the gods.

He glanced out the French windows that overlooked the terrace leading down to the pool, and froze. There had been a flash, almost a suggestion of something white out there, something pale and ghostly, and immediately his mind went to Rufus. As difficult as it was to believe he was dead, the thought that he'd return to haunt Renwick was even more ridiculous. But then, if anyone would turn into a mischievous, vengeful ghost it would be his half brother, Rufus.

For a moment he stopped to consider why he would think Rufus would want revenge. As far as Alexander knew, his half brother adored him—he'd have no reason to wish him ill.

He moved closer to the window, looking out. He wouldn't be seen—there was no light behind him and the brightness of the moon was blinding. He could see that almost formless white shape flit through his gardens like a hummingbird. A white, pure hummingbird, with long, golden hair halfway down her back.

She'd turned that lovely back on him. She was wearing only a shift and it clung to her body like a glove. She'd tilted her head upward, spreading her arms as if calling to the moon, her lover, to come to her. He was frozen, mesmerized, watching her. It was as if he'd happened across a fawn in the woods, a shy woodland creature. Or more likely a unicorn. She looked so silvery white in the moonlight, more like a goddess than the girl he knew she was.

She turned, not even glancing toward the house. She was practically naked—he supposed the dark heap at her feet was the rest of her clothes. She was standing at the head of the pool, watching as it shimmered in front of her, and he held his breath as he realized she was wet. The water made her shift cling to her body, outlining every curve, every valley and shadow. She'd been in his pool, and his entire body grew painfully hard at the thought. She'd been in the water, and he hadn't been with her.

He slipped out the door silently, into the shadows before she could realize anything had changed. She jerked her head back toward the house, her eyes searching, her body tense, and then she relaxed, seeing nothing.

She was thinner than he'd realized, though still rounded in the prettiest places. He couldn't quite reconcile the tart-tongued whore with the innocent schoolgirl act, and now the moon goddess had joined her roles. Who else could she play?

She was humming beneath her breath, so softly he couldn't make it out. She was moving, swaying, and the song got just a little bit louder, until he could make out one of Johann Strauss's new waltzes. She hummed, took a few steps and then turned, dipped, and moved on. She was dancing, he realized, dancing alone in his gardens, her body damp from his pool, and he wondered if she knew he was watching her. She'd know soon enough.

He kept to the shadows along the complicated system of terraces, out of her sight as her pretty voice moved on to another waltz, something slow and almost sexual. He wanted to stay in the shadows, watching her, he wanted to take her and . . . he just wanted to take her. He recognized the waltz now, and some odd, quixotic part of him made him suddenly move forward, into the moonlight, taking her in his arms and swinging her into the waltz and for a brief, unreal moment she danced with him, perfectly, like a London socialite.

And then she froze, her humming strangled in her voice as she stumbled against him, and they came to an abrupt halt. He kept hold of her, lightly, but he wasn't about to let her go, particularly as she tried to push away from him. "You aren't supposed to be here," she said, sounding almost panicky.

The panic had to be feigned—it was ridiculous. "Why not?" he said in a low voice.

"You were supposed to be gone for at least two days." She was calming down now, the tight edge gone from her voice.

"Where was I supposed to be?" he questioned lightly. He could smell the water on her skin, and he wanted to lick her shoulder, her neck, he wanted to pull down the wet shift and suckle her. Through the thin, damp cotton he could see nipples, dark against the sheer fabric, puckered against the cold. Waiting for his mouth.

"They told me you were off with your whores," she said.

She sounded almost jealous, which was absurd, given that the women he would have been with were her sisters in the world's oldest profession. "I decided I'd rather have you," he said, holding her quite mercilessly, looking down into her dark blue eyes that shouldn't have held so much intelligence. He put his other hand at the back of her neck, sliding it beneath her damp curtain of hair, and tilted her face up so that he could kiss her.

"Don't you dare," she said in a furious whisper.

He was so startled at her vehemence he almost loosened his hold on her. Almost. "Why not? You're bought and paid for."

If she wasn't clamped against his body she probably would have slapped him. Her outrage was so complete that it was hard to believe it was feigned. She was so very good at this. "Bought and paid for?" she echoed furiously; her struggles, which had momentarily died down, began in earnest again. "You conceited jackass! Who do you think you are? I was told you kept your hands off the people in your employ. Clearly you think nothing of exerting that unfair advantage over me, but I have no intention of letting you get away with it. Let go of me."

"Did Mrs. Lefton send you or did she not?" he demanded, growing weary of all this.

"Of course she did," Sophie said instantly. "Why else would I be here?"

"Why indeed?" he murmured to the heavens. "And did she explain fully what your duties would require?"

She hesitated for a moment, and he knew exactly what was going through her head. She was deciding which of her complicated schemes she would play out. "Of course," she said finally.

"In detail?"

"I've already told you, yes. In detail," she snapped, but she was looking uneasy.

"So I'm tired of waiting. Take off your fucking clothes."

CHAPTER TWELVE

SOPHIE STOPPED PUSHING AGAINST him. The more she fought, the tighter his grip, and he was a very strong man. He was also out of his mind. What kind of employment agency would send a woman out to . . . to . . . she wasn't even going to think his crude word, but the idea was absurd.

He was angry now—she could feel it radiating through his taut body. She was angry too, but it was getting her nowhere. Maybe he'd listen to reason. Maybe it was the time for honesty, much as she despised sinking to that level.

"My lord," she said in a quiet, firm voice. "I see I'm going to have to explain the situation. I'm not really a cook."

He raised one of his black, satanic eyebrows but he didn't frighten her. At least, not much. "Oh, really?" he drawled with great sarcasm. "You astonish me."

Sophie took a deep breath. "I'm actually a . . . lady. Well, at least I was, until circumstances changed." She couldn't tell him her real name—he knew better than anyone the scandal involving the Russells, the scandal that had brought him this house and possibly his fortune.

"Ah, yes," he said thoughtfully. "I expected something like that. It was either going to be that or the shy schoolgirl, which has never appealed to me. Innocence, even feigned innocence, is annoying."

"Unfortunately for you, I *am* innocent. A virgin, in fact. So you really don't want to waste your time with someone like me."

Some of his anger had faded, and now he was looking faintly amused. "So I should toss you back in the stream like a fish that's too small and go looking for something larger?"

She wrinkled her nose. "Not an elegant way to put it, but yes. I'm sure there are any number of women around who'd fall at your feet."

"Oh, would they?"

"Of . . . of course," she stammered. He was no longer hurting her, but she knew the minute she tried to escape, his grip would tighten once more. "You're very handsome, you know."

"Yes, I know," he said blandly.

She could kick him, she thought wistfully, holding still. "And you're wealthy, and you have a title. Most women would do anything to be the recipient of your . . ."—she struggled for the word—". . . attentions, dishonorable as they are."

"But not you?"

"Not me. I have other plans." Most of her momentary panic had fled, leaving her more uneasy than frightened. This wasn't a man who'd force himself on her.

"Such as?"

She ground her teeth at his polite question. "If you let me go I'll answer your question."

He didn't bat an eye. "You'll answer the question anyway."

"You're a brute and a bully."

He shrugged. "As I said, you picked the game. What are your plans?"

It wouldn't give anything away to tell him. "I plan to marry well," she said. "I'm very pretty, you know, and I usually have men flocking around me."

"I imagine you do. Such a problem for people like us—all the people falling at our feet. It makes walking difficult."

She wasn't amused. "I . . . I intend to marry someone extremely wealthy and well bred. Probably with a title."

The damned man rolled his eyes at that, and her anger pushed the last of her fear away. "Of course you do, love. Why not one of Queen Victoria's sons while you're at it? I'm afraid the Prince of Wales is taken but there are younger ones, and Bertie may come down with a fatal disease. You could end up queen of England."

"This isn't funny," she said stiffly.

"Well, you're just going to have to put up with my amusement if I have to put up with your games. So how do you want me to play it? Am I to be a tender suitor who sweeps you off your feet? A bandit who kidnaps you? Perhaps a pirate?"

"Why don't you be yourself," she said sweetly. "An impossible ass."

He laughed. "As you wish, my innocent one," and before she realized what he was doing he'd scooped her up in his arms and started toward the house.

For a moment she was too shocked to react, and then she started to struggle until his soft, implacable voice stopped her. "If you keep kicking and hitting me I'll feel totally justified in returning the favor."

She kept very still. "You would, wouldn't you? Hit a helpless female."

"Never. But you're not a helpless female." He must have left one of the French doors ajar, because a moment later they were inside, and he was starting for the stairs.

"I could scream," she warned him. She wasn't sure if he really would hit her back but she wasn't going to take any chances.

"You could. But the sound doesn't carry to the servants' quarters from here."

"Your stepmother would hear."

"True. She'd love to catch me despoiling a virgin. Should I invite her to join us?"

"You're disgusting."

He set her down on the stairs. "That is a rather foul thought, isn't it?" he said in a deceptively amiable voice. "Where do you want to go? There's my room, of course. It's not fancy but it's quite comfortable. Or I can take you back to your bedroom next to the kitchens."

"And leave me there?"

"Of course not. There's also a pretty little house I had chosen for you. I believe it used to belong to someone's maiden aunt until she died. I had it freshened up, and we can do anything we want there. You can scream as loud as you like and not bother anyone."

Aunt Tillie's cottage, Sophie thought with a pang. "Why would I want to scream?"

"Oh, I do promise I can make you scream, precious," he purred.

She stared at him. "You already make me want to scream, sir. In frustration."

"I'll take care of that too. Where are we going?"

"I'm going to my bedroom and my very narrow bed, alone, thank you. You are going straight to hell."

"Ah, princess," he said, "I think it's going to be more like heaven." His mouth came down on hers.

Oh, God, the other kisses had been disturbing enough. Each time he kissed her she seemed to go a little farther on the road to inescapable madness. This one was a little rough, a demand rather than a question, his hands hard on her, but, instead of freezing, her heart leapt in immediate response. She didn't even want to think about what she was doing—she pulled at her hands that were locked between their bodies, and slid them around his waist, holding on as he ravished her mouth.

It was hypnotizing, it was heartbreaking, it was everything she wanted and nothing she could ever have, and she deserved it.

Just this once she deserved at least a taste of him, of the man she'd watched for so long, the man she'd dreamed about. She wanted, needed, his mouth, his skin, his touch. Surely she could risk that much. She softened her mouth beneath his, and then opened it as his tongue brushed across the seam of her lips, opened it for his tongue.

The shocking pleasure swept over her, and she wanted to melt into his skin. She wanted to kiss him back, but she didn't know how. All she could do was stand in his arms and let him ravish her mouth, closing her eyes so she could revel in it.

He suddenly broke the kiss, looking down at her, his breath coming in quick rasps. "Who the hell are you?" he whispered, looking shaken. Her wicked Dark Viscount, shaken by a kiss she had barely managed to respond to.

For a moment she could think of nothing to say. She'd tried to tell him the truth but he hadn't believed her. In the end, what did it matter? Tomorrow she'd be gone. "Sophie," she whispered. "I'm Sophie."

A faint smile curved his mouth, one of almost relief. "So you are," he said, and picked her up in his arms once more, moving up the stairs quickly. She realized then that his white shirt was open, baring a triangle of burnished skin, and she imagined his shock if she moved her head downward and put her mouth against him.

Action followed thought immediately, and she pressed her face against his bared throat, breathing in the delicious scent of him. And then, because she couldn't help it, she tasted him, her tongue tracing a small path.

It was a good thing they'd reached the top of the stairs, because with a strangled sound he dropped her, pushed her up against the nearest wall, and pressed the lower part of his body against hers. She should have been frozen in disgust, knowing what that hard ridge of flesh was, but instead it made her burn. Her thin, damp chemise was made of such fine silk that its touch on her flesh was one more arousal, brushing against her aching breasts, rubbing between her legs with the thrust of his hips, and she cried out, as something shook her, some strange, terrible need that she couldn't fight.

"Do that again," he growled in her ear, "and I'll take you right here, right now, and I don't give a damn who walks by and sees it."

She felt drugged, dazed, but she tried to focus on him. It was hard, because he was pushing against her lower body in a slow, insistent rhythm; that hard, clothed part of him against her soft, silk-covered flesh. "You didn't like it?" she asked dazedly.

"You know damned well, my sham innocent, that I liked it far too much. I wanted your tongue everywhere on my body, and if you tease me like that I'm not going to wait. If your game includes taking me in your mouth the first time, then you have my blessing, but I'm taking more than that. I'm taking everything."

"Everything?" she echoed dazedly. She ought to run. This was the disaster that had been looming, that she'd known was coming. Not Alexander Griffiths. But her own, totally demented need for him. It was what she should have run from. It was what she was staying still for.

Her sisters hadn't told her about this. No one had. She'd been advised on the technical details of mating, which was far more warning than most girls received, but she had two older sisters to fill her in, though to her knowledge neither of them had firsthand experience. And they'd talked about love, and shared interests, and companionship, and comfort.

But no one had said anything about a fire in your blood that burns away any common sense you might have once possessed. No one said you could want a man's touch so much that your body was in an uproar, parts that you didn't even name seemed to be aching with longing. No one had said you would throw everything away for a man who mocked you and teased you and then spoke to you in clipped tones like you were a servant, and yet all he had to do was touch you . . .

She no longer knew where she was in the house where she'd spent almost her entire life. He was moving her now, his body still clamped to hers, moving her backwards, and she lost all sense of direction, caught up with the feel of him pressed against her, the sight of his chest, that warm, exotic color that should taste like the sun. They came up against a door, and it opened behind her, and they were in darkness, the curtains pulled against the bright moonlight.

She heard him kick the door shut, and the next thing she knew he'd picked her up, walked a few paces, and sent her sailing through the air to land on a large bed. "Sorry if my virgin princess wants a more tender wooing, but you've teased me long enough." His voice was harsh, and she heard the sound of clothing being torn off.

Clothing. Coming off. Oh, God, she was in trouble. She started to scramble off the bed, but he caught her ankle, hauling her back and coming down over her. She was spread sideways across the mattress, and he was over her, pressing her down. Shirtless, all that skin against her, and he was hot, while she was cold, wanting to shiver in the darkness.

She closed her eyes, stilling the fight that was coursing through her veins. She was no match for him physically. She'd have to outwit him. With most men that would be easy enough, but Alexander was far more intelligent than the pretty young fribbles she'd danced with in her triumphant season in London. She could see it in his fierce, mocking eyes.

There was no way she was going down without a fight. She was going to win this battle, against him, against her own incomprehensibly wanton desires, simply because she had to.

She lay still beneath him. He didn't move either, but he was breathing deeply, and she suspected, given his ease in carrying her one hundred pounds or so up the stairs, that it wasn't from exertion. She closed her eyes and gathered her meager defenses.

He lifted his head and looked down at her. "You really are a giant pain in my arse, Sophie. If you weren't so damned irresistible I would have sent you straight back. But Lefton knew what she was doing when she sent you."

Again with the employment agency? Why was he so obsessed with it? "In truth I don't think I'm suited for this position," she said in what she hoped was a matter-of-fact tone.

"And which position would you prefer? There are so many variations even I haven't tried them all, and I defer to your professional knowledge."

She stared at him. "What in God's name are you talking about?"

He sighed. "Sex, my dear. Copulation. Fucking. What we're finally about to do."

"Oh, no we're not . . ." she started, before his mouth silenced hers. She couldn't do this. She would lull him into thinking she was compliant, even eager to participate in this, and then run whenever his attention happened to wander. *A good plan*, she thought almost dazedly, the soft, almost familiar bed beneath her, the strong, hot body on top of hers, the mouth ravishing hers as he tried to steal her resolve. He was luring her, she knew it, seducing her with his increasingly intimate kisses, by the heat his very presence seemed to bring forth in her.

She was no helpless twit to lose her sanity in the face of an overwhelmingly gorgeous man. And yet she was. Was it his kisses—he kissed differently, more intimately, with his mouth open, with his tongue seeking hers. She'd gotten over the shock of it—she was drawn by the almost hypnotic power of it. *This must be how rich heiresses are compromised by penniless rakes and forced into marriage,* she thought dizzily. Even the most stalwart of females would have a hard time resisting a kiss like this one.

But she was the one who was penniless in this situation. She tore her mouth away from his, gasping for breath, and fixed him with a fierce look. "I don't understand you," she said. "Why me?"

She had to fight the sudden lurch of her heart at the flash of anger in his eyes. Whether she wanted to admit it or not, there were times he could frighten her. She wouldn't let this be one of those times.

But annoyance wasn't enough to make him move from her. Oddly enough, he wasn't too heavy, just enough to keep her there but not enough to hurt her, and she realized he must be taking some of his weight on the arms that trapped her. "Why you?" he said. "You're here."

His flat, irritated voice was enough to make her buck beneath him, trying to get him off her, but it was a waste of time. "Just give me half an hour and I'll find you someone else," she said.

"Do we really have to play this game?" His voice was weary.

"What game?"

He sighed. "All right, my precious, have it your way. You're a lady in disguise as a simple servant, and I'm the wicked seducer you can't resist. Just tell me one thing. Do you want it rough or gentle?"

Her eyes shot open, staring into his cynical ones. "I don't know what you're talking about."

"We'll see how things go then, shall we?" His mouth caught hers again, silencing her protest. She managed to get her hands free, and she slid them up to push at his shoulders, but the shock of his hot, sleek skin stopped her. He was warm, pliant beneath her fingers, and he kissed the side of her mouth, his teeth tugged on her lower lip, and she let out a shaky little moan.

"That's right, you little hellion"—he moved his head to whisper in her ear—"I promise you, I can make you forget any game you ever wanted to play and give you the ride of your life."

"Don't," she said desperately, clutching at his shoulders, holding on to him.

"Don't what?"

"Don't talk." Just for a moment she wanted to lose herself in the feel of his skin, his mouth, without the sarcastic words tearing her from her dream.

149

He laughed then, and to her surprise he rolled to his side, bringing her with him, so that she was no longer trapped. It should have been a relief, but like a fool she didn't try to pull away. Her eyes had begun to get used to the darkness, but even so close she could barely see him. She felt his hand on her calf, catching the whisper-thin chemise in his hand and starting to draw it upward, and when she reached down to stop him, he simply caught her hand in his and brought it to his mouth, kissing it. "Don't you ever get tired of fighting?"

"Don't you?" she countered in a whisper. *Put your hand back there*, she thought. *Don't let me stop you.*

She had no idea whether he was a mind reader or not, but he slid his hand back down her leg to catch the shift again. "You don't want me to tear this pretty thing off you, do you? If that's the game you want to play then you should wear cheaper clothing."

"I don't want to play any games," she cried.

"Good. Neither do I."

She had no idea how he managed to move so fast, so deftly; his hands slid up the sides of her body and stripped the chemise over her head, tossing it away in the darkness, and she was alone with a man, in a bed, wearing nothing at all.

She should tell him to stop. She should tell him exactly who she was—he would jump away from her as if she were pure poison. She'd wrapped her arms around her body, instinctively, protectively, and neither of them moved.

"It's up to you now, Sophie," he whispered, his voice a little rough in the darkness. "No more games. Yes, or no?"

He was so close she could feel the heat coming off his body; she could still taste his mouth on hers, feel the touch of his surprisingly calloused hands on her arms. She could roll away from him, hit the floor, and run. She knew it with an instinct old and sure as time. He would let her go. He'd let her go the first time she ran; he would let her go this time as well.

But she didn't want to run.

For a moment she didn't move, trying to will common sense back into her brain. It was gone, vanished in the darkness, and there was no way she could summon it back. It didn't matter; none of it did. The only thing she cared about was Alexander, beside her, waiting for her answer. There was only one answer she could honestly give.

She unwrapped her arms from her body, reached up, and cupped his face, holding him with her strong hands, her thumbs gently caressing his mouth, and she heard the word in her own voice, the word from her own heart, not her nonfunctioning brain. "Yes."

For a moment he didn't move, and she had the sudden fear that it had been the chase that mattered—once she gave in, stopped playing the game, as he called it, he would lose interest.

And then he let out a pent-up breath. "Thank God," he murmured, and kissed her with such sweetness she wanted to weep. His arms came around her, and she was suddenly dizzy as he rolled her over his body, so that she rested on top of him. Her bare breasts were against his warm skin, and instinctively she rubbed against him.

He slid his hands up, and the feel of them on her breasts was so exquisite she took in a quick breath. His thumbs brushed against her nipples, and she jerked in surprise, feeling it directly between her legs.

"Don't worry, my precious little virgin," he said. "I'll make your first time good for you."

She felt relief flood her. He believed her. He wouldn't hurt her—he would take care of her, cherish her as any lover would. It didn't matter if his voice was ironic—he always sounded that way. It didn't matter that he wasn't her lover, or her husband. For now he would be.

She slid against him, her hips up against his, feeling the hard ridge beneath his trousers, a perfect match for the ache between her legs. It would be all right. She ran her hands up around his neck and pulled him closer.

Her nipples were hard against his thumbs in the warm night air, and he knew he had her. Knew that she'd be wet between her legs, and he wanted to put his mouth there, wanted to with such a fierceness that he could barely fight it. She was the one being paid—even if it gave him pleasure, he wasn't going down on someone who serviced men for a living, no matter how good an actress she was. It was a pleasure he would have to reserve for someone else.

Her breasts were a different matter. He wanted to taste her, to suck on her, and with a groan he pushed her onto her back, leaned down, and took one hard, small nipple into his mouth.

He felt her entire body jerk, a reaction that couldn't be feigned, and he ran his tongue over her, then latched on, using his teeth just slightly, and sucked, hard, as he ran his hand down her stomach, and he felt her buck beneath him, her hands on his shoulders, clinging to him.

She had soft, perfect skin. Pampered, delicate, and he wanted to lick her all over. She tasted like the cool, clear water that he swam in, and he wanted more. His fingers slid through the soft curls covering her, and he felt a second flash of emotion hit her body. He moved his hand down, his fingers touching her wetness, and he was the one who groaned in sheer, delicious anticipation.

Her arms were around him, holding him to her as he sucked on her, her fingers clutching him, and as he slid one finger inside her she bucked again, her hips reaching for the pleasure she knew he could bring her. He lifted his head, releasing her breast with a soft, popping noise, and her fingers dug in, not wanting to let him go.

"Equal time, precious," he murmured with a soft laugh, and caught the other distended nipple between his teeth.

The sound she made, low, keening, needy, was music to his ears, and he pushed one finger inside her. She was so delectably tight, despite the dampness he was coaxing from her, and he pulled out one finger and slid two in. There were things women could do, to make their bodies tight, almost virginal again, and Sophie must have made use of whatever herbs or powders provided that effect. He didn't need it—this had been her game, not his, but either way it didn't matter. It was where he wanted, needed, to be.

He had to move this along. He couldn't remember ever being so aroused in his life. He needed to get inside her and fuck them both senseless, a fast, hard, heavy release that would get some of the pent-up frustration out of him. Then he could go slower, take his time, let her practice her skills on him. He had a few skills of his own he'd learned in his travels when he was younger, and he had every intention of giving her as good a time as she was giving him. But right now he was ready to explode.

She was making no effort to undress him, caught up in the sensations of his mouth and his hands. He took his fingers from her sex, hearing her cry out with pleasure. He hadn't even touched her pleasure spot yet, and she was already shaking with need. He pulled her hand from his shoulder and set it on the buttons that were now tight over his swollen cock, and instead of setting to work she tried to jerk away.

He wasn't having it, and he gave her nipple a small, warning nip with his teeth as he brought her hand back, and this time she didn't pull away. She rested her fingers against him for a moment, like someone checking a hot stove to see if it would burn, and then she moved, slowly touching him with a delicate, exploratory hand that almost made him spill. She caressed him with her fingers, slid her hands down, as if to figure out the size of him, and if it had taken her any longer he would have reached down and ripped the damned buttons off himself.

But he felt her reach the top one, and he moaned, running his tongue over her, and she moved to the next button.

This was the way it was supposed to be, give and take, his move increasing her need, her move building his own passion. It was no wonder it felt as if they would end up bursting into flames. This was it, the way it should be, the way it never really was.

But not with Sophie. She'd reached the fourth button, and damn, he wanted her mouth on him, so much he shook with it. But she was still playing her game, not his, and in impatience he reached down and released his cock, catching her hand and placing it on him as he felt her try to move away.

Oh, Holy Mother of God, that was a terrible move, he thought with a groan, as her cool fingers slid along his skin. He'd underestimated how her deceptively shy touch would affect him. It was a good thing she wouldn't take him in her mouth this time—he'd spill at the first touch of her lips. Even the thought of it was making him ready to burst.

Her soft, seemingly innocent touch was driving him mad, and he pushed his fingers back inside her, into the sleek tightness of her. His thumb found her and he rubbed.

She shrieked, her hand clamping down on him almost painfully, and if he didn't know better he would think she'd never felt a man's hands on her before. She was aroused, maybe as hot as he was— there was no way for her to fake the wetness between her thighs, and he wanted to see her come, wanted to make her as helpless and lost in pleasure as he planned on being. She'd teased him, kept him dangling on a string for too long, and he was going to do a bit of the same to her, bring her to the brink and then pull back, so that she knew what frustration was like. He circled her with his thumb, bringing her wetness with him, and before he could stop her she came, hard, her body clamping down on his fingers as they thrust inside her, her entire body rigid as she exploded with a silent scream.

He couldn't wait any longer. He gave her a moment, until she fell back limply on the bed, then covered her, shoving his pants down and moving between her legs. His cock felt huge, and he set it where his fingers had been, rubbing the head of it against her, mingling his wetness with hers, a joining of readiness neither of their bodies could deny. He started to push inside her.

He felt the jolt of shock run through her, and her hands caught his shoulders, digging in. But she didn't push him away—at least that little bit of playacting was over with. He paused, his cock just barely inside her, fighting to control his need to rut. "You want this?" He knew she did—her body didn't lie nearly as well as her mouth did. But he needed there to be no mistake about what was going on between them. The game was ending. *Les jeux sont faits.* The game is played.

There was a breathless, endless pause. And then the one syllable he needed in her hoarse voice. "Yes."

He slammed into her, driving deep and hard, so needy that there was no more polite maneuvering. He was unprepared for her reaction. She screamed, this time out loud, convulsing against him, and it wasn't in pleasure, but pain. He froze, deep inside her, blessedly deep, her body clutching his, throbbing around him. Women had told him he was bigger than most men, and she'd done something to make herself tight, and he should have remembered before thrusting into her so hard, but he hadn't been able to resist. He'd hurt her, he should do something, but he heard her shattered breath beneath him, and her legs moved around him, accommodating him, and he could no longer think, didn't want to think. He only needed to move, to thrust, to find the release so long delayed. He buried his face in her neck, forcing his body to slow, hard thrusts. He was slick with sweat and so was she, and she was clinging to him tightly, holding on, gasping as he thrust, back and forth, a heavy rhythm that was almost costing him his sanity. He wanted her to come again, but something was off, something was wrong, and all he could do was drive himself home and then deal with it.

He pulled her legs tighter around his hips, driving into her, and finally he was there, and he wanted to spill inside her, so badly, but he pulled out, letting his seed pulse on her stomach as he sank against her with a deep groan, his whole body shaking with the power of his release.

He didn't know how long it was before he realized she was holding him almost tenderly, her hand stroking the back of his neck with delicate, strong fingers. He nuzzled against her, purring like some huge jungle cat. When he could he lifted his head to smile down at her, to kiss her, and then he stilled.

He had always been able to see well in the dark—his night vision was extraordinary. He could see her face, the shocky whiteness of it, the dried tracks of tears down her cheeks, the dark, confused pools of her eyes. She looked like someone who'd been assaulted.

He pulled away from her in sudden horror. She'd said yes, damn it. She was a hired whore, a woman good at playing games. He didn't like this game at all.

"What . . . ?" he said hoarsely.

And then she smiled at him, a beatific smile that warmed her eyes, even if his uneasiness still lingered. "Come back," she whispered, a siren call drowning out his sudden misgivings.

He could no more resist than he could stop his heart from beating. He sank down beside her, into her arms, held with such tenderness it made him ache. A moment later he was asleep.

CHAPTER THIRTEEN

SOPHIE COULD TELL WHEN his breathing slowed and he sank into a deep sleep. His muscles relaxed, and she knew she could let him go and he wouldn't notice. She didn't want to. She wanted to burrow against his big, strong body and hide. She felt . . . so many things. Shame. Anger. Pain. A strange churning inside her that seemed to claw at her, demanding something. She should hate him. He'd ruined everything. But all she could do was hold him to her, her fingers in his long, silky hair.

She knew, deep in her bruised heart, that this had been her fault, not his. She was the one who had let sheer, overwhelming animal attraction distract her; she was the one who had held him and told him yes. She could come up with all sorts of excuses, but in the end she had to answer to herself. And she knew that no excuse would absolve her of this.

She'd ruined her life for a moment of pleasure. Well, to be sure, there had been more than a few moments, and while the tearing pain when he'd thrust all the way inside her had been like cold water on a bonfire, there had still been a kind of primitive joy in the possession, even as it hurt.

It always hurt the first time, Bryony had informed her with the knowledgeable voice of a confirmed virgin. It hurt a lot more than she'd thought, but then, Alexander hadn't made any effort to ease it for her. She could be angry with him about that, she thought, as she stroked his smooth, damp skin. But in the end she knew that she was the one to blame.

This was such a strange feeling, as if that rough, erotic joining had forever changed her heart and soul. This was a random coupling for him, but it was something more for her. A gift, a promise, a connection that wouldn't be easily broken, no matter what happened next.

And nothing would happen next. She had to leave, just as she'd planned, and pretend this had never happened.

Let go of him, she told herself, but her arms didn't seem to be paying any attention to her brain. *Move away, pull yourself together, and assess the damage.* She couldn't. Soon enough she was going to have to disappear, get away from here and try to regain some semblance of her life. But for just a few moments more she wanted to sink into the feel of him.

A murky light was beginning to seep through a crack in the curtains, and sudden shock made Sophie release him and roll on her back, looking upward. Looking up at what she'd always looked up at during her years at Renwick—the top of the coffered ceiling. She was in her old room, her old bed. She'd just been deflowered in the very bed, perhaps the very sheets, where she'd formed such romantic fantasies about it. The handsome, deferential lordling, shy and adoring, the coupling that had been long on bliss and short on detail.

Instead she'd been roughly taken by a cynic, a sarcastic creature with demonic eyebrows and the eyes of a lost soul, damn him. The sooner she got away from him the better, or she'd start to romanticize the whole thing. This should have cured her of the notion that she was falling in love with him. This was reality.

She wanted to kiss him again. She wanted to crawl under his body, feel him all around her, his heat, his strength.

She had to go.

She inched away from him, rolling over on her stomach as she stared blindly into the darkness. This was no time for longing for the impossible; this was a time for action. She pressed her face against the cool sheet. It smelled like Renwick, it smelled like Alexander, it smelled like sex, a perfume of pain and complexity that wrung her heart.

But her heart could have nothing to do with it, she reminded herself. Escape was what mattered, before he woke up, before anyone woke up. Fortunately she was already packed.

She slid from the bed, but he slept on, like a rock. It took her a while to find her discarded shift, and when she did, she pulled it over her head. It was still slightly damp from her dip in the pool, and she shivered, but there was nothing she could do about it. She closed the door quietly behind her, and her bare feet were silent as she ran down the hall and the front stairs she'd played on when she was younger.

When she stepped outside, the grass was cold and wet with dew, and she was shivering by the time she found her discarded dress and petticoats. His shirt lay there as well, and she was so cold she pulled it on against the early morning chill. Prunella and Gracie would be up any time now, getting started on the early morning baking, and Dickens was right about one thing: The staff knew everything. She needed to run.

She didn't wait to get dressed. She couldn't find her shoes anywhere, and finally she gave up, slipping inside the kitchen to grab her valise. At the last minute she took a hunk of cheese and a loaf of yesterday's bread, suddenly famished. And then she was gone into the early morning mist.

Alexander was not a man who woke up quickly. It took him a damned long time; he came awake in stages, helped by large amounts of coffee, and woe betide any fool who yammered at him before he was good and ready to hear another human voice. Dickens knew this full well, and had continued to live a good long life because of it.

He didn't even want to open his eyes. He could smell her. Smell the tangled perfume of sex and Sophie on the sheets beneath him, the air around him, and in his morning thickheadedness he remembered something was wrong, but he couldn't remember what. His body was humming pleasantly, still happy from the bone-shattering release of last night, so powerful that it had knocked him out and he hadn't been able to continue with all the things he'd wanted. But it was morning, and he was going to have to say something to her and not growl.

He was hard as a rock, of course, and not just his early morning erection. Maybe he could just take her first before any unpleasant memories fought their way through. He opened his eyes to the dim morning light. It had to be only a bit past seven. Very carefully he rolled over onto his back, ready to take her in his arms.

He was alone in the bed. Suddenly he was wide awake, as if he'd been up for hours with half a pot of coffee inside him. He sat up, looking around the room. His trousers and smalls were in a heap on the floor, but there was no sign of her shift, or of Sophie at all. She'd run off, the coward, and there was nothing he could do but roll out of bed.

He yanked open the heavy curtains, letting in such a flood of light that it assaulted his eyes and his head. He'd had too much to drink last night before he made the fatal mistake of finding Sophie almost naked, dancing in the moonlight.

Fatal, he thought. *Why the hell did it feel fatal?* He was just taking what was bought and paid for, and he'd gone out of his way to make certain she'd been willing, which on the face of it had been absurd.

It hadn't felt like a transaction. It had felt as if he were in bed with someone he cared about, not a hired companion. Part of her damned games, and even in the heat of everything, she hadn't dropped that mask. He glanced over at the bed in frustration, and froze.

There was a dark stain on the sheets. He shut his eyes. He wasn't going any closer—the maids would strip the bed and the whole thing was none of his business. But he knew he couldn't ignore it. Opening his eyes, he moved back to the bed and looked down.

The smear of dried blood where he had taken her was unmistakable. He could tell himself she'd had her monthly courses, yes, that was the reason she'd been standoffish, but he knew that was a lie. He remembered the blessed tightness of her, her cry of pain when he'd pushed through, and the impossible, damnable truth was staring him in the eyes.

He heard Dickens rap softly on the door and without thinking Alexander slid back in bed, pulling the discarded covers up over the telltale sign.

"Good morning, your lordship," Dickens said in a quiet voice used to keep a wild animal at bay, carrying his breakfast tray. He came over to the far side of the bed and set it down, right over the spot that was burning a hole in Alexander's brain. Dickens poured him a cup of coffee from the heavy silver pot, and Alexander grabbed for it, amazed that his hand was steady as a rock.

"I'm afraid breakfast is a bit below expectations, but I regret to tell you our cook has disappeared. When Prunella went to wake her, there was no sign of her, her bed hasn't been slept in, and all her belongings are missing."

Alexander met his butler's eyes angrily. There'd been just the faintest bit of accusation in the man's voice, and Alexander's guilt bit at him. He took a deep gulp of coffee and burned his tongue, but he swallowed it anyway. "So what the hell do I have to do with it?" he demanded.

"Indeed, sir," Dickens said smoothly. "I wondered the same myself."

No one but Dickens would have dared to say something like that to him. Alexander ignored him. "Draw me a bath. I've got work to do today. And you'd best see about finding us a new cook, one who won't flit off in the middle of the night. Have you checked to see whether she ran off with any of the silver?"

Dickens's disapproval deepened. "No, sir. I'll get right on it."

A servant, even one of Dickens's tenure, wasn't supposed to be sarcastic, but Alexander ignored it. Dickens got away with a lot more than a regular servant. Alexander lifted the silver cover and then dropped it back on the unappetizing meal. "And take this rubbish away. Tell Prunella if she can't manage a decent breakfast then she can take herself off as well."

Dickens stiffened. "Yes, my lord. Would you prefer I send her to you so you may inform her yourself?"

"Go to hell, Dickens."

"Yes, sir."

By the time he was bathed and dressed and Dickens had shaved him without cutting his throat, Alexander's head had cleared. It was a relief she was gone, he told himself as he settled behind his desk. She'd been a distraction instead of a convenience, the exact opposite of what he'd told Lefton he'd wanted, and he was well rid of her. He was going to have a word with Mrs. Lefton, and never make the mistake of trusting even a professional like that overpainted harridan to choose a bed partner for him.

By the time it was late morning he'd been doing an excellent job of not thinking about Sophie more than once or twice every few minutes. When Dickens knocked on the door he felt an unaccustomed relief in the distraction.

"You have a visitor, my lord," Dickens said in austere tones.

Alexander raised his eyebrows, waiting.

"I've put her in the small front parlor. Do you wish to see her there or shall I bring her to you?"

"Her?" he echoed, puzzled. "Do you mean a lady?"

"No, sir," Dickens said in a stiff voice. "A female."

"A servant?"

"No, sir."

"Damn it, Dickens, I'm in no mood for guessing games!" he snapped.

"Nor am I, sir," he shot back, and suddenly Alexander felt like he was sixteen years old and his valet-cum-bodyguard had caught him in some minor wrongdoing.

Alexander rose, shoving some papers off the desk, and stalked to the door his man was holding open. "You and I are going to have to have a serious talk about all this," he said in a dark voice.

Dickens didn't back down. "That we are, sir. One of the upstairs maids informed me about the sheets."

For the first time in perhaps a decade Alexander Griffiths felt color warm his face. Pushing past Dickens, he stalked down the hallways to the small front parlor kept for inconsequential and unwanted guests.

The woman was standing there, her back to him as she surveyed the view from the window, but she turned swiftly at his approach and managed an exceedingly graceful curtsey. A sight better than Sophie's uneven attempts, he thought, then cursed himself. He had to stop thinking about her.

The woman was tall, with dark hair and a calm expression. She was attractive rather than beautiful, her clothes were expensive but not quite *comme il faut*, and the application of paint on her face was skillful. With sudden dread, Alexander knew who she was, and he wanted to turn and run, not listen to her. But he'd never run from anything in his life, and he'd never refused to face the consequences of his own actions.

"Good morning, your lordship. I'm Melinda. Mrs. Lefton sent me."

"She did?" He was amazed he didn't sound as hoarse and sick as he felt.

"I'm sorry it's taken such a long time, but she wanted to make sure she had the right candidate for you." She had a pretty smile, and in another lifetime she would have done very well. She took a look at his face and her smile faded slightly. "If I won't suit then it's no problem, my lord. The carriage is still waiting, and she can send someone else."

"I-I've changed my mind." He never stammered.

The woman didn't even blink. "Of course, my lord," she said immediately. Her well-bred voice couldn't quite disguise the cockney beneath it. "Would you like Mrs. Lefton to send someone else?"

"No." Without another word he turned on his heel and left her to Dickens to take care of, while he walked straight through the house and out into the gardens.

The day was slightly overcast, but still warm, and he would swim this afternoon. Swim until he wiped all memory of last night from his mind. He stood at the edge of the terrace, staring out over the length of the pool, and it was there Dickens found him.

"Your lordship."

Alexander turned his head. "It took you long enough. Are you going to tear a strip off me for my bad behavior, Dicky?" He used the old nickname from his adolescence, when his father had first brought the retired boxer to look after him.

But Dickens didn't unbend. "No, my lord. I merely wished to know if you had any idea where Miss Russell had gone."

Alexander blinked. "Who?"

"Miss Russell, sir. I believe you called her Miss Sophie." There was no inflection in Dickens's voice; nonetheless Alexander felt flayed. "The staff and I are worried about her. She left no word and I'm not sure she has any place to go."

He turned, burgeoning anger replacing at least part of his guilt. "What secrets have you been keeping from me, Dickens?"

The man didn't flinch. "It wasn't my secret to tell."

He was feeling sick inside. "Miss Russell," he repeated slowly. "Sophie Russell. I suppose it's too much to hope she has nothing to do with the previous tenants of this house."

"Who else would she be, your lordship?" Dickens was beyond disapproving. "Miss Sophia Russell, late of Renwick and Curzon Street, London, daughter of Mr. Eustace Russell. A proper young lady whom I believe you took advantage of last night."

Alexander's pungent curses flew through the air as he felt his world contract into one narrow path. Dickens stood impassively in the face of his profanity, saying nothing until Alexander had finally come to a halt. "Indeed, sir," Dickens murmured. "We need to find her. I've had a few of the footmen out making inquiries in the village, but no one has seen her, and the cottage where she'd been staying with her old nanny has been occupied by some of your tenants whose own cottage burned last fortnight. She has no place to go."

A slow, righteous anger was beginning to fill Alexander, an anger that wiped out any of the guilt that had been bothering him. He'd been tricked, cheated, lied to. Hell, a proper young woman had allowed him to seduce her, had participated willingly enough, leaving him with no choice at all. The Russell daughters had been cast adrift without a paddle, so to speak, and he'd just been fool enough to give them a lifeline.

Why else would she have shown up here, pretending to be someone else? Of course, she probably had no idea who Mrs. Lefton was, and she'd been annoyingly standoffish, but each time he'd put his hands on her she'd melted obligingly. He had no idea whether it had been a trap or not—at that moment he was just too angry and uncomfortable to give her the benefit of the doubt.

He could refuse to marry her, of course. There was no elderly relative to force him to do the right thing, and few would condemn him. He hadn't paid much attention, but he knew Russell's daughters had taken on their father's disgrace and were considered outcasts from society. No one would blame him if he did nothing, and he didn't give a damn if they did. They already blamed him for killing Jessamine—he hadn't been welcome in society for years, and it had been no loss to him. Whether Jessamine had fallen or jumped from the roof at the manor house had ceased to matter, any more than the approval of a group of gossiping, overbred idiots. They had judged and condemned him already—seducing and abandoning one semi-respectable virgin would hardly matter.

Semi-respectable. He felt like a fool, to be gulled like that. He'd known something was off with her, but each time he'd questioned her she'd assured him that Lydia Lefton had sent her. She wouldn't even know who Lydia Lefton was.

Damn the lying little bitch! He ought to wring her neck. It would be nothing more than she deserved if he simply forgot about her, let her go wherever she wanted, to find some other man to gull. She'd learned how to do the deed, after all. She'd already done it to get him to marry her—it was a short step from blackmail to doing it for money, and she'd been a quick learner.

And goddamn him. He turned on Dickens, coming up to him. "If you want to hit me, go right ahead," he said in a quiet voice.

"I want to thrash the hell out of you as you deserve," Dickens said, the threat almost comical in his gentrified voice. "But I'm too worried about Miss Russell. I can wait until we've found her."

"You and what army?" Alexander shot back.

"I'm still man enough to give you a beating when you deserve one," Dickens growled, sounding more like the prizefighter he'd once been and less like the proper butler he'd turned into.

Alexander glared at him. "Go ahead and find her, then. I'll be waiting."

"And when we do? What next?"

"How the hell should I know?" Alexander snapped.

"It might be a good thing for you to decide by the time we bring her back," Dickens said severely, turning his back on his employer and stomping off.

Alexander let him go. Dickens was always punctilious about proper etiquette between a servant and his master, even in a relationship as long-term and intimate as theirs. He had to be greatly moved to let the veneer of decorum drop.

Alexander turned and faced the garden once more, cursing beneath his breath. He knew what he had to do, whether he was ready to admit it to Dickens or not. All he wanted was to strip off his clothes and wash everything away in the coolness of the water. Instead he was saddled with this impossible mess.

He looked up then, at the tor that towered above the grounds of Renwick, at the spot where he'd felt the spying eyes, and suddenly he knew, without question, who had watched him all those weeks. And he knew where Miss Sophia Russell, recently despoiled, proper young lady, was.

He went down the steps and started across the lawn.

CHAPTER FOURTEEN

SOPHIE DROPPED TO THE grass, exhausted. The fitful sun had burned off the heavy morning dew, but her bare feet were still cold, and she tugged her skirts down to wrap around her toes. She'd dressed in the woods, doing the best she could, but the corset had defeated her and she'd simply shoved it in the valise. She was going to have to do something about shoes. She'd only had the one pair, and she'd been too panicked to do a thorough search. Maybe she could get word to Prunella and she'd find them. After all, she could hardly take the train to London with no shoes on her feet.

She had absolutely no idea what she was going to do once she got to London. None of their extended family resided in the city, so she couldn't look for help in that direction, but there were a number of old friends who might not turn their backs on her. Not all of them could refuse to help her.

Unless, of course, their parents knew she'd found herself in a man's bed without the countenance of marriage. But with luck it would take time for her destroyed reputation to follow her, and it might even remain a secret. None of the servants had wished her ill, and God knew the Dark Viscount probably wouldn't want to repeat the experience. She hadn't known what to do, and certainly men preferred an experienced partner in such things. Alexander wouldn't think twice that his unsatisfactory lover had run off, and if by some horrible chance he found out who she really was, he'd be even more certain to keep quiet about it. Not that he struck her as the sort of man who'd let society force him to do the honorable thing.

Six months ago it would have been simple. He'd compromised her; he would marry her. But she was probably no longer considered a proper young lady, and the gossips would probably say she was no better than her father, curse them. Father hadn't been amoral; he'd been set up. Though in truth she couldn't say the same thing about herself.

She lay down in the grass and looked up at the shadowy sky. There was a storm coming in, and she'd brought no umbrella with her. She was going to be soaked by the time she reached the coaching inn, and she would still have to deal with the matter of shoes.

She had just enough money for a ride on the public coach to either Plymouth or London. London seemed the better choice. While Maddy might still be in Plymouth and was undoubtedly the person she most wanted to run to, if Maddy had already left there'd be no one to turn to. In London there were dozens of old friends, and surely at least one of them would give her shelter. Surely.

She closed her eyes with a soft moan. She could still feel his hands on her body, his mouth at her breasts. She could feel him inside her—she was still uncomfortable down there. Bringing up her arm, she mashed it against her breasts, trying to give herself some sort of relief. She wasn't going to be able to forget last night until her body stopped giving her reminders. The rough red burn on her skin that had come from his whiskers. The bruising on her thighs where he'd held her as he'd thrust into her, over and over again. The constant tightening inside whenever she thought of him, pushing into that place, taking her, claiming her, loving her, making her wild.

Ruining her.

Well, in truth, she was already ruined. First her father's disgrace, then her masquerading as a cook and living under the same roof with someone as notorious as the Dark Viscount, degenerate, recluse, wife-murderer.

Not that he'd been particularly degenerate with her, at least as far as she knew. She imagined women would consider him a very good lover. She was certainly in no position to judge—it all seemed dreamlike to her in retrospect. Perhaps, after a long enough time, she might be able to forget it ever happened. It didn't even need to put a damper on her practical plans for the future. She'd had so many men flocking around her during her season that it should be simple enough to choose one of them with enough money and position to bring her back to where she belonged. To be sure, the fortune hunters might fall by the wayside, and the high sticklers might consider her tainted by the lies that had been told about her father. But that still left more than a few to choose from, and her maid had told her there were ways to fake virginity. In fact, said Doris, few men had the wit to notice anything at the time. Clearly Alexander hadn't.

Had Doris known she was going to fall from grace, known that her mistress was a helpless wanton? Or was Doris just being helpful on the off chance that something happened?

Sophie groaned, rolling over on her stomach and putting her face in the grass. She missed her kitchen, the smell of food and the freedom to create anything she wanted. She missed her small rooms in the basement; she missed Prunella and Dickens. Most of all she missed . . . no, she didn't! She was well rid of Alexander Griffiths.

The ground beneath her pressed against her tender breasts, pushed against that soft spot between her legs. She rolled back with a groan, staring up at the darkening sky. Sooner or later she was going to have to move.

But maybe she'd wait just long enough to watch him swim, one more time. There was no denying he was a beautiful sight. Maybe this time he'd finally divest himself of his smalls.

She could feel heat burn her face. She might not know what the man looked like without his clothes, but she had a far more intimate acquaintance with his body. In her less than pristine condition she would probably have to settle for a less than stellar husband, and in truth, she couldn't remember a single man from her social whirl in London who was half as bewitching as the Dark Viscount. Somehow with his gray eyes, his high cheekbones and strong nose, his devastating mouth that could be so hard and so soft, somehow he had managed to be the most beautiful man she'd ever seen, and she was well and truly ruined, not just in terms of her body and her reputation. She was ruined for another man. She hadn't just given him her virginity; she'd given her heart and soul to a cynic.

Oh, there would be a good man, sooner or later—she had no doubt of it. She was still pretty, and the sins were laid upon her father, not her. She could probably have either a good-looking younger man without title or a great deal of money, and they could live on love, or she would marry an older man, less attractive but more endowed with worldly goods, and she could enjoy herself in the style she was used to. But either way, they wouldn't be him.

The dark clouds were scudding across the sky, mirroring her mood. She had to come up with a plan, and she would. She closed her eyes as thoughts danced round in her head, and she tried to catch one, to focus, but it slipped away, and she was asleep.

She didn't dream, but she felt the sun begin to warm her bones, and she settled in deeper, shifting on the hard ground. Time passed, and suddenly she was cold again, something was blocking the sun, and she opened her eyes to see a dark monolith standing over her. She blinked, trying to focus, and she struggled to sit up.

She looked straight into the Dark Viscount's stormy eyes and everything inside her turned to stone.

"Oh, bloody Christ," she said.

"Watch your mouth, Miss Russell," he said coolly. "Anyone would think you were a lowly tart with language like that, instead of a proper young lady. Or perhaps *proper* is the wrong word for it. A spying, cheating, lying trollop might be a better description."

She stared up at him in instant fury. "Trollop!" she echoed, unable to argue with the lying or spying bit. "I was a virgin until last night."

"So I noticed. I'm assuming that was part of your plan. Sneak into Renwick under false pretenses and seduce the master of the house so he has no choice but to marry you."

Her outrage grew, and she managed to scramble to her feet without a complete loss of dignity. "Seduce you?" she snapped, furious. "You idiot clodpole, in case you didn't notice, you seduced me. And I wouldn't marry you if you were the last man on earth. I just needed a place to stay while Nanny was in hospital." She certainly wasn't about to tell him she suspected him of destroying her father. Somehow he knew her name, but he might not know her connection . . .

"You sound so very self-righteous, Miss Russell, for the daughter of an embezzler. I'm sure you could have found better pickings than me for this little game. Why not go for a royal duke? I'm assuming this blasted estate must have something to do with it. You're willing to barter your virginity to own it again?"

He was so damned big, towering over her, and the difference was even worse with her lack of shoes. "You're a bully," she said. "I . . . I was wrong." It devastated her to admit it. "I shouldn't have come, but I couldn't think of anywhere else to go at the time, and then things got complicated."

"And you fell madly in love with me," he said with heavy irony. "So that you couldn't bear to leave my side."

She jerked her head up at his words, and she was filled with a horrific thought. He was mocking her, of course, but did he have any idea that he might be far too close to the truth?

She pulled herself together. She'd had lots of experience arguing with her sisters, particularly Maddy, and she never gave in without a fight. "I have no interest in you," she said icily, pleased with herself. "You're a deluded popinjay, to think you were ever part of my plans."

"So you admit you have a plan then. Did that include watching me swim day after day? Were you disappointed I didn't strip down completely?"

The truth of that was unmistakable, and she could feel the heat flush her face. There was no way he could know that, no way she was admitting that. "Don't be ridiculous."

"Then why were you up here, watching me?"

"How did you know . . . ?" she began, and then could have kicked herself.

He didn't look gratified. "I could feel your eyes on me, even from a distance."

She wasn't ready to give up. "Oh, so that's why you preened and strutted like a peacock?"

A trace of amusement lightened a bit of the anger in his eyes. "No, you little hellion, I'm just that glorious. Why were you watching me?"

She went for a bit of the truth. She glowered at him. "This was always my favorite place to walk to, and I always went out while Nanny napped. Is it my fault that her naps and your public disrobing happened to coincide?"

"It was hardly public—I had an audience of one," he drawled. "So tell me your plans, Miss Russell. I admit I'm mildly curious. I'd like to know what they are before I throw you to the curb."

"There aren't any curbs in the countryside," she said, a pathetic triumph. "And my plans are simple. I've been trying to find a way to get back to London. I have dozens of friends I could stay with"—a rash exaggeration—"and I'll have you know I was quite the sought-after young lady last year. I could have had my pick of a dozen men."

"That was when you were an heiress."

Bastard, she thought grimly. "I was hardly a wallflower with only my fortune to recommend me," she said. "In case you hadn't noticed, I'm beautiful." Saying the words out loud felt odd, but it was simply the truth.

"Oh, I noticed," he said softly, and a chill went down her spine.

"And what were you going to do when you got your lovely, deceitful self to London?"

If she'd had shoes on she'd have kicked him. She could hardly pull his hair as she and Maddy had done with their big go-rounds—even though he wore his long, he was too tall for her to reach it. "I was going to find someone rich and handsome and titled and marry him!" she shot back, not caring how venal she sounded. And then the simple truth of what she'd said hit her, and she wanted to disappear.

"But luckily for you, you found someone rich and handsome and titled right in your former backyard," he said, his voice dripping sarcasm.

She had no argument but a weak one. "What makes you think you're handsome?"

"What makes you think you're beautiful? We'd make a lovely couple if I ever planned to take you to London, but since I hate the place, I'm afraid you'll be staying right here."

"I'm not staying anywhere. I'm leaving."

He shook his head. "You're the one who started this game, Miss Russell. You have to play by the rules. You managed to get me to despoil you, and I have to do the honorable thing. We're getting married, immediately, much as the thought galls me."

"I'm not marrying you!" Her voice rose in sudden panic. This was all wrong; the sweet pleasure of last night had become something ugly and twisted. "And what do you mean, I got you to despoil me? I tried to stop you."

"Not very hard. I've never taken an unwilling woman in my life. Admit it—this is what you planned."

"It was not!" She needed to get away from him before she cried. She was very near to tears now, and that would only complete her shame. "If I wanted to marry a lord, I'd hardly pick one who murdered his first wife."

The moment the words were out of her mouth she froze, horrified. What had she done?

He didn't move, didn't even blink at the horrid accusation. "That's the good thing about being saddled with an unwanted wife. I can always toss you from the battlements as well."

"I'm sorry . . ." she began, feeling wretched.

"Oh, don't be sorry, Miss Russell. You're only saying what everyone has been thinking. In truth, I'm sure we'll have a lifetime of connubial bliss."

Why did that sound like a threat? "I'm not marrying you. I don't care if you . . . if you . . ."

"*Fucked you* is the term, I believe."

She glared at him. "If you deflowered me," she said firmly. "No one need know. I won't marry you."

He let out a derisive laugh. "Deflowered? What books have you been reading, Miss Russell? Whatever they are, they aren't in touch with reality. My reputation is already shit, and I have my own reasons not to seek out a new disgrace. You're marrying me, whether you like it or not. And don't think I'm one of your besotted suitors. I already know how bad you are in bed. I'm doing my duty and nothing more, and you're going to have to pay the price for your indiscretions."

The rest of his words faded in the distance. How bad she was in bed? What did that mean? That he didn't want her? That last night had been a disappointment, not the transcendent experience it had come close to being for her? That she had wasted herself on someone who had found her wanting?

He was watching her in silence. She set her mouth in a tight line, refusing to look up. If she did he might see the sudden sheen of tears in her eyes, which were simply tears of exhaustion, she reminded herself. They had nothing to do with his cruel, hateful words.

He moved closer, too close, and she tried to back up but he caught her arm in his hard grip. "Come along, Miss Russell. I have a wedding to arrange, and you need a warm bath and a change of clothes."

She didn't listen to him. She couldn't fight him—his grip was unrelenting. "My . . . my valise," she said, unable to argue anymore.

It was in reach, and he caught it up. Without another word he started down the path that had been hers alone, the track to her sanctuary, and she stumbled after him, wincing as the stray stones and twigs bit into her feet. When she'd come up here, she'd come at a slow pace, avoiding the sharp bits on the path, but he was pulling her so fast that she had no choice.

There were halfway down the track when a particularly sharp stone dug into her instep, and she staggered, falling against him. "Watch yourself," he snapped, and then paused. "What the hell are you wearing on your feet?"

She was hardly going to lift her skirts to show him. "I . . . I couldn't find my shoes."

He had no such qualms. He reached down and caught her skirts, pulling them up high, and even as she tried to slap his hands away she could see that one foot was bleeding. "You are such an idiot," he muttered, and picked her up in his arms.

It happened so fast she had no chance to avoid him. She struggled for a moment, until his harsh words sank in.

"If you don't stop that I'll spank you, and under these circumstances I don't think you'd enjoy that at all."

She immediately stopped struggling. "I can't imagine any circumstances under which I'd think I'd enjoy it."

For some reason that brought a sardonic grin from him. "I

forgot you're not a whore. I think that's one of the first ways I'll educate you."

"What are you talking about? I don't need any education."

"Let's end this discussion, shall we?" he said as he continued down the path, for all as if she weighed nothing. She remembered the previous night, when he'd carried her up the broad staircase in Renwick, and her insides began to warm, until she heard him continue. "It's making me hard, and my only choice would be to disgrace myself in front of Dickens or take you for a quick shag in the woods. And I can think of better ways to spend my time."

She kept her face averted, refusing to flinch at his casual cruelty. "The sooner I get back to the house, the sooner I can be on my way," she said icily. "And if you have a problem, think of capons. And castrati."

His laugh sounded almost devoid of anger. "Even if you're a dead bore in bed you'll be entertaining out of it," he said, continuing down the path.

· ·

He was being a right bastard, Alexander thought, the delicious bundle in his arms stiff with anger, and he didn't know why. To be sure, he had every right to be furious. She'd lied to him, time and time again, trapping him into marriage whether it had been her intent or not. He was furious with her and with himself—he'd known there was something off about her, but every time he questioned her about Lefton she'd insisted the old abbess had sent her for his pleasure.

He still didn't need to be quite so vicious to her. He didn't need to pretend that the night before hadn't been . . . memorable in more ways than one. Perhaps it was simply that it had been too long since he'd had a woman, but he knew he was fooling himself. He could still taste her, feel her body clench around his, and he was going to have to dunk them both in the pool to deal with his erection if he didn't stop thinking about it.

He had more important things on his mind. To marry her locally would require the calling of the banns for three weeks, and he wasn't in the mood to wait, or to deal with her arguments for that long.

The arguments had to be as specious as her connection to Lefton. She'd admitted her goal was to marry a rich and titled man, and she'd managed to get herself compromised by one. Of course she'd done everything she could to put him off, but he had no idea whether that was simply part of her game or a real aversion to him. It could simply be the natural reticence of a properly reared young lady—he hadn't been around one in a while.

Damn her, he thought, speeding up as he approached the house. And damn him. This was a right holy mess, one that could have been avoided if she'd simply told him who she was. Better yet, if she'd never come near him in the first place. Now it was up to him to clean it up, as quickly and discreetly as possible.

One of the footmen was waiting at the door, opening it for him as he swept her inside and dropped her valise. He paused a moment, trying to decide where to take her, when she spoke in a stiff little voice.

"I'd like to go back to my rooms by the kitchen. And I'm capable of walking," she added pointedly.

"I'd rather not have you tracking blood all over my carpets," he said.

"Then Tim can carry me."

Alexander jerked his head up to give the footman a piercing glare. They had all probably known who she was, and he ought to sack the lot of them. "I think I can manage," he said dryly. He started for the servants' stairway. He had no intention of leaving her down there, but for the time being it was easier, and someone needed to look after her feet. She wouldn't be walking far on them, and that would give him time to sort things out.

Everyone froze as he descended into the kitchen, and the guilt on every face he happened to notice assured him that they were all intimately aware of his cook's real identity and his damned infatuation with her. "Her feet need bandaging," he announced in a gruff voice. "Where are her rooms?" He had a general idea of how the kitchens were laid out, but the sleeping arrangements of the servants had been Adelia's purview until she'd collapsed in histrionic grief over her precious son.

Dickens stepped forward, all dignity, as if he hadn't been lying to his master for days now. "This way, my lord. And Prunella, if you would join us with bandages and carbolic. Agnes, continue with the preparation for dinner—Prunella will rejoin you in a moment."

Sophie stirred in his arms, ignoring him as if he were nothing more than a carriage transporting her. "What are you working on for dinner?"

"Just what you wrote down, miss," Prunella replied. "Everything's going well, and I'm planning to do the sauce just as you showed me."

"If I'm stuck here for the night I may as well help you."

He wanted to growl, like an angry bear. "You're stuck here for a lot longer, and you'll stay in bed. Your feet are in worse shape than you realize." He followed Dickens into a set of plain rooms, the front door paneled in glass. Her bed was indeed narrow, and all sorts of wicked thoughts entered his mind as he dropped her down.

She glared up at him. "Go away."

If she heard Dickens's shocked intake of breath she didn't react.

"I'm going. I've had my fill of scrambling in the woods looking for you. I have better things to do."

She wanted to snap some kind of comeback to that, but she kept her mouth shut. *Smart girl.*

There was one obvious silver lining to this particular cloud. Adelia was going to be livid when he told her he planned to marry again.

With that to look forward to, the day wasn't so bad after all.

CHAPTER FIFTEEN

"OH, MISS!" PRUNELLA SAID, fluttering around her. "Whatever did you do to your poor feet?"

Sophie sent up a silent thank-you that she hadn't asked a more pertinent question. There were other parts of her body that were almost as uncomfortable. "I couldn't find my shoes," she mumbled, suddenly feeling guilty.

"Never you mind, Prunella." Dickens's reproof was gentle. "She's had a rough time of it. You just take good care of her and I'll have a talk with his lordship. I expect you'd like a cup of tea and something to eat, Miss Russell."

There was no need to stop him from using her last name now. "That would be lovely, Mr. Dickens."

"Just Dickens, ma'am," he said. "I'll have someone see to it, and I'll send Tim to look for your shoes."

Once he'd left she could pull her skirts up to her knees. Her feet weren't that bad—a bit bruised and a little bloody, as far as she could tell beneath the dirt and mud.

"I'll draw you a nice hot bath, Miss Russell, and then we'll see about bandaging those feet."

The bath was the closest thing to heaven Sophie could imagine. Her feet stung when she first stepped into the steaming water, but sinking into it was like being wrapped in warmth. She slid down, up to her chin, letting the hot water reach the soreness between her legs, and she breathed a sigh of pure pleasure. Until she saw Prunella looking at her in shock.

"Whatever did he do to you, miss?"

Sophie could feel her face flame, and she glanced down at her body beneath the clear water. There were marks, definite marks, on her breasts, her chest, and probably more places. Her pale skin always bruised easily, not to mention the redness from his unshaven stubble, or the fact that her lips felt swollen. "I . . . uh . . ."

But Prunella had already turned away. "Begging your pardon, Miss Russell," she said.

For the first time Sophie felt ashamed. "I'm sorry, Prunella," she said helplessly.

Prunella turned back. "Oh, no, miss! It's not your fault. Men are the very devil, and resisting one who's caught your eye is well-nigh impossible. I just hope he didn't hurt you."

Sophie remembered that sudden sharp pain when he thrust inside her. And then she remembered the burgeoning of feeling that had come over her despite the pain, and her insides clenched as she remembered his mouth on her breasts, and she felt her nipples contract in the warm water, which shouldn't be right. She tried to sink lower, but if she went much farther she'd end up with a mouthful of water.

"Of course not," she muttered, wishing Prunella would go away.

Prunella must have been a mind reader. "I'll leave you be, then, miss, unless you'd like some help washing?"

Sophie tried not to look too relieved. "I'll be fine. I'd just like to soak a bit."

"A good idea, miss. It'll help the aches and pains."

Sophie had the strong suspicion she wasn't talking about her feet.

• •

An hour later she was bandaged, dressed, and hobbling around in a pair of slippers two sizes too big for her. Dickens had even found her an entirely unnecessary cane, which she used anyway to favor her right foot, which seemed to have suffered a turned ankle as well as the cuts. She was sitting at a stool in the kitchen, working on the evening's pastry, an elaborate tart made from dried apples and fresh ginger. They still hadn't found her shoes, and the viscount was right—she wouldn't be doing much walking for at least a day. That didn't mean she could afford to sit around waiting. There was no way she could be near a kitchen and not be involved, and working with the pastry had calmed her shattered nerves just a tiny bit, and enabled her to plan. Clearly she had to find a way out of there, and fast. She was hardly going to spend the rest of her life married to a man who despised her, particularly one capable of such casual cruelty. Not that she cared what he thought of her, but she was hardly going to stay around someone who thought she had manipulated him into marriage, someone he had tried and found wanting.

Not that last night had felt casual. She'd been caught up in a storm of emotion and desire, and she could have sworn he was too. Otherwise why had he bothered?

"Miss Russell, you'll be taking dinner with his lordship." Dickens had just descended the stairs, and while his words were proper, his eyes were troubled. "And he's directed me to move your things to one of the guest bedrooms."

"No," she said flatly.

"I'm afraid you have no choice in the matter. He said to tell you that if you don't cooperate you won't get your shoes back."

"He has them?" she said angrily. "Blast the man! So I'm supposed to whore myself out for a pair of shoes?"

Dead silence in the kitchen, and Sophie could have kicked herself. It wasn't as if they all didn't know what she'd been doing last night, but they'd studiously ignored the fact, treating her with the kind deference they had from the very beginning.

Prunella was the first to speak. "I don't believe the master had any such idea in mind. He's a reasonable man if you just speak to him."

"Are we talking about the same man?" Sophie shot back bitterly. "The one who won't let me leave here?"

"He's looking out for you, miss," Dickens said.

Sophie made a rude noise of disbelief. The more time passed the more the astonishing pleasure of last night faded, and her regret was so strong she wanted to weep with it. If she were the type to weep, that was.

"Do you need Tim to carry you upstairs, miss?" Dickens continued, obviously not about to let her escape.

She made one last adjustment to the pastry, then slid down from the stool. "I can manage." She didn't bother to disguise her annoyance. It wasn't his fault, of course, but she had no doubt at all he'd instruct Tim to haul her upstairs kicking and screaming, if she kept being stubborn.

She was in a miserable situation, she thought, leaning on the cane as she slowly made her way up the winding stairs to the ground level, but fussing about it wouldn't help. She needed to be calm, patient, and look for her best chance of escape.

She automatically started up the second flight of the servants' staircase when Dickens stopped her. "No, Miss Russell. You need to use the main staircase."

She resisted her instinctive, long-suffering sigh and followed Dickens into the empty hallway where she and her sisters had once played hide-and-seek. "Do you think the viscount really means it?" she asked him.

"Means what, Miss Russell?"

"Means that he's going to make me marry him," she clarified. "Because I have no intention of letting him."

Dickens paused on the staircase, turning to look at her in shock. "Why not, miss? I've been with his lordship for more than twenty years, and I can tell you there's not a finer gentleman in all of England."

And there wasn't a more deluded butler in all of England, she thought, and then the arithmetic started to connect. "How old is he?"

"Thirty-four, miss."

"Too old for me," she said flatly. "And why did he need a butler when he was fourteen?"

"I was hired more as a companion and a valet." There was something odd in Dickens's voice, some secret there.

"Why does a fourteen-year-old need a valet? Was he extraordinarily messy?" She rather liked the thought of him covered in mud.

"No, miss." They'd reached the second floor and Dickens paused by her sister Maddy's door. Sophie closed her eyes for a moment, wishing desperately that the last few months hadn't happened, that the door would open and Maddy would be there, and they'd immediately fight, and make up, and fight again, and all these terrible things would disappear . . .

Dickens opened the door for her. "The master thought this might be appropriate."

Maddy had always gone in for pretty things, and the room was decorated in soft shades of pink that had complemented her rich, dark hair and creamy complexion. It had always made Sophie slightly bilious, but suddenly it felt familiar and beloved. "It's fine," she said, limping inside and looking around.

"He also wished me to tell you that there are appropriate garments in the dressing room, and that I should take your current dress and burn it," Dickens said. "The bathing room is down the hall and . . ."

"I know where everything is," she said. "I lived here all of my life when we weren't in London."

"Of course, Miss Russell. I beg your pardon—I forgot."

She gave him an absent smile as she looked around the pink room, then started with shock. "Humphries!" she cried.

"Miss?"

But she'd moved, a little too quickly for her protesting ankle, and scooped up that slightly battered-looking stuffed toy that was tucked into a corner of the room on its own small chair. She hugged him to her, and he smelled like her sister, like the rose perfume she favored, and Sophie wanted to cry.

But Dickens was watching her, and while he wasn't the enemy, he clearly sided with the viscount. She turned. "This is Humphries. He belonged to my sister when she was young."

Dickens was staring at the slightly battered creature with distaste. "Exactly what is it?"

"A hedgehog. It always went well with Maddy's personality," she said. Hobbling over to the bed, she dropped down with a total lack of grace, then hid her wince as the soreness between her legs protested. "So how long do I have to be in this prison? Can I come back downstairs and oversee the cooking?"

"Prunella and the girls have things well in hand. You should rest, and then change for dinner. I don't know if Mrs. Griffiths will be joining you, but I expect the occasion will be semiformal since it is en famille."

"I'm not changing my clothes."

"I didn't check to see if there were matching shoes . . ." Dickens's voice trailed off suggestively.

She gave him a grumpy look. "You're as bad as he is."

There was just the glimmer of a smile in Dickens's eyes. "Don't worry, miss. I expect this will all work out quite well in the end."

"As long as I get away from here I'm sure you're right."

Dickens said nothing, merely giving her a slight bow before leaving, and Sophie flopped back onto the bed. It was soft, luscious, and it felt like hers, and then she remembered when she'd last been in her own bed and let out a groan. She wasn't going to think about it. Wasn't going to think about him.

She got to her feet, moving carefully across the thick Persian carpet that Maddy had adored, and walked to the window. The room was a little stuffy from having sat unused for so many months, and fresh spring air might help, but the moment she reached the casement she froze.

It was the wrong time of day, but Alexander was swimming. She stared down at him as he surged through the water with an uncanny grace. She'd never been so close when he was in the water, and she could see his body quite clearly. Were there male mermaids? Mermen? If there were, they would look like Alexander. She leaned against the window dreamily, watching his strong shoulders and arms as he plowed through the water. There were all sorts of folktales about selkies, creatures who were seals in the water and humans on land, but Sophie had never been one to put much store in folktales or stories. Now she was beginning to wonder.

There was something almost hypnotic about the way his body moved, and she couldn't pull her eyes away. She still didn't believe he'd felt her spying on him during the last few weeks—someone must have seen her climbing the tor every day and told him.

His strong body drove through the water, and suddenly she remembered that body in her arms, driving into her, again and again and again, and her strange sort of joy in his possession. A joy he hadn't shared, apparently. She was being ridiculous, watching him like some heartsick ninny. But she couldn't pull herself away.

He stopped abruptly at the far end of the pool, pulling himself up and shaking off some of the excess water from his hair, for all as if he were a spaniel, she thought, trying for mockery and failing. The sun gilded his skin, and the droplets of water sparkled like diamonds.

He turned, reaching for a towel he'd dropped on the ground, and she took the time to admire his back. And then he turned and looked directly up into her window, directly at her.

It was too far for their eyes to meet, and she immediately fell back into the shadows. There was no way he could know for sure, and he was probably just looking at the house. But she couldn't rid herself of the suspicion that he'd been looking into her eyes, knowing she was watching him, just as he'd seemed to know she was watching him from the ledge far above Renwick.

Arrogant, preening bastard, she thought, moving to the bed and climbing up into the middle of it. It was a warm day, and she was feeling suddenly overheated, so she unfastened the top buttons of her somber dress. Humphries sat on the bed, and she hugged him to her, breathing in the familiar smell of him, trying to shut out everything else. It was going to be all right in the end, wasn't it?

Maybe if the Dark Viscount drowned.

Oddly enough she slept. She had nightmares, of course—she could see his body, the water glistening on his skin, in his hair. She'd never seen him from the back before, and it had been a revelation. She'd known the front of him was undeniably glorious, but his back was almost better, the contours of it, the way the wet, almost transparent, smallclothes clung to his . . . well, she'd better not think of that. And from the back she didn't have to see his annoying, ironic smile. She could pretend he was someone else entirely, the handsome fairy tale prince she'd been planning to find in London to solve all her family's problems. Not this unlikely troll who'd invaded her garden and ruined her life.

Then again, she didn't believe in fairy tales, folk legends, or even trolls, though Alexander Griffiths came close.

It was dark when she awoke, but someone had come in and lit the lamps, so she scrambled out of bed and turned them up. She was rumpled and frumpy and her feet hurt, and on the off chance there really were shoes in the dressing room she hobbled over to it.

She took one look at the myriad of dresses and slammed the door again, without even bothering to look for shoes. Half of those dresses would fit her, because half of those dresses had been made for her. They were still there, along with everything else they had left behind at Renwick, even including poor old Humphries—they'd been allowed nothing. She wondered for a moment if her favorite doll was still in residence, then knew that was a lost cause. He had taken her bedroom with its glorious view of the tor and the hills beyond it, and he would have had anything overtly feminine tossed out. She hadn't had a good look at the room during her desperate exit—had it only been this morning? She didn't have the sense that he'd changed it much, though he'd probably repainted the sunny yellow walls. His bloody lordship wasn't much for sunshine and good cheer.

There were no shoes in the room. Just as well—they wouldn't fit over her bandages, and her feet were much happier with the warm woolen hose covering the thick wrappings. The only problem was they made her shorter, and the Dark Viscount had a tendency to loom. She'd deal with it.

She heard the warning gong, and she knew she was supposed to present herself in one of the reception rooms to make polite conversation and flirt. At least, that was how it went at any house party.

But this was no house party. This was disaster personified, and if she found any chance to get away from him she'd take it. For now she wasn't going anywhere, not with bandaged feet and no shoes. And the staff, so protective and helpful while she was trying to hide her identity, seemed to think a forced marriage with their infuriating master was just the thing. No, she was on her own again.

But a marriage couldn't be accomplished that quickly. They had to call the banns—that gave her three weeks to find a way to leave. Time enough for her feet to heal, time enough for her to come up with a practical plan. If she'd had a little more time to figure out what to do after Miss Crowell whisked Nanny Gruen away she might not be in the mess she was now. Coming to Renwick had seemed like a good idea at the time. She must have been demented.

At least she could be certain that he wouldn't be taking liberties with her during the next three weeks. He'd made it clear that he'd found bedding her less than enthralling. No, she would be safe from him during the time she was forced to remain there. So why did that bother her so much? She had always had dozens of men at her feet—she didn't need or want Alexander to be one of them.

The bell rang again, a second warning, and she knew she had to stir, or the brute might storm up here and drag her down to dinner. Besides, she was interested to see how they managed without her. Not that she'd been in the kitchen long enough to effect much of a change, but Prunella had the basics—she just had to listen to her instincts.

There was a beautiful gray shawl with lavender trim hanging in the dressing room. Sophie had always coveted that shawl, and of course Maddy had flaunted it. It was amazing the two of them loved each other, considering how much they fought. She wrapped it around her against the coming night chill. After all, the colors were suitable for demi-mourning, weren't they? Not that she was going to return to colors any time soon. Not, at least, until she found answers about her father. She just wasn't going to find the answers here. Alexander might be many horrid things, but he wasn't a thief and a murderer. At least she could trust her instincts on that, even if they'd failed her every other way.

She was descending the last few stairs when a harried Dickens headed for the gong in the hallway, prepared to summon her once more, but he looked up when he saw her and she could recognize the relief that flooded his body. He straightened his burly form. "Lord Griffiths awaits you in the blue parlor, Miss Russell."

She didn't even wince. The blue parlor had been Bryony's. She'd run the household, more efficiently than any housekeeper might, and her desk was there, presumably still with her books and her inkstand and pens. Sophie followed Dickens's burly figure, trying not to limp.

The room hadn't changed much. A few of the more feminine adornments were gone, and the pretty watercolors had been replaced by hunting scenes, but it still felt like Bryony. God, she missed her sisters! What were they doing, who were they with, what had they found out? Anything at all?

Dickens had been right—Alexander Griffiths had dressed for dinner, and he was a glorious sight. It didn't seem fair that he should be quite so beautiful, and she paused to look at him objectively, searching for flaws.

He was too tall, for one thing. She was the shortest of the three sisters and she was not pleased with that fact. She didn't like men towering over her.

He was clean-shaven when most men had some sort of facial hair, and the smoothly scraped skin highlighted his sharp cheekbones and strong, stubborn jaw.

His mouth was too noticeable, always with that merest hint of wry amusement that drove her mad. His dark hair was far too long, his dark eyebrows slanted up in a way that could only be called satanic, and his gray eyes were too far-reaching. The mockery was in those eyes as well, and Sophie stiffened her back.

As for his clothes, they were elegant, well tailored, and slightly worn, as if he couldn't be bothered to replace his evening attire. Money certainly couldn't be the reason, and he wore the slightly tired-looking jacket with a carelessness that made her judgment seem frivolous.

Plus, his manners were appalling. He was leaning against the fireplace, his arms crossed over his chest, and he made no effort to stand up or come forward. He simply stayed there, watching her with deceptive laziness as she entered the room.

"I told you to change your clothes. And don't tell me they don't fit—I gather at least some of those fripperies once belonged to you."

She fixed him with a steady eye. "Have you forgotten? I'm in mourning—it's far too soon to discard my blacks."

He didn't seem moved by her reproof, merely letting his eyes run down her body with slow, deliberate fascination. Then he spoke. "Turn around, would you?"

She looked at him suspiciously. "Why?"

He laughed. "Foolish little girl. I promise I won't touch you."

Doesn't want to touch me, she thought, slowly turning her back to him, continuing on around until she faced him again. "So?"

"So I wanted to see if your backside was as pretty as it felt in my hands. It is."

As yet she'd been unable to control her instinctive blush at his outrageous words, but she simply ignored the heat that rushed to her face. "Ever the gentleman," she murmured. "Will your mother be joining us for dinner?"

His eyebrows drew together, his mockery vanishing for the moment. "She's my stepmother."

Sophie smiled sweetly. "Oh, yes, I forgot. The two of you are so much alike that it's easy to make a mistake."

It should have been an effective blow, but she'd overplayed her hand. He laughed. "I do try to pattern my behavior after hers at all times. But I'm afraid we'll be dining à deux tonight. You can beguile me with tales of your larcenous father."

Before she could say anything, Dickens himself appeared in the door. "*Madame est servie*," he announced, and Alexander pushed away from the wall, moving toward her with insolent grace and holding out his arm.

CHAPTER SIXTEEN

SOPHIE DIDN'T WANT TO take his politely proffered arm. She didn't want to touch him, feel the warmth of his skin beneath the fabric, the strength of his muscles, but refusing would only set her up for more trouble, and she suspected he would insist on the formality simply because it bothered her. She reached up and put her arm on his, as lightly as she could. She hadn't thought to look for gloves, and of course he wasn't wearing any, and their hands were skin to skin. She couldn't control her tiny jerk, but he said nothing, leading her into the dining room.

There were two places set, one at the head of the long table and one to his right. Exactly where she used to sit when there were no guests, at her father's right hand and Maddy at his left. Bryony had sat at the opposite end. That should have made things easier, but as he pulled the chair out for her, she couldn't rid herself of a strange feeling of unreality. Where were her sisters? Where was her father?

At least Alexander didn't insist on mealtime conversation. Instead he watched her, and she almost wished he would talk about the weather. In desperation she made a few attempts, but his replies were monosyllabic as his eyes focused on her, and if she hadn't been so hungry she would have lost her appetite.

Prunella had outdone herself. Course followed course, and each one was exquisite. Sophie might have put a little thyme in the fish bouillon, and the butter molds were not as precise as they could have been, but all in all it was delicious.

Alexander ate sparingly, never taking his eyes away from her, and it became more and more difficult to concentrate on the food. Finally she set her fork down, very carefully, instead of throwing it at him, and met his inimical gaze. "Are you watching to make sure I have acceptable table manners in the unlikely case that I agree to marry you? I assure you, I had a governess until I was sixteen and I spent the next two years at a finishing school in Switzerland. I'm really quite civilized."

"Are you, indeed?" he said gravely. "In fact, I'm trying to make sense of you. And yes, you will marry me," he added in a voice that brooked no opposition.

She decided to ignore that part. "Make sense of me?" she echoed. "I'm perfectly average."

"That, you most decidedly are not. For one thing, you're quite beautiful and we both know it. There's no need to be coy and bashful about it."

She raised one eyebrow. "Have you ever seen me coy or bashful?"

"Point taken. But you're also very young, younger than I thought. Perhaps it's your self-important way of carrying yourself, but you seem more like a woman in her late twenties."

"Ah, just what a woman wants to hear—that she looks old," Sophie said blithely. "And if anyone is self-important, it's you."

He laughed, clearly pleased to have goaded her. "So what makes a very young woman lie her way into a household and continue to come up with the most amazing untruths, no matter how harmful they were? And for that matter, where in the world did you learn to cook? Tonight's meal was good, but nothing compared to the miracles you've created in my kitchen. Most young women don't have such practical skills. If the men in London had known there was cooking behind that gorgeous face, you wouldn't have ended the season without a husband."

The wineglass was close enough that she could have thrown it at him. It was so tempting. "I had a number of very flattering offers," she said, unable to hide her irritation. "I turned them down."

"You were right to hold out for marriage." His voice was dulcet.

She reached for the wineglass, considering it. "Offers of *marriage*," she corrected in a tone as sweet as his. "As for my skills, I learned the basics in the kitchens of this very house, and then my finishing school in Switzerland honed my skills. It was felt that anyone who ran a great household—and that's what we were being groomed to do—should be able to accomplish what she hired other people to do."

"You went to a school for housekeepers? I didn't know they even had such things."

She toyed with the crystal stem, thoughtful. "Finishing school," she corrected him calmly, not reacting. "And might I be allowed a question?" It was that or fling her wine at him, she thought.

He leaned back, that smile lurking at the corner of his mouth, and she was suddenly drawn to it, remembering the sweet softness of his lips, and then the fierce tug against her breasts, and she felt such an odd, aching warmth fill her that she took the wineglass and drained it. So much for using it as a weapon—she'd simply have to throw the crystal itself instead of the missing wine.

"Of course," he said. "What is it you'd like to know? Our arrangement should be relatively straightforward. We won't be living in London—I despise the place. I'm not sure how many nights I'll require you in my bed—it will depend if I have another arrangement in place. I'll settle a generous allowance on you as my viscountess, but not generous enough to enable you to leave at any point. And I'll have people watching, not just Dickens."

If any of this mattered she'd be furious, but she'd be long gone before he could institute such draconian measures. "No, my lord," she said. "I was curious about another matter entirely."

"Call me Alexander," he said amiably. "Given our previous intimacy I think it's appropriate."

She would call him Alexander when hell froze over, even if that's how she had started thinking of him in her mind. "I wanted to know why you decided I was fair game as a bed partner when every member of the house assured me you never . . . what delightful term did they use? Oh, yes, soil your own nest. Prunella and Dickens insisted you would never touch me."

"Clearly they were wrong. And if you're going to start preening, thinking your exquisite self made me lose all control, then you've failed to take into account your absolute insistence that Mrs. Lefton sent you."

Now the feeling inside her wasn't a pleasant longing; it was dread and guilt. She needed more wine; she needed something to focus on rather than his face. "I'm sorry I lied, but I could scarcely say I simply turned up for the job."

"Did I not, over and over again, ask you if you came from Mrs. Lefton?"

"Yes, but . . ."

"And did you not answer, most emphatically, yes?"

"You know I did. So I lied about the employment agency. It's hardly the greatest crime in the world, and it doesn't absolve you of . . . of . . ." If she accused him of ruining her it would merely make him more determined to put her through a hellish sham of a marriage.

"Of what, my precious?" His voice was silken.

"Of taking advantage of someone in your employ," she finished.

"But you're failing to take into account a major factor. Mrs. Lefton does not run an employment agency for domestic servants. She runs a very elegant cathouse in London, and everyone who works for her is a whore."

Sophie sat there, stunned. "You mean you sent away for a prostitute, like ordering a delivery of coal? Sight unseen? You simply asked for someone to fill your bed?"

He was unabashed. "Well, actually, I had another bed planned for her, in a cottage on the estate, but then you arrived, took over the kitchen, and insisted that Mrs. Lefton had sent you. I assumed your coy, missish ways were simply part of a sexual game you liked to play. Many people enjoy them, and I went along with it reluctantly. Every time you were too believable, I checked on whether Lefton sent you, and you always said she did. Your double entendres were quite lascivious, though I guess they were single entendres after all, and when you were talking about making me melt with delight you really *were* talking about pastries."

Coy? Missish? She was just ready to fling her wineglass at him and see the fragile crystal shatter against the strong bones of his face, when Tim entered with the next course, pheasant with truffles, and there was nothing she could do except fume.

"I told her to put toads in it," she said grumpily.

"How delightful of you," he murmured. "I think from now on you can be my official taster. If you or anyone else decides to poison me, you'll go first."

"Such a kind gentleman," she cooed.

"Always, my love," he said, taking her reluctant hand that rested on the white tablecloth. Before she realized what he was doing he'd placed a soft kiss on the back, and she snatched it away.

"You'd best watch it, my lord," she said with the syrupy tones she'd used before. He called her coy and missish? She'd live up to his demoralizing words. "I might fall madly in love with you, and just think how inconvenient that would be. Not to mention unfashionable."

"Oh, we needn't worry about fashion," he replied. "We won't

be going into town. In fact, you won't be going anywhere, so no one will notice as you fawn over me."

If only she'd learned how to shoot, she thought wistfully. She knew just where they kept the guns, and while murder, no matter how tempting, might be a bit extreme, she could always shoot off a toe or something. There was something about the Dark Viscount that made her feel extremely violent.

But she'd never bothered with guns, unlike Bryony, who'd regularly gone hunting with their father and hit her target far more often than he did. Sophie had spent her time with her laces and ribbons and powders, too busy being a girl to learn how to protect herself or get revenge.

"I will endeavor not to embarrass you with my excess of devotion," she said between clenched teeth.

Picking up his wineglass, he leaned back in his chair to survey her. "Oh, I might not mind. Devotion is always so flattering, and you're halfway to being in love with me already. Don't bother fighting it. Some men are simply irresistible."

She reached for her own empty wineglass to throw but Tim managed to whisk it out of her reach, refilling the glass, and by the time he set it down again she'd thought better of it. She needed Alexander to trust her. It was the only way she'd escape.

Tim disappeared into the butler's pantry, leaving them discreetly alone for a few minutes, and Sophie turned a patently false smile on Alexander. "My heart's delight," she said sweetly, "have you talked with the vicar about the calling of the banns?"

His response was equally florid. "Oh, my passion flower, I have not. Indeed, I doubt I can wait three weeks to make you my own, and I have decided a special license is just the thing."

Sophie's artificial smile faltered. "A special license?"

"My solicitor can see to it, I imagine. I find that the prospect of you sleeping in a separate bed is less than appealing."

All artifice fled in the face of such imminent disaster. "No."

He sighed. "Do we have to go over this again, my pet? You're making a fuss over nothing. Considering that you've been watching me, nearly naked, for weeks, including today, I can only conclude you find my body interesting. You enjoyed yourself in my bed, for all your protestations. I'm experienced enough that I know when a woman reaches her peak, experienced enough to make certain she does."

She tried to control her panic. "But not experienced enough to recognize when a woman is a virgin," she shot back.

"It was outside the realm of possibility. Lefton charges good money for virgins—she wouldn't have sent me one without securing a very large sum in advance."

"You're disgusting."

He shrugged. "Not particularly. I have no interest in the frightened, untried efforts of a novice. Did you know that some men used to believe that taking a virgin would cure them of the clap? Bad luck for both of them."

"Would you stop talking about prostitutes and . . . disease?"

"Of course, my love. I had no idea you were so squeamish." He was enjoying this, she thought, though his motives eluded her.

"You don't really want to marry me," she said. "Why are you insisting?"

"Perhaps it's because you dislike the idea so intensely, and I'm a contrary man. Perhaps I simply want to fill my bed. Perhaps I don't want society to think I'm without honor."

"Society thinks you murdered your wife. Seducing and then marrying someone who's already beyond the pale will hardly redeem you."

"So tactfully put," he said softly. "I have my own reasons, and you don't need to know all of them. Are you going to throw that wine at me?"

The last question was added so smoothly that it took her a moment to react. "What?"

"You've been considering it most of the evening. The only question is whether you'll toss the contents or the entire glass."

"The only question," she said, "is whether I'll sit here for one more moment and let you toy with me like a cat with a mouse."

He threw back his head and laughed, free of his usual mockery. "I have yet to see someone less like a shy little mouse than you, my pet. And I'm hardly a tame pussycat."

She felt as if she couldn't breathe, as if life were closing around her like some evil cocoon and it would either smother her or release her as an entirely new, unrecognizable person. She needed to get away from him, from his long, elegant hands, his stormy gray eyes, the way he watched her. She needed to remember who she was, Miss Sophia Eulalie Russell, the toast of London. *Before everything had fallen apart*, she thought.

She knocked over her wineglass as she stood abruptly, but fortunately it was empty. She'd lost track of how much she'd had to drink; she knew only it was too much, given her stressful circumstances right now.

He'd risen when she did, polite for a change, and if he felt any concern for her he didn't show it. "I didn't . . ." he began.

The door to the dining room slammed open, shutting off his words, and Mrs. Griffiths stood there, trembling with strong emotion. "How dare you!"

Sophie had startled at the abrupt entrance, but Alexander didn't betray any reaction. "Good evening, Adelia. I hadn't realized you wished to join us."

"I don't wish to join you, you philandering reprobate!" she snapped. "I was told you plan to marry this creature."

Alexander's faint smile didn't falter, but there was a sudden coolness in his eyes. "Miss Russell and I plan to marry as soon as I can arrange it, yes. Did you wish to offer your felicitations?"

"I wish to tell you I won't have it!" The woman's face was flushed with anger, and her massive chest heaved. "You cannot marry a cook. It would make me the laughingstock of my friends. This . . . this trollop needs to be sent about her business. Since you can't keep your hands off her you can set her up in town or something. I refuse to have her on the estate. You will get rid of her immediately."

Alexander dropped back into his chair, reaching for his wineglass. He barely glanced up at his stepmother. "Sit, Sophie," he said without inflection.

Sophie wasn't fooled into thinking this was a casual request. She sat, even though it went against a lifetime of training to sit in front of an older woman.

He glanced up at his stepmother from beneath heavy lids. "First off, my dearest Adelia, you don't have any friends. And how would marriage to a chef make you the laughingstock of these putative friends, considering you yourself are the daughter of a butcher?"

The woman's color went from dark pink to purple, and she made spluttering noises of protest as Alexander sailed on, unperturbed by her reaction. "Secondly, you have absolutely no say in whom I have in residence, who I marry, or who I fuck."

"How dare you—?" she raged again, but Alexander overrode her.

"Thirdly, if you call my wife a trollop, if you treat her with anything but complete respect, I'll kick you out of this house. You're here on sufferance, and because I promised my father I'd look after you. You gambled away your widow's jointure, you lost your house in a game of whist, for God's sake, and you've thrown yourself on my hospitality and sense of duty. But deathbed promises and duty carry me only so far. Do not annoy me in this matter, Adelia, or it will be the worse for you."

The woman seemed to have her emotions in check, but there was a dark, calculating expression on her features. "You seem to forget we're a household in deep mourning, Alexander. A wedding is out of the question."

"We're not having a wedding, Adelia, but a small ceremony.

And God knows my reputation is always in shambles. No one will blame you."

The woman took a deep breath. "Very well, Alexander. As you wish. I presume you are traveling to London to obtain a special license, before this . . . fiancée of yours begins to breed. When do you leave?"

Sophie said nothing, watching all this with interest. Her father had once passed on a saying—the enemy of my enemy is my friend. Adelia Griffiths seemed dead set against the marriage, though Sophie had no idea why. It didn't matter—Adelia might be called upon for help if Sophie needed to make her escape.

Alexander was eyeing his stepmother with seeming indolence, leaning back in his chair. "Tomorrow, in fact. Just a quick trip to secure the license, and then I'll return."

The stony gaze in the woman's eyes was pure hatred, so deep that Sophie felt slightly ill at the rancorous emotion in the room. Alexander looked as if he didn't give a damn, as usual, but she could feel his malice as well.

"As you wish," Mrs. Griffiths said, smoothing her skirts with an unconscious gesture. "Of course I will bow to your wishes, and if you don't wish to listen to my words of caution . . ."

"I don't."

Mrs. Griffiths didn't let the mask slip from her countenance again. "Then you must allow me to arrange for the ceremony. Even though it will be small, there will still need to be some kind of organization. A wedding breakfast, for instance. If only Rufus were still with us . . ." She let the words trail off with a sigh. "But that wasn't to be. Not to worry, Alexander. Your fiancée and I will plan a lovely little ceremony while you're gone . . ."

"I'm afraid she's coming with me."

Sophie jerked her head up at those words. "I am?"

Adelia screeched, "She is?" at the same moment.

He gave Sophie his doting smile, the one that made her hands curl into fists beneath the table. "I couldn't bear to leave you even for one night, my precious."

"But you weren't—" Sophie began.

"I wasn't going to tell you about the trip—I thought it would be a lovely surprise for you. We can get you properly outfitted."

She already was properly outfitted, if she wasn't in mourning. Granted, her lost wardrobe was six months out of date, but some of those dresses hadn't even been worn before the disaster, and fortunately the fashions hadn't changed that much this season. Sophie had managed to find a copy of the latest fashion magazine to ascertain what was de rigueur while she was living with Nanny, even though she'd known that part of her life was gone.

"I'm in mourning," she said again in a low voice meant only as a reminder to Alexander.

It caught Mrs. Griffiths's attention anyway. "In mourning?" she echoed. "And yet you've been lifting your skirts—"

"Adelia." Alexander didn't raise his voice, but the chill in his words stopped the old woman mid-spate. She tried to plaster a pleasant expression on her face.

"Ah, poor lamb," she said, and no one missed the effort the words cost her, the faint tinge of sarcasm.

The woman was a menace, Sophie thought, and the very notion of staying alone with her in this big old place made her uneasy. Besides, getting to London had always been the problem—escaping there would certainly be much easier than getting anywhere from the middle of the countryside.

"When can we expect the two of you back?" Mrs. Griffiths said, sounding positively jovial, making Sophie even more uneasy.

"When you see us. I've explained this to you before, Adelia. I need to look into Rufus's death. It's possible a mistake was made."

"I assumed you were lying to me to simply twist the knife in my heart over my lost boy," Adelia declaimed. "If there was truly any hope you would have left for London immediately. You may not value your stepmother, but you've always had a soft spot for your brother."

"Half brother," he corrected, which struck Sophie, a fascinated witness, as odd. If he loved his brother, why did he choose words to distance him?

"Your half brother," Adelia said acidly.

"I only received word recently and I've been busy."

"Busy forn—" Adelia wisely stopped speaking. "I trust you will send word the moment you hear anything?"

"I will."

"And I presume you won't allow me to accompany you? You need a chaperone. Shouldn't your soiled dove have at least the pretense of virtue?"

Alexander shuddered dramatically. "I would rather eat poison, Stepmama."

For some reason Adelia's flush face paled. "As you wish," she said again. She glanced over at Sophie. "I wish you joy of this . . . this monster."

"Oh, she'll receive a great deal of joy, I promise you," he murmured.

Adelia strode from the room as abruptly as she entered it, her massive bosom heaving in indignation, and Alexander turned to look at Sophie in the candlelight. "I do regret foisting that creature on you, but I find that ignoring her works fairly well. I plan to rid this house of her as soon as I discover what happened to my brother."

For some reason Sophie felt a moment of pity. "She's just lost her son—it's no wonder she's a little . . . difficult."

Alexander's sardonic smile only annoyed Sophie more. "Trust me, my dearest, Adelia was always, as you say, a little . . . difficult. I've always had the strong suspicion she tried to poison me when I was fourteen, and my father had grown disillusioned enough to consider it a possibility. Hence the arrival of Dickens. You'd best watch your step with her."

She stared at him in shock. "Tried to poison you? You must be mistaken. And if your father believed it a possibility, how could he have allowed her to remain in the household?"

Alexander shrugged. "He was infatuated with her. I'm assuming she was very talented in bed."

Sophie flushed, remembering just how untalented he'd claimed her to be. "Then why have you allowed her to live in your house once your father was gone?"

"Ah, you're getting curious about your new family, my pet. My brother happened to adore her, and I respected that. But I have no illusions—she's a dangerous woman, and you'd be wise to watch your step around her."

Sophie stared at him. At least that was one thing she wouldn't have to worry about. She had no intention of ever seeing the woman again. Once in London she would run—there were a dozen ways to escape. So she simply nodded, rising.

"I'm tired, my lord," she said. "And if you truly mean me to go to London then I'll need to pack. I'm afraid you'll have to eat the rest of your meal in solitude."

She half expected him to stop her, to take her arm and drag her back down into the chair. Instead he took the little silver bell and rang it, and Tim appeared immediately.

"Escort Miss Russell to her room, Tim, and see that she has everything she needs," he said, and Tim replied with a dutiful nod, holding out his liveried arm.

"Miss Russell?"

She had no qualms about taking it, and she hoped Alexander would remember her reluctance to take his. "Good evening, my lord," she said, sinking into the merest hint of a curtsey.

"À bientôt, my precious."

CHAPTER SEVENTEEN

SOPHIE WOKE EARLY THE next morning, just after dawn. Her tenure in the kitchens must have ruined her ability to sleep in, she thought, surveying her closet and the dresses she had once loved so much. There were a number in the lemony yellow she adored, but she hesitated. Surely that color was far too cheery. She pulled out a gray-blue ensemble that wasn't a far cry from demi-mourning, but really, why was she bothering?

She'd already lost any semblance of proper behavior—her adherence to the etiquette of mourning was a waste of time. She'd been compromised, both in the eyes of the world and in her own heart; she'd lived under the roof of a bachelor, even if no one knew about it. She'd spent . . . time in his bed. She was a ruined woman and she might as well defy convention completely. After all, she'd never been one for simply following along, obeying the rules.

She could only hope one of her sisters had returned to London. If worse came to worst she could always take the train to Plymouth and a hackney to Devonport, assuming they even had hackneys in Plymouth.

She looked down at the blue dress in mild disgust. She'd always hated the dress, but Bryony had insisted she needed something subdued for funerals.

She hadn't had it for the small, shabby ceremony they'd held for their father in Marylebone. But then, she'd worn black, the same hated dress she'd been wearing for the last few days.

She wanted to burn it. She was leaving her old life behind, the hidden, shamed, mournful part. And she was leaving the Dark Viscount in the dust—it didn't matter what she'd felt two nights ago, that strange, restless longing that seemed to have taken up permanent residence in the pit of her stomach. She wasn't going to take the life he thought he could force on her, for whatever odd notion of propriety he might have, and he struck her as someone who didn't give a damn about propriety.

She could always get another job in a kitchen. She could certainly write her own brilliant references, and a cooking job could provide a safe haven for her until she could find her sisters.

Her first act when they got to London would be to secure a newspaper and see what positions were available. But first, she had to find a pair of shoes.

She shoved the gloomy dress back into the cupboard and took out a new dress of lemon yellow, with matching petticoats and froths of lace. Her French-made undergarments were all there as well—Alexander must have simply moved in with all their belongings still intact, and no one had bothered to get rid of them. Someone, however, had bothered to get rid of her Italian leather shoes, and her annoyance grew.

She opened the door quietly, half expecting someone to be standing guard, but the hallway was shadowed and empty, and she knew exactly where the service staircase was. She disappeared behind the baize door and made her way down into the cheerful chaos of the morning meal.

The moment she stepped down into the kitchen everyone stopped talking, and they all rose from their breakfast, standing at mute attention, and for a moment Sophie wanted to cry.

It was Prunella who came forward. "I do beg your pardon, Miss Russell. We hadn't realized you'd be up quite so early, or Gracie would have brought you a tray."

Yesterday afternoon she had still been one of them. This morning she wasn't, and she felt her heart break. "I rather thought I might have breakfast down here. With all of you." She ought to go away, she thought, feeling defeated.

And then Dickens spoke up. "Gracie, set a place for Miss Russell, will you? Up here by Prunella and myself. I'm sure we can all squeeze in to make some room. We're having porridge and kippers, miss. What would you like Prunella to prepare?"

Gracie quickly brought a place setting as the rest of the servants moved down. "I'd like what everyone else is having," she said, switching the plate so that she was on the far side of Prunella on the bench, rather than taking one of the chairs. "And a cup of coffee strong enough to strip paint, and I want to hear what the latest gossip is. And does anyone know where my blasted shoes are?" She put the *blasted* in purposefully, just to relax things a bit, and after a moment everyone sat down again, and conversation resumed.

It wasn't as comfortable as before, but it was worlds better than dinner with the viscount and his stepmother popping in. Before she left, Gracie presented her with a pair of shoes. She'd outgrown them, and they were a bit small on Sophie, but they would do in a pinch. Then Prunella looked at her uncertainly, but Sophie simply grabbed her and hugged her. She did the same with Dickens, much to his horror.

"Don't let him terrorize you, Miss Russell," he said in a choked voice. "And we'll be looking forward to your return."

But she wasn't going to return, not to these kind, hardworking people, not to the house she grew up in. She was running so far and so fast that no one would ever find her.

• •

Two hours later she curled up on the seat of the elegant brougham, closing her eyes and pretending to sleep. Not that she would normally have been so indelicate as to draw her legs under her skirts, but Alexander had failed to return her shoes, and when she'd protested he'd simply picked her up and carried her out the door and across the drive to the waiting carriage, dumping her inside with a total lack of ceremony. The borrowed shoes were tucked away inside a shawl so he wouldn't take those as well, and she didn't want Alexander looking at her feet—it felt far too intimate. It didn't matter that he'd touched almost everything else; he hadn't actually seen her body. The room had been dark, thank God.

He was reading a newspaper, and she wondered how she would get it away from him to look for suitable positions until she could catch up with her sisters. He seemed to be taking his own sweet time about it, and she wished she'd brought something, anything, to keep her mind off her predicament.

Failing that, she could do nothing but brood and come up with far-fetched plans. First she would need to discover where Bryony had worked. The Earl of Kilmartyn had a house somewhere in Mayfair, but of course Sophie had never paid any attention.

And Maddy was somewhere near the coast, in Devonport, an area of Plymouth. She had been gone for more than a month—it was anyone's guess whether she was still there. If she wasn't, wouldn't she have tried to return to Nanny Gruen's house? And what would she have found there?

No, Sophie needed a bolt-hole, someplace safe from Alexander's ridiculous plans for her. For some reason it seemed paramount that she avoid marrying him, though if she sat down to consider it rationally she couldn't come up with a good reason. In fact, he was exactly what she'd planned to find, only better. He was titled, he was wealthy, and on top of that he was beautiful, or at least she found him so. He'd given her a taste of pleasure so exquisite in his bed that she felt a little damp and dizzy when she thought of it. What was the problem?

"Are you plotting nefarious things, my sweet?" came his dulcet voice, and she raised her eyelashes to survey him, looking for something to criticize, such as his eyes were too close set, his nose was too big, his teeth were bad.

His eyes were beautiful, that lovely dark gray astonishing her once again. His nose was straight, his teeth were fine, his mouth . . . his mouth . . .

"Doing my best," she said briskly.

"Plot all you wish. It won't do you any good."

She looked at him. "Why are you insisting on this marriage?"

He set the newspaper down and leaned back. He was properly dressed, with stiff collar and cravat, watching her with amusement. "Why do you think?"

She considered it. "I really cannot imagine why. Oh, I'm beautiful. It would be a waste of time to deny it, but I expect you could find someone equally as pretty without too much difficulty."

"I didn't think you considered anyone to be equally pretty," he drawled.

"I'm not vain; I'm realistic," she said.

He raised an eyebrow.

"All right, I'm vain *and* realistic," she amended. "But the fact remains that if you want a beautiful wife, there are others just as qualified."

"Perhaps I like your particular arrangement of features?" he suggested.

She made a face. "Marriage is hardly a temporary proposition. Within a year or two you won't even look at my face."

"Try a week or two."

She glared at him. "You clearly don't like me; you found me dull in bed, though how in the world you could expect me to be anything else is beyond me. Where was I supposed to learn the fancy tricks I expect are necessary to keep your . . . interest aroused? They aren't in books, or I would have read them."

"Maybe you haven't been reading the right sort of books."

She ignored that, though her curiosity was piqued. Were there really books like that? She forged ahead. "Maybe I haven't. I have no reputation to begin with, thanks to my father and whoever tried to—" Belatedly she remembered that he was, technically, one of the suspects, and she halted.

"Go on. I'm finding all this fascinating. You have no reputation, thanks to your father and . . . who? Do you suspect things weren't as they seemed?"

"Of course I do," she snapped, thoroughly cross. "And you needn't act surprised—anyone connected with the Russells knows we're protesting the findings of the police and the court."

"Ah, yes, that reminds me. Could it be mere happenstance that you managed to infiltrate my household under an assumed name? Simply because Renwick was close at hand? Or did you have another, more devious reason to sneak in here? Do you suspect me of murdering your father and stealing all his money? And then setting it up to look as if he was the embezzler?" He seemed no more than idly curious.

She hesitated, then decided to answer truthfully. "You did get the house, after all."

"Why should I care about the house? Granted, it's been in the family for generations until my great-uncle lost it so precipitously to your father in what was most likely a rigged card game, but there are other houses, and I'm hardly a sentimental man."

"What about the large sum of money you seem to have come into?"

"My, my," he said. "You are very well informed about my business, aren't you? In truth, I happen to have one talent in this world, and that seems to be making money."

"Then why didn't you display this talent before you took possession of Renwick?"

"Because I didn't have the money to play with. The only people who can afford to make money are those who can afford to lose it."

"There shouldn't have been any money attached to the house."

He looked at her with a bland expression, but it seemed to her as if his eyes darkened. A moment later that look was gone, and he was entirely affable. "I'm afraid someone else will have to answer your questions. I have no idea where the money came from. So you think I killed your father for his money?"

"Of course not," she said irritably. "You were always our least likely suspect, despite the fact that you—" Again she halted. What was wrong with her today? The man made her tongue run away with her.

"Despite the fact that I murdered my wife," he supplied easily. "Well, I'm glad that was good for something. Do you still doubt me?"

"No."

"Why not?"

She fumbled for the words, when she had been considered the wittiest beauty to grace the London scene. "Because you're not that sort of man," she said.

"I'm gratified. So who are your other suspects?"

"I don't wish to talk about this."

"I do. We have a long ride ahead of us and I've finished with the paper."

"May I read it?" She couldn't hide her eagerness.

"Of course. When I get bored with your conversation."

"You," she said, "are a rat bastard."

He exploded with laughter. "And you, my dear, have spent too much time around the stables. I assume that's where you heard such insalubrious terms?"

"I learned them from my sisters."

He chuckled. "And here I thought the Russell sisters were so straitlaced. There are three of you, are there not? Though no one ever saw the eldest one. Where are they now?"

"I don't know."

"I don't like lies, my sweet," he said.

"I'm not lying. Do you think I'd still be here if I knew where they were?"

"I think you wouldn't have any choice in the matter. So we have discussed my reasons for marrying you . . . ."

"Not entirely. You could marry someone with money," she suggested.

"I don't need it. I told you, I have a gift for making it on my own."

"You could marry someone with a pure reputation."

"I don't care about reputations. You should know that."

"Then why are you insisting on marrying me?" she demanded.

"Let's turn this around, shall we?" he said in his elegant voice. "Why don't you tell me why you keep refusing my very handsome offer?"

....

He really was being a rat bastard, Alexander thought. He shouldn't be enjoying this so much, but Sophie had that effect on him. In fact, he enjoyed her so much he'd probably be better off letting her escape, but he couldn't bring himself to allow it. He set the paper down beside him, stretched his legs out, and watched her as she struggled through her justifiable outrage. "Because I hate you!" she finally said.

"What a pathetic answer. And entirely untrue—you'll have to do better than that. Why should you hate me? I'm rich and titled, just as you required."

"I wanted an elderly peer who'd die off and leave me alone," she shot back.

"I'm afraid I can't help you with that," he murmured. "I am a bit older than you are, but I intend to live a long, long time. Right at your side, my precious."

He watched her fume, and wondered whether he'd still be able to drive her into a passion when they were elderly. He hoped so.

"I don't—"

"Don't come up with another lie, please," he said. "It's tedious. Why don't you want to share my bed and board?"

"Because I didn't happen to like your bed, and I prefer my own board," she snapped.

"Well, then, I suppose I'll simply have to change your mind." She was light enough, and it was a simple matter to reach across and lift her into his arms. She wasn't expecting it, so she didn't fight, and he held her in his lap, a mass of billowing skirts and infuriated womanhood.

"You are a beast," she said in a low, furious voice.

"And as you've pointed out to me numerous times, you are a beauty. See how well matched we are." He put his finger under her stubborn chin, lifting her face to his. "So let's see how easy you are to train."

She tried to elbow him in the ribs for that one, and he swallowed his laughter. There were times when he was his own worst enemy, but she was just so delicious. He lowered his mouth to hers, half expecting her to bash him in the head, or at least bite him, but the moment his lips touched hers she stilled, like a startled woodland creature confronted by danger, and all his humor fled.

He slid his hand up to cup the side of her face, pulling her even closer with his other arm, and she melted against him, flowing, her mouth soft and welcoming, opening for him when he deepened the kiss. She tasted of cinnamon and coffee, delicious, and he lost himself in the kiss, in her response, as he lured her tongue into his mouth with sweet seduction.

He lifted his head and looked down at her, bemused. He knew the answer to the question she kept asking, and he was damned if he would tell her. He was marrying her because she made him feel alive, he was marrying her because he'd never wanted a woman so much in his life, he was marrying her because in her arms he felt like he'd finally come home for the first time in his life.

He kissed her again, and because he no longer had to hold her in place he slid his hand down her neck, his fingertips tracing a pattern on her warm, creamy skin. God, he wanted to lick her all over, he wanted to claim every inch of her. He wanted to show her that the small release she'd had before was nothing compared to what he could give her, and he wanted to drown in her response.

The neckline of her sunny yellow dress was demurely high, her breasts guarded by layers of cloth and whalebone. He let his fingers trace one, and she startled for a moment. He lifted his head to look down at her. "Hush, Sophie. You're like a fortress with all these layers. I won't do anything but touch you."

She stared at him, her dark blue eyes slightly dazed, and then she reached up and pulled his head down to hers again. He would have laughed in triumph but her mouth was too wonderful, and he cupped her breast in his large hand, his thumb finding the nipple beneath all that armor with unerring instinct, rubbing, gently at first, and then harder, pinching slightly until it was like a button beneath the cloth, and she was squirming on his lap, needing more.

He tore his mouth away, finally moving it to her neck, kissing her soft skin, sucking at her, biting her, and she responded with a low moan, her arms tightening around him as she tried to get closer. God, he wanted her breasts in his mouth; he wanted to suck at her like a hungry pup. He wanted to push her down on the carriage seat, shove up her skirts, and slam into her sweet, moist depths, finding his own, mindless release.

He wouldn't do it. He'd already taken her too hard, when he thought she'd been experienced. The next time he got inside her he was going to take his time.

But he could get her ready. It didn't matter that her delicious bum was seated directly over his straining erection—it provided a wicked stimulation on its own as she squirmed. He held her safely in one arm as his hand slid down her leg, reaching the hem of her heavy skirts and touching her stockinged foot.

He'd forgotten he'd stolen her shoes to keep her from running, and for a moment he smiled at the brilliance of it. Her foot was small, sensitive, and he rubbed it, his thumb beneath the arch, and her reaction was electric. Who would have thought a woman would like her feet rubbed this much, he thought, increasing the pressure, and she moaned in pure pleasure. He put that information in the back of his brain for further use, but he had more interesting destinations in mind. Taking the hems of her dress and petticoats in his hand, he began to draw them upward.

Her moan of pleasure turned into a sound of distress, and he returned his mouth to hers for a brief, caressing moment, feathering her lips with his. "Hush, love. I promise. I'll only touch you."

He looked into her dazed blue eyes as if he could command her agreement like the great Mesmer, and to his relief and astonishment she finally nodded. He kissed her again, a brief, hard one. "Good girl," he praised her, and lifted those ridiculous layers of skirt higher still.

Why did women wear so goddamned many clothes? After they were married he would take her away someplace, maybe a secluded cottage, and she could dance around in her shift the way she had in his garden, when he'd finally succumbed to his . . . obsession.

It was easy enough to simply slip his hand beneath all these layers, to move up her silk-covered leg to the ribboned garters that tied them in place. And the silky flesh above it. She wore the very latest in Parisian underwear. Her knickers were of a fabric so soft it was practically nonexistent, but he moved past, up her lovely thigh to his ultimate goal.

She jerked again when his fingers found her, the soft curls between her legs, the dampness between her thighs, and he wanted to lick her there. He would, sooner or later, but now he let his fingers dance over her, letting her get used to his touch.

She'd settled back again, her bum rubbing against his cock, and he stifled his groan of pleasure. Please God she didn't suddenly move the wrong way and cripple him for life, he thought absently, but even that thought couldn't make his raging erection subside. He knew how to pleasure women—and he rubbed that spot just below the curls with deft, delicate pressure. She climaxed immediately, a short burst of release, and he smiled against her flesh. It hadn't simply been his kisses today that had brought her to her peak so quickly. She had to have been thinking of him, remembering, to be this easily satisfied.

But he had no intention of stopping there. He held his hand still, against the lovely plump folds of her sex, and then he slid one finger inside her.

She squeaked, moving again, and he wondered what would happen if he came in his trousers, against the skirt of her dress. She was still so tight, reminding him that she'd been a virgin until he'd taken her. Guilt was long gone, only triumph that she was his, would be only his, and he moved his finger gently, rubbing inside the slick channel, preparing her, as his thumb touched her spot once more.

She started to climax, and he pulled back. She was clutching his shoulders, her fingers digging in, but at this she bucked, making a sound of distress at his withdrawal. He slid two fingers inside her this time, the wetness easing the way, and he felt her clamp around him, felt her shake.

He rubbed again, just enough for another small climax to hit her, and he pulled back. She made a soft cry of need, and a fierce possessiveness washed over him, one he didn't want to consider or question. *Mine* roared through his blood, and he pumped his fingers into her, feeling the start of another climax. He wanted more from her, he wanted to make her cry and scream with pleasure, he wanted to give her such pleasure she could never forget it no matter how far she tried to run. He pressed his thumb up against her, rubbing the dampness around her, rubbing that bundle of nerves, and he felt it through his own body: the sudden rigidity of the soft armful, the gasp of shock, the explosion that rushed through her, and he covered her mouth with his to drink in her cry of completion.

He made it last. He knew how; just as one peak subsided he touched her again and another washed over her, and he did it again and again, until she was trembling in his arms, her face buried against his neck, and she was sobbing, demanding, overwhelmed.

He brought her down gently, and she collapsed against him, a sodden little heap of femininity in his arms. He was still hard—there hadn't been any unexpected accidents, which frankly astonished him. He could have come just from watching her face. He withdrew his hand slowly, caressing her as he did so, smoothing the soft cloth of her knickers, trailing down her leg and pulling her skirts down. He caught her foot once more, slowly rubbing it, and he felt the last of the tension leave her body. He took her other foot, giving it the same sort of attention, and smiled at her response. She purred like a kitten against his neck. He could feel the dampness of her tears, which probably infuriated her. She struck him as a girl who didn't like to cry. *No, not a girl, not any longer. A woman.*

He held her, simply held her, as the well-sprung carriage made its way toward London. He could wait that long. Once inside the town house he could carry her directly up to bed and finish what he'd started. Surely he could manage to hold out that long. At least there would be no one there but the small, discreet staff he always kept on. He would feed her in bed, he would eat her in bed, he would indulge them both in an unending orgy of pleasure that would never stop.

And then, tomorrow, he would marry her, whether she liked it or not.

CHAPTER EIGHTEEN

SOPHIE OPENED HER EYES. They felt sticky, odd, and she reached up to touch them. It almost felt as if she'd been crying. Slowly, but far too surely, memory came back to her. She was curled up on the carriage seat next to Alexander, his arm around her, her head tucked against his shoulder, and she remembered what he'd done to her.

She shoved at him, hard, only succeeding in falling off the seat. He caught her in time, pulling her back up into his arms, and a weak, wicked part of her wanted to sink against him. She was stronger than that.

This time when she scrambled away he let her go, watching her as she ended on the seat opposite him, in the farthest corner away from him.

"You lying bastard," she said.

He raised an eyebrow. "That's hardly the response I usually get for such unselfish behavior on my part. Gratitude would be far more appropriate. And I didn't lie. I told you I would only touch you, and that's what I did. And you certainly didn't do anything to discourage me. In fact, I vaguely remember hearing a *please* somewhere in there."

"You're disgusting."

He laughed. "And you're a prude."

She glared at him. She was the furthest thing from a prude that she could imagine, but he made her feel like a nun. Why had she let him do *that* to her? How could she have been so willing, so wanton?

It was his kisses, she decided. She gave him a disgruntled look, calming down a bit. "Do you put some kind of poison on your lips?"

He raised both eyebrows this time. "I beg your pardon?"

"Every time you kiss me, my wits desert me."

She expected mockery, but after a startled moment he simply smiled. "Well, that's a start."

Talking about it wasn't a good idea, she thought. It led to dangerous waters. "How far are we from London?"

"About two hours out, I expect."

"And are you going to return my shoes, or will you be carting me up the front steps like a character in a French novel?"

He made a face. "More like a gothic novel, where I carry you off and imprison you in my lair."

"You've already told me that's what you're doing," she said.

"Well, I was going to put you in a nice, airy bedroom to yourself for the time being, but if you prefer a lair . . ."

"Do you have one?"

"Oh, yes, I keep a lair, a dungeon, and an oubliette in every one of my houses. You never know when they might come in handy."

She ignored his amusement. "How many houses do you have?"

"Reconsidering me as marriage material? Wise girl. I own Renwick, a house in St. John's Wood, a manor house in Yorkshire, and a farm in the Lake District, and I believe there's a run-down hunting lodge just over the border in Scotland. You have to understand that my elderly uncle only recently succumbed to a long life of wretched excess and I haven't had time to inspect all the honors and dignities that go along with my title."

"Honor," she scoffed under her breath.

"Not that kind of honor," he said reprovingly. "Besides, I'm on a trip to London to marry the innocent child I accidentally despoiled, and if that's not honorable—"

"Not when she doesn't want to marry you. And I'm not a child," she snapped, then realized how childish she sounded.

He always did this to her. Got her wound up, so that she blurted out inappropriate things and did things she should never do if she had half a brain. Which she appeared to be lacking, every time he touched her. What an idiotic, weak-willed female she was!

"Need we go over this again?" he said, sounding bored.

She closed her mouth. They'd been arguing about that very thing when he'd pulled her into his arms and proceeded to demonstrate quite clearly why she should want to marry him, and she didn't dare risk giving him the excuse to put his hands on her again, any more than she wanted to risk temptation.

"Since you refuse to listen, no," she said, straightening out her crumpled skirts, trying to forget what had happened beneath them. "May I look at your newspaper while it's still light?"

He smiled. "Of course, my precious." He handed it to her, and she turned past the front-page advertisements to the articles and society columns, waiting for him to stop paying attention to her.

He didn't—he was watching her with lazy interest, as if waiting for something. It didn't take long for her to realize what he was expecting.

There were no advertisements in the paper apart from those on the front page. He'd taken those pages out, the polite inquiries for domestic servants and lost dogs, cutting off that avenue of escape. She didn't let her expression change. "The paper seems thinner than usual." It was no more than a casual comment.

"I took leave to remove sections before we left that would be of no interest to you," he replied.

"How kind." She couldn't keep the acid from her voice.

"I am always at your service, my love."

She wanted to grind her teeth in frustration, but she kept her expression as impassive as his. As soon as he returned her shoes and turned his back she'd be gone. She could buy a newspaper anywhere, or find an employment agency. Or take the train to Plymouth and hope for the best. She had countless options.

So why did the thought of leaving him dishearten her? Why was she, the most practical and levelheaded of creatures, suddenly so confused?

She wasn't going to give him the satisfaction of knowing he'd bested her in the question of the newspaper, so she forced herself to read an extremely dull article on the arguments in a minor parliamentary issue, a look of intense concentration on her face. She glanced up once, but he hadn't even noticed. His eyes were closed, and whether he slept or not, she didn't think hurling herself out of a carriage would be a solution.

She set the newspaper down with a sigh, and if one corner of his mouth quirked in the trace of a smile, she ignored it. Once they reached London the possibilities would be endless. She could wait till then.

* * *

Astonishingly enough, the bumpy roads got worse as they neared the city, not better, and feigning sleep certainly wasn't the answer. Sophie glanced out her window as they drove through the city, wondering where her usual excitement had gone. When she was young, indeed, a few months ago, she had always been breathless with anticipation when they left Renwick for the London town house on Curzon Street, the town house that was now a burned-out wreck. She had found her time in the country to be more penance than respite, and she'd done everything she could to make her father return to the city.

None of that thrill remained. She looked at the houses, the people, the lamplighter making his rounds, the dung- and mud-filled streets, and she thought of the theater, shopping, riding in the park, all the things that she'd loved. And she wanted to be back at Renwick.

The carriage stopped sooner than expected, and she looked out her window into the gathering dusk. Shadows had invaded the carriage, and she couldn't see Alexander's face, but he seemed to recognize the place.

"My shoes?" she said.

The coachman opened the door, and Alexander climbed out first, then turned and reached a hand for her. She held up one bare foot.

"Yes, they're quite lovely, but I think you're better off without shoes for the time being. And you shouldn't have taken off your bandages."

"I didn't need them, and . . . oof!"

He'd reached in, caught her arm, and hauled her out, not into his arms, but over his shoulder, starting up the stairs as if hauling an unwilling bride was an everyday occurrence in the area. For all she knew, it was.

She considered struggling, but he'd probably slap her on the bottom, and she simply wanted to get out of sight as quickly as possible, so she stayed very still until the front door opened for him, and a butler welcomed them in, not even batting an eye. "Welcome home, sir. We've been expecting you for some time."

Alexander let her down, and her body slid against his in a most undignified fashion that she wanted to feel again. "You have?" he said, looking perplexed. "I didn't send word I was coming."

"No, but—"

"Alexander!" came a new voice from behind Alexander's tall frame. "I knew you'd show up sooner or later. And look at the pretty present you brought me. Or are we going to share?"

The man's voice was light, charming, and Alexander stiffened with shock. He slowly turned, still blocking her view. "Rufus," he said in a hoarse voice. "You really are alive!"

"I am indeed, brother mine. Bloody but unbowed."

Alexander was looking as if he'd been struck by lightning. He stared at his brother with a dazed expression, then shook his head, as if to clear his brain. "Why didn't you come to Renwick?" he demanded.

"And deal with my mother's histrionics? I think not. So tell me, who's the delightful little crumpet who's hiding behind your skirts, so to speak?"

Alexander moved then, and Sophie took her first look at Alexander's recently deceased brother, who apparently wasn't dead after all.

He was a handsome man—anyone related to Alexander would probably have to be. In fact, he was possibly prettier than Alexander was, with large eyes and a generous, smiling mouth, a tousle of dark hair with an artfully arranged curl over his forehead. He was a bit too thin, and his face was pale, as if he'd been ill, but he made her an extravagant bow that almost sent him tumbling.

Alexander caught him immediately, and the man gave his brother a rueful smile. "My blasted leg," he said, then glanced at Sophie. "Beg your pardon, beautiful stranger."

"She has an affection for bad language," Alexander said. "Sophie, may I present my Lazarus of a brother, Rufus Griffiths? Rufus, this is Sophia Russell, my affianced bride."

Did she imagine that fleeting expression of shock that washed over Rufus's pale face? She must have, because a moment later he'd limped toward her and taken her hand in his, kissing it with great panache. "So I'm finally to have a sister? When did all this happen? I've only been dead a few weeks."

Alexander laughed, but the sound was uneasy. "I want to hear what happened to you. One moment you're on a grand tour, next we hear you've gone overboard on some pirate's ship, which I always took leave to doubt. What in heaven's name happened to you?"

"Ah, the stories I could weave you," Rufus said with an airy wave of one pale hand. "But first, how did you hear I'd drowned?"

"Apparently your man was in Plymouth, though God knows why, and word came from London that you'd been lost overboard. But I don't understand why your man wasn't with you, and why Plymouth, of all places?"

Plymouth, Sophie thought. What an odd coincidence, that her sister had been so close to him. They might even have passed each other on the street.

Rufus smiled at them both impartially. "Simple enough, brother mine. My man had some kind of emergency. I didn't pay it much attention—I think someone in his family died—so he abandoned me to the clumsy care of an Italian valet. You cannot imagine the florid things he wished me to wear. As for Plymouth, I was planning to end up there on the final leg of my journey."

"So where did the pirate come in?"

"Where do pirates always come from?" Rufus said musingly. "I think that will make for excellent dinner table conversation. Miss Russell, I expect you would love a chance to freshen up. You look as if you'd been wrestling a tiger." He glanced at his brother and laughed softly. "Oh, dear, have I been indiscreet?"

Alexander's smile didn't waver, but Sophie didn't miss the sudden irritation in his eyes. "My brother is right—I've been a poor host. Wilton?"

The butler, who'd properly blended into the background, stepped forward. "Yes, my lord?"

"Would you see Miss Russell to the room next to mine? And have one of the footmen take her luggage up there."

"She has luggage?" Rufus said. "I assumed you'd found her selling apples on the corner. She doesn't even have shoes."

Sophie smiled at Rufus Griffiths, gritting her teeth. She had never been fond of overly charming people—perhaps that was why she was so irrationally attracted to Alexander. And Rufus wasn't too pleased with her, either. He didn't want his brother engaged, she could tell that much, no matter how much he was trying to hide it. That could prove extremely useful.

"He likes me better without shoes," she said sweetly. "He knows I'd be tempted to throw them at him."

Rufus laughed. "Oh ho, so it's that way! Your legendary charm has won the fair lady. Are you sure you want her in the adjoining room—she might slit your throat in the middle of the night. I suggest you lock your doors."

"What fun would that be?" Alexander countered lightly. "Besides, I've kept her away from sharp instruments."

"You don't happen to have a knife, do you, Mr. Griffiths?" she inquired.

"Call me Rufus, my dear. After all, we're going to be brother and sister, are we not? Alas, I do prefer my brother in one piece. If you feel so murderous, then why ever did you agree to marry him?"

"I didn't," she said flatly.

Rufus beamed at her. "This becomes even more interesting than my excursion with pirates. I look forward to hearing all about it. And when is the happy occasion?"

"Tomorrow. You can be one of the witnesses," Alexander said.

He didn't seem to notice Rufus's fleeting expression of sheer malice before he smiled that charming smile. "I would be honored to do so. Though that's a bit soon, isn't it?"

"I don't believe in wasting time. Miss Russell is without a chaperone or any kind of protection, and the sooner we're married, the less gossip there'll be."

"I don't need protection," she shot out, but Rufus gave her a calculated smile, moving closer.

"Don't let my brother bully you, Miss Russell. I promise I'll keep him in line," he said, reaching for her hand again.

She let him take it, noticing how her skin crawled when he touched her. It was a strange reaction—the man really was more beautiful than Alexander, his smile brilliant, his eyes clear and guileless. And yet she didn't believe him. Something was off, and she wasn't sure what, but Rufus Griffiths was the very last person she'd go to for help in getting away from Alexander.

Unfortunately, he might be her only choice. She gently disengaged her hand, giving him her practiced smile that was as false as his was. She could only hope hers was more believable. "I look forward to hearing about your adventures on the high seas, Mr. Griffiths," she murmured. She turned to Alexander. "And I look forward to the return of my shoes. You'd hardly want a barefoot bride, would you?"

Was it her imagination, or was there tension in the large entryway of the town house? Alexander had been happy and relieved to see his brother alive and well—there was no doubt about that. But some of that had faded, and there was an undercurrent that she couldn't quite define.

Alexander gave her his cool, mocking smile, nothing like the effusive charm of his half brother, and yet more believable. "The idea has a certain charm, but I may relent. Expect to see them in the coach on the way to the church."

"Rat bastard," she muttered beneath her breath, just loud enough for Alexander to hear. She turned her back on both of them, following Wilton up the broad stairs.

Alexander watched her go. In fact, he actually liked her without shoes—she had a way of scampering, like a young girl, not moving with the usual dignity that hard leather imparted.

"Can't keep your eyes off her, can you, brother mine?" Rufus's silky voice intruded. "It must be love."

Unwillingly Alexander turned his gaze back to the prodigal son, managing a flinty smile. "Do you really think I'm capable of falling in love, Rufus?" he drawled.

Rufus laughed. "Oh, most definitely. You've done your best to become cynical and cold-blooded since Jessamine's death, but deep down you're an incorrigible romantic. I'm only surprised it hasn't happened sooner."

Alexander had stripped off his hat and coat and handed them to a waiting footman. "Don't be ridiculous. I need a drink—what about you?"

"Always," said Rufus. "And you can tell me all about how you two met, and when you realized she was your one true love."

There were clear signs of Rufus's occupancy as they walked into the drawing room. Not that the staff wasn't diligent about keeping things spotless, but things had been moved, several valuable trinkets he'd acquired during his travels after Jessamine died had disappeared, and he had no doubt where they'd gone. Rufus was always in need of money, despite his generous allowance.

"Why are you limping?"

"Bit of an accident, old man." Rufus brushed it off. "Driving too fast, as usual. I'm much better now—I don't even need a cane. But I don't want to talk about me, I want to talk about you and your grand passion."

"Hardly." He poured them both whisky, then glanced around for his favorite chair. It was no longer there, but he didn't bother to ask where it had gone, avoiding a seat on the tufted sofa that was now pulled close to the fire. The room was too hot, and he wanted to open a window, but Rufus had already sunk into the leather chair that was nearest the healthy blaze, so he took one farther away.

"Well?" Rufus prompted, propping his injured leg on a footstool. "What does my mother think of the upcoming nuptials? I'm surprised she didn't come with you. Or did you tell her she couldn't?" he added with his usual perspicacity.

"Can you imagine your mother and me in a carriage for eight hours? Only one of us would be left alive," he said lightly. For some reason he didn't want to talk to Rufus about Sophie. In his grief over his brother's death he'd forgotten one salient point. He didn't completely trust Rufus.

"My money would be on my mother," Rufus said, raising his glass. "Cheers."

"Here's to Lazarus's return from the dead," Alexander murmured.

"Here's to your upcoming nuptials. So what happened? You swore you would never marry again after the debacle with Jessamine. That silly chit was never right for you. In fact, it was a good thing she took a dive off the battlements, though I suppose you still must be plagued with guilt. A wife who kills herself is always a bit lowering, don't you think? But tell me, who is this little chippie?"

He could feel his joy at Rufus's resurrection continue slipping away. "Hardly a chippie, Rufus, and considering she's going to be my wife, you might mind your manners."

"Oh, I seldom do, particularly in the safety of my very own home," Rufus said carelessly. "Don't try to put me off—I won't have it. I want details."

Strange, Alexander thought. He was hardly a possessive man, and what he owned he shared, but when Rufus referred to the town house Alexander had inherited along with the title as "his very own home" the phrase sat oddly. "It's simple enough," he said, taking another sip of the whisky. "She's a properly brought-up young lady. I accidentally compromised her, ergo I marry her."

"Accidentally?" Rufus echoed dubiously. "How does one 'accidentally' compromise someone? You tripped and ended up between her legs?"

A flare of protective anger flashed through him. "We're discussing my wife, Rufus," he said mildly enough, but there was no missing the note of warning.

Rufus, however, was unabashed. "When did you get so nice in your ways? We've discussed women in all their delightful detail all our lives. We even discussed Jessamine's problems in the marriage bed. Why is this pretty little tart off limits?"

"She's one of Eustace Russell's daughters," he said, resisting the urge to punch his frail, long-lost brother.

"Even more so, then. That family has been thoroughly disgraced. One daughter disappeared; another ran off with a married man who murdered his first . . ." Rufus let the words trail off, as if he suddenly realized what he was saying.

But Rufus always knew what he was saying. "Murdered his first wife," Alexander finished for him. "Well, then the daughters will have that in common, won't they? Perhaps when the third one surfaces we can find a wife-murderer for her too. But explain this to me—if the one ran off with a man who murdered his wife, how can he still be married? Or is he planning to go through a whole slew of them?"

Rufus grinned, unabashed. "No, Kilmartyn would have been a widower by the time the girl ran off with him. Too bad you don't listen to gossip—it was a nine days' wonder."

"But you were abroad at the time. How did you happen to hear about it?"

"Oh, I've always been more interested in gossip than you have, and word travels to all the expatriates and consulates all over the world. The sun never sets on England, old boy, and it never sets on any juicy scandal. Didn't your blushing bride tell you about them?"

"I don't know if she knows where her sisters are."

"Been too busy doing other things?" Rufus suggested, smirking. "You really don't have to marry her, you know. Fuck her all you want—the Russells are no longer considered to be a decent family, and as far as I know there are no relatives to look out for any of them. Certainly no angry uncles, cousins, or brothers to horsewhip you."

Alexander had forgotten how much he disliked Rufus's smirk. "How do you happen to be so conversant with Eustace Russell's family? I wouldn't have thought that kind of financial scandal would have been of much interest." Once again he was feeling uneasy. Something wasn't right here, and he was remembering how often he'd felt that way in Rufus's presence.

"Oh, some raddled old English lady in Italy told me more than I'd ever want to know about Russell's lineage, and unfortunately I have a tendency to remember everything," Rufus said easily.

That didn't sit right either. Rufus never wasted his time with raddled old ladies, even for the sake of gossip—he was most often downright rude when he grew bored. Alexander watched him closely as he continued. "Since my inheritance effectively put her out on the streets I feel a certain responsibility."

Rufus laughed. "That's my brother. Always feeling responsible for everyone, even for sorry creatures like me and my mother. I'd forgotten the Russells owned Renwick—that must have been awkward."

He was lying. Rufus had always been a brilliant liar, but for some reason Alexander had always been able to tell, even when their father had been convinced. Rufus knew perfectly well who the Russells were.

"Not awkward at all," Alexander said, taking another sip. "Are you going to let your mother know you're among the living?"

"Oh, I sent her a note. That's why Wilton expected you. In fact, I sent it days ago. It must have gotten lost in the post."

"It wouldn't be the first time," Alexander said easily enough. In fact, almost all of Rufus's purported letters never made their destination, and Alexander had long stopped believing in their existence. "How long have you been here? When did you return to England?"

"Oh, not that long ago," Rufus said. "Though granted, I was in rough shape when I first arrived—it was little wonder that it took me a bit before I could put pen to paper. But here you see me, hale and hearty once more, or close enough to it." He drained his glass, then managed a dramatic yawn. "Though I must admit I do get tired. I usually nap before supper. You don't mind if I go up for a bit, do you? Wilton already knows I like supper at nine thirty, though if your buxom bride needs sustenance earlier I'm sure Cook will provide. By the way, I hired a new one. Cook, that is. Mrs. Parker was dreadfully unimaginative."

Mrs. Parker had been in his employ for over fifteen years, and a good, loyal worker. Alexander didn't show any discernible reaction as his annoyance and disquiet increased. "My buxom bride probably won't eat out of sheer stubbornness. She's not as convinced that we need to marry as I am."

Rufus raised his eyebrows. "Oh, really? Why ever not? Granted, you're nowhere near as pretty as me, but you're still well enough, and you've got both money and the title. What has she got to complain about?"

Alexander was about to mutter, "Ask her," when he thought better of it. "As I said, she's stubborn. We'll be married tomorrow."

"You have the license already?"

"It shouldn't be a problem to get one. With enough money and connections it's merely a formality."

"And you have both, dear boy, don't you?" It almost sounded like malice in Rufus's voice. Alexander watched him covertly. When had everything turned upside down in his life? His brother had reappeared, and with him all the doubts and uneasiness that had plagued Alexander for the last few years.

On top of that, Alexander had become . . . perhaps *infatuated* was the right word . . . with a pretty little doll of a female. A pretty little doll with a sharp tongue and sharper claws, someone who made him laugh and never bored him. Perhaps that was it. He was simply marrying her out of boredom.

It didn't matter. Right then he wasn't terribly comfortable in examining his feeling and motives. Tomorrow he'd be a married man, and they'd go from there.

And one thing was abundantly clear, though he wasn't sure why. He was keeping her well out of the reach of his once-dead brother.

CHAPTER NINETEEN

HALFWAY ACROSS TOWN MADELEINE Russell Morgan lay on her stomach on the rumpled linen sheets, the body of her husband collapsed half on top of her.

"You're an evil woman, Maddy," he said in her ear, just slightly out of breath. "It's no wonder I love you."

Maddy smiled against the soft feather bed. She was too sated, too lazy to do more than make an agreeable noise, and a moment later Luca had rolled over onto his back, pulling her with him so that she was sprawled atop him.

"I wanted to sleep," she complained. It wasn't convincing, since she couldn't resist rubbing her face against his chest, all that warm, solid skin, but Luca was used to ignoring her complaints.

"I wear you out, do I?"

"Um-hum," she said, settling happily against his shoulder.

"And what about me? Keeping you busy is worse than looking after an entire crew. When I go back to sea I'm going to consider it a vacation."

She felt his hands drift down her back, and she wiggled against him, trying to get closer. "What makes you think you're going anywhere without me?"

"We've had this discussion before—I go dangerous places." He lifted her so that she lay straddled across him.

She raised her head to look down at him, her dark hair drifting down over his body. "I've been in dangerous places before, with you and without you. I can face anything you can." He was right, it was an ongoing argument, but it was one she had every intention of winning.

He reached up and caught her face in his long, hard hands that could be so gentle, and so deliciously rough. "I don't want anything to happen to you. Going to sea is a dangerous business, and there's never any guarantee we'll make it back safely."

"And how do you think I'd feel if you died?"

"You're strong enough," he said fiercely. "You can live without me."

"Yes," she said. "But would I want to?" She pulled away, fixing him with a stern look. "Listen to me, Luca Thomas Morgan, whatever name you want to go by. I was brave enough to infiltrate your house to find out whether you were a thief and murderer. I fought off nasty fiancées and hired killers and the crazy man who killed my father, and most impressive of all, I managed to make a rogue, half-gypsy, half-street-urchin former pirate fall in love with me. I can do anything if I put my mind to it. Except live without you."

He pulled her down to kiss her, hard and deep, and moments later they were lost in each other once more, the question unanswered as always.

• •

It was three hours later when Maddy awoke once more. Sooner or later they were going to have to get out of bed and deal with things. Luca had shipping business to conduct, while Maddy needed to see if she could find out where her two sisters had disappeared.

Nanny Gruen was in hospital and Sophie had disappeared, according to Miss Crowell, and there was still no word from Bryony and her new husband, even though the Earl of Kilmartyn was no longer being sought for questioning in the death of his first wife and her maid. Maddy and Luca had come first to Kilmartyn's town house on Berkeley Square to see if they'd returned, and Collins, his butler, had insisted they stay. The house was empty, and according to the butler the new Lady Kilmartyn would be horrified if her sister and her husband didn't make use of the house.

She put her arms around her husband, ready to wake him, when her worst nightmare came to fruition. The door to their bedroom was slammed open, light streaming in from the gas lamps in the hallway.

Maddy shrieked and tried to dive under the covers as Luca came up, a knife already in his hand, when a familiar voice broke through.

"Oh, good God, Maddy!" Bryony said in her brisk, older-sister voice. "Tell your husband to put down his knife and put on some clothes."

"Though I can see why she married him," drawled an unfamiliar male voice. "Darling Bryony, I may start feeling inadequate."

"Behave yourself, Kilmartyn!" Bryony said, but there was pure indulgence in her voice. "The day you feel inadequate is when hell freezes over." She turned back to Maddy, her eyes running over both of them. "Thank God the two of you are here. I was afraid you might be down in Plymouth or even worse, out at sea. When you can manage to get dressed, come down to the library. We need to figure out where in the world Sophie's gotten to."

Maddy heard the door close once more. Luca was making an odd, choking sound, and she cautiously peeped out from beneath the enveloping sheet to see her husband laughing, *laughing* at what had just transpired. A moment later he'd turned the gaslight up full, looking down at her and laughing again.

"You should see your face, love," he said. "It's bright red. Is the rest of you that same lovely color . . . ?" He started to pull the sheet away from her body and she slapped at his hands.

"Stop it," she hissed. "What's my sister going to think?"

"I expect they know what we were doing," he said amiably, sitting back down on the bed. "I don't suppose we have time for a bath. We both fit so nicely into that tub."

"Luca!" She probably was red all over, she reflected. She felt hot beneath the sheets.

"All right, but we'll have to get a bigger tub in Devonport." He reached for his discarded clothes. "You want me to call for some water for you?"

"No!" She was mortified. Bryony was older than she was, and had always been the voice of reason and proper behavior. To have been caught in bed with a naked man, even if he was her husband, was beyond embarrassing, and Maddy wanted to pull the covers over her head and stay there.

He turned and knelt on the bed, reaching for her. "Sweetest one, I expect they do just what we've been doing."

"Ew!" Maddy said. "I don't want to picture that."

"Well, your sister's already had proof when it comes to you," he replied cheerfully, and, sinking forward, Maddy hid her face in the covers and moaned.

They dressed in record time, making do with the tepid bowl of water left from earlier in the day. Maddy didn't bother with a corset, shoes, or her hair—Luca was right; it was a lost cause. She slid her arm through his, more for courage than anything else, and they descended the wide front stairs to the first floor and the library.

Bryony was sitting on the sofa, curled up against a stranger. No, not a stranger—Maddy had met him when she'd visited the shipyards with her father. It was Adrian Bruton, the Earl of Kilmartyn, her sister's husband.

Her sister Bryony, who'd insisted she'd never marry, was sitting there positively glowing with happiness. Maddy blinked. It was almost as if she'd never really seen her sister before. She was a beautiful woman.

Fortunately for her new brother-in-law, he was looking at his wife with complete adoration. The two of them rose when Maddy and Luca entered the room, and Maddy had the vain hope that the heat in her face came from the small fire that was taking the dampness from the air and not an embarrassed flush.

The polite introductions that followed were almost comical, Maddy thought, giving Kilmartyn a fierce perusal. He was quite good-looking, though of course he couldn't hold a candle to Luca's dark beauty, and Maddy could remember vague tales of his libertine reputation.

"I should warn you," Maddy said in a quiet voice, once they'd all taken seats, "that if you hurt my sister, I'll have my husband gut you like a herring."

"Herring are too small, darling," Luca said solemnly. "I'd more likely gut him like a shark."

"How about a swordfish?" Kilmartyn suggested. "I rather fancy the sword, and then I'd be more edible."

"Sharks can be very good eating," Luca offered.

"There will be no gutting of anyone!" Bryony said.

"Speaking of eating, I'm starving," Kilmartyn announced.

"In due time, Adrian," Bryony said, casting her husband a sneaking glance. She turned to Maddy. "Do you have the slightest idea where Sophie is? She's not in the cottage at Renwick—the place was deserted."

"Oh, lord," Maddy groaned. "And who knows what kind of trouble she could have gotten herself into this time?"

"I told you to stay with her," Bryony said severely. "It wasn't safe for you to go gallivanting off on your own, nor was it safe to leave Sophie behind without someone to rein her in, and we both know Nanny's not that good at saying no to Sophie."

"In case you've forgotten, you'd disappeared, and I can only presume that Lord Kilmartyn's name is off our list of suspects, or you'd never have married him."

The man beside her brightened. "Is that true, darling? Did you truly believe I was capable of such a villainous scheme?"

"Of course you're capable," Bryony replied. "You just didn't happen to do it."

Maddy ignored their byplay. "I decided we couldn't just sit around and wait, so I went after Captain Morgan to see whether he had anything to do with it. And I made an excellent housemaid," she added with an air of triumph.

"And was the old gentleman guilty?" her sister asked.

"Why does everyone persist in thinking me an ancient mariner?" Luca demanded. "I'm only thirty-three."

Bryony looked at him in shock. "You're Captain Morgan? I thought you said your name was Luca."

"It is," he replied unhelpfully.

"It's a long story. We go by the name Morgan," Maddy said.

Bryony looked from one to the other. "Do you love her?" she demanded, sounding like a disapproving parent.

"Bryony!" Maddy wailed.

But Luca simply laughed. "Do you think I'd put up with her if I didn't?"

Bryony nodded. "And there's no need to ask you, sister mine. I've never seen anyone so foolishly besotted."

Maddy wasn't about to take this without a fight. "Have you looked in a mirror?"

Bryony, calm, sensible Bryony, actually blushed, and a feeling of satisfaction warmed Maddy's insides. Now if they could just find Sophie . . .

"Then do we assume, since neither I . . ."—Kilmartyn glanced at Luca—". . . nor the pirate captain is guilty in your complicated conspiracy theory, then the man who took your country house is the culprit? Don't look so surprised, Mrs. Morgan—of course I know everything."

"Viscount Griffiths," Maddy supplied. "And there's no guarantee—you three were just the most likely."

Kilmartyn's smile was dazzling. "And of course you could be wrong about me or the captain. I may have seduced Bryony with my abundant . . . er . . . charm, and convinced her of my innocence when I was actually a hidebound villain . . ."

"Don't be ridiculous," Bryony said, her ravishing smile taking the sting out of her words. "We don't have time for games. We need to find Sophie."

"Yes," agreed Maddy. "And besides, no one ever fools Bryony. Trust me, I've tried."

"So the question is," Luca interrupted, his businesslike tone at odds with his gypsy lilt, "did your sister head to London or Devonport to find us, or did she go after Griffiths on her own?"

"We don't know how bad the situation is. Sophie's not used to being on her own, and who knows what kind of monster she's gotten herself involved with if she decided to go to Renwick. The man supposedly murdered his wife."

"Ah, a fellow in arms," Kilmartyn said cheerfully.

Bryony cast him a stern glance before continuing. "And we know accusations like that can have little to do with the truth. We need to send word to Renwick, as well as back to Devonport, to see if anyone's seen her. There was that private detective we hired after Father died . . ."

"He was clearly rubbish," Kilmartyn said. "We can find someone better."

"I know someone," Luca said suddenly. "He can find out almost anything if given enough incentive. He and I go way back, and he tends to get quick results. I'll go talk to him."

He rose, and Maddy looked up at him in shock. "Now? It's the middle of the night."

"It's the best time to find people like the Wart," Luca said. "And don't even say it. You're not coming with me—you'd stick out like a peacock in a group of nuns. Not only would it be dangerous, but he's more likely to talk freely if it's just me."

"And I've got someone in mind if your friend doesn't work out," Kilmartyn offered. "But unlike the pirate captain's delightfully sordid acquaintances, I need to wait until morning to call on him."

"Would you mind not calling me 'the pirate captain'?" Luca said plaintively. "It sounds ridiculous."

"That was rather the point, old man."

Only Maddy could hear Luca's soft snarl. He bent down and kissed her, hard, and a moment later he was gone.

There was a brief silence. Bryony glanced speakingly at her husband, and Kilmartyn laughed. "All right, I am not totally obtuse. You wish to speak to your sister without me around, do you not? Are you going to reveal secrets of the marriage bed?"

Bryony turned a fiery red. "Of course not."

Kilmartyn's smile was angelic. "Just make certain to praise me lavishly. Having seen the pirate captain in the altogether makes me wonder if I have . . . er . . . fallen short in some way."

"Go away, Adrian," Bryony said in a patient voice. "I'm certain we have better things to talk about than your manly attractions."

"Well, then, I'll go on down to the kitchens and see if I can convince Mrs. Harkins to feed me, shall I?" Bowing extravagantly, he left, and Bryony turned to look at her sister.

"Well?" she said.

Maddy was confused. "Well, what?"

"Tell me about him! He's quite gorgeous, though not nearly as pretty as Adrian," Bryony said, moving to sit next to Maddy on the sofa. "Did he know who you were the moment he saw you, or were you able to fool him for a bit? And when did you fall in love with him? How long have you been married; tell me everything!"

Maddy looked at her doubtfully. Living the life of a recluse, Bryony had always seemed muted, shy, quiet, except with her immediate family. Now she was bright and happy, humming with energy.

"Only if you'll tell me about Kilmartyn, who is, by the way, very nice to look at, but nowhere near as handsome as Luca. Then again," she added fairly, "I haven't seen him naked, so I can't make an informed comparison."

The sound of their giggles followed Kilmartyn down the hall of the house he'd once hated.

CHAPTER TWENTY

Sophie sat curled up on the window seat of her allotted bedroom, surveying it with a doubtful eye. The room was lovely, done up in dark shades of blue that probably matched her eyes. Very bad paeans had been written about her golden tresses, her dark blue orbs, her ivory skin tinged with rose blush.

She'd never been much for poetry, particularly the bad stuff written by her admirers. She could just imagine the kind of thing Alexander would write in her honor.

> "My bride is like a red, red rose,
> Full of thorns and beetles . . ."

Not that he'd even go to that much effort. She leaned back against the wall and surveyed her toes, wiggling them. She needed her shoes, though she had to admit that going without them felt quite . . . freeing. It was an illusion—she needed her shoes if she was going to have any chance of escaping from Alexander and his ridiculous insistence on marrying her.

He still hadn't given her a reason why he was doing this. Then again, she hadn't told him her reasons for refusing him. She didn't want to examine those reasons too closely, for fear she might weaken. Marriage to the Dark Viscount was far too tempting simply because she . . . no, she wasn't going to think about that, about him. She was going to find some way to get out of there, and she had a strong suspicion that his brother would help her cause.

She didn't like Rufus Griffiths. She wasn't sure why—he was perfectly charming. She would have to get over her instinctive distrust of him. He was her most obvious ally. He'd made it more than clear he didn't want her to marry Alexander. She needed to discover if he'd back up that dislike with action.

She stared out into the gathering darkness. It stayed light for a long time during these spring days. Even this late there was still just a hint of a glow on the horizon, past the spires and rooftops of the massive city. There were still people she knew living here—she just couldn't trust them to take her in. She could probably find writing utensils in the small escritoire over by the door—she should start composing some glowing recommendations. She'd need them to find work until one of her sisters returned. Though how they'd go about finding each other was another question.

London was the largest city in the world, teeming with people, and if she was working in a kitchen she would hardly be moving in the same circles that even the disgraced Misses Russell would be. How in the world would she know if her sisters came anywhere near the city?

She would deal with that later. After all, as a cook all her daily needs would be met, including, most likely, uniforms. She would have a bed, enough to eat, warmth when needed. Any money she made, including the money she had remaining from the small bit that Maddy had left her, could be used toward finding her sisters.

In the meantime she simply had to face things as they happened. There was no way Alexander could get a special permit tonight, nor would anyone be willing to marry them at such an absurd hour, so she was safe, at least for now. Tomorrow was a different matter entirely, and she had to find a way to turn Rufus from an enemy to an ally, though the very thought was uncomfortable. She didn't like him, and she didn't know why.

So, one more night. One more night, and she'd be free, never to see Alexander again, never to feel his touch, his kiss. She put her face down on her knees and sat there, dry-eyed and miserable.

....

Rufus Griffiths sat alone in the library that had been his own for the last few weeks, pondering his good fortune. Just when everything seemed lost, the one Russell daughter he hadn't been able to find had been delivered into his lap. Clearly it was a sign. He must have done them in the wrong order. Not that he would consider he'd made a mistake with the eldest daughter who married Kilmartyn or the bossy one. He had done everything he could to kill Bryony and her new husband. Kilmartyn should have been charged with his wife's murder—it had been planned out so carefully—and Bryony's as well. But bad fortune had plagued Rufus, things out of his control. He'd brought them both to the charred remains of the house he'd burned down, the house where he'd interred Kilmartyn's bitch of a wife's body, along with her maid, and if things had gone as they should have, their corpses would all be down in the ruins of the Russell town house, and Rufus would have disappeared with nothing to ever connect him to Eustace Russell and all that lovely money he'd managed to embezzle with the help of Kilmartyn's wretched first wife.

But instead the back end of the house had collapsed beneath him, and he'd barely managed to crawl away. He'd endured shards of wood in his leg and a wrenching twist to his hip that made walking excruciating.

Kilmartyn and the Russell chit had escaped to the Continent before he was able to walk again, and despite everything, the police decided Kilmartyn hadn't murdered his wife after all, the idiots. Rufus had planted so much evidence only a fool could have missed it.

And then, to make matters worse, he'd failed . . . no, he'd miscalculated with the middle one. It had been surprisingly easy to trace Maddy Russell to the household of Thomas Morgan, the former privateer who had been Eustace Russell's favorite captain. Rufus had hired the best people to get rid of her, but they'd failed, twice, and when he'd given in and gone after her himself he'd almost died. Had it not been for some damned Frog fishermen he would have drowned.

But once more fate had been with him, proving to him that he was following a righteous cause. He'd been biding his time in the house that should have been his, brooding, when he should have trusted fate would bring things around and drop the third Russell sister right in his lap.

This time he would allow nothing to chance. This time his mother would be proud of him, proud that he'd come up with his own plan, and it worked. Perhaps it was simply that her convoluted plotting had been flawed. He didn't want to think it—she was everything to him. But this was beautiful in its simplicity.

It was more than obvious that the pretty little brat didn't want to marry his half brother. He couldn't imagine why—he despised Alexander but he had no illusions. Alexander was everything he was not, or so his mother had always told him. But the girl would want help in getting away, and he'd provide it. Over the rooftops, where a slip was such an easy thing. And once again Alexander would take the blame for it, and this time he wouldn't escape from the trap Rufus had set. One murdered wife was a misfortune; two murdered wives was unacceptable.

They hanged peers for murder. It would put a blot on the title, but Rufus had little doubt he could charm his way out of the shadow. He'd be noble and grieving for a bit, then slowly recover and take his place in society, and no one would ever guess the complicated machinations that had gotten him there.

There was still the problem of the two older sisters, but he was unworried. They would either present themselves, as this one had, and the answer would be simple, or they would never return. Kilmartyn and the eldest one were on the run, and they might never hear that the charges had been dropped.

For all he knew, the pirate and the middle one had perished in the storm that had sent him overboard into the howling sea. He had been saved, but then, he was blessed. The dark force that had always watched over him could have already sealed their fate.

He was at peace. He no longer had to hide, and be afraid of his mother's disapproval and her lashing tongue. Even if he hadn't done her bidding, he had triumphed anyway, and Alexander was finally destroyed, the money from Russell Shipping was safely invested with the rest of the viscount's estate, and Renwick was once more theirs.

She would be very pleased with him, and that was all that mattered.

Alexander didn't bother sending a servant to inform Sophie that dinner was about to be served. She'd probably refuse to come, and throw something at the poor footman. Alexander was good at dodging things, and he wanted to make sure the room was sufficient. It was too close to his, a challenge to his determination not to bed her again until they were legally married, but he didn't dare let her sleep any farther away from him. London offered too many opportunities for escape.

He climbed the two flights of stairs slowly, turning things over in his mind. There was something disquieting about this house, about Rufus, about Sophie. It was as if everything was out of step, and he couldn't quite decide what was wrong.

He reached his own bedroom, went in, and washed up. He still had the scent of her on his hands, and he liked it far too much, but there would be other times. Moving to the adjoining door, he opened it.

She was sitting in the window seat. She was sound asleep and he stood there, watching her. She really was exquisitely beautiful. She looked as fragile and lovely as a porcelain doll, with her perfect skin, her sweet mouth, her golden curls, but he knew just how deceptive that was. She was as fierce as Boadicea, the female warrior who'd fought off the Romans. She was tricky and deceptive and determined, and their clash of wills was evenly matched. He was going to triumph, at least in the matter of marriage, but it was never going to be easy with her. Then again, he'd never been interested in easy.

He moved into the room, only half hoping she'd wake and they could start their bickering once more, but she slept on, shadows of exhaustion beneath her soft eyelashes. He took the chair nearby, settling into it quietly, and watched her breathe.

He ought to let her go and he knew it. She wanted freedom, or at least she believed she did. He could change her mind—she was halfway there already—but why did he want to? If he really loved her, he would let her go.

And he did. Love her, that was. He wasn't sure when it had happened, and he had no idea why. She was scrappy and contrary and vain and . . . delicious. Maybe it was when he found her asleep on the tor, proof that she'd been watching him for weeks. Maybe it was when he'd found her dancing in the garden in nothing but her shift, and he'd taken her in his arms and danced with her. Maybe it was when she came, and wept, and she was a woman who didn't weep.

It made no sense, but he loved her. And if he told her so it would give her one more weapon against him. She didn't recognize that they were . . . *soul mates* was a ghastly phrase, but it suited them. They belonged together; he knew it with an absolute certainty.

248

She seemed to know that they didn't, with the same kind of certainty. Which one of them was right?

He still had no idea why she was refusing exactly what she'd wanted. She wanted a wealthy, titled husband, and he was hers. On top of that, he had already shown her he could give her the kind of pleasure she'd never felt before, and he knew she found him physically appealing, no matter how she tried to hide it.

So why was she fighting it?

If she told him no he'd have to let her go. It didn't matter that he needed to satisfy the dictates of honor—no one knew she'd lived beneath his roof without benefit of a chaperone, that he'd touched her, kissed her, taken her. If he couldn't seduce her into doing what he wanted then he couldn't, wouldn't, force her.

He should let her go, he told himself again, watching the soft curve of her breasts as they rose and fell beneath the pretty yellow dress. If it were up to him he would always dress her in yellow, or in nothing at all.

He should let her go.

He couldn't.

CHAPTER TWENTY-ONE

SOPHIE CAME AWAKE WITH a start. She'd fallen asleep in the window seat, and her neck hurt; her entire body was stiff from a day in the carriage and then falling asleep in an uncomfortable position. Alexander must have plumbing in this house . . . a long, hot bath would do wonders for her amour propre.

She heard a deep, growling noise, and it took her a moment to realize it was her stomach. She'd refused to eat in the carriage, which meant she'd had nothing since breakfast, and she was a girl who liked to eat. Or was she now officially a woman? What made the difference in the eyes of the world—being compromised or being married? If it was marriage, then she was definitely still a girl and would be for a while, if she had any say in the matter.

She stretched, slipping down off the window seat and glancing around her. The gaslights were turned down low, but she could see the room quite clearly. She ought to change for dinner, she supposed, but she needed a bath more than anything. The bathing room was at the end of the hallway, and she quickly filled the tub and got in, soaking in the warm water.

She'd had odd dreams while she slept. She'd dreamt that Alexander watched over her, not the mocking, overbearing Alexander, but the man who'd kissed her, who'd taken her to bed, who'd danced with her in the moonlight. If he had been watching her it would have been to make sure she didn't escape, but she couldn't rid herself of the feeling that he'd watched over her with . . . caring. She laughed to herself at the notion. That would hardly have been Alexander.

If she hadn't realized she was starving she would have stayed in the bath forever. She put the yellow dress on once more—at least it had only a light wearing—and stepped into the hallway, to see Alexander waiting for her.

"Dinner's ready," he said, his eyes traveling down her body with a slow, deliberate caress.

She ignored it, and the small shiver it sent down her spine. "Good," she said in a clipped voice at odds with her inner warmth. "I'd change but since I'm shoeless I decided you prefer informality."

His mouth curved in a faint smile. "Maybe I just prefer your bare feet."

"Did you ever consider that my feet might be cold?" They weren't, but she wanted to make him feel guilty.

"I could warm them for you."

She remembered his hands on her feet in the carriage, the delicious sensation that had spread through her. A very different sensation from what he'd done beneath her skirts, but nonetheless wonderful. "They aren't cold," she said quickly.

"I didn't think so. It's been warm the last few weeks." He held out his arm. "I believe my brother awaits us."

His brother, she thought. The man who could help her, even if she'd rather cuddle up to a snake. She looked into Alexander's dark, beautiful face, and put her hand through his arm. "Lead on, Macduff."

She'd had worse meals, including the one Rufus Griffiths's mother had interrupted. Alexander's brother was doing his best to be the charming, amusing center of conversation, and Alexander laughed at his slightly malicious stories, but Sophie had the sense that he was uneasy as well. Perhaps it had nothing to do with his brother and more to do with second thoughts about marrying her.

The thought should make her rejoice. Instead her appetite fled after a few bites, despite the fact that Alexander had a decent cook, and she sat in silence, wiggling her toes beneath the table as she tried to come up with a plan.

She needed to leave him before he decided to let her go. Pride demanded it. Which meant tonight. She still had the tight slippers Gracie had given her, and while St. John's Wood wasn't in the very heart of London, she certainly could find a hackney, even at this late hour. She could excuse herself, and instead of going to bed she could simply walk out the door before he realized it, and never see him again.

God, he was beautiful in the candlelight! But animal attraction wasn't a reason to marry someone, and yes, she had to admit there was a powerful animal attraction going on between them. She looked at him and wanted to rut, to roll in the mud with him, to do all sorts of unspeakably wonderful things with him.

But that wasn't a reason for marriage. Neither was the appeal of his dark humor, or his kindness toward his servants, or his clear intelligence, or his unexpected gentleness. Having her heart jump every time he drew near, the unexpected trembling when he touched her, the need to be near him, to see that smile devoid of mockery. All of it meant nothing, nothing at all.

She was no romantic young chit, despite appearances. She was practical, hardheaded, and she knew what she needed to do. As long as she stayed around the Dark Viscount all those qualities went out the window, and she felt helpless to resist him.

She manufactured a discreet yawn, but even that was so ill mannered she was half-ashamed of herself. She had been so inculcated in society's rules that breaking each one felt like an act of treason.

"Are you simply exhausted, my precious?" Alexander said solicitously. "You've had a long and tiring day."

She forced a polite smile. "Indeed. I should retire and leave you both to your brandy and cigars, but I think I will go straight to bed rather than have coffee in the drawing room. It's after midnight, and I don't think I can keep my eyes open."

"There's no need to leave on our account, sister," Rufus said with his charming, slightly smarmy smile. "You don't mind me calling you sister, do you? I've always wanted one, and dear Jessamine was with us for so short a time. They were barely married a year before she was . . . before she fell to her death." He glanced at Alexander, looking suddenly contrite. "Oh, dear, perhaps I shouldn't have mentioned her."

Alexander was sitting back in his chair, calm amusement in his eyes. "She knows, Rufus. I don't think you could surprise her with any of my horrible secrets. Her opinion of me couldn't sink much lower."

There was just the faint hint of regret in his voice, as if he really believed she disliked him. Not only believed it, but hated that fact. Ridiculous. If it was true, it was simply because she was making his life difficult by pretending to . . .

Pretending to what? She wasn't going to waste her time thinking about such things. Once she was gone, and safe, she could ponder what was going on in her own stupid mind. Infatuations were easy enough to deal with—she'd squashed a number of them in her time.

But this didn't feel like an infatuation.

"I am very tired," she said, giving Rufus an apologetic smile when she'd rather kick him. With shoes. "If you gentlemen will excuse me?"

The footman moved toward her chair, but Alexander was already there, moving so swiftly from his lazy pose that she was astonished. His hand on her arm as he helped her was . . . she wasn't going to think about it; she wasn't.

It took all her self-control to come up with her false smile, the one with an edge of anger to it, when she felt no anger at all, just regret, and a strange kind of grief. She wasn't going to see him again, ever.

"Do you want me to escort you to your room?" She had no idea whether he was mocking her or simply being polite, but she wouldn't look at him to see which it was.

She shook her head, determinedly pulling away from his light touch. "I'll be fine. I just need a good night's sleep."

He was watching her, she knew it, but she had no idea what he was thinking. "Indeed. Tomorrow will be a busy day."

Tomorrow, when he thought she'd marry him. Tomorrow, when she'd find another way to live. Without him.

"Good night, gentlemen," she murmured.

She made her way up to her room with a stately grace that should have fooled anyone watching. The moment she was in her room she began searching for her valise. She could scarcely walk out on the streets of London at this hour wearing a pale yellow dress.

The valise was nowhere. At the last minute she opened the armoire and found her dresses carefully arranged, with the shawls and hats and necessaries folded on the shelves. Everything but shoes.

She'd been far too precipitate in getting rid of her black dress— it would have been perfect for disappearing into the night, not to mention applying for a job. There was a dark violet dress that would have to do, and she changed quickly, tucking her wayward hair into a bun at the back of her head and wrapping the borrowed shoes in a gray shawl. She peered out the window into the street below. It was empty, but she'd heard the occasional carriage go by, and doubtless it was more populated a few streets away on the larger boulevard they'd passed. She had enough money for several nights in a hotel, though she hoped she would only have to spend one night there before she came up with a reasonable plan.

She didn't dare sit on the bed—she really was tired, and she might fall asleep and not awake until morning, when it would be too late. She picked the window seat again, looking out into the night, until she heard Alexander come up the stairs.

There was no lock on the adjoining door, but she'd shoved a chair in front of it to stop anyone from entering. To her mixed emotions, he didn't even try. Leaning back against the paneled casing of the window seat, she listened to him move about, readying himself for bed, and she steeled herself for his approach.

There was a soft rap on the adjoining door, but she said nothing, holding her breath. He could probably force it if he wanted to, and then all would be lost.

"Good night, Sophie," he said softly, and she heard him walk away, heard the creak of the bed and the rustle of bed coverings. She closed her eyes, trying not to picture him, trying not to long for him, trying not to feel regret.

She already knew he didn't snore. She waited a good long time, until she was certain he was asleep. Opening her door silently, she slid out into the darkened hallway. That was one good thing about stockinged feet, she thought. No one would hear her.

She'd already noticed a side door in one of the drawing rooms, and that was her goal. She had to avoid any servants wandering around, but at this hour most of them would have retired. She made it down the three flights of stairs to the ground floor without incident, and slipped into the darkened room.

If there was any moon that night the omnipresent London fog covered it, and the room was almost pitch-dark. She moved carefully, feeling her way, but the place was unknown to her, and she stubbed her toe on something hard and immovable. "Bugger," she muttered, appropriating Bryony's favorite curse. *That hurt!* So much that she sank down into the chair whose leg had attacked her and rubbed her damaged toes for a moment as she tried to sharpen her night vision.

The room was full of large, ominous shapes that she knew were simply pieces of furniture. There was a faint light coming from one corner that she recognize as the French door leading outside, and she breathed a sigh of relief. She'd only had a glance at it when Alexander had carried her in but her memory had served her.

A soft, rustling noise broke her abstraction, and she froze. Was someone still about? She held very still, but the sound had stopped, and she shook herself. They must have mice or rats here—most houses did. She could send Alexander a polite, anonymous note suggesting he hire a rat catcher.

She grinned in the darkness. It would drive him mad. She liked driving him mad, just as he seemed to appreciate returning the favor. If she married someone like him she would never be bored.

Right now boring sounded wonderful. She didn't want to question or doubt; she just wanted peace and safety. One night wasn't so much to ask, was it? She would figure things out tomorrow.

Wincing at her wounded toes, she rose and drifted across the dark room like a ghost. The door to the side garden was locked, of course, but the key was in it. The housekeeper should retain the keys, she thought, another example of a bachelor-run household. He really needed someone to take things in hand.

She could add that to her note, she thought, cheering up. Turning the key, she slipped out into the dark, foggy night.

The flagstones on the terrace were cold and damp beneath her bare feet. There was enough moonlight filtering through the clouds that she could see the heavy stone balustrade, and she sat down and pulled on Gracie's shoes. The first foot was difficult; the other one with the stubbed toe was painful enough that she let out an unconscious little yelp, then froze. Had someone heard her?

After a moment she relaxed. They were all asleep, and no one would even notice she was gone till late tomorrow morning. Unless a housemaid brought tea in early, but even so, there'd be no way to trace her in a huge city like this, and Alexander wouldn't bother. He'd be free of her, he would have done his duty and attempted the honorable thing, but her disappearance would acquit him of any more effort on her behalf.

There was something wet on her face, and she brushed it away angrily. The fog must be so heavy that it made her eyes water. She rose, holding on to the stone balustrade, and stepped down into the garden.

It was large, and she imagined quite beautiful in the daylight. Even at night the scent of early roses was evocative, reminding her of Alexander. The fragrant roses in the air as he'd caught her in his arms and danced with her. She would never again smell roses without thinking of that night.

Damn it, the fog was getting worse. It was making the tears stream down her face, and wiping it away didn't seem to be doing much good. She blinked a few times, trying to stifle the hiccupping noise that sounded oddly like a sob, and headed for the back of the garden, where there must be a door to the mews.

There wasn't. She moved carefully along the entire wall, but there was no opening at all. She started up the side wall, being careful not to trample any of the early flowers, sliding between the wall and shrubbery in case the door was hidden by an artful display, until she reached the back of the house. Nothing on that side—just the high brick wall.

Avoiding the house, she moved along the opposite wall. Who would design a garden with no egress or entrance? But there was nothing, nothing at all. She was trapped.

She wasn't going to give up that easily. There were trees, young ones, since the house was new, but long ago she'd been adept at climbing. Nanny Gruen had moaned more than once about her torn skirts and scratched arms.

With more half-blind experimentation she found a tree she decided would do. The branches were low enough, and even if they weren't terribly thick, the tree was young enough and sturdy. If she could just make it to the top of the wall she could drop down on the other side without much difficulty.

She hadn't counted on her skirts. It had been many years since she'd climbed a tree, and she was only partway up when her petticoats caught on something and wouldn't let go. She yanked as hard as she could—they could rip for all she cared, as long as she could continue her ascent. The walls were a good ten feet tall and very thick, and the tree was a foot or so away. She needed to get up high enough that she could swing over to the top of the wall, which had a wedged top rather than a nice flat surface, damn it. If she landed she might go tumbling over anyway, and falling without being prepared could lead to problems.

The tears had stopped—even though the fog had thickened to an almost-impenetrable layer, it seemed to have ceased bothering her eyes as she concentrated on the problem—and she wiped the last of the moisture from her face with the hem of her dress. A lady never went out without a handkerchief. Then again, a lady never crept out in the middle of the night wearing a maid's shoes.

The petticoats were refusing to budge. She reached down with one tentative foot, trying to see what was holding her, and her shoe fell off, into the darkness below.

Sophie froze, wanting to weep. Then again, if she were honest with herself she'd already wept, hadn't she? Why did she keep lying to herself? What good did it do? She was stuck up in a tree, with one shoe gone. She couldn't free her petticoat, she couldn't climb higher, and chances were she'd break her leg if she managed to jump down on the other side.

She couldn't climb down either and regain the missing shoe—the petticoats were holding her prisoner. She tried to reach under her skirts, to untie the tapes that held them, but she started to lose her grip on the tree. She was standing on one weak branch, clinging to the slender trunk, and she leaned her head against the bark wearily.

She didn't even hear him approach, but then, for all she knew he'd been in the garden the entire time. "Has Cinderella lost her slipper?" Alexander said softly from directly beneath her.

For the first time she was feeling entirely defeated. She had done everything she could, and nothing was working out. "Go away," she said miserably. "You were supposed to be asleep."

"You were supposed to think that," he replied steadily. "You'd best come down. You'd never make it across to the wall, and I'm afraid the other side is a drainage ditch full of very unpleasant water."

Blast. She was well and truly trapped. "I can't get down," she said, trying not to sound like a complete fool. "My petticoats are caught in the bushes."

"Allow me." She felt a tug on her skirts, a moment of freedom, and then another hard tug that had her falling directly into his arms.

He caught her, amazingly enough, not even staggering beneath her weight. "You may as well give up, Sophie. I'm going to do the right thing whether you like it or not."

Those were the last words she wanted to hear. "What kind of idiot puts a walled garden in the back of his house and then doesn't put a door in it?" she said, knowing she sounded peevish and not caring.

"One who's careful about letting stray people in. Or out, in this case." He was still holding her. She couldn't see anything in the darkness but the gleam of his dark eyes, and she couldn't read much from his voice. Was he angry? As weary as she was?

"You can put me down now," she said in a small voice.

"I could," he allowed. "But I don't think I will. God, you feel even lighter than before. You barely ate enough to keep a bird alive today. Are you planning some kind of hunger strike to get out of marrying me?"

"I haven't been hungry. *Please* put me down."

"No." He was moving through the foggy darkness with the surety of a man who knew exactly where everything was. She hoped he got smacked in the face by a branch, but he didn't even brush against any of the foliage. She still had only the one shoe on, and she doubted he'd rescued the other. She was back where she'd started.

Or worse. She was in the arms of a man determined to do his duty, and she didn't want his duty or his honor. She wanted love. His love. And she would never have it.

He kicked the door open, and she realized that despite his light words he was angry. Very angry. He moved through the darkened house at a reasonable pace, but she could feel the tension rippling through his body. He was wearing only a loose white shirt and trousers, and it was too thin a barrier between her face and his flesh. It didn't matter. She was tired of fighting—she'd done her best to free him from his damned obligation, and tomorrow she would rise and fight some more. But for now all she wanted to do was put her head on his shoulder, her face in his neck, breathe in the scent of him for one last time.

She wanted to rub her cheek against the soft linen of the shirt, but at least she resisted that temptation. If he was surprised by her sudden acquiescence he didn't show it, moving up the flights of stairs at a steady pace.

The cool, clean scent of his skin was so seductive, and she knew she was lost. She was going to let him make love to her. The damage had been done, and she deserved one last night of pleasure, one night with the man she longed for and wouldn't have. In the darkness there was just the two of them, and she could feel his heart beat beneath her, feel her own rapid one. He was going to carry her to his bed and strip off her clothes and send her soaring. And then he would hold her, and kiss her, and she would tell him what she wouldn't tell herself, tell him that she loved him. If he would only hold her. She needed to wake up in his arms, to know he would be there. But he wouldn't.

They reached the third floor, and her heartbeat picked up, hammering against her rib cage. Her pulses were racing, and she held her breath as he reached the door to his bedroom.

And passed it. Moving on into her room, he kicked open the door and dropped her on the bed. "I presume you're not going to be tiresome and try this again," he said in that cool, ironic voice of his. "Otherwise I'll take you to my room and tie you to the bedpost."

Yes, please, she thought mournfully. "I won't try to leave." Her voice was lifeless. He didn't want her. It was duty and nothing else.

He glanced at the adjoining door and saw the chair wedged under the handle. "That was a wise precaution on your part, my sweet. I have only a limited amount of self-restraint and you're testing it."

He left without another word, slamming the door behind him. It bounced open again—when he'd kicked it he'd managed to break the catch. It didn't matter. Nothing mattered. She threw herself back on the bed in misery and stared up at the ceiling.

She could hear him in the next room, cursing. Things were being slammed around, and she winced at each thud and crash. What had made him so angry? He'd brought her back, she'd promised not to leave, he'd gotten what he wanted. Hadn't he?

She sat up and looked at the adjoining door and the chair wedged beneath it. One of those thuds had been against that door, and the chair had shuddered beneath it. What had he thrown? Or hit? What was he doing?

She climbed down off the bed and carefully removed the chair, but the noise next door had subsided.

The dark lavender dress was miserable to get out of—it had been made for her when she still had her own maid, and if Doris was busy then Maddy would fasten her. It had taken her too long to get dressed earlier, and getting out of the blasted thing was torture. She yanked at it, and heard the buttons pop and roll across the room. The fabric was too new to rip, but the buttons were enough, and she shoved it down, unfastening her petticoats at the same time, stepping out of the annoying pile and kicking it.

She hadn't bothered with her corset—the idea of escaping had been difficult enough. Stripping off her garters and stockings, she was left standing in her shift and bloomers and nothing else. She couldn't quite bring herself to remove the bloomers, but she could practically see her breasts through the thin cambric.

She took her hair out of the bun, shaking it free, then looked at herself in the mirror. The room was almost dark, and the creature who looked back at her was a stranger, a beautiful, wild, and wanton stranger. Her mouth curved in a smile, a wicked smile. She was tired of thinking, tired of games, tired of pretending. One last night. If the worst happened and he managed to drag her to the altar she could simply say "I don't," and no cleric in the country would marry them.

But that was tomorrow, not tonight. Tonight she would break one more rule. She would go to him, because she loved him, the rat bastard. If he let her.

She half expected the door to be locked between their rooms. But it opened easily enough, with no betraying noise. The gaslight had been turned off, but there was a lamp in the room, sending out a small pool of light, and she wondered whether he was asleep. She pushed the door open all the way, until it hit something, and she stepped into the room.

There was a large book on the floor, which had clearly been thrown against the door. He was lying on the bed, in the thin drawers that he swam in, and there was a book on his lap, but his eyes were on her, dark and intense.

"I promised I wouldn't run tonight," she said, her voice shaking a bit. "And I always keep my promises. But I'm afraid I'm having a hard time keeping that promise. You're going to have to tie me to the bedpost after all."

Slowly Alexander closed his book.

CHAPTER TWENTY-TWO

SHE WAS THERE. SOPHIE was really there, standing in his bedroom wearing nothing but her shift and bloomers. Even in the shadows Alexander could tell that much. Her blond hair cascaded down her back; her dark blue eyes were huge, luminous. Nervous. She had actually come to him.

"Is this some kind of trick?" he said warily. "Are you planning to knock me over the head with something?"

She took a step closer, shaking her head. "You're too tall for me to reach. I suppose, if you really want me to, you could always bend down and I could find something to hit you with." There was just the tiniest tremor in her voice as she tried to sound nonchalant. His darling Sophie, dressed in almost nothing, coming to his bed of her own accord, and she wanted to sound casual. God, he loved her.

"I think not," he said in a relatively normal voice, considering how relieved he was. "I'd rather have all my faculties when I'm with you." He climbed off the bed, moving toward her. The room was littered with the things he'd thrown in a frustrated fury. He'd decided to let her go. If she hated the idea of being with him that much, if she was willing to risk the damage to her reputation, then holding on to her was wrong. No matter how much he wanted, needed her. Loved her.

But she was here. On her own. Watching him warily.

She cleared her throat. "What were you reading?"

He controlled his instinctive laugh. "So we're going to discuss literature, are we? Is that why you came to my room?"

"We can do anything you want."

His heart stopped, and then started again, a slow, hard pounding that he could feel through his body, his blood pumping through him, filling him. "You know, the idea of tying you up is absolutely irresistible, my love, but I think we need to wait till later for that kind of play. We still haven't enjoyed all the basics."

Her gorgeous forehead wrinkled in confusion and she didn't understand what in the world he was talking about. It didn't matter. If she wanted, he could teach her, but there was no need—just looking at her fulfilled his most erotic fantasies.

He stopped a few feet short of her. He was wearing his smalls and nothing else, and they left nothing to the imagination, including his fierce reaction to her presence. She glanced at him, her cheeks reddened, and she looked up, keeping her gaze focused on his shoulder.

"Come here, Sophie," he said softly. He'd moved around to the other side of the bed. All she had to do was take two steps and he would lay her down amidst the sheets and coverlets and devour her.

There was only a second of hesitation. She came to him, willingly, lifting her face to his, and he bent and put his mouth on hers.

God, she tasted sweet, so sweet, as her arms went up around his neck and she moved against him, her body soft, her nipples hard. She opened her mouth for his tongue, and he tasted every part of her, coaxing her to kiss him back. The feel of her small tongue in his mouth was beyond pleasure.

But he wanted far more. He needed to take his time with her, and he would. He would make love to her, with her, he would tup her, shag her, fuck her. He would give her everything and take everything in return.

He broke the kiss, and she was out of breath, panting slightly. "You have to remember to breathe, love," he whispered.

"I just need practice."

Did she say that to make him happy? It didn't matter. He caught her waist in his hands and turned her back toward the bed. "I think you need to lie down for this."

She looked worried. "For what? Will it hurt?"

"Stage two in your realm of experience, my love. And it won't hurt at all." He pushed her down on the mattress, her legs hanging over the edge, and reached beneath her shift to the tapes that held her drawers together. They were loosely tied, and as he pulled them down she didn't protest, but her body was tense, worried.

He knew just how to relax her. He parted her legs, and before she knew what he'd planned he'd put his mouth between them.

She gasped in shock. "Oh, no, you mustn't . . . you shouldn't . . ." Her voice trailed off as he reached the spot that was the center of women's passion, his tongue teasing it, and she gasped, her hands no longer pushing him away, her fingers on his shoulders, clinging to him. Slowly she loosened her tight grip, slipping her fingers up to run them through his hair, a shy caress, holding him to her, accepting him.

If her mouth was sweet then this was ambrosia. He loved the taste of women, the smell of them, the way they reacted. This was different—somehow it seemed as if all his experience had been leading to her. He'd learned how to pleasure women just so he could pleasure her, take her, give her everything she ever wanted and more.

His fingers parted her, another indignity that made her jerk against his mouth, and he slid a finger inside her tight sheath, so wet, so ready. He used his mouth, his tongue, his teeth, sucking at her, licking her, biting her with sharp little nibbles that made her gasp in delight. Her hands were no longer gentle on his scalp; she was pulling at his hair, making the most delicious sounds of need, like *please* and *more* and *yes*. He wanted more; he wanted to spend hours with his mouth on her, but when he slid two fingers inside her she climaxed, arching off the bed with a scream. She tried to cover her mouth, to still the sound, but he managed to catch her hands.

"Let it come," he whispered. "Scream as loud as you can." He slid his fingers through her wetness, up to the top, rubbing her, and watched her as everything left her and she did scream, a hoarse, sobbing sound of such wild pleasure that he could have come from watching her.

He pushed her up on the bed, following her and wrapping her in his arms as she shuddered and trembled, errant stray convulsions still rippling through her. She hid her face against him now, suddenly shy, and he smiled when she couldn't see it. *Mine*, he thought. He'd claimed her, and he would never let her go. *Mine*.

•••••••••••••••••••••••••••••••

Sophie lay wrapped in his arms, her face tucked against his chest, her entire body shaken. It was too much; it was not enough, and she was too embarrassed to let him see her face. She'd lost control completely; she'd screamed. It didn't matter that he'd told her to. She'd lost every bit of restraint she'd ever had, exploding with a frightening kind of ecstasy, and now she just wanted to hide her face against him.

He wasn't going to let her. He'd wrapped his body around her, and she could feel his erection jutting against her, hard as iron. Why had he done such a strange and indecent thing to her? Why had it felt so overwhelmingly wonderful?

She was beginning to catch her breath, though her heart was still beating like mad, and she finally felt brave enough to turn her head and look up at him. He was leaning back against the pillows, stroking her hair, and there was a smile on his face. The one she loved, the one without mockery.

"Why did you do that?" The words were out of her mouth before she realized it, and she could have died of shame. It was bad enough that he'd done it, and she'd responded the way she had; talking about it made it even worse.

His smile widened, and she felt something clutch at her heart. "Because I knew you would like it. And because I like it."

"You do?"

He kissed her forehead. "Oh, yes. It's one of my favorite things to do. You'll have to get used to it."

The thought of him doing it again, and often, made her shiver. "It gives you pleasure?"

He kissed her mouth, and she could taste herself on it. It was strange, erotic, and she wanted to hide in the darkness again. "It gives me great pleasure," he said, his voice rumbling in his chest.

She put her face back down, hiding. She liked the darkness better—then she could pretend that no one could see; no one could know. But he could see her quite clearly; he would know everything about her reaction to the things he did.

She wanted to touch him. She wanted to touch that part of him that invaded her body, that part where all this desire seemed to be centered. But she didn't want the light. She could do it in the dark, touch him, stroke him. The very thought was giving her pleasure, and she finally understood why he had put his mouth on her.

She lifted her head, still shy. "Could you put out the light?"

He laughed, but it was a gentle laugh, without the ironic edge he usually had. "No."

"Why not?"

"Because I want to see you."

"I'm more comfortable in the darkness," she said miserably. He was so close, his cock was so near, and she wanted to touch it, but the light frightened her.

"Please," she said.

"Sophie, we're going to make love in the fields in the middle of the day, on the desk in my library, in the pool, on the floor of every damned room in this house and Renwick and every other house I own. I'm going to take you on the damned kitchen table, cover you with lemon sauce and whipped cream and then lick it off you. We may even try that here if I can get rid of the new cook. You're going to have to get used to the light, because I want you, badly, and I can't imagine ever *not* wanting you. I'll take you every way I can, and in ways that haven't been invented yet."

His words only made it worse, this need to touch him. He was arousing her, deliberately, when she didn't need the arousal; she was still so shaky from his mouth that she thought he only had to touch her and she would explode again.

She put her hand on his stomach, and he drew his breath in sharply. It was a flat stomach, golden from swimming in the sun, and there was a faint tracery of hair moving down into the drawers. She could see the shape of him, pushing against the fabric, and she felt some of her nervousness melt away.

Very slowly and carefully she put out her hand, as if she were approaching something dangerous, and touched him through the thin cloth.

He muttered something, closing his eyes, and she knew he liked it. What else would he like?

The buttons were strained tight over his erection, and she wanted to tear the clothing off as she'd ripped off her own dress, but she resisted. She glanced up at Alexander. He was leaning back, his eyes closed, tension rippling through him. Did he like this? Did he want her to do it?

It didn't matter. She certainly hadn't wanted him to do such a scandalous thing to her, and the feeling had been beyond anything she could imagine. She wanted to give him that same feeling; she wanted to see him, to touch him, to taste him.

She began to unbutton him, very carefully, starting from the bottom. When she finished, he sprang free, and Alexander groaned.

His hand was on her shoulder, and he slipped it beneath her hair, cupping her neck, kneading it, calming her, arousing her.

She looked at his cock, studied it. It was totally different from the statues and paintings she'd peeked at. Those had been small, droopy things. This was huge—no wonder he had hurt her. His skin there was pale, and there were veins bulging around it. The top was smooth, round, with a drop of liquid on it. She put one finger to it, and it came away sticky. *Interesting.*

She encircled him with her hand, sliding it down over the veins, the skin sliding with her, and then she touched the sack beneath, gently, and he hissed out something.

But he held very still, and she took that as permission. She liked this part of him, this private part that no one else could see or touch. He took her hand and placed it back around him, and then moved it, showing her what he liked, and the heat blossomed again inside her. She rested her head on his stomach, watching his cock as they moved their hands together, up and down, up and down, and it seemed to grow even larger. He leaned back on the bed, his other hand kneading the back of her neck, and she felt him shiver in pleasure.

She lifted her head slightly, and his grip loosened, ready to release her. Or stop her, she wondered. She wanted this. Her body wanted this. At last she understood. She leaned forward and put her mouth on his cock.

He let out a string of such blasphemous profanity that she might have pulled away, but he'd tightened his hand on her neck, not forcing her, but holding her, caressing her, as she took him into her mouth, as much as she could, sucking on him, tasting the sweet flesh, letting her tongue run along the veins.

"Up and down." His voice was hoarse. "Please, Sophie. Move your mouth."

She smiled, triumph rushing through the erotic haze that surrounded her. She wanted everything; she wanted his pleasure to burst into her mouth so that she could drink it. She was pagan, wicked, and she sat up for a moment, ripping her shift as she yanked it over her head and threw it. She needed to be naked, she needed the light, she felt like an animal and she liked it.

She drew him into her mouth again, sucking hard, and his hands threaded through her hair, caressing her scalp, as she slid down to capture all of him that she could, so much that she wanted to choke on it, and then, sliding back up, her lips closed tightly around him.

She heard his guttural moan, and she felt it between her legs, a strange tightening when he wasn't even touching her. She sank down again, taking a little bit more this time, and Alexander cried out. She could make him climax this way, she knew she could, and it was what she wanted. She sucked hard, up and down his shaft, never able to take it all but coming close, and she stopped thinking, lost in sensation, drowning in it, tasting it . . .

"No," he cried in a hoarse voice, pulling her away as his hips bucked. He yanked her up beside him, collapsing back on the pillow, holding her there beside him while he tried to regain control.

"Why did you stop me?" she said, frustrated, needy. "I wanted to."

"You don't know what happens when I come. You're too inexperienced for this."

"I know what happens. I felt it on my stomach." She thought for a moment. "Is it poisonous?"

His laugh was raw. "No. It's harmless, and it's a good way to avoid babies."

She thought of his cock, hard, waiting. "I like babies," she said.

He was silent a moment. "So do I."

Everything was still for a moment. Could she risk it all, give him the ability to destroy her, break her heart? Ah, but she already had. This was nothing but admitting the truth she already knew, deep inside. And she suspected he knew it as well. "But we don't have to have a baby immediately," she said calmly. And she tried to dive back down.

He hauled her back. "You're a very wicked girl, aren't you?"

She considered it. "I think so, yes. Except you're the wicked one. I don't feel wicked except when I'm with you, so it must be your fault."

"It must be," he agreed, taking a deep breath, and he turned her underneath him. "I don't want to come in your mouth, not this time. I want to fuck you; I want to come inside you, again and again, until you're filled up with me. I want to fuck you until neither of us can move, and then when we're rested I want to do it all over again. You're mine, and I can do anything I want with you, as long as it pleases you. And it will. I promise."

His hard body was pressing her into the mattress, and she tried to open her legs for him. She had never felt this way in her life, empty, needing.

"Not that way," he said and turned her over onto her stomach, pulling her on her hands and knees. She could feel him behind her, the rounded top of his cock pressing against her, rubbing her wetness around them both, and she pushed her hips back, needing him inside her.

He began to slide into her, but this time there was no pain. Just a tightness as he pushed in, slowly, and tilted her hips back, trying to get more.

He had his hands on her hips, holding her still as he sank into her, and his pace was driving her mad. "Do it," she said hoarsely. "Now."

It seemed to break whatever hold he had on himself. He thrust all the way into her, deep and hard, and it felt so good, so necessary, and she exploded once more, her body clamping down around that part that she'd taken into her mouth so lovingly, ripples of reaction shaking her.

She felt his hands cover her breasts, and when he pinched them lightly the last bit of her mind vanished. She howled and sank down into the bedclothes, covering her head with her arms as he began to thrust inside her, hard, so hard, so gloriously hard. "More," she said, though she didn't even know what she wanted.

But he knew. He was moving faster now, harder, the hands on her breasts holding her in place, keeping her from being flattened by his heavy thrusts. She clawed at the sheets, so lost in pleasure she was aware of nothing but Alexander with his body around her, inside her, thrusting, and she climaxed again, so lost that when she wanted to scream nothing came out. It was just them joining together, sweat and fluids and love and mess and nothing mattered but his arms around her, his cock still thrusting back and forth inside her as the night shattered around them both, and she felt him spill inside her. And she was gone.

When he finally pulled away she felt the loss of him so keenly that she wanted to weep. She couldn't, of course. She never cried.

She collapsed flat on her stomach on the bed, and he covered her, his much-bigger body pushing her down into the bedclothes.

He was like a hot, heavy blanket on top of her, and she loved it. It didn't matter that he was so much heavier than she was; she wanted to sink into him, be a part of him, dissolve into nothingness and let him absorb her. Crazy ideas kept flitting through her head, thoughts that belonged in the darkness that he'd brought to light. He lifted off her and turned her over, pulling her into his arms, so tightly that air couldn't get between their sweat-soaked bodies. He pulled one of her legs over his hip to get her closer, and she collapsed into him, as the last, final shudder racked her body. She wanted to stay this way forever, full of him, replete. Everything felt so right, for the first time in her life. This was where she belonged. With Alexander, who didn't love her.

She pushed the thought from her mind—she pushed everything out of her mind, concentrating on his sleek skin, his arms tight around her, the pounding of his heart as it slowly returned to normal. She listened for the heartbeats, *ba-thump*, *ba-thump*, and then she fell sound asleep.

•••••••••••••••••••••••••••••••
···

Alexander looked down at her. She'd fallen asleep—she was exhausted, poor baby, and he'd made it worse. If he had to use sex to keep her with him then he'd gladly make the sacrifice, but the truth was he could have sex with anyone. He wanted only Sophie.

She could learn to care for him. He had to count on that. By coming in here she had accepted his offer, no, his demand. She would marry him, and she would learn to love him.

They had fucked, they had rutted, they had made love. Had Rufus heard them? Knowing Rufus, he would have been listening if he could. It didn't matter. Rufus would find his own way in the world—he always had several schemes going. The last one, whatever it was, obviously hadn't worked out too well, but Rufus was his brother, not his responsibility, and nothing to worry about. Rufus's monstrous mother was a different matter.

But he wasn't going to think of Adelia when Sophie was lying naked in his arms. He didn't think he'd seen anything more erotic than the way she'd ripped off her chemise before taking his cock in her mouth. He still couldn't believe she'd done that. He was getting hard again—in fact, he hadn't come down completely from the first time. But he would let her sleep. He would hold her in his arms, smell the scent of roses mixed with sex, and dream about all the things they could do together.

Perhaps lick hollandaise sauce from her stomach and then carry her sticky body out to the pool and take her again. The possibilities were endless.

CHAPTER TWENTY-THREE

RUFUS VOMITED. HE HADN'T wanted to, but the rage and betrayal were twisting his insides, and he had no choice. He'd heard them. Alexander would know that he'd heard them. Alexander, whom he'd worshiped for so long, Alexander, whom he killed for, stole for, all so his idol could have the perfect life.

She'd warned him. She'd told him he'd be untrustworthy, but Rufus hadn't listened, and now he was vomiting his betrayal into a waste bin.

He knew what he had to do, and he wouldn't hesitate again. He'd planned to wait until all the extraneous details were dealt with, but the two Russell sisters had survived. It didn't matter. His mother would know how to deal with it, once he finished what she'd planned. He would lure the Russell girl onto the roof, and suspicion would fall on Alexander.

He'd idolized his brother for so long, loved him so much he'd been determined to be like him. He hadn't liked other people interfering, and the first time he'd killed had been surprisingly easy. Not that he'd planned to drown his father—he'd been caught in a strong current and his father had jumped in after him. Holding the old man under the water had been almost too easy, and it meant he no longer had to share Alexander's attention with anyone.

Jessamine had had to die for any number of reasons, chief among them that she couldn't be allowed to bear Alexander an heir. It would cut Rufus out of any chance of ascending to the title, and his mother had no plans to ever let that happen. Rufus had been more than happy to do her bidding, and it had been easy enough to lure Jessamine up onto the battlements. She'd had a crush on him, and he'd nurtured it, and one little slip had taken care of things.

But Alexander wasn't the man Rufus had thought he was. He made mistakes; he was troubled by ridiculous concerns like honor. The Russell girl had bewitched him, and there would be another wife to be gotten rid of. It was getting too complicated. His idol had fallen, and there was only one solution. He would have to take his place.

Rufus wasn't as strong as his brother, particularly since the accident, but he could still manage to take care of things. Alexander trusted Rufus enough to get close, and a bullet in the brain at point-blank could easily be arranged to look like a suicide. He was adept at forging Alexander's name—he'd been doing it for years on debts and bank cheques. A note expressing his guilt and despair over committing a second murder would raise no troubling questions.

He would slip into Alexander's life perfectly. Once, long ago, he had worshiped his older brother. Maybe he still did. But that was weakness. His mother thought he could take Alexander's place. No, he could *become* Alexander. If he did, Alexander would live on, in him, and he would feel no guilt. It would be . . . glorious.

· ·

Sophie was alone when she woke. Of course she was. Cautiously opening her eyes, she looked around her. No sign of him. She buried her face in the pillow as mortification overcame her.

What had she done? She'd been an animal last night, worse than the basest whore. She had wanted him so badly that nothing else mattered. How could she have done such things?

She moaned into the pillow, then jerked her head away. It smelled like him. That lovely, subtle scent of skin and wool and leather, and she felt a tightening deep down, and she wanted him again. She wanted to do the same things with him, the shameful, secret things; she wanted to stay locked in this bedroom for days and never leave the bed or him.

But he had left her. The one thing she'd wanted was to wake in his arms. She'd wanted words, not the hot, sexual words he'd used, but words of love. Or at least affection. And he'd said nothing.

He'd held her as she fell asleep, her practical mind argued. He hadn't left the bed. But then, each time she'd awakened he'd been hard and she'd been eager, so eager that she was sore between her legs. So in truth, he'd stayed with her only as long as he could tup her, and when it was morning he'd left.

But he'd stayed . . . no, she couldn't look for something that wasn't there. The man was an inexplicable mix of ridiculous honor and undeniable lust. Who would have thought she'd prefer the lust part of him?

She sat up. Bright light was filtering in through the curtains— she had no idea what time it was. Everything was topsy-turvy, nothing made any sense, and she wasn't sure if she wanted to laugh at the absurdity of it or weep. She would do neither. She would get up, bathe and dress, and move on with her life. Which would include walking out that front door, barefoot if she must. She couldn't marry a man who didn't love her. Not when she was so desperately in love with him.

She climbed out of bed, and every muscle, including unexpected ones, protested. Her shift was her first priority. She remembered what she'd done with it, and she groaned again. And then she saw the silk dressing gown that lay on the end of the bed.

She slipped it on, then almost pulled it off again. It was like wrapping herself in Alexander. The Dark Viscount, she'd called him, because of his reputation, his looks, his saturnine demeanor. It had been a stupid name, one born of childish imaginings. But she wasn't a child anymore; she had seen to that. She could have pulled herself together after the night at Renwick, even after the interlude in the carriage. But now she would never be the same.

She didn't care, she thought, straightening her shoulders. If she had to do it all over again she would. She wouldn't trade her putative future with an ancient, wealthy lord for a moment of last night. She could spend the rest of her life in someone's kitchen, perfectly happy with her memories and the pleasure of creating glorious things to eat.

She shoved the sleeves of the dressing gown up, but they slid down again, and she had to pick up the hem so she wouldn't trip on it. The door to her room was ajar, and she went in, moving a little slowly.

A strange maid was standing there, folding delicate, lace-trimmed underclothing, and for one heart-stopping moment Sophie was afraid the girl was packing for her. Alexander had changed his mind—he refused to marry such a wanton. But the girl smiled and bobbed a curtsey as she tucked the clothing into the large armoire, and Sophie wanted to smack herself. She wanted him to change his mind, didn't she? To admit the truth, that he didn't care for her.

"You're up, miss," she said. "I'm sorry I didn't hear you or I would have had your bath drawn already. It won't take but a moment. And I'll have a tray sent up, shall I? It's gone past three and you must be famished."

"Three?" Sophie said, and then stopped with shock at the raw sound that came from her throat. She cleared it, and tried again. "As in three in the afternoon?" It was a little better, but not much.

"Yes, miss. You were that tired, and his lordship said no one was to bother you until you woke on your own."

Sophie took a deep breath. "And where is his lordship?"

"Dunno, miss. He went out early this morning and hasn't come back. He doesn't tend to tell the servants where he goes or when he returns. Mr. Griffiths said I was to tell you not to worry if his lordship doesn't come back. He'll make sure you're looked after."

The words were like a stone in Sophie's heart. She sank down in a chair as the girl disappeared.

She deliberately straightened her back. Food and a bath would go a long way toward making her feel human again. Until then she shouldn't rush into any decisions. She should try not to think at all, because life at that moment was too overwhelming.

Her curtains were pulled, and it was an overcast day. It always seemed to rain more in London, which was so unfair, given that in London one's clothes had to be smarter, one's hair had to be more elaborate, and no umbrella was big enough to protect the intricacies of proper dress. She wouldn't have to be worrying about such things in the future, which was a mixed blessing. She'd always liked dressing up.

There were drawbacks as well. She wouldn't be able to walk in the countryside, of course, unless she found a position away from London. Indeed, that would be the smartest thing, far away from people and places she'd known. But she would need a place fast, and London was her only option, at least until her sisters reappeared, and she couldn't count on them for rescue. She had to make her own way. The three of them had faced disaster, and each of them had to find her own way through.

The bath was a heavenly respite from her muddled thoughts. Once the girl, Gemma, had left her, Sophie leaned back and opened her legs, letting the water soothe her. The girl had put some sort of herbs in the bath as well, and the effect was wonderfully soothing, so blessed that Sophie refused to get out until the water grew cold around her.

Gemma must have been sitting outside the bathing room door, listening, for the moment she rose from the tub the girl knocked and slipped inside, taking a large towel and wrapping it around her. "I thought you were going to shrivel up like a prune, miss, you were in there so long. You've got a tray of cold meats and cheese waiting for you in the room, and I've set out some clothes for you to approve. I hope you don't mind. I'm just an upstairs maid, not really a lady's maid, but I was told to look after you until they could find someone permanent, and I'll do my best."

"You'll be fine," she said. If life were different, if she were going to stay, she'd be happy to have Gemma as her permanent maid, a step up in the servant hierarchy for the girl. But she wasn't.

Gemma's instincts had been unerring—the outfit she'd chosen had been one Sophie had worn to make afternoon calls. The skirt was gathered in the back and flat in the front, the blouse pleated and ruffled and laced, with a fitted jacket that had a slight military flair. It was neither too fancy nor too plain, and it would suit her.

"And these, miss," Gemma said, holding in her hand a pair of shoes.

"Where did you get those?" Sophie demanded, shocked. They were one of her favorite pairs, left behind when they'd been evicted with only the clothes on their backs. She could walk for miles in those shoes.

"His lordship told me to make certain you had them."

His lordship had sent them? His lordship, who had disappeared without a word and might not be back for days? For a moment, in the bath, she had considered facing him, explaining why she couldn't marry him.

But she could hardly have told him the dismal truth. That she wouldn't marry him because he didn't love her. He would laugh at that, at her, and she didn't think she could bear it.

It was no longer an option. He'd given her the shoes and disappeared. That was message enough.

"Mrs. Griffiths asked to see you," Gemma said once the shoes were buttoned. "I told her you were having a nap, but she said 'wake her.' Which I wouldn't do, not ever, but I thought I should pass it along, because that old witch, if you'll pardon my language, would just as likely climb the stairs and barge in here if she wants to. You'd probably be better off if you saw her."

"Mrs. Griffiths?" Sophie pictured the ghastly woman with her tiny eyes and thin mouth beneath the mounds of maquillage. "When did she arrive?"

"A few hours after his lordship left," Gemma said, shattering Sophie's errant hope that it was his stepmother who'd driven him out. "I think she's here to stay."

"Oh, of course. She wanted to see her son."

"And quite the reunion it was, miss, with her wailing and sobbing and Mr. Rufus looking like a little boy. And then they went into his lordship's study and were very quiet for a long, long time."

Sophie managed a wry smile. "I don't suppose someone tried to eavesdrop?"

"Oh, no, miss!" Gemma said, but Sophie had her doubts. "But then Mr. Rufus went out, and she demanded to see you."

She could refuse, but Gemma was right. Mrs. Griffiths was someone who didn't take no for an answer. "Do you think we could put her off for a bit?"

"No, miss. And she's really quite insistent."

"I know how difficult she can be for the staff," Sophie said, rising, remembering the demands the old woman had made. "Where is she?"

"Still in the master's library. He hates it when anyone goes in there, but Mrs. Griffiths doesn't pay that no mind. There'll be hell to pay if he comes back while she's still here. He doesn't even want her in the house, much less his library."

And who could blame him, she thought. "Will she be staying here?"

"It depends on whether his lordship returns today or not. He's given orders that she's not to be allowed in here, but there's not really much the staff can do, particularly with Mr. Rufus here."

Sophie nodded. Mrs. Griffiths was a force of nature, and she had no choice but to face her.

She found the woman ensconced behind Alexander's desk, riffling through his papers. She didn't rise when Sophie entered, but as an older woman she didn't have to, though the gesture would have been polite. "You wished to see me, Mrs. Griffiths." Sophie summoned all her best behavior.

It didn't do her any good. The old woman looked up at her with acute dislike. "I did. I wanted to look at the creature who lied and tricked her way into my stepson's bed."

Sophie simply stood there, unmoved. Mrs. Griffiths's nasty streak was the least of her worries.

"Aren't you going to say anything?" the old woman prodded, her eyes dark and vicious.

"Is there anything in particular you wish me to say?" Her voice was cool and calm, a far cry from Mrs. Griffiths's raging tones.

"You should be ashamed of yourself," she spat. "Oh, I know all about you. Just because you're the daughter of a shipbuilder you think you're some highborn lady, when in truth you're nothing."

Better than the daughter of a butcher, Sophie thought, but wisely kept her mouth shut.

"If I were you I would be too ashamed to show my face," the woman continued. "You should . . ."

"Mama!" Rufus appeared in the doorway, his too-pretty face lined with concern, that errant, deliberate curl ruffled. "You mustn't talk like that. This is not Sophie's fault."

Sophie looked at him in surprise. She hadn't thought she'd have a champion in Alexander's brother, particularly since Rufus had been so attentive to him the previous night and faintly malicious toward her.

"Then whose fault is it?" Mrs. Griffiths snapped.

"You know Alexander has his weaknesses. It's happened time and time again. He grows infatuated with someone, insists on marrying the most inappropriate of females, and then abandons them for me to get rid of. Don't you remember the actress?"

Sophie refused to let a flicker of reaction cross her face, even though her heart seemed to have suddenly contracted into a dark ball of pain.

"Of course. I remember them all," Mrs. Griffiths said in a calmer voice, albeit laced with contempt. "I'm tired of my son having to clean up his messes, especially after all you've been through."

"There's no need to berate the poor girl," he said, coming forward and taking Sophie's arm gently. She didn't resist. "This is not her fault. I'll see to her. We all know he would never marry her, and he's unlikely to return for days until he's sure I've taken care of things. You should go up and rest. You know travel always makes you bilious."

Sophie would have smiled at that, if she had any emotion other than pain available to her. She felt frozen. She was being a fool, she tried to tell herself. She'd already determined to leave, hadn't she? Or had she been hoping he'd return and take her in his arms and tell her that he loved her, that he'd never let her go?

She didn't believe in fairy tales. In fact, she never had, and the only reason Alexander had for marrying her was for the sake of his reputation, something he'd always said he didn't give a fig for. And she'd been a fool, to let dreams creep into her heart when she wasn't looking.

She let Rufus gently tug her away, but at the last moment she turned back to glance at the horrible woman who had taken over Alexander's desk. Mrs. Griffiths had a smile of supreme satisfaction on her face. Of course she did—she'd won.

It made no sense, but Sophie didn't care. She simply let Rufus lead her, up the stairs to the second-floor salon, settling her down in a comfortable chair as if she were an invalid. "I'm so sorry about my mother," he said with an anxious expression. "She has a tendency to speak her mind, but she's unaware of the details of Alexander's . . . tendencies."

"Tendencies?" she echoed dully. She felt lost, broken. She really didn't want to listen to Rufus's malicious gossip. She simply wanted him to leave her so she could escape.

"I'm afraid he's done this time and time again. In fact, there has been an occasion or two when I haven't been able to intervene in time. The results were . . . tragic."

She roused herself enough to look at him. "What do you mean?"

"I'd rather not go into details. The problem is, if you simply disappeared there'd be too many people looking for you. It would be a different matter from a young companion or an actress."

"Are you saying he killed them?" Her voice sounded flat and strange to her ears.

"Of course I'm not," he said quickly. "Don't ever tell anyone I suggested such a thing—I'll deny it. It's just that . . . for your own safety I think it would be best if you left as soon as possible."

"I have every intention of doing so." She pulled the cold blanket of nothingness around her. "In fact, I'll leave immediately."

"It's a little more difficult than that. The servants have been ordered to keep guard on you, not let you go anywhere. If you tried to walk out the front door someone would stop you, and you'd end up locked in a room he keeps for that purpose."

This was unbelievable. The picture Rufus was painting, of an unbalanced madman seducing and then disposing of women, was absurd. If he didn't want her there, why would he tell the servants to guard her? None of this was making any sense.

But Rufus continued. "I think there's just something wrong with him. I don't know what caused it, but it happened when he was about twenty, and all conscience seemed to leave him. His poor wife was the first victim of his . . . problem. I just couldn't bear it if there were any others."

He sounded so earnest, so worried for her. She still didn't trust him, but she couldn't even trust her own heart. She had to get away from this place so that she could think clearly. "Then what do you suggest I do?"

"Are you afraid of heights?"

"No," she said flatly.

"Then there's an easy path over rooftops. I used to take it all the time when I was young and wanted to escape supervision. I still use it when I don't want people spying on me. You would have no trouble."

She glanced out the window at the rooftops of London. Some were peaked, some were flat, some were adorned with ridiculous gargoyles, while still others had windows positioned to let in light. There were chimney pots all about, and she wondered how in heaven's name she would manage to navigate such a treacherous terrain. It didn't matter. She had to get away from here.

"I'm ready," she said.

He blinked. "I'm not, I'm afraid. I need to make certain my mother is comfortably settled, and then I'll show you the way."

"I thought your mother wasn't allowed here?"

"Alexander won't return for days. He's always hated my mother, but he doesn't mind if he's not around."

She didn't bother to question it. Rufus's lies were none of her business. "Just tell me the way to go. I don't need you to show me."

"I couldn't let you try it alone. I've worked out the path after many attempts, and one wrong move could send you tumbling to your death. I feel duty-bound to see you safely from this house."

Duty again, she thought. She despised the very word.

"Promise me you'll stay here until I check on Mother. No one else will trouble you and I'm determined to keep you safe. Please."

She had already made promises that had gotten her into nothing but trouble, but this one was easy enough. She wasn't afraid of heights, but she wasn't madly enamored of them. The cliff at the edge of the tor had been more than enough for her. She could wait until Rufus showed her the way.

She had enough sense to know that altruism wasn't his sole motivation. He didn't want the scandal, and she suspected he didn't want Alexander having a wife or even a mistress. Not that either of those seemed a real option, not when he'd gone off somewhere. But Rufus was driven by self-concern as much as anything else, and for that reason alone she trusted him to get her out safely. No matter what tales he was spinning—and they were, on the face of it, ridiculous—it reminded her that she needed to be gone from here. If for some reason the servants were watching, then she'd climb the Alps to get away.

"Promise me," Rufus said earnestly, and she believed him. Almost.

"I promise," she said.

Rufus gave her his flashing smile and pressed her hand meaningfully. "You won't regret it."

CHAPTER TWENTY-FOUR

"She's where?" Bryony's usually calm voice was just short of a shriek, and Maddy lifted her head in surprise. Luca and Kilmartyn had just returned from some mysterious visit to the East End of London, and she was staring at the men in shock.

"Why are you so surprised, Bryony?" Maddy said from her comfortable spot on the sofa, catching her husband's eye and smiling at him before turning to her sister. "Sophie's just been waiting to kick up her heels. We should have known she'd go after the viscount."

"Are you sure?" Bryony said. "Are you absolutely positive?"

Luca strolled over to Maddy and gave her a kiss, and she reached up and smoothed his long hair away from his face. She hated staying behind, but Bryony had been too edgy to be left alone, and the four of them could hardly traipse through the London slums.

Luca turned and looked at his sister-in-law. "The Wart never fails me," he said.

"And exactly who is this Wart?" Bryony's eyebrows rose.

"One of the captain's criminal confederates, my darling," said Kilmartyn, leaning lazily against the door. "I'm sorry you couldn't come with us down to Seven Dials—it was fascinating. Depressing

286

as all hell, but fascinating. It appears Mr. Dickens's novels are closer to the truth than we realized."

"Right now all I care about is my sister," Bryony said firmly, and Maddy had to admire her. In the past few weeks Bryony had blossomed from a quiet, shy recluse into a strong and secure woman, and Maddy supposed she could thank Kilmartyn for it. She held herself like a woman who was loved.

"Of course you do," Luca said soothingly, moving near Kilmartyn, and Maddy stifled a groan. The two of them got on far too well, and if it ever came to an argument between the women and the men they would be well matched.

But in this case it was their sister, and it was up to Maddy and Bryony to see to things. "She pretended to be a cook, and now she's in Griffiths's house over in St. John's Wood, with no chaperone, under her own name. She's ruined," Bryony said.

"It was your idea that we enter service," Maddy pointed out, perhaps unfairly.

"Do you think I don't know that?" Bryony said miserably. "We have to get her out of there. That's the most important thing. Then we have to find out if she wants to marry him. If she does, that will be up to Adrian and the captain to ensure it happens."

"My pleasure, love," Kilmartyn drawled, and Luca nodded. Maddy could almost be sorry for Sophie's Dark Viscount. Did she still think of him that way? Maddy could only hope he'd turned out to be a prince in disguise.

"The one thing I can't imagine is Sophie actually working for a living," Bryony said. "She detested any kind of work or exercise."

"Actually, she changed," Maddy said. "She suddenly started taking long walks, disappearing for hours, when she'd always hated the outdoors. And her cooking was ridiculously good."

"I don't think it's her cooking that the viscount is interested in," Kilmartyn said dryly.

Bryony rose. "The longer we wait, the more difficult this is going to be. We need to go get her."

Maddy was already on her feet when Luca said in a placating voice, "Why don't you let us go and retrieve her? We're more than capable of dealing with any resistance, and it might be better if you weren't seen."

"You aren't capable of dealing with Sophie's resistance if she doesn't want to come with you," Maddy warned him.

"She knows I'm married to Bryony, and she'll take my word that you and the captain are wed. I would think wishing to be reunited with her sisters would trump any infatuation she might have."

"True enough. Sophie was never infatuated in her life—she thought men were tedious. If she's developed any affection for the viscount I'd be astonished. Nevertheless, we're going with you. I, for one, don't intend to wait one second longer than I have to before seeing her again," Bryony stated, fixing him with a stern expression.

"But you'll stay in the carriage," Kilmartyn said firmly.

Bryony had learned to lie in the last few months, Maddy thought. "Of course," Bryony said, her eyes wide. "Anything you say."

• •

"Have you convinced her? Or have you buggered it up again?"

Rufus flinched beneath his mother's harsh tones. "She's ready whenever I am," he said. "She believed everything I told her."

His mother's smiles were never warm, but there was a trace of approval in this one. "Good boy. And we're fully prepared to deal with Alexander. I found the gun in his desk drawer, and I've loaded it for you. It will be easy enough to sneak up on him. He'd never suspect you."

"He won't be happy if you're here," Rufus said doubtfully.

"He won't even be thinking about me once he hears that she's fallen. He'll be distraught, and you could even suggest she committed suicide. As long as you do your job it will all go swimmingly. Just make certain she falls into the garden, not onto the street. That would cause too much of an uproar, and we're going to have to live all this down once you inherit the title."

"You forget I have experience in tossing Alexander's females off a roof," Rufus said with an attempt at dignity.

"Ah, yes, poor Jessamine."

"She didn't love him," he said. "She was always flirting with other men, even with me. She deserved her fate."

"And so does that little trollop who conveniently happens to be one of the Russell girls. I would be quite cross with you if I weren't pleased with how all this came together. Clearly it was meant to be. I have every expectation that the same opportunities will arise once more with the two others. And if you find you're tired of killing, there's always the chance we don't need to worry about them, but I believe in being thorough. It is only when you deviate from my plans that things go wrong, my boy. If you'd done what I told you, they would have died when you burned down their town house, and it would have been over with when you killed Lady Kilmartyn. But you miscalculated and they escaped. Very sloppy."

"Yes, Mama. I promise I'll finish it. I haven't grown tired of it."

"You will redeem yourself, I have little doubt, and then you will come into your own. You're much more suited to the viscountcy— Alexander would rather strip off his clothes and dabble in the water like a child. This way it all works out as I had planned. First we took Renwick back, along with enough money to support it, and everyone assumed it was Russell who'd stolen it. That will be followed by Alexander's disgrace and death, and no one will even remember the trouble in the house of Russell."

"It doesn't do to underestimate him, Mama," Rufus felt compelled to say.

"He is no match for me," she said simply. "Neither was his father."

"My father as well," Rufus said.

"You aren't still fussing about that, are you? Once you succeed in killing your own father, you find that you're quite able to do anything at all," she said simply. "He was so weak I could have taken care of it, but I wanted you to have the experience. It made you stronger."

"Yes, Mama."

"If you can kill your father then you should have no trouble at all killing your brother."

"No, Mama." The thought suddenly came to him—her equation worked out quite simply. He should have no trouble killing his mother either. The thought brought an unexpected cheer to his heart.

"You should take care of it, my darling boy. You should do it now. We can't be sure when Alexander will return, and it needs to be done."

"Yes, Mama." He rose obediently, but to his surprise his mother rose as well. "You're coming with us?"

"Not onto the roof, of course," she said. "But I wish to observe and make certain there are no mistakes this time. I should have a good enough view from the servants' quarters."

"Yes, Mama. And I plan to make certain she lands on the stone wall, so that she dies quickly. It's four flights down—I have no doubt that it will be sufficient."

Mrs. Griffiths sighed. "It is too bad we can't use the street, but we can't risk the attention. Someone might look up and see you. She might scream when she falls. I don't suppose you could break her neck before you toss her."

Rufus shuddered. He'd done that once, at her behest, and he'd hated the cracking noise. "I'll do my best."

Mrs. Griffiths smiled at her son fondly. "That's all I could ever want, darling boy."

• •
. . . .

Alexander was ready to punch someone, anyone. Applying for the special license had been simple enough; finding a cleric or magistrate was an entirely different matter. He'd been across town and back at least six times, tracing down one possibility after another, and it was well past teatime before he found someone willing to take care of it. He simply had to convince or drag Sophie to the magistrate's office at the Old Bailey to have it done, and he could imagine her reaction. Sanctifying a marriage among thieves and murderers was hardly a good way to start a marriage, but then, the two of them were hardly an ordinary couple. The magistrate had been so delighted to oversee an act of joy rather than his usual duties of sending men to prison, hanging, or the hell of transportation to Australia that he'd agreed, though he insisted he couldn't do it before tomorrow morning.

Alexander had little doubt he could convince Sophie. He was still in a haze from the night they'd spent together, the sheer joy in her as she discovered her sensuality, explored his body, and let her own be taken and pleasured until she was a helpless bit of femininity, beyond movement or speech, curled in his arms trustingly, holding him tightly even in her sleep.

She might even love him. At the very least, he was utterly sure he could get her to love him, and the pleasure they took in one another was a good start. She would say yes; he was sure of it. He'd done everything he could to show her how much he wanted her, needed her.

Of course, his inner devil pointed out, *you didn't say the words.* Women liked words, and he hadn't given them. It had been too long since he'd felt this way—if, in fact, he ever had. He'd been infatuated with Jessamine, but that had been a boy's fascination.

With Sophie he felt an almost mystical connection, though he refused to believe in such things. He'd felt it the first time he'd seen her, and been fighting it ever since. He loved her anger, her sweetness, her smart mouth, and her fierce sexuality. And by God, he loved her cooking. He could worship at her feet if he wasn't afraid she'd stomp on him. And that was still another reason why he loved her. She was afraid of no one; she would do anything, risk anything.

She was also damned volatile, and she could have viewed their long night together with belated embarrassment, and he hadn't been there to soothe her. She might have decided he was pond scum once more, and try to escape, particularly since he'd given back her shoes.

But he trusted her. If she left he would find her. If she left he had the very strong suspicion she'd find some reason to come back. She was as drawn to him as he was to her, and he didn't think she could just walk away, any more than he could.

He'd left her alone with Rufus. For some reason the notion troubled him, making him quicken his pace. There was something off about Rufus in the last few years, something strange and excitable that worried Alexander. There was no reason why Rufus would harm her, though he'd made it clear he thought the idea of Alexander marrying her was insane. Then again, Rufus was his heir, and Alexander had sworn off marriage after Jessamine's death. Rufus could have gotten used to thinking of himself as the future Viscount Griffiths.

No, Rufus wouldn't hurt her. He wasn't like his vicious mother. He could blacken Alexander's character with his malicious tongue, but Alexander could take care of that by taking Sophie in his arms and speaking the words he was so wary of. Words that were so easy and so hard.

He quickened his pace. The house was too close to get a hackney, too far to get there fast. He strode through the streets at something very close to a run.

CHAPTER TWENTY-FIVE

"Are you ready?" Rufus ducked his head inside the door, his charming smile leaving Sophie unmoved. She was about to make her escape over the rooftops of London from the man she loved, the man who had either abandoned her or, if she were to believe Rufus's outlandish tales, might even kill her, and the only person she could turn to was Rufus Griffiths, a man she disliked and distrusted.

She couldn't shake the agitation Rufus brought out in her whenever he was near. Perhaps it was simply her confusion about this entire situation, and it had all devolved onto Alexander's hapless brother.

But there was nothing hapless about Rufus; she had no doubt of it. From his charming, self-deprecating smile to his one perfect curl on his forehead, he was artifice personified.

He was offering to help her, and she couldn't afford to be picky, to let an unexpected queasiness get in her way. She rose, feeling like her old self in her dress, with the almost-new corset Gemma had found among her belongings. She'd lost some weight, probably from the missed meals, and Gemma had been set to tighten that instrument of torture still further when Sophie had begged her to stop. At Renwick she wouldn't have to wear a corset, or shoes, or do anything she didn't want to do. At least, not in the perfect Renwick she pictured in her mind. She could even take off everything and slip into the pool. She wanted that glorious feeling of the cool water all around her again, this time with bright sunlight overhead.

But that was all a fantasy, and she was much better off not thinking about it. She had to look ahead, not behind.

She followed Rufus, watching the slight limp that he'd tried to disguise, and she wondered how he'd been hurt. That had never been explained, nor had his connection to pirates, but presumably he'd shared the story with Alexander. She didn't need to know. *Forward*, she reminded herself. *Not back*.

"This way," he said, opening a door toward the end of the hallway that she hadn't even seen. It was cut into the wall, and she realized it was a servants' entrance. "We don't want to risk anyone seeing us—they'd try to stop you."

The steps were narrow, winding, and he reached behind her to pull the door shut, his arm brushing against her body. Even with all the layers of female armor she felt a flinch of fear shake her, and she wondered what would happen if she simply went back, if she ignored Rufus's warning and faced Alexander whenever he returned. Rufus was undoubtedly lying about some of the things he'd told her. Everybody lied at some point or another, and it was clear Rufus was jealous of his brother.

"Come along, Miss Russell," he whispered, and she turned forward, ready to follow him. But for some reason, purely instinctive, she gave a little kick backwards, and the door opened just a crack.

Rufus didn't notice, and she hadn't an earthly idea why she did it, but for some reason it seemed necessary as she followed Rufus up into the darkness.

It ended in a large, barren room. There were windows at either end, boxes and odd pieces of furniture in storage, but the shadows were too deep under the eaves to see. There were probably a thousand rats up here, she thought, shivering. She could feel their eyes on her in the darkness.

There was a narrow door beside one of the windows, and Rufus had already pushed it open, hurrying her along, as if he didn't want her to look too closely into the darkness. *I'm not afraid of a few rats*, she thought defiantly, but followed him nonetheless. The less she thought about it, the easier it would be.

She walked out the door and immediately froze, slamming herself back against a brick chimney. She'd been envisioning a nice, flat rooftop, easy to traverse, but this one was slanted at a fairly sharp angle, the next roof was too far away to jump, and she could see no way down, even if she managed to get across them without falling.

Rufus had already pushed the door closed behind her, or Sophie would have turned around and dived back inside. She wasn't afraid of heights, but this was different, with all of London laid out before her, the street miles below. She glanced behind her, and the garden seemed equally far away.

A wind was whipping through the rooftops, pulling at her hair, tugging at her voluminous skirts, and she clung tighter to the brick. Alexander's house was one of the few with a hut-like wooden entrance on top of the roof, presumably so the climbing boys could get to the chimneys. A window looked out over the roof, and once more she felt beady, ratlike eyes watching her.

"Are you sure this is a good idea?" She had to raise her voice a bit for Rufus to hear her. A light drizzle had begun, and she wondered if it would make the slate tiles slippery. That was all she needed.

"Done it a dozen or more times," Rufus said cheerfully, his hair flopping in the wind. "Just give me your hand."

He held out his own, but for the moment she couldn't move. "Just let me gather myself," she said shakily. "I hadn't realized it was this high."

"Don't worry about it," he said with a peculiarly sweet smile. "Don't even think about it. It won't take but a minute."

She reached out and put her hand in his and began inching across the pitch of the roof. Her heart was pounding wildly, and she realized she was afraid, terrified, in fact, when she'd never been afraid before. She looked up at Rufus, and she knew for certain that she'd been a fool.

"Come on," he called to her, lifting his voice above the wind. "You're better off on the far side of the roof. You don't want people seeing you up here—they may make a fuss, call attention to us, and then the servants would try to stop you. It could be dangerous up here if you don't know what you're doing."

She glanced down, way down, into the street. There was some kind of commotion going on right in front of their house—people milling about, angry voices rising up to her. And then someone turned his face up, way up, to the roof, and even from that distance she knew it was Alexander. Alexander, coming for her. Alexander, who cared for her.

"I've changed my mind," she said. "I think I'll go back in."

The door opened behind her, and she started to turn, full of relief, when she looked into Mrs. Griffiths's dark, ratlike eyes. "No, you won't, missy," she said, slamming the door behind her and moving out onto the roof, sure-footed as a spider climbing a web.

Sophie edged back from the chimney, reaching for the door, but there was no handle, no way to pry it open. Mrs. Griffiths held up a large iron key. "It's locked and this is the only way we'll get back in. I'm afraid you won't be coming with us." She turned to look at her son. "Come along then, Rufus! What's keeping you? It's a simple enough job—get on with it."

"She's on the wrong side, Mama," he said plaintively, sounding eerily like a small child. "You said I must throw her into the garden."

Mrs. Griffiths sighed loud enough to be heard over the wind. "Then take her and throw her. You're a man; you're strong enough."

"Why are you doing this?" Sophie cried out, though she knew the answer.

"That's a remarkably stupid question," Rufus said petulantly.

"I should be the viscount, not Alexander. It was only an accident of birth that put him first."

"He must be at least five years older than you!" she cried.

"Eight, to be exact," Rufus said, ignoring logic. "I'm the chosen one."

She stared at him in disbelief, trying to fight the panic that was surging through her. "Chosen for what, exactly?" She couldn't keep the caustic note out of her voice, when she should have been placating, and she wanted to kick herself. Except if she did, she'd end up falling over the edge of this treacherous rooftop.

"Don't be difficult, Sophie," Rufus said. "It was all preordained. Fighting against it will only make it worse. Your father didn't struggle. I broke his neck and it was over in an instant. I could do the same for you. There's no way out—make it easy on yourself." His soft voice was almost persuasive.

Sophie stared at him in shock. "It was you? You killed my father? For God's sake, why? He never hurt you—you didn't even know him!" Her cry was caught and carried by the wind, and she wanted to scream in pain and disbelief.

"I needed the money and I needed a scapegoat," Rufus said simply. "And I needed Renwick."

"We needed Renwick," his mother corrected in an icy tone far removed from Rufus's wheedling. "Now get on with it, or I'll do it myself."

The last of Sophie's fear drained away as sheer fury filled her. These two . . . monsters had destroyed her life and the lives of the people she loved. There was no way she was going to let them win. She clung tightly to her chimney, trying to decide who was her weakest opponent. Mrs. Griffiths was a mountain of a woman—if it came to a battle she would win by brute force. Rufus had a bad leg, which had to affect his balance on this precarious perch. If she could fling either of them over the edge she'd do it without a moment's regret. She took a tentative step toward Rufus. "I'll scream. I'll scream so loud Queen Victoria will hear it."

"No one will hear it," said Mrs. Griffiths coldly. "The wind will carry the sound away, and if anyone happens to notice, it will be too late. They'll just assume it was your scream as you fell in your foolish attempt to escape. Or your suicide, whichever works best. We can decide that later. Right now we just need you dead."

There was no room for panic, just determination. Alexander was back, and he'd seen her. He hadn't disappeared for days. Even now he'd be coming for her. She needed to stall these two, just long enough for Alexander to reach her. She could probably manage to fight off Rufus, but Mama was a different matter.

Sophie began to edge her way forward, carefully on the slate tiles, staying on the front side of the building. She had good balance, and now that the fear had been replaced by a cold rage, she felt her way without hesitation, moving farther and farther away from Rufus and his monstrous mother.

"Rufus!" His mother's bark of fury was enough to startle both of them. "Get on with it. We haven't much time."

"But . . ."

"No excuses. You've done it before with Jessamine and you said you enjoyed it. Do it now."

Rufus suddenly looked resolute, like a child facing some inner demon, and he took quick steps and reached for her. She dodged, and her shoes slipped. She went down on her knees, scrabbling at the tiles, and managed to stop her fall. She lay there, panting, clinging to the side of the roof.

"Mama!" She heard Rufus cry out.

"Grab her arm and haul her to the other side!" his mother said, all exasperation.

She felt Rufus come near, cautiously reaching out for her, and she tried to move her arm out of the way but she began to slip. He grabbed her and hauled her up onto her knees, stronger than she would have imagined.

The door to the attic slammed open, and Alexander was there, on the roof, and there seemed to be a hundred people behind him, all talking, familiar voices, calling her name, shrieking in fright.

"Let go of her!" Alexander thundered, his voice rising above everyone. She didn't dare look. She was kneeling at the very peak of the roof, with Rufus holding both arms, ready to fling her into the garden.

He wouldn't reach her in time. Rufus would kill her, and Alexander would be alone and she couldn't bear it.

At that very moment Rufus was staring at his half brother, a look of horror on his face. "Alexander," he said, stammering slightly, like a boy who'd been caught with his hand in the cookie jar. "You weren't supposed to be here."

"Damn you, Rufus, what the hell are you doing?"

"Don't you understand that she has to die?" he said plaintively. "It's part of the plan. We can't let her mesmerize you."

"What are you talking about?" Alexander's voice had quieted, as he tried to calm his half brother. "Whose plan?"

"I'm supposed to be the viscount," Rufus whined. "You know it. You stole it from me, just as you stole everything from me."

A frown of confusion lined Alexander's forehead. "I'm eight years older than you are, Rufus. Of course I got the title, for all it's worth."

"It's not fair. You don't even care about it, when it really belongs to me."

"There's nothing I can do about it, old man," he said gently.

"That's why I have to take care of it. And you. I'm sorry, Alexander, but this is the way it has to be." He started to yank at Sophie's arms, pulling her toward the far edge.

"No!" Alexander screamed, and it startled Rufus enough that his hold on her arms loosened slightly. It was all Sophie needed.

She didn't hesitate for a moment, slamming her head into his damaged leg with a satisfying thunk. He crumpled, releasing her, and for a moment he squatted there, teetering on the edge with a look of complete disbelief. In the next he went over the edge, his screams echoing in the night as he rolled down to disappear over the far side of the roof. There was a horrible, crunching noise, of bones shattering, and the screaming stopped. All was silence.

And then she was being pulled up, into Alexander's strong arms, as the drizzle fell around them, and she clung to him, so tightly she felt she could never let go. She heard words, soft words from him, but none of them made any sense. The sound of his voice, the racing of his heart, was enough. She was safe, she was home, and she wanted nothing more than to melt into his hard body, to lose herself in him.

He tipped her chin up, staring down with his stormy gray eyes. "Aren't you ever going to learn to listen to me?"

She tried to say something, but she was beyond words, so she simply gripped him tighter and pulled his head down, kissing his hard, beautiful mouth.

He kissed her back, and if he hadn't been holding on to her she would have tumbled over the side as sheer rapture washed over her. When he kissed her, nothing mattered; the world disappeared.

It was a new voice that broke her dream, an achingly familiar one, and she lifted her head in time to see first Bryony and then Maddy emerge onto the slippery roof, with two men beside them.

Sophie's sense of unreality grew proportionately, and for a second she wondered if Rufus had won, if she was the one who'd died and this was some strange sort of heaven. And then she heard Maddy's familiar voice say, "I should have known you'd get yourself into a mess," and she knew it was real; everything was real. If she were anywhere else but in Alexander's arms she would have turned and rushed to her sisters, but right now he was her rock, her safety, her heart.

"She got herself out of it," Bryony said, clinging to the arm of an elegantly dressed man who could only be Lord Kilmartyn. She had no idea who stood with Maddy but he looked like a gypsy, the complete opposite of what Maddy had always wanted.

"Be careful!" Sophie warned her sisters, her arms still tight around Alexander as the wind buffeted around them. "You'll fall. Go back inside."

"Not until you're safe," Bryony said, moving farther out onto the street side, holding on to Kilmartyn.

Sophie released her death grip on Alexander reluctantly, knowing she had to head for the door, for her sisters, when she heard an eerie scream.

She'd forgotten one important thing. They weren't alone on the roof. Alexander hadn't even known the old witch was there, but a moment later Mrs. Griffiths emerged from behind the massive chimney, shrieking like a madwoman. "You killed him! You killed my baby!" she screamed. She shoved her way past Maddy and the gypsy, almost sending them tumbling, and came straight for Sophie, madness in her small rat's eyes.

Sophie stared at her, frozen, unable to move. Alexander was still holding her hand, but if he tried to stop the woman he'd likely go over himself. She tried to move, to draw the woman's attention, and Alexander released her arm, ready to let her go.

Until he moved, with such quick grace she almost missed it. He stepped in front of her, fast and deft as some circus performer, his foot went out, and Mrs. Griffiths went screaming over the front edge of the town house, ending with a loud crashing noise and the sound of frightened horses.

Lord Kilmartyn peered over the side of the roof, then turned to Bryony. "I'm afraid, dear one, that we're going to have to buy a new carriage," he said languidly.

And for the first time in her life Sophie fainted, directly into Alexander's arms, knowing she was home.

CHAPTER TWENTY-SIX

THEY WOULDN'T LET HIM stay with her, those chattering sisters of hers, Alexander thought, watching as they surrounded the chaise in the drawing room where he'd put Sophie and crowded him out of the way.

"We need a doctor," he said harshly.

"No, we don't," said the woman he assumed was the new countess. "She's just fainted."

"And I believe your late, lamented family is beyond mending," Kilmartyn drawled.

Alexander looked at him with dislike. "You're talking about my half brother."

"He's talking about a murderer who would have happily killed our sister and probably you as well," said the younger sister. "I'd dance on his grave."

With that Alexander walked out of the room, closing the door behind him. His hands were shaking, and he wasn't quite sure why. The most important thing was that Sophie was safe. After that, nothing else mattered.

"Your lordship?"

Alexander turned. Dickens was standing there, a sympathetic look on his stolid face. Alexander looked up at him.

302

"There, there, lad," Dickens said, in a rough, fatherly voice. "They were a bad lot and you knew it full well, much as you tried to give the boy the benefit of the doubt. You couldn't save him, even years ago. He was under the old witch's thrall and there was nothing you could do." Alexander took a deep breath. "I knew there was something wrong. His stories just didn't add up, but he was my brother . . ." His voice broke for a moment, and then his mouth hardened. "I should have gotten rid of Adelia and her pernicious influence long ago. But he loved her, and I loved him."

Dickens shook his head. "Nothing you could do," he said again.

"I need to call the police, do something . . ." He felt dazed, shattered, and all he wanted was to go to Sophie and have her wrap her arms around him, but there were too many sisters getting in the way.

"Don't you worry, your lordship. I've already notified them, and they're outside right now, removing the bodies. I'll see to the garden after they're gone, but they want to talk to you."

"Of course they do," Alexander said, trying to pull himself together. His eyes finally focused on Dickens. "I don't understand— why are you here?"

"I followed your stepmama, of course. I knew she was up to no good. Mr. Wilton is outside directing the constables while I see to you. When you're ready to speak to them just let me know. And remember what's important. You're in love with that little girl, whether you admit it or not, and you almost lost her. If you don't do something about it now, today, you may still." He fixed him with a fierce gaze. "Be the man I brought you up to be. Your brother's gone and there's no bringing him back, and in the end it's a mercy and you know it."

A mercy, Alexander thought, remembering the small boy who had followed him with worshipful eyes, the young man who'd already been old in the ways of sin, the man who was ready to commit fratricide for his mother and his own greed. It didn't matter—he had the right to grieve him anyway, whether his death was convenient or not.

And then he thought of Sophie. Sophie was the one who'd knocked Rufus to one side, sending him spinning off the roof instead of falling to her death. How would she feel about killing someone, even if he had been trying to kill her? He needed to hold her as well, to tell her it was all right, that no one would hurt her again. He wouldn't let them.

He straightened, taking a deep breath and shaking off the demons that hovered around him. "Thank you, Dickie," he said. "I'll go kick her yammering family out of the house long enough to tell her the truth. You're right; I love her. And I'm not letting her go."

Sophie was lying on something hard and uncomfortable when she regained consciousness. Her head ached, and there were too many people talking, too many people arguing, fluttering about her. She wanted Alexander and no one else, and his deep voice wasn't among the cacophony.

"Go away," she growled in a low voice.

"She's awake!" Maddy said much too loudly.

"Sophie, darling, are you all right?" Bryony was kneeling beside her, touching her with delicate hands as if to ensure that she was really there. Sophie did her best to tolerate it.

"I'm awake," she said, opening her eyes and searching for Alexander. He was in one corner of the large room, speaking to a pair of uniformed police officers; Bryony was beside her with Maddy next to her; the men who'd accompanied them were nearby, conversing among themselves; and she saw to her shock that even Dickens was there.

"Dickens?" she said, before she even spoke to her sister.

"I was worried about you, Miss Russell," he said, stepping forward, an abashed expression on his rough-hewn face. "And I figured his lordship would need all the help he could get."

"Thank heavens," Sophie said, sinking back on the settee. It was particularly uncomfortable—trust a man to furnish a house with the wrong furniture, she thought randomly, staring at Alexander. He looked pale, drawn, and she wanted to go to him, to pull his head down to her breast and comfort him. He looked as if he'd survived a bloody battle, and she wondered what he was thinking. He'd killed someone.

Then again, so had she, and she didn't have a moment's regret. She always prided herself on being practical, and there'd been no other way out of it, but Alexander might not be quite so sanguine, considering it was his half brother. In fact, he might be blaming her . . .

"Oh, darling Sophie, you've been through so much," Bryony crooned, interrupting her worried thoughts.

"Not that it wasn't your own fault for going off like that," Maddy added.

"Oh, for heaven's sake, stop trying to pick a fight!" Bryony snapped. It was so blessedly familiar that for a moment Sophie wanted to cry. "We need to get Sophie home, take care of her. She's been through a huge shock."

Alexander turned at her words, suddenly intent. His eyes met hers for a moment, and his were dark, tormented, and he quickly looked away.

"You'll be all right," Maddy said to Sophie with rough affection. "Just don't think about it."

Sophie looked up, confused. "Don't think about what?"

Bryony and Maddy shared a glance, and Bryony decided to answer truthfully. "Darling, you killed a man. Not that he didn't deserve it, but it must be shattering for you."

Sophie shrugged, her eyes still on Alexander. *Look at me*, she thought. *Come to me, put your arms around me, and send my sisters away. Tell me nothing matters; tell me you love me.* She glanced back at her sisters. "Oh, that," she said vaguely.

Bryony made a choking sound and Maddy laughed. "Now what would Nanny Gruen say?" Maddy said mockingly.

"She'd probably say 'well done,'" Sophie said, still watching Alexander. He looked pale, shocked, and she wanted to hold him, but after her clumsy words he might not want anything to do with her. She couldn't take them back. She wasn't going to pretend to be anything other than who she was. She'd been through enough, and she was tired of being tactful. Either Alexander wanted her or he didn't—if he was going to reject her because she'd done what she had to, then there was nothing she could do about it. She would have to live with his decision.

"Oh, God, she's just like her sisters," the gypsy murmured to Lord Kilmartyn. "How could there be three of them?"

"How could the world have survived thus far?" countered Kilmartyn.

"I don't understand who that crazy old lady was," Bryony said. "And what in the world was Rufus Brown doing, trying to kill you? He should have died when the old house collapsed."

"You knew him too?" Maddy said, astonished. "He went overboard the *Maddy Rose* during a storm after trying to kill me. What in the world did he have against us?"

"He wasn't Rufus Brown, he was Rufus Griffiths, Alexander's half brother, and that was his mother," Sophie said without emotion.

Maddy turned fascinated eyes toward Alexander. "He killed his mother?"

Look at me. Please, look at me and tell me you forgive me. "His stepmother, you idiot," she said flatly. "It all had to do with Renwick, I think, and Alexander's title. He was behind Father's disgrace, and he's the man who killed him."

A shocked silence filled the room, and Maddy rose and sat down hard on one of the uncomfortable chairs. "But why?" she said finally.

"There was no money with Renwick," Alexander said in a flat, cold voice, the first time Sophie had heard him speak since she'd regained consciousness, but he kept his gaze averted. "I expect he thought he would kill two birds with one stone."

Kilmartyn spluttered with laughter. "Not well put, old man."

"I'll have to see about returning the money," Alexander continued after shooting a glare at Kilmartyn.

The Earl raised a languid hand. "No need. I replaced it all, and it barely makes a dent. I have a gift for making money."

Alexander eyed him sourly. "As do I."

Kilmartyn beamed at him. "How splendid! We're both financial wizards and we're both suspected wife-killers. What else can we bond over?" He turned to look at the gypsy. "Luca, I don't suppose you murdered a wife sometime in your past?" he said hopefully.

"Afraid not," the man said wryly.

"I didn't kill my wife," Alexander said through clenched teeth. "I suspect Rufus or his mother did."

"Oh, I didn't kill mine either, much as she deserved it," Kilmartyn assured him. "I can thank your brother for that as well." He gave them all a wicked smile. "Seriously, I am grateful." He inspected the sleeve of his elegant coat, picking at an invisible piece of lint. "I still think Luca needs to have some wretched skeleton in his past."

"I have more than enough," the gypsy said. "And I'm not killing Maddy."

"Oh, do be quiet, Adrian," Bryony said, giving him a reproving look devoid of rancor.

"Excuse me," Sophie said, tired of all the noise. "But who is that man?"

Bryony followed her gaze. "That's my husband, of course."

"That one was easy," Sophie said in a dry tone. "Who's the other one?"

"That's *my* husband," Maddy said with an undeniable air of pride. "Captain Morgan, but you can call him Luca."

"But I thought he was old!" Sophie said in bewilderment.

"Sweet Neptune's briny pants!" swore the captain. "Why does everyone think I'm old?"

"Our coach got . . . er . . . damaged," Bryony continued, ignoring him as she stroked Sophie's wind-tangled hair away from her face. It was a soothing gesture she remembered from when she was very young. For the first time she didn't want her sister's hand, she wanted a larger, stronger hand. She looked at Alexander again. The policemen had left, but he hadn't moved, hadn't come any closer. She'd killed his brother and she'd showed not an ounce of regret. Maybe he couldn't forgive her.

"It'll take a little while for a hired one to arrive here, but Adrian's made all the arrangements. You can come back to Berkeley Square and we'll look after you."

"No." The word was short, sharp, and clear, and everyone turned to look at Alexander. Sophie felt a surge of hope fill her.

"I beg your pardon." Bryony was all stiff outrage, clearly already a countess.

"I said no. She stays with me."

"I don't think so," Maddy chimed in with a martial gleam in her eye. "She's gone through enough. She needs her sisters around her."

"I compromised her," he announced. The other two men were following this with rapt attention.

Maddy rolled her eyes. "Of course you did. And we don't care. Sophie is our sister and she can do exactly as she pleases."

"I've spent the entire day running around London, getting a special license and finding a magistrate to marry us, though perhaps not in the best neighborhood," he added. "We're getting married first thing tomorrow morning."

"Entirely unnecessary," Bryony said briskly. "We don't care about scandal and neither does Sophie."

"Would you let me speak for myself?" Sophie broke in, her voice firm, looking at her sisters huddled around her, looking at Alexander standing so far away. "I would think it would be my decision."

"Of course, darling," Bryony said. "You'll come with us, won't you?"

Sophie looked at Alexander, and this time his eyes met hers.

They were dark, stormy, full of intensity. "Where would we be getting married?" she asked.

He held very still. "The Old Bailey. In the criminal courts."

"How fitting," Kilmartyn drawled. "I can't miss this."

"And exactly why do you want to marry me?" Sophie said, no longer caring that her sisters and their husbands were a fascinated audience.

He looked like a cornered fox. "I compromised you."

"We don't care," Bryony and Maddy practically spoke in unison.

"I do." He was the picture of immovable stubbornness.

"Would you be quiet?" Sophie snapped. "This is between the two of us and the rest of you have no say in the matter." She turned back to Alexander. "Sorry, but that's not good enough. Tell me why I should marry you. One reason. And I want the real one. You give me an excuse and I'll go with my sisters." It was a risk, a very real risk. But she couldn't take him any other way without destroying her heart in the process.

Everyone was very still, her sisters staring at Alexander, Kilmartyn and the captain watching him with very real sympathy.

"Might's well do it," Captain Morgan said. "There's no way out of it."

"Trust me," Kilmartyn added, "these women are hardheaded."

"Do you think the two of us could have a little privacy?" Alexander sounded desperate.

"No," came four voices, almost in unison.

Sophie rose, walking toward him. She felt nervous, shaky, but she wasn't going to let him see her uncertainty. She knew his answer, but there was always the chance that he didn't recognize the truth. That, or he'd refuse to say the words. But she couldn't give in—she'd drawn a line in the sand and she couldn't back down. She stopped when she was just out of reach, looking up at him. "So?" she said.

"Witch," he muttered beneath his breath. "Because I love you."

She smiled at him, a wide, brilliant smile, and he smiled back, all the darkness gone from his eyes. "I love you too," she said, and went into his arms.

EPILOGUE

THE OLD BAILEY WAS the center of the criminal courts of London, smack-dab next to Newgate Prison. As the bride was led in, her future brother-in-law murmured, "It's a good thing they no longer do hangings right outside here. It would dampen the festive mood."

Luca was looking extremely unhappy. "I've been here a little too often for my liking," he muttered.

Kilmartyn looked at him in admiration. "As a pirate?"

"No, a pickpocket." He followed the wedding party inside, looking over his shoulder every now and then.

It was a strange and glorious celebration. The magistrate, Sir Duncan McGrew, also known as the Hanging Judge, presided over the ceremony, the groom had a pirate and a reprobate lord stand up for him, Sophie had her sisters. The police gathered round, bringing their felons and miscreants with them, and there was a tear in many a criminal's eye at the end, when the shouts of *huzzah* were so loud Sophie thought her eardrums might burst. She looked up at her new husband as he placed a dutiful kiss on her lips and she smiled.

"This wedding," she said, "is absolutely perfect. Let's see you try to improve on this." Reaching up, she caught his head in her hands, yanked him down, and kissed him as hard as she could.

Sir Duncan was required to read the riot act before everyone peacefully dispersed, some to a prison cell, some to a hangman's noose, and some to their marriage bed.

"Do you think they'll be happy?" Bryony asked her husband as she slipped into bed beside him.

"I have absolutely no doubt at all," said Kilmartyn, "but right now I'm more interested in our happy ending."

Bryony's smile was dazzling. "So am I, love. So am I."

ABOUT THE AUTHOR

ANNE STUART IS A grand master of the genre, winner of Romance Writers of America's prestigious Lifetime Achievement Award, survivor of more than thirty-five years in the romance business, and still just keeps getting better.

Her first novel was *Barrett's Hill*, a gothic romance published by Ballantine in 1974, when Anne had just turned 25. Since then she's written more gothics, regencies, romantic suspense, romantic adventure, series romance, suspense, historical romance, paranormal, and mainstream contemporary romance.

She's won numerous awards and appeared on most bestseller lists, and speaks all over the country. Her general outrageousness has gotten her on *Entertainment Tonight*, as well as in *Vogue*, *People*, *USA Today*, *Woman's Day*, and countless other national newspapers and magazines.

When she's not traveling, she's at home in northern Vermont with her luscious husband of thirty-six years, an empty nest, three cats, four sewing machines, and one springer spaniel, and when she's not working she's watching movies, listening to rock and roll (preferably Japanese), and spending far too much time quilting.